MAPS OF
THE SOUL

A   ᵃagih is a renowned Libyan novelist and playwright, b   ᵢ Libya 1942. His first collection of short fiction in A   was published in 1965. His award winning trilogy C   ᵣs *of the Night* was published in its English translation iₙ   ᵌ5. His other works include several collections of short sₜ   ᵉs, plays and essays. *Maps of the Soul*. He lives between T   ᵒli and Cairo.

AHMED FAGIH

MAPS OF
THE SOUL

DARF PUBLISHERS
LONDON

Published by *Darf* Publishers 2014

Translated by Thoraya Allam and Brian Loo
Revised and Edited by Ghazi Gheblawi
First published in Great Britain in 2013 by DARF Publishers LTD
277 West End Lane, London, NW6 1QS

www.darfpublishers.co.uk

ISBN 9781850772712

Printed and bound in Turkey by Mega Printing

Typeset in 11.5/14pt Bembo by Palimpsest Book Production Limited,
Falkirk, Stirlingshire

CONTENTS

BREAD OF
THE CITY

ONE

It was a terrifying sight: the ground was covered in blood and strewn with beheaded corpses.

Your sixth sense had failed. You could only see and hear one thing: the steps of the executioner as he drew near you, heralding death, your head about to be cut off, like those of your companions who had met the same fate just minutes ago.

They had bound you and your companions by your hands and feet in iron chains that made your wrists and ankles bleed. They pushed you against a wall made of tree trunks held together by hemp rope and strips of monkey hide, which formed a fence around the wide dusty yard, into which the scorching sun beat mercilessly.

There were a number of huts scattered inside the yard, which the Abyssinian fighters had taken over as one of their military bases in the mountain hollow. The tree trunk you had been tied to had a protrusion that pressed hard against your back and its sharp tip thrust into your back between your shoulder blades. All you could do to prevent it from stabbing unbearably between the vertebrae of your spine was to shift your body slightly, after which the protrusion settled somewhere on your right shoulder causing you merely immense pain. You suffered and cried in silence.

A tall Negro emerged from the nearest of the huts reserved for the guards' use. His emaciated body seemed hollowed out, as though he were a skeleton. He was naked save for a wrap, which was mottled like a tiger's skin and concealed his genitals. His teeth shone brilliantly in the sunlight, big, white. There were small spaces between each tooth, making them look like the prongs of a pitchfork.

He stood examining the prisoners with an imbecilic expression on his face, before moving with quick steps, pacing in front of everyone, scrutinizing their faces more closely, one after the other, his eyes narrowing. His grotesque mouth remained gaping in lustful astonishment, as though in disbelief couldn't that so many enemy soldiers had fallen into his hands so that he might do with them as he pleased.

You were with a group of recruits from the Italian army, although the only Italian among you was the regiment commander, while the rest were Somalis, Eritreans, and Abyssinians, except for two Libyans. The Negro chose to stop in front of a prisoner of his own nationality, whom he seemed to know. Perhaps the prisoner had fought alongside him before he joined the invading army. A hopeful, pleading smile lit up the prisoner's face as he uttered the name of his old companion in a choked, servile tone, "Sanko".

The only response Sanko gave, however, was to spit in the beseeching face. The humiliated man was unable to wipe the spit from his face because his hands were bound. After completing his round of inspection, Sanko stood at the head of the line of prisoners and began to laugh hysterically, without any apparent reason, and without any of the prisoners making a sound. The only noise that followed was the buzzing of the big green flies that had settled in swarms on the faces and bodies of the prisoners. No one could shoo them away, because of the chains of steel that bound your hands. The flies relished the absence of cleanliness and hygiene, happily finding enough variety of sordid food to satiate their countless armies.

After exhausting his fit of hysterical laughter, Sanko held his hand out in the air, palm up, fingers straight. His facial features hardened, and the whites of his eyes shone like the whites of the eyes of the dead, while beads of sweat on his black brow and temple shone like fireflies in the dark.

A soldier came forward bearing a knife long as a sword and placed it in Sanko's outstretched hand. Sanko began feeling the edge of the knife methodically with his fingertips, then he whirled around muttering a few angry words in Amharic, at which one of the guards fetched him a file to sharpen the knife. The screeching of metal set your nerves on end to the point that you began to gnash your teeth and struggled to control your trembling body until the sound stopped.

Everything suggested you were witnessing the preliminary rituals of a massacre where you would be among the victims. This was what all of you had been expecting ever since you had been taken prisoner ten days earlier. As for why the slaughter had been postponed all this time, it must have been spent bargaining with the Italians through the open lines of communication with their army's leadership, which had now probably refused to comply with the Abyssinians' demands. This was the opinion held by some of your more seasoned companions. Of the prisoner before him, and slashed his throat. The severed head let out a shriek whose echoes reverberated in the seven heavens, or so it seemed to you as you raised your head dizzily towards the dome of the world where the echo resounded, the death rattle of the decapitated prisoner.

Many prisoners, who like you were backed up against the tree trunks, couldn't repress their screams of terror, but you managed, even though it swelled in your throat like a serpent. You shut your eyes and recited, "'I testify that there is no God but Allah and that Muhammad is the Messenger of Allah'", while your fate awaited you. You kept your eyes closed through the hysterical screaming as Sanko fulfilled his role as the King of Death.

Sanko was carrying out his work methodically. He would slay a prisoner, then step over to the second prisoner beside him only to spare him and fall upon the third prisoner with his long knife. You didn't understand why he chose such an arbitrary way of murdering his victims. Perhaps he relished the amusement of leaving some alive in order to return to them later with a renewed lust for carnage. Or perhaps he spared them for use in bartering with the Italians in one of the prisoner exchanges that happened frequently between the two sides.

Your sole concern at the time was to know the number of prisoners that stood in the terrifying gap between you and the murderous Negro, so that you could work out whether you were to be among the living or the dead. Sanko didn't differentiate between Libyans, Somalis and Abyssinians. His only consideration was to kill the prisoner before him and spare the next. Your panic increased when you saw that you would be amongst the dead. Perhaps you had counted wrong, you said to yourself, trying to cling to hope. So you counted them a second time, then a third, then a fourth, but no promise of redemption or salvation was forthcoming. Your death was inevitable.

He would spare this African to your right, and the African to your left, and then kill you. He slit the throats of men as though he were slaughtering sheep rather than human beings. He moved closer, until there were only two prisoners standing between you. He would slay the first, skip the second, then move on to you. Shaking, you started to recite the Surat Yasin, which you had often recited for the souls of the dead and is full of verses pleading for mercy and forgiveness.

You felt ashamed at being overcome by fear and by the sweat that you couldn't stop from flowing down your forehead and into your eyes and your mouth. Why did you care about fending off fear when your end was nigh, when you knew that once the electricity that provided you with energy and life was cut off, perpetual darkness would follow?

The herald of death drew closer until you could see him carrying out his barbaric ritual for one last time. There was only one victim left standing between you. That prisoner looked as though he were already dead. He was a fellow countryman named Abdullah from Tripoli, who had come with you to Abyssinia. ` You had befriended him on board the ship that brought you to this land. You knew that he suffered from the sort of chronic headaches that even red hot scythes, the only remedy in his village, could put an end to, though they had left many scars on his neck and temples. Here he was, this poor man, this wretched creature, about to find at last a permanent cure for the pains in his head. His eyes bulged, and his mouth, covered with spittle, hung open as though lightning had electrocuted him and frozen him stiff.

Your distress made you forget any compassion you might have felt for him. You had been educated in the traditions of war, whose first lesson to you was that when the head of a companion fighting beside you goes flying, you touch your own head and thank the heavens that it was someone else's. This time, however, the situation was different, both your head and his head would go.

Sanko reached out and grabbed Abdullah's scalp with one hand, leaving the other free to slit Abdullah's throat. Your slaughtered friend let out a gurgle like a lowing cow, and jets of blood burst from his neck, splattering your head and face. You bumped your head hard against the tree trunk. You shook it fiercely, trying to get the blood from your eyes. Through the drops of blood hanging on your eyelashes, you saw the killer wipe his knife on the slain man's clothes; then you watched him move, leaving the African behind to stand before you. It was the moment of reckoning. He looked you squarely in the eyes. You mustered all your courage and tried to return his look with a stronger one, focusing, trying to hide your weakness and your fear.

As often happened in times of danger, your thoughts turned to one of the pious men of your village for aid, namely Sidi Abdelsalam al-Asmar, who lay resting in his mausoleum in the town of Zlitin, may God be pleased with him. You said his name three times. Thousands of miles of desert, forests, rivers, mountains, and seas lay between you, but no distance could prevent your plea from reaching him, and no obstacle could thwart him from answering if he so desired.

You raised your eyes to the open sky above the yard, as if casting about for the path your soul would follow to the world of eternal silence, seeing what awaited you beyond the black screen of death. Soon, the suspense of waiting to learn the answer to that ultimate question would be over. Mere seconds remained before that unknown world, and all its secrets and cryptic mysteries would reveal themselves to you. The sun's rays streamed down in columns, hurting your skyward eyes. The Negro of Death reached out his hand, to deal with you as he had dealt with your friend Abdullah when he had grabbed him by his scalp. You wanted to save him the effort, and save yourself the ordeal of having your head thrown back, so you lifted your head and arched it back as far as the tiny distance between you and the wall would allow. You stretched your neck as far back as you could, tautening your bare throat, giving the knife a chance to carry out its work easily, without requiring the killer to grab you by the hair. You could taste the bitter acridity of fear as you took your final constrained breaths. You shut your eyes, trying to flee from the horror before you. Time and space slowed and stopped, the air fell still, movement ceased, and the hands of every clock in the world froze at the final second of your life.

The world turned in your head, spinning rapidly, linking the day you had come into the world – a day you knew only through the stories of the older women in your family – with these final moments, when the time had come for you to leave this world. No one had celebrated your birth with happy songs as it had coincided with the Italian army's invasion of your village, Awlad Al Sheikh. Their arrival had been violent, accompanied by vengeful raid operations into the houses of resistance fighters. Aptly, perhaps your treacherous life would now also come to an end amidst bloody violence and suffering.

But as this final vertiginous and ecstatic reverie peaked and faded, you realized that something had kept Sanko from delivering the fatal swipe. Why had that split second between raising the knife and swinging it down to your throat dragged on for ages? You noticed your fellow prisoner was smiling because he had been skipped over by the Negro of Death – in fact he was almost laughing from the great joy he felt at being saved. You were thus stunned to hear a terrifying, eerie scream come from him. You opened your eyes to behold what had happened. The murderous Negro had for the first time changed the system he had started with, leaving you alone for no logical reason, and turning upon the African who had been laughing just a moment ago. He had grabbed his scalp instead of yours, and the man, for the first time, emitted a terrifying shriek when he saw the blade of the knife, which glittered in the sunlight before descending onto his throat. A bloody curtain burst across your vision, obscuring the disc of the sun, as if you had fallen into a blood-red swoon. Had you been saved? As Sanko the butcher passed you by and continued applying his long knife to the necks of other victims, it appeared that you had been saved by the whimsy of a murderous madman. Was that happiness you felt? Indeed it was, selfish and blissful happiness, and not an iota of sadness for your deceased neighbour.

An absurd situation resulted. Yet you remained watching the slaughter unfold, a massacre by all measures, but you realized that the good fortune had stayed the butcher's knife and saved you. As you began to gag nauseously at the human blood on your face and in your mouth, which was attracting more flies than you thought possible, you realized that Sidi Abdelsalam, whose intervention you had sought, had delivered you from this massacre. The sun was now directly overhead and seemed to pierce your body and soul with the force of a personal divine interrogation.

You saw what had happened to you as a preliminary drill for some other life that awaited you in the heart of hell. With shattered nerves, you followed the scene progressing in the yard as Sanko the killer moved from prisoner to prisoner until he had completed his task. He cast the bloodied knife on the ground and let out the chilling war cry of Abyssinian warriors, which you had previously heard on the battlefield. The rest of the guards took up the cry, then other soldiers both inside and outside the fence joined in. Your mind folded into itself in a stupor, as your body collapsed in its shackles.

But the day had come to an end and you hadn't died, didn'tor become another piece of that congealed block of blood that mixed with the dirt in the yard. Neither had you learned why that man, with all the appearance of a human skeleton coated in black tar, spared you at the last second from putting his knife to your jugular. The answer would remain forever a mystery, a symbol of the absurdity of fate that permeated your existence.

The blood bath was over and for today, you and the others were no longer prisoners that needed to be rescued. However, the effect of that day's events scarred your heart and mind, leaving a black, indelible stain on your memory. You were like who had come back to life after having traveled to the land of the dead.

That day, the taste of blood in your mouth forever spoiled your appetite. That moment changed your views on a variety of subjects, becoming a dividing line between two eras and two different lives. You felt as though you had grown decades in a single second, and your way of thinking changed accordingly. Your vision of the meaning of life broadened, just as your understanding of hope and salvation, failure and success, good and evil, happiness and misery, pain and pleasure — even life and death — shifted. In that pivotal moment, all of these concepts assumed a single meaning, futility.

TWO

It had all begun with a truck that stopped in the market square during the midday stillness. The shopkeepers had closed up, and with the driver's help, you crept onto the truck and hid amongst the sacks of coal. You endured hours of inhaling coal dust and listening to the buzzing of flies. You were smothered by the heat of the sun. The sweat you wiped from your brow was mixed with coal particles. You whispered prayers and incantations so that nobody would discover you, until you heard the truck starting, and felt it beginning to move. It drove down the hill that linked your village to the main road, which led to the capital. You waited a few minutes before raising your head over the sacks of coal and breathing God's fresh air. When you looked back you saw the buildings and palm trees of your village receding in the distance and you realized with a heavy heart that a chapter in your life had come to a close, and that a new chapter was about to begin.

You had been forced to leave the village, but you didn't regret it, because even before the incident that eventually compelled you to leave, you had been burning with desire to get out of the village before you died of boredom.

Otherwise. it would have been left to the flies, bedbugs and fleas someday to put you out of your misery. You had reached the age of twenty-four and nothing you could see offered any promise of change.

You shepherded a flock and had learned the Quran by heart at the Sunni Mosque, after which you had become the teacher's assistant. You would follow him with a pitcher to pour water on his feet during his ablutions, more like a servant than an instructor. Despite your education and the price you had paid for it in lashes and rebukes, you continued to roam with your flock like any uneducated shepherd boy.

You realized that your life would continue in much the same way if you remained in the village, and that all you could ever achieve through your education was the honorific title of Sheikh Othman. The only thing to set you apart from the rest of the villagers was that they would approach you in the market, in the mosque, or at your home, requesting you to read letters for them, or to write messages for them. And you always made a point to sign the letters "Greetings from the writer of this letter, Sheikh Othman", even if the addressee didn't know you. It was your way of proving your existence and boasting of the favour you had done them.

Writing and reading other people's letters for free was the only way you could put what you had learned to good use. All that you were able to profit by your education was a handful of eggs that your teacher, Sheikh Abdullah, passed on to you from the gifts of his students' families, for this was all the people of Awlad Al Sheikh were able to give to their childrens' teacher. The most you could dream of was to one day take your teacher's place if he passed from the world of the living before you, or you could compete with Sheikh Baraka in writing out amulets by the shrine of Sheikh al-Kabir. To yearn after any other ambition was hopeless, even if you were to read every single book from the oldest to the most recent and acquire all the knowledge therein.

Before Sheikh Baraka discovered you at the deserted well with Aziza, the daughter of Nafeesa the water carrier, you had met her many times before at the same place. Aziza was a young black girl with delicate features unlike most women of her race and colour. She was a few years younger than you, and you had known her since she was a little child trailing after her mother as she brought water to the villagers' homes. In time, Aziza began to help her mother carry water, and her breasts developed along with a host of other enticing feminine qualities. She would always look your way with a tempting, beckoning glance and one time you had met walking towards the abandoned well. You walked along with her on the deserted path, under the shade of palm trees, and expressed your desire to meet with her alone. She acquiesced.

The well itself had been filled in long ago, leaving two sides still standing, between which was an empty space that you had made into a special, secret place for you to study, contemplate, and pray. You had covered it with palm branches and made it into a hut, where you left a straw mat and a water-jug.

After that first rendezvous with Aziza, you transformed the hut also into a place for clandestine rendezvous. Because it was surrounded by palm trees and still near the functional well that Aziza drew water from, it wasn't hard for her to claim she was going out to the well and from there to sneak between the palm trees into this secluded area, and later to fill the clay jar with water before returning to the village, to conceal what had been her real motivation.

Your preliminary meetings with Aziza passed without any physical contact because, in spite of her admiration for you and her willingness to meet with you alone, she wasn't ready to make the relationship a physical one. When it finally did happen, the contact was restricted to a few kisses for several meetings, before moving on to something more, but with one essential condition, she insisted that she had to remain a virgin. Indeed, the intimacy between you took place without violating this condition, which you also wished to observe in order to avoid complications, as well out of a sense of compassion for the girl. Moreover, it didn't keep you from enjoying the act. The relationship didn't trouble your religious conscience as it didn't fall under the category of full sexual intercourse, which Islamic law considers among the gravest of sins.

When Sheikh Baraka raised the cover of palms over your hut, it seemed that he had been standing outside eavesdropping at first and had wanted to catch you red-handed. You were half-naked and locked in an embrace, and he began to shout, calling upon the people to come see the Quran teacher Al Sheikh Othman Al Sheikh committing lewd obscenities with Aziza, the daughter of Nafeesa the water carrier. But before anyone else could arrive, you had both dressed quickly. Aziza covered her body in her wrap and fled between the palm trees back to the village, while you remained to face Sheikh Baraka in the presence of the people who had been drawn by his vociferous bellowing. One of the first to arrive was an elderly farmer who denounced Sheikh Baraka as a liar,

saying he had seen nothing more than the girl bringing
you a pitcher of water, and that Sheikh Baraka's perverse
mind made him think there was something immoral going
on between the two of you.

Meanwhile Sheikh Baraka was screaming and swearing
that he had seen you in the act of adultery with Aziza the
black prostitute. Apparently, he had been keeping an eye
on you for a while and had heard a rumour about a relationship between you and Aziza, so he had lain in wait,
observing her movements until he figured out when she
would come to the abandoned well and followed her to
carry out his plan. The problem was that he had chanced
across Haj Badran near the well, someone who enjoyed the
respect of the villagers and who corroborated Sheikh
Baraka's testimony. After that, it was hard to find someone
who would believe your denials.

You realized you were fated tp be driven from the
mosque, cursed vehemently by your family members, beginning with your father, mother and step-father, and perhaps
turned out of your home too. You rummaged around your
pocket and found a small amount of money. You knew of
a truck loaded with coal bound for the city that would
arrive from the countryside and stop for a while in the
market square. You didn't hesitate to follow through with
the plan that would extricate you from your predicament
and take you out of the village. You haggled with the truck
driver, eventually paying him to find a secure place for you
among the sacks of coal where you could hide until the
time of departure.

The motive behind Sheikh Baraka's actions had been
revenge. All you had done to arouse his enmity had been
writing a single amulet for which you had been recompensed

merely two eggs. You used to go to the shrine of Sheikh
Al-Kabir looking to earn extra income by writing amulets
for men and women seeking spiritual cures.

Sheikh Baraka was renowned for writing amulets and
everyone went to him. You, on the other hand, after hours
of waiting, couldn't find anyone but this single old woman
who had failed to secure a place in the sea of people
surrounding Sheikh Baraka and thus settled for an utterly
unknown young man to write out her amulet for the
treatment of a headache. Instead of the four eggs she had
brought to pay for Sheikh Baraka's amulet, she gave you
only two since she considered an amulet written by someone
like you to be only equivalent to half of an amulet written
by the better Sheikh. He might have contented himself
with driving you out of the vicinity of the shrine of Sheikh
Al-Kabir, but that wasn't enough for him. Ultimately, he
decided to drive you out of the village completely so as
to rid himself of all rivals.

Meanwhile, you saw an opportunity in these events to
leave the village and its restrictive environment, which
oppressed you like a weight on your chest, in order to seek
out a wider space where your dreams could roam unin-
hibited. Such a place could only be the capital.

You had never been to Tripoli, although you had heard
much of it. You knew that the villagers who visited it
returned in a state of the utmost awe and captivation,
mentioning its name as if they spoke of a magical charm
that brought happiness, or as if they spoke of freedom itself,
which brought with it the liberty to do whatever one
pleased. Even though you knew nothing of the capital, it
was enough that you knew Awlad Al Sheikh and all the
boredom, monotony and suffering that came with it. You

knew intimately the dirt and sand that blew into your mouth and eyes when the summer and winter winds came up from the south, so freezing and chilling that you had always wondered why that distant ancestor of yours who was the first to settle in this locality, hadn't chosen some greener and lusher place than this arid and desolate spot.

All the evidence led you to believe that he must have been a criminal wanted by the law, who sought to escape to a place where the servants of the state would be power-less to reach him. So he had chosen this wasted, depressing place between the mountains as his sanctuary in order to hide among its bare, rocky hills and the sandy, rust-coloured horizon, which was broken only by more sand dunes. At the foot of these hills, by the few washes and creek beds fed by infrequent rain, your ancient outlaw grandfather planted a few date seeds that grew into a palm-grove and fed a generation or two of his descendants. But as time went on, and the clan grew, it became impossible to feed all those hungry mouths on the dates of these palm trees.

You once dreamed that you were sitting on a luxurious sedan chair with blue silk curtains, carried by seven strong black men on their shoulders. They took you up a moun-tain, on top of which waited a woman in a rose gossamer gown that fluttered in the wind. You awoke from your slumber happy, certain that those slaves were the servants and guards of success, bearing you up to the lofty heights where the Lady of Success and Happiness waited for you. But realistically, what success, what fortune could one find in a desert village that maps didn't even deign to mention?

You had forgotten this dream and only remembered it as you leaned against the sacks of coal in the truck making for Tripoli with you in the rear. The black sacks came to represent the slaves in your dream, the truck a luxurious sedan chair, and Tripoli, which loomed on the horizon, the Lady of Good Fortune awaiting you atop the mountain. There was no other city in this desert country where dreams might come true.

You had developed a mental image of life in the city as the opposite of life in the village, the opposite of its misery, silence, and emptiness. So you came to Tripoli a stranger, without knowing anyone, or what life had in store for you, or how to behave in such a city. All that you had was the image in your head that the villagers' imaginations had created, brilliant lights that turned night into day, where everyone rode carriages and carts drawn by horses with saddles engraved in gold and silver. You imagined a city where scantily clad foreign women strolled down the streets, unveiled, baring their arms and legs, making a show of their feminine charms, wearing make-up and perfumes that wafted from their wrists and temples. Sometimes it went further than that, especially at the swimming pools or the seaside beaches where their bodies would be almost completely naked except for an area that could have been covered with something the size of a mulberry leaf.

The villagers' imaginations drew a picture of a city where on holidays and special occasions the courtyards and streets hosted concerts and dances, where the government distributed food and drinks for free. There were also horse and motor races and countless other sporting events, not to mention promenades, gardens, theatres, the cinema, and markets and shops stocked with all the food, drinks and fruit a person could desire all year round, imported out of season from every corner of the earth. And there were rose gardens and fountains from which water trilled and sang, coming out in fanciful shapes and forms to entertain the people and evoke merriment in their hearts. This was a city of the wealthy: people who lived in castles, wore the finest silk and ate with golden spoons.

Yet the central myth behind Tripoli was the sea, that infinite vastness of water that dazzled everyone from your village who saw it. Normally they were fascinated to see a puddle of water left by the rain before the earth dried it up. Then they saw the swelling sea with its mighty waves, and the ships ploughing through its rising crests.

The sea surrounded Tripoli on three sides and was the subject of old wives' tales that you had heard as a child from the women of your family before you slept. Promenades clustered all around the sea, and channels reserved for pleasure boats, and beaches reserved for swimming. Naturally, you arrived in the city with a burning desire to see such a sight.

Still, when you heard all the talk of the city, you were also able to distinguish imagination from reality. You knew that the city wasn't all promenades, castles and diversions, that there was more than just dancing, and free food at festivals. You knew there was oppression, drudgery, poverty and misery, but you also knew that whoever possessed diligence, industriousness, and intelligence could achieve riches and success there.

You were prepared to exert as much effort as you could to achieve success in the city, realizing that as soon as you arrived, your first task would be to find a job during the day in order to secure some roots in the city, so that you would not be carried off by the first gust of wind. You would need a source of income and a place to live, and from there would you begin your ascent.

You didn't have any relatives in the city, so you didn't have anyone to be your guide and support in the first days. This meant that you would have to rely on your own faculties and energies to guide you.

All you knew about the city was that there was an agency that served as a way station and resting place for people who went back and forth between the city and the oases. It was called the Shushan Agency and was situated near the Tuesday Market. Therefore, this is where you chose to painfully stretch your numb, creaking, limbs off the truck and brush as much of the coal dust from your clothes and skin as you could. You looked around in startled awe, immediately transfixed and sensitive to the details of life in the metropolis.

The Shushan Agency consisted of a stretch of land surrounded by a wooden fence, which was used as a place to stop cars and load goods. They had built a hut out of tin sheets and wood planks where those without anywhere else to go could sleep. It was important that from the very first moment you arrived on the Shushan Agency's doorstep, you were assured a place to rest your head over-night, free of charge.

The first thing that struck you as you began to acquaint yourself with the city of Tripoli, was how greatly the people here differed from the people of Awlad Al Sheikh. They wore clothes of multifarious foreign fashions rather than the uniform traditional garb that the people of your village wore. Their complexion didn't resemble the swarthy faces you were used to. Instead, the people here were fair and ruddy. It wasn't difficult for you to surmise even in the very first days of your arrival that Tripoli wasn't, as you had thought, an Arab-Libyan city, but that it was actuallyan Arab-Italian city through and through. You had begun to compare the people here with the villagers of Awlad Al Sheikh thinking they were all of the same Libyan descent. But they weren't Libyans, they were Italians, for there wasn'thing Libyan about the way they went about the wide streets, or sat in elegant cafés and restaurants, or went shopping in grand-looking stores, all the while speaking in their foreign language, and stamping life with an Italian air that hadn'thing to do with Arab origins.

Bewildered, you set out to find the Libyans of the city, crossing streets, searching the faces of people sitting at pavement cafés, circling through the markets, shops, and promenades without coming across one Arab street, café or restaurant, not even a shop with Arab customers. The few Libyans that were there, were lost in the midst of the Italian masses. You didn't even hear the call to prayer until the day after you spent the night at the agency, after you discovered the surrounding alleyways whilst wandering through the back streets looking for a mosque. It was here, along these back streets that the Libyans got around town after the Italians took over the city and its broad, beautiful, lit streets.

You also discovered that the city had its own unique fragrance, which you had inhaled the moment you arrived. It was more distinct in the mornings, though you couldn't pin it down to a single scent, for it was a cocktail of many different aromas. The fragrance of roses and flowers from the gardens was mixed with the smell of ovens baking sweets and cakes, with the tang of olives and soap factories, perfume shops and vegetable markets, the scent of fried food from the restaurants and cafés, and the herby smell of shops selling medicinal folk remedies.

That was the first breath of air that wafted your way when you woke and went out to greet life in the city.

Distilled from every environment, that unique fragrance was the essence and aroma of life, for it sprang directly from life, from its diversity, its stench, its all-encompassing totality, just as the people, their markets, streets, houses, and squares sprang from the city. Even the trees wore the stamp of the city, giving them a different appearance from the palm trees that grew in your village. Trees that were more familiar to you looked nothing like they did in the country-side. Their leaves and branches looked as though they were made out of paper, like the fake trees adorning the window displays of the Italian shops. Even their trunks were stripped of that rough covering you thought was characteristic to all palm trees. There were no fibres or stubble, and probably no dates either, as the reason for their existence was merely to decorate the street, whereas in the village they were a source of sustenance and livelihood.

The trunks of some of the trees had been painted white with a reflective substance for reasons having to do with the flow of traffic, so that when the street lights or car lights fell upon them at night, the tree trunks would shine.

As for the other trees, known as decorative trees, they were trimmed and pruned until their branches, leaves, and smooth trunks all seemed alike, matching each other with mechanical precision, exemplary models of order and crafts-manship. They stood in two parallel lines that defied the natural freedom and chaos of the countryside. Perhaps they even defied the dignity of trees themselves, for the trees in the wild were there to carry out the functions intended by their crea-tion, namely to be of benefit to people and animals. Here, on the other hand, the trees were planted for mere show.

Workers were employed full-time to prune and trim the trees, leaving them perpetually neat, elegant, and beautiful, so that they could put decorative paper on their tops, and hang film advertisements and pictures of actors or singers on their trunks, or hang coloured lamps from their branches during holidays and festivals. That was all the city wanted of the trees.

Your arrival in the city coincided with an Italian holiday, perhaps it was some king's birthday, or the anniversary of his ascension to the throne, so you rejoiced at the occasion to commemorate your own arrival to Tripoli and the commencement of a new phase in your life, bidding farewell to the life of a country boy and embracing the life of a city youth.

In the square by the Shushan Agency, you saw a crowd gathered around some games and entertainers, so you headed that way. One of the entertainers was standing on a tall platform beside the Wheel of Fortune, a large wheel with an arrow fixed to it. The arrow would spin over a display of numbers ranging from one to a hundred, and people bet on which number the arrow would stop at with a payout of one to one hundred for whomever fortune smiled upon. There were other people who were playing a game involving shooting arrows at targets, and at the edges of the square were swings and wooden horses, which could be ridden for a paltry fee. You rode the horses and the swings and put up half a lira for the Wheel of Fortune, then lost it without feeling any disappointment. You were enjoying the festive, celebratory atmosphere which had no equivalent in Awlad Al Sheikh.

Then you went to Pasha Mosque to see the ancient mosque, with its fine carpets, high domes, the splendid minbar, the beautiful engravings on the ceiling and walls, and the Quranic verses written inside the domes in gold lettering. You began to wonder in astonishment how the

Italians, given their leaders' reputation for foolishness and irreverence, left this imposing Islamic edifice standing. No sign or mark of disturbance or desecration marred the mosque, unlike what had happened to many other Islamic monuments, including the Sunni Mosque in Awlad Al Sheikh, whose walls the Italians had destroyed in a battle, and whose library they had burned.

Next you went to the Turkish Market, the Musheer Market, and the Rabba Market. Tripoli, meaning three cities, derived its name from these three markets, whose fame and prestige increased generation after generation. There you enjoyed the merry shapes and colours that the native calligraphers, masters of their trade, drew on plates, saddles, and plaques. You saw a new face of Arab-Islamic Tripoli, a beautiful face that shone through these traditional arts and crafts, one that was more authentic and vibrant than the dingy alleyways whose shabbiness was saddening.

Some of that splendour was also evident in the fine, surrounding architecture, and decorative fountains from which water shot high into the air, tracing curves that joined with other curves drawn by the blue veins of the fountains' marble. You also saw public fountains in the squares erected by the municipality, open at all hours for men and women to drink their fill from the waters, which then slid downhill into cisterns that eventually came to the sea. Soon, you arrived at the sea.

You watched the sea crashing against the walls of the Red Castle, and you saw a tongue of stone parallel to the castle, jutting into the sea. You walked along it until you were also in the middle of the sea. The waves raced around you, spraying you with water, and you were brimming with excitement. You had heard much about the sea. With attentive ears you had picked up your mother's stories about the seven seas that the hero of legend crossed to save the Sultan's daughter. You memorized the Quranic verses that spoke about the sea that the pious man, Al-Khider, crossed in his boat. You had been bewildered by the story of Allah's prophet Jonah, who was snatched up by the whale and lived in its stomach, neither dead nor alive. You listened with glee to the fate of the Pharaoh as he chased the prophet Moses, who split the sea before him to cross safely with his people, but then sent the waves down to drown and kill the Pharaoh and his soldiers.

But your imagination had never pictured the sea as you saw it before you now, and you said to yourself that the awe and wonder written on the faces of the villagers who had seen it wasn't strange at all, for your feelings were no less of wonder and awe than theirs, having come from that desert of drought, thirst, and oppressive heat. You did know that the water was salty, unsuitable for drinking or watering plants, but nevertheless you felt intoxicated by the presence of so much water and by the roaring waves that washed over the headland of rocks that you stood upon. You felt the beauty of that intoxication overcome you whenever it used to rain and you would go out to the public square of Awlad Al Sheikh with your friends, dancing, letting the showers land on your faces, and singing:

> O rain! O dear Aunt!
> Pour over my braids of hair,
> Anointed with oil from the olive tree.
> O rain, pour, pour,
> Pour over Al-Qubi's house.
> He has nothing to his name,
> But a scrap of meat and a smoking pipe!

The people of the city had built promenades for themselves along the edge of the sea, a Corniche for strolling, and beside it Summer resorts whose grounds were covered in sand for people to recline upon after swimming to their hearts' content. Aspects of the sea made it seem almost like a counterpart of the desert, that vast space of red sand contrasted with this range of blue curving waves crowned by white foam, both stretching on seemingly without end. Each of them was a frightening enigma, a maze, and as the well-known saying held, nothing compares to the treachery of the sea but the treachery of the desert.

THREE

Your first day in the city was filled with amazement and discovery. Your second day was filled with a fear of the unknown, and this fear grew with the third and fourth days, as you began to knock on the doors of offices and agencies looking for clerical work. You discovered that no one was in need of your knowledge of the Arabic language, because all commercial transactions in the markets or the government departments were carried out exclusively in Italian, and that there were no positions anywhere for someone who hadn't mastered reading and writing this language.

The only food that you could afford to buy in the city was a loaf of bread with a cup of tea. Anything more substantial would use up your remaining money in a single day. So you went to the New Gate where there was a station for horse-drawn carriages and a circle of people drinking tea. A man was sat in the middle of that circle before the burner preparing tea from a large pitcher and distributing three rounds of red tea in small elegant cups to those around him. You sat with them and sipped your cups of tea like them, and when the last cup came it was tea mixed with slipping through the cracks in the wooden slats and sheets of metal, and you hadn't a single franc left.

The new clothes you had arrived with had become dirty. Your shirt collar was filthy and some mud had stuck to your Arab trousers, leaving nothing but your waistcoat, which would at least give you a somewhat presentable appearance for when you met the owners of shops and offices asking them for work. You really didn't know how you would find time to wash your only shirt, and if you did find time you would have to remain wrapped in your cloak until the shirt dried, something that would have to wait until after you had secured some sort of work, no matter how lowly or degrading. Any job was better than standing in front of the mosque begging for charity.

It would suffice to be granted enough pay to buy a loaf of bread. That was all you wanted. It would not be hard to begin your day without tea or breakfast, but what about lunch and dinner? If you didn't find work, what would you do about tomorrow and the next day now that you had cut the strings that once tied you to your village? There was no going back now, a matter to which the other men staying at the Shushan Agency couldn't relate. They took pity on you and, seeing the plight you had got yourself into, knew no remedy other than for you to return to your family in Awlad Al Sheikh. They broached the topic with you, and when they found you insistent on staying and continuing to suffer daily, they looked at one another, shaking their heads with the collective phlegmatic wisdom of the ages, and hummed the melancholy folk song that says that whoever tastes the bread of the city can never leave.

You didn't explain that your problem was different, that

it wasn't you who refused to return to your village, but the village who had ejected you and wasn't prepared to welcome you back, leaving you no choice but to face your fate in the city by any means possible. Telling them all this would be embarrassing and disgraceful. You were happy that the story of your flight from the village was unknown to these people.

Some of the porters at the Tuesday Market harassed you when you tried to lend a hand with the sacks and boxes of goods being loaded onto a cart. Even they had rejected you from their menial craft, perceiving your actions as a threat to their livelihood. In crude, rough voices, they ordered you to seek your fortune elsewhere.

As you passed through the markets, you saw people sitting around large bowls of food. You stared at them enviously, then tore your gaze away and moved on. The longer you looked, the more your hunger would grow. You could have found a discarded tomato on the ground of the Tuesday Market and made that your breakfast, but you refrained from picking up something so covered in dirt, and the entire day passed without a morsel to eat.

Night came and your stomach began to pang.. The pain was no longer due only to hunger. It was a different sort of pain, as though hot pincers were gripping your entrails for short agonizing moments, then stopping, only to return with renewed intensity. Your desire to find food of any kind to stop this torture was so great that you considered plucking the leaves off any tree you might happen across, even one of the trees planted for decoration on the streets, just to chew on something to stop the convulsions in your stomach. But you also feared you might make the pain worse rather than better if you ate something, for this was not the result of today's fasting, but also of the four days before when nothing had entered your stomach but loaves of bread and cups of tea. But now even those items of low nutritional value were unattainable.

Nevertheless, you went to the tea circle where you had already been, to see the tea maker lighting a lantern beside the burner so that he might see better while he prepared the tea. He had placed a turban around his head to protect him from the night-time dew. It was April, and Spring had just begun, however the warm weather of the mornings couldn't withstand the waves of evening chill, which turned the Spring weather to Winter. You had felt the cruel aching cold whenever you returned to the shelter at the agency, throwing yourself onto the mangled mat, holding your knees up against your chest and trying to ward off the cold with your light papery cloak. Nothing worked, so you had been forced to resort to using card-board from shipping boxes to cover your body.

You had come to the tea circle this time without any money, hoping to get a cup of tea from the proprietor by promising to pay him later. Then, because drinking tea alone would only serve to increase the pain in your stomach, you would try to get him to loan you five bara with which to buy a loaf of bread. You had high hopes that this man would agree. From the very first day, you had felt that he sympathized with you, which was what incited you to continue coming here to the exclusion of all the other circles of tea makers, as a kind of camaraderie developed between the two of you.

He had started to call you by your name whenever he handed you your tea, while you began to call him Uncle al-Sharif. Why were you embarrassed, or even afraid, to approach him then? It was not as if you were asking for his daughter's hand in marriage, it was only a franc, which you would pay back. It was certainly a better option than starving, and more dignified than begging. Even so, the task was difficult for you, because it was the first time in your life you were asking a stranger for money.

You remained still, hesitating for a while, moving your gaze over the men sitting in the circle before moving towards him slowly so as not to startle him or draw people's attention to your plight. You began to get closer to him without anyone taking note of your movements until your shoulder touched his, and you put your mouth beside his ear. You wet your throat again and again, you recited the Fatiha and the Surat Ikhlas to yourself so that your efforts would succeed. Finally you put your trust in Allah and began your speech by greeting him, although the turban that was wrapped around his head and ears prevented your whispered voice from reaching him. You were forced to raise your voice and risk being discovered by one of the men sitting around him. Hunger is an infidel, as they say, and it was hunger that forced you to swallow your pride and tell him what you had come for as quickly as you could.

He didn't reply, but merely raised his head and shouted, "Yousef!" His son, who helped him hand out the cups of tea, appeared above the heads of the sitting men. He was a young man in the middle of his teens, and his father spoke to him in a sentence you didn't understand even though you heard it perfectly, "Take this man to Abdullah's place."

Yousef took you to a bakery up against the city wall in the opposite direction. Abdullah was the owner of this bakery, and had just finished putting the loaves of bread he had prepared onto the boards in front of the oven. A young black assistant greeted customers, gave them their bread, and took their money, placing it in a drawer beside him. From the bakery's entrance a man came burdened with a heavy load of firewood and straw, which he placed on top of another pile of firewood. The bakery owner reached into the drawer to give the firewood porter some money, and asked him to stay there for a few seconds.

He then turned to you, placing a hot loaf of bread between your hands, he said, "Are you truly looking for work?" You answered him around a chunk of the burning bread that you had already put in your mouth, "Yes, yes." From the next day onwards, gathering straw and firewood from the public parks, the rubbish dumps, or the forests surrounding the city, and transporting it to Abdullah's bakery became your regular job. Every morning you came to work. While shepherding sheep in the mountains and valleys of Awlad Al Sheikh had been far easier, the difference between was that shepherding doomed you to follow sheep until old age overtook you, whereas here gathering firewood was just one step to help you over the threshold and begin life in the city.

You practised your new profession with this thought in mind, and without sharing the enthusiasm of your co-workers, who viewed their employment as the chance of a lifetime. Take for example the man who led you out to the forest the first time. Like you, he came from the countryside, but all he wanted was an opportunity to make some money, even if he frittered away an entire decade doing it. Then he could return to his village and open a grocery shop, or a bakery of his own. That's why he worked two shifts a day, one at dawn, and the second in the afternoon, working until dusk. You, meanwhile, contented yourself with just one shift in the morning, because the point of working was to meet your costs of living temporarily until you found work commensurate to your education.

FOUR

You woke up with the dawn call to prayer and went to the Senoussi Mosque to pray before heading to the forests and rubbish yards around them. You would not return until the middle of the day to collect your four francs. Then you took advantage of the remaining afternoon for your own chores, like washing your clothes. You also borrowed some francs from Abdullah, the owner of the bakery, to buy a jilbab befitting your new profession, and this way the clothes you brought with you from the village would stay in good condition. This free time also gave you the opportunity to look for less exhausting work worthier of a man who had memorized the book of Allah.

You were now guaranteed an amount of money that met your basic needs, and the Shushan Agency could still provide you with a place to live for a few more days, though it was a refuge for travellers and wayfarers, and not a place for permanent accommodation. Anyone who stayed there for more than two weeks would be warned of the necessity of finding another place to sleep.

You continued roving around the large boutique shops, hoping they might need a worker for accounting or a sales assistant to take customers' measurements, and you went to restaurants and cafés, hoping they might need a waiter, but without any luck.

During one of your rounds, you saw people in a funeral procession heading towards the cemetery, and remembered that among the tombstones and memorials of the graveyard there was one job that you and few others had perfected. The burial ceremony required someone to read the Surat Yasin, so the deceased would be blessed and granted mercy. So you hurried to the cemetery of Sidi Munaider and sat in front of the nearest open grave into which its new occupant was being interred. Without knowing who the deceased was, or asking the family's permission, you raised your voice and chanted the Surat Yasin.

Your voice came out sweet and resonant, imparting a touch of majestic solemnity to the death, and spreading peace and tranquility in the hearts of the family and friends of the deceased. You saw the people listening closely to you in silence and amazement, and you felt increasingly certain the family of the deceased would reward you with something. But the burial rituals concluded and the companions of the deceased left the cemetery without even bothering to place a franc in your hand, leaving you without anything but words of thanks and praise.

The same thing occurred a second and third time before you realized that no one was going to pay you for reading the Surat Yasin, and what you had first estimated to be an additional source of income, would gain you nothing but words from the family of the deceased, wishing peace and mercy upon your own dead ancestors.

You knew this for a fact after you stumbled across someone from your village one day. His name was Abdel

Mowlah, and you had just come out of the Mizran Mosque after afternoon prayers, intending to follow the family of a deceased person from the mosque to the funeral, when you saw him at the threshold to the mosque's entrance as you were putting on your sandals. He was wearing a long jilbab of the cut worn by Issawi dervishes and his head was wrapped in a white turban. He held a crutch in one hand, while the other was stretched out to beg alms from the mosque-goers.

When he saw you, he tried to hide his face behind the fringe of his turban and turn his body towards the far wall. But you, inexperienced and naive, failed to understand that he was trying to hide the shameful fact that he was begging. You leapt over to him, taking his outstretched hand and shaking it, both happy to have found someone from your village after two weeks in a city where you knew no one, and grieving at the same time for his condition.

The people of your village had been proud of this man, who used to be an important merchant. Curious, you asked him what had brought him to this state of affairs, but he shook his head, putting off answering for another time. A distant family connection related you to this man, but in fact the entire village was tied together by some distant relation, for all of them sprang from the first person to lay roots in the land, Sheikh Al-Kabir, whose famous shrine was in your village. That meant that both you and Abdel Mowlah were descended from the Sheikh, and what disgraced him, also disgraced you, and what bettered his standing and reputation also bettered yours.

Neither you nor anyone else would have ever thought that Abdel Mowlah was in Tripoli. He had told everyone that he was a cloth merchant, which he transported from Fez to Kano and many other African towns, returning from them with ivory, ostrich feathers and ostrich eggs. So it got into everyone's heads that he was on one of his distant travels to the unknown reaches of the African continent. It would never have occurred to you that you might meet this important trader begging in front of Mizran Mosque.

You knew his family, and knew he had a wife and three children who lived a life of luxury and comfort. They wore new clothes on holidays, owned a rubber ball for the children to play with, which the other children in the village longed to play with, since they had only sack-cloth balls. As Abdel Mowlah's family was one of the few that could afford a meal with meat in it at least once a week, you considered them among the more fortunate in your village. So how could he provide a life of riches and prestige for his family, despite his humiliating position in the city? You realized that he had never in his life undertaken any journeys, nor any trade, not of ivory, feathers, or eggs, and that it was all a ruse to avoid shame and scorn. But was the begging profession truly capable of earning so much that a man could shower his children with money like this?

Abdel Mowlah walked ahead of you, and you followed behind him on a long journey from the modern and affluent parts of town, through the suburbs of Bu Mushmasha and Bu Harida, and onto the Sidi Khalifa area, and the crowded huts of Bab Akkara, at last entering a shanty-town district of huts made from branches and corrugated tin, where he had built himself a rickety, rusty domicile.

When you arrived, the tin hut was still radiating heat absorbed by the midday sun. You ducked your head when you entered so as not to hurt yourself on the sharp metal edges and protrusions. You instantly felt its heat and narrowness strangling you.

You wanted to ask him again why he contented himself with this life, but he preempted you, ignoring the curiosity that shone in your eyes.

He said, "Why did you leave Awlad Al Sheikh and come to the city?", gripping your shoulders in his hands and shaking them violently, as if you had committed some grave crime.

Clearly the irony of the situation was lost on him, for it would have been more befitting if he had directed the question to himself, but from everything you had seen you realized that in actuality he was directing it to himself as well. Through this question, he was saying that he had been forced to come to this city, to earn insult and humiliation with his own two hands. He had come knowing that there was no place for him, just as there had been no place for you, and he knew that these immigrants came from Italy to Tripoli to remake Libya for themselves according to their standards, making it a place for their enjoyment, and theirs alone. He knew that they didn't welcome any natives among them, except as workmen, servants, or beggars.

Abdel Mowlah had come to Tripoli after his camel had died. He had used it to transport commodities between the south and north of the country. And because he didn't have enough money to purchase a new camel, he fell into his current dilemma, for which he saw no other solution but to leave and never show his face in the village again. His family had become used to a life of leisure, which he had been able to save for through his work as a desert merchant, so he had journeyed to Tripoli looking for a chance to restart his work in trade, and to find any temporary work that could earn him enough to buy a new camel. This required him to move back and forth between many different jobs, but while he made enough to meet his bare necessities, they didn't leave a surplus he could send to his family. So he began trying to make extra money by begging.

By day, he orked as a porter at the harbour, or as an occasional construction worker or a stone-mason at the Al-Dahra quarries. Once the sun set and the evening prayers were done, he would would lurk enshrouded by darkness for people coming out of mosques, begging for alms to send back to his village.

Abdel Mowlah told you that it was under the influence of a man from the desert who had come to the city for work that he became a true beggar, and found himself going to a new place to beg. This companion had informed him that there were better people who would be more generous to the wretched and unfortunate than the people at the mosques were, namely the patrons of the nightclub in Musheer Market. But because an evening in front of the nightclub waiting for the customers to come out went on until the small hours of the morning, it became impractical for him to wake up for work at the harbour or quarries, which left him free to beg full-time. Habit and repetition made him forget humiliation and disgrace until all he cared about was that he made plenty of money without suffering or exertion.

Abdel Mowlah burst into bitter tears in front of you before he could finish his story. You didn't know what you could say to console him and only managed a melancholy silence. He had told everyone he was a merchant who traded in the desert regions between Fez and the heart of Africa, neglecting to realize that his presence in front of the mosques of Tripoli would not remain hidden for long from the eyes of his village. He couldn't return to the village

– nor in any other place – and find work more profitable than begging.

Abdel Mowlah continued to sob as he told you that he was trusting you, and knew you would conceal the circumstances you had found him in from the villagers of Awlad Al Sheikh, sparing him the scandal and infamy that would surely ensue. You said that you couldn't guarantee that others from the village who came to the city would not expose him, but you promised that you would never do such a thing.

For several years, Abdel Mowlah had refused to enlist in the Italians' police force or army, despite the guaranteed wages. But now he might find himself forced to go to them, for working with them and joining the police or army was no longer considered an act of betrayal against one's nation as it had been during the times of resistance and warfare. At that time, Lkbyans in the Italian army had feared to find themselves on the front, bearing arms against their brothers fighting in the resistance. But now that this was no longer a danger, and the resistance had been defeated, working with the Italians was no longer deemed disgraceful in most of the country.

You thus hastened to tell Abdel Mowlah that despite surrendering to the reality of life under occupation, the people of Awlad Al Sheikh still considered enlisting in military service with the Italians to be a loathsome, despicable thing, and whoever did so was disowned and turned out. You expressed your sympathy that a man could find himself torn between the humiliation of begging and the disgrace of becoming a soldier for the Italians.

He got up suddenly, shouting in your face that this curse would haunt you too if you didn't return immediately to Awlad Al Sheikh. You would find yourself in his exact position, facing a difficult choice between begging and donning the Italian military uniform.

You replied in a confident voice, "Perhaps death is easier than either option."

No sooner had you uttered the sentence than you regretted it. The situation was already laden with wretchedness, and there was no need for further humiliation, if only for the sake of the man before you, torn by hardship and shame.

Abdel Mowlah said quickly, "You can at least kill yourself if you want. Suicide in a situation like this is an act only single men such as yourself can commit. As for me, it would be a crime my children would pay for. They are my flesh and blood and I would be leaving them behind, so how can I kill half of me and leave the other half to a life of suffering?"

Evening had begun to creep into the place, bringing a refreshing breeze that drove away the heat of the day. The man brought out a mat and spread it out in front of the hut. He sprinkled some water around the mat to settle the dust, which passing feet might disturb, and invited you to sit with him while he busied himself lighting the little stove to prepare tea. The dirt indeed settled, but the water that he sprinkled over the earth made tiny puddles, and whenever the neighbours' children stepped in them, chasing after one another in play, they splashed your face with muddy water.

The little charcoal stove emitted thick smoke while Abdel Mowlah blew on it, aided by a piece of cardboard to fan the fire. He placed the tea kettle on the stove and then went into the hut. He came out carrying the sack he used to beg. He emptied all of its contents onto a length of cloth, among which were dried figs, dates, three pieces of bread, onions, carrots, cucumbers, peppers, two squashed tomatoes, and a handful of unshelled peanuts. He sorted them out by type, then prepared a knife and plate to cut the onions and tomatoes with some cucumbers and green peppers, making a salad known by the people of the city as "Charmoula", which was the favourite dish for supper in Tripoli.

Abdel Mowlah placed the tea in front of you and handed you a piece of bread, inviting you to partake in the food, saying, "Blessings are abundant, as you can see, so don't be bashful and eat your fill."

You excused yourself from eating or drinking anything, especially after a flock of sheep led by a young shepherd passed by, splashing the remaining water onto you and the bowl of charmoula. Your hand would not consent to reach forth and take any of this "abundant blessing", as Abdel Mowlah had called it.

The sight of the food and the way Abdel Mowlah gobbled it down upset your empty stomach, which turned with a great rumbling noise, demanding other kinds of food than this.

"Blessings are abundant as you see." The sentence rang wickedly in your head. It was as if the man were boasting of what he had attained through begging. The whole thing disgusted you. You got up and left him, hastening back to the Shushan Agency.

You knew that you had exhausted your right to sleep at the agency. One of the truck drivers who supervised the agency had told you that you could stay no more than one or two days at most, making it necessary for you to find, in this short period of time, a hole in which to take cover, or perhaps a crack in the city walls in which to sleep. If it came to that, you would be no less determined to find a place of shelter than the rats, lizards and cats who made the city their home.

The next day, after collecting firewood, you went on your daily rounds in search of work, keeping in mind the problem of finding a place to sleep. In Kushat al-Safar, you came across an old man making shoes. He raised his eyes to you and searched your face with his two narrow eyes while you stood in front of his store gazing at the many beautifully decorated oriental shoes he displayed on a wooden shelf in front of the store. In the casual tone you used on such occasions, you asked him if he had any work for you. But before he was able to reply, your sixth sense told you that this man, with his kind, fatherly look, was the man that you had been looking for, and that you would find in him the solution to your problems. Your sixth sense became certain of this when he took a nail from between his lips and hammered it into the heel of the shoe placed over an iron foot and asked, "Where are you from, my boy?"

For the first time, you heard a response that didn't indicate an outright refusal. The man had asked you which village or city you came from, so he must be interested in you, giving you and him a chance to talk together and get to know each other.

Beside him, you saw a chair meant for customers to sit in when he measured their feet, and you felt that after that question, you were entitled to use it. So you sat down after shaking his hand and answered his question, saying, "My name is Othman al-Sheikh and my village is Awlad Al Sheikh to the south of the Western Mountain."

"And who does not know Awlad Al Sheikh, if only because it produced the legendary hero 'Al-Fourty'?" said the man.

Al-Fourty was the nickname the people had given the highwayman who had harried the government in recent years. After the Italians defeated the resistance, the highwayman launched a one-man crusade on them. He would seize cars loaded with weapons headed for the south and redistribute some of the captured arms to the poor people of his tribe in the desert regions. The people therefore considered him a hero and named him Al-Fourty in the Italian language before he fell into the hands of the police, who took him to the city so that he might be tried and given a long prison sentence.

"Are you from the south or the north side of Awlad Al Sheikh?" asked the man.

You realized that the man was well-informed about your village, for only the villagers themselves, or someone with a sound knowledge of the area would realize that the clay and plaster houses, clustered together tightly, were divided between a north and a south side of town.

You said, "It's obvious that you know Awlad Al Sheikh well, sir. I'm from the north side."

"Then you are a drinker of donkey milk!" said the man.

In the days when rivalry and enmity had broken out between the two sides of the town, the people of the south side started a rumour that the residents of the north side drank donkey milk, which caused them to be born stupid, lazy, and dim-witted.

You laughed when you saw that he was laughing and had spoken to you amicably. Still, a little apprehension washed over you because this conversation linked you to highwaymen and dim children weaned on donkey milk. It seemed out of keeping with work that required someone reliable, trustworthy, and intelligent. You relaxed a little when he asked you if you knew how to read and write, because he needed someone to record the names of the clients who owed him money, and those to whom he owed money, and when you told him that you had completed the study of the Quran, his face lit up with satisfaction, though he didn't say a thing.

He went on to mention some of the well-known merchants from your village, whom he had previously done business with, finding them to be models of honesty and integrity. He made special reference to three in particular, and you told him that you knew them, and that everyone in the village was a cousin to you, meaning that even those merchants were relatives of yours.

"Then I can complain about you to them if you neglect your work," he said jokingly.

You were so happy that you almost got up from your seat to kiss his hands out of gratitude because he had accepted you as a worker in his shop without asking you how much you wanted in wages. It was a tiny shop, seeming no wider than a hand's breadth, but no matter. You would spend long hours with your back and neck bent over, holding nails in your mouth like the old man, who had developed a hunch in his back from the excessive bending he did whilst driving the tiny nails into the heels and soles of shoes. It didn't matter, this job was meant for you, even the metal foot standing in front of the store owner had guided you to him.

You later found out that your master's former assistant

had started his own shop on Gharby Street. This sparked dreams of you one day owning your own shop, making shoes and having your own assistant. You gazed for a long while at the shop, which acquired a new beauty and elegance.

The shoemaker specialized in making a type of Tripolitanian shoes with elaborate engravings and designs. Women's and men's shoes with roses in gorgeous colours made from a fine transparent fabric gave the shoes a distinctive look. He hung the shoes around him, covered the walls with them, and sat among them looking as if he were in the middle of a rose garden rather than a shoe shop. He had placed some of them on a wooden shelf attached to the store front to the left of the door, and another similar shelf to the right. The shop was like a museum of traditional arts and crafts.

You wanted to ask him to let you start that instant, but before you could open your mouth, he told you that you would begin in a couple of days, when the next month of the Christian calendar began. But his words didn't deter your resolve to begin work immediately, starting tomorrow. You told him that you would be willing to work tomorrow without pay, thinking more of finding a place to sleep than of wages. Moved by your enthusiasm, the man noddedin consent.

Leaving the shop, you saw Tripoli with new eyes, not those of someone who had been looking for work since the minute he arrived, but those of someone with a good job who had earned the right to walk through the streets the way anyone else might, cheerfully watching the people, looking at the buildings and markets and shop windows, enjoying a leisurely stroll without any goal other than relaxation and sight-seeing.

Until then you hadn't eaten a single hot meal in Tripoli, nor a complete meal even after working as a firewood gatherer because you had placed more importance on the jilbab you had bought, and you were left with only enough money for your habitual dinner of bread and tea. At that moment you felt your empty stomach hankering for a sumptuous plate from the popular street restaurants from which wafted aromas of garlic and spices. But it could wait, because despite your stomach's craving for food, you were overcome with joy at now having a job and shelter, and because you felt that whatever your stomach ached for, whatever you saw through the windows of sweatshops that made your mouth water, whatever you saw in store fronts which sold clothes which you yearned to wear, was yours for the taking in the future. You were in no hurry, for you had acquired permanent work to earn money, and you would soon be able to eat this food, and wear those clothes like the people of the city, and felt you at at last become one of them.

With great enthusiasm for your new profession, you began your work the next morning in the shop of Haj al-Mahdy. You discovered that overhead in the shop was a space where Haj al-Mahdy stored his thread and leather, the raw materials of his trade. He had made a false ceiling for the store, half a metre from the real ceiling. You saw that it was big enough to hold you and if you climbed a few wooden steps, went in hunched over, and wormed out a place between the leather skins and looms, you could sleep there. It didn't matter to you that the shop lacked all amenities necessary for a person's life, because the nearby mosque of Sidi Mahmoud, which was open night and day, would make up for these shortcomings. As for food, you would have to live on dry meals and wait for the occasions when the Haj ate dinner in the shop and shared with you hot food that he brought from home.

You didn't forget your friend al-Sharif the tea maker, and you would have to visit him, this time with a loaf of Italian bread, the kind called panini, in your hand. There was also no harm if your ambitions extended so far as to look forward to the day when your riches would allow you to eat at Bura'y Restaurant, which was widely renowned for its grills.

The Haj sat you down beside him so you could observe every minute detail of his craft. The first task he entrusted you was to take a pair of scissors and cut out leather strips according to the marks he had drawn with a pencil. Because he didn't know how to read or write, he had depended on his previous assistant to write down the names of his clients who bought on credit, especially the store owners who sold his shoes and couldn't afford to pay for the shoes before selling them.

The Haj turned his ledger book over to you to begin hadn'trecording the names of new customers. While closely watching him, you were delighted to discover that he wasn't just wasn'ta shoemaker, he was an artist. He possessed a talent and imaginative ingenuity that enabled him to place the colours and ornamental designs with precision and skill, affixing the fabric flower in just the right way to make the shoe even more beautiful and elegant. You even tried to imitate him when you were alone in the shop, but you couldn't embroider a single thread, and you realized this wasn't something one couldn't learn through simple imitation, but that it would take a lot of hard work and talent.

You quickly fell into the rhythm of life in the

commercial centre of the old city of Tripoli. You became one of the people of the market, one set of hands among many producing traditional crafts and goods. You no longer had to fear returning to the desert and to the life of a sheepherder, and you no longer worried about sharing Abdel Mowlah's fate as a beggar.

However, the initial excitement of finding work and shelter soon disappeared as you felt your life become hostage to the confines of the shop, which was only four metres squared and where you spent every waking hour. You went through the daily routine of your personal chores in this tiny square. Despite that, you were pleased with yourself, because although you left the shop only to shower and pray in the mosque, or when the Haj sent you on a small errand to the neighbouring store, this tiny, narrow space always gave you a feeling of calm, safety and stability. Indeed you felt proud to belong to a profession far superior to those lowly trades that you had wished for whilst collecting firewood in the forests, or whilst you wandered around the Tuesday Market, or amongst the city's cemeteries, associating with firewood collectors, grave-diggers, and porters.

Another reason for your pride was that Haj al-Mahdy's shop was the most refined and distinguished in Tripoli, as it specialized in making the shoes that grooms bought for their weddings, and that brides from the upper class boasted of wearing. Thus, the cream of the city's elite was eager to do business with him.

In a matter of days, you saw proof of that and through your work with Haj al-Mahdy, you acquainted yourself with the the upper-class ladies of Tripoli. A lady of the higher class, often of a superior type of beauty, would come to the shop wearing a sparkling white cloak tautly across her body, so tightly that it brought out the curves of her body in a provocative manner, and her heels tapping on the pavement in a sing-song rhythm as if she were playing a melody. The tantalizing scent of her perfume preceded her, and she would always have a black servant in a jilbab in tow, with a handkerchief covering her hair, and a palm-branch basket in hand, in which the lady could place her purchases.

No sooner would such a lady cross the threshold than she would remove her veil from her face to scrutinize the shoes. Out came the crystal-clear, unblemished skin and two wide brown eyes with long beautiful lashes streaked with kohl. Her eyebrows were drawn meticulously like two crescent moons glowing with a dark light, and her lips were painted in luscious red, giving her sensuous mouth the appearance of a rose kissed by the moisture of morning dew.

Usually gold earrings hung from her ears, her hands were dyed in henna and festooned with delicate gold rings, and on her smooth arms she wore tinkling bracelets of gold and ivory. She spoke with the sweet Tripolitanian accent, which was accompanied by coquettish, seductive gestures and movements that aroused a man's desire and sent tremors through his body and heart. But these ladies aroused more than lust. They were dazzling beacons that signalled the potential refinements and beauty of the very situation of being human.

One day in contrast, Haj al-Mahdy sent you to a tannery in the Arab district known as Bab Akkara. It was a poorer district where the odour of the tanneries, which smelled like dead dogs, reached you from several miles away, and where people lived in shacks and huts made from sheet metal, and in tattered tents with their cattle. There were swarms of flies and their feet slipped in the muddy streets. The children were like skeletons in rags, urinating and defecating without shame in front of their huts. You returned from that errand feeling nauseous and disgusted with humanity.

On another occasion, the Haj sent you to a store on Mazzini Street, owned by an Italian who sold coloured thread and employed a Libyan assistant named Numan. When in the Italian centre of the city, you could see the huge difference between the Arab quarter and the Italian quarter. Here, you were in a park from which emanated fragrant perfumes and beauty, full of lights and colours. The pavement seemed so smooth and shiny you could see your reflection in it. Even the walls and the trees of the district exuded happiness, like the faces of its residents, and except for a few Arab workers, all of the people were Italians. They wore clean, stylish clothes and sat around tables arranged across the pavement. They walked the streets individually or in groups, men with their arms around their women, or holding their hands and walking along the flowerbeds that adorned the thoroughfares.

When the cannon atop the Red Castle fired its traditional shot to salute the flag, you obediently stood to attention and raised your hand to salute the Italian flag. If you hadn't done so, it would be considered a slander to the symbol of Italian rule and you would be punished by law. Afraid the Italians might harass you, you started to come to these areas only when dressed in clean elegant clothes like the Italians wore, and like them you went bareheaded. During your first days in Tripoli, you were often approached by policemen asking you to leave the street because your Libyan attire was not to their liking. You would hide in the first blind alley you came to and re-emerge when the policeman left.

As you worked and were able to dress more smartly, and to know the ways of the Italian Quarter, solitary chores and pleasure strolls became one of your favourite consolations.

FIVE

When Thuraya, the daughter of Haj al-Mahdy, would bring his lunch to the shop, she would dispel the dull repetitive routine of your work. He would invite you to partake his meal, usually a dish of macaroni or couscous, with beans and peas. Once, a plate came with two small cuts of meat on it, confirming the family had prepared a portion specifically for you.

Even though she always covered her face with the hem of her cloak, you could easily see her face when she put the plate down. You thought Thuraya's was beautiful and innocent, like the faces of children, round and wheat-coloured, shining with happiness, sparkling with something inexplicably joyful and beatific. Perhaps it was the smile that adorned her face, or the dimples that augmented that smile. She came with a smile, left with a smile, and said hello with a smile, never staying for more than a few seconds, for she would leave the food and then depart, not picking up the empty plate until she brought the next meal.

There were always scraps of food left in the dishes, and you would return at night to wash them, so that she would find them clean and empty when she came to pick them up. There had never before been anything more worth the suffering of waiting, than those brief sweet moments when Thuraya came and her smile shone among the shoes.

At first you hadn't been aware of the secret of her beauty, because in the beginning you would raise your eyes towards her, only to drop them to the ground again out of shyness and fear of her father. Then, gradually, you began to let your gaze linger and took advantage of the rare times her father would be at the mosque for noon prayers when she came. You exchanged a few words with her and were able to look at her without embarrassment, until a degree of familiarity developed between the two of you. Then you started to read a new silent meaning in her looks. You also tried to answer with your own silent language, expressing the extent of your affection for her, and your admiration of her beauty. Your heart pounded with happiness when you saw reciprocity in her eyes, and you told yourself that fate had led you to this shop and found you work and shelter only to enable you to meet this girl who single-handedly that made life bloom in your hart like a flower in Spring.

Thuraya transformed the drudgery of a day filled with repetition and irritation into one full of the anticipation of future happiness. The tiny space of the shop became transformed into a wide open space, big enough to hold a smiling future in which you saw yourself as the owner of one of the houses in the old city with a woman to share your life there, a woman with a pure and innocent smile like Thuraya's, two almond-shaped eyes like her eyes, and two enchanting dimples on her cheeks. A woman for you to dwell with, and to dwell with you, as the Quranic saying has it.

The strength of these emotions wreaked havoc on your heart, like two armies warring across your chest. You went to lengths to show loyalty and sincerity to Thuraya's father. You didn't want to be a mere shop assistant, you wanted to be like a son to him. You hoped your efforts to endear yourself would succeed in creating a reciprocal fondness that see you accepted as his son-in-law and make him the father you wanted him to be, for your affection towards him was sincere. Your respect and love for him increased daily. He was a pious and righteous man, who didn't brag, lie, or put on airs, and he performed the five daily prayers at the appointed times at the Sha'ib al-Ain Mosque.

When you first joined his shop, he was keen to return quickly from his prayers so as not to leave the customers waiting for him, but then he began to trust you to deal with customers while he enjoyed chatting with his friends after prayer on the stone bench outside the mosque, leaving you in charge. You saw this as proof that he now trusted you like a son. You never saw him withhold something from you, or refrain from giving you your due, instead he treated you with a generosity that only increased your admiration for him.

One day, while you were alone in the shop, a violent earthquake shook the earth and everything above the false ceiling fell onto your head. You managed to pull yourself out, pushing the piles of thread and leather from you, and left the store, which you imagined was about to fall on you. You found the shoes that had lined the wooden shelves outside the door had fallen all over the ground. You were about to gather them up and return them to their place when you saw all the people in the street, screaming and reciting the Quran in horror, repeating "There is no God but Allah and Muhammad is His Messenger," as if they expected death to come at any moment. They were calling after one another, and you heard someone urge you to quickly come along with them. You didn't know where they were headed. Perhaps there was a shelter like in the days of the war, when people would flee from the bombs and cannon fire. So you left the store open, left the shoes scattered on the ground, and ran off with them.

Soon you arrived at Durouj Mosque, which was nearby. The mosque was crowded with men, women, and children, but they made space for the newcomers. You didn't see why the walls and ceiling of the mosque should be more secure than those of any other building, but you understood that the reason was less about the strength of the building than about the belief that the mosque would offer the best protection as the House of God. The second point was that if the earthquake destroyed the mosque, collapsing it onto the heads of those taking refuge there, at least their deaths would be more honourable here than in some other place. The forgiveness and mercy of God would be granted to everyone who met his Lord beneath the ceiling of a house of worship where God's name was uttered night and day.

The earthquake and its immediate danger were past, but the threat of mortal injury still hung over the people smothered in the densely packed crowd. They were afraid the earth would start shaking anew and wanted to stay for a little longer to reassure themselves that no new tremors were coming, especially because several smaller aftershocks had followed the powerful initial quake. Some individuals, who had tired of being jostled in the crowd, decided to risk venturing into the street, risking a death unblessed by God's angels in the mosque.

You could wait no longer and left the mosque with them, for you were racked with worry about the shop you had left open and the shoes scattered across the width of the street. You returned racing to the shop, expecting to find the shoes had vanished. But they were still there, everything was in its place, even though life had resumed as normal in the street. People old and young walked by the shop, without anyone thinking of stealing the shoes, despite there being beggars and bare-footed urchins among the passers-by. Perhaps the earthquake had reminded everyone of death and the Day of Judgement, because you were certain that at any other time if any one of those people had found shoes lying in the street while no one was tending the shop, they would have stolen the shoes and picked the shop clean without the slightest hesitation.

Thuraya continued to come to the shop when her father was gone for the noon prayers, and the silent relationship between you progressed to a stage of bold declarations when you told her that you had seen her in a dream and you hoped some day this dream would become true.

You were being earnest. You were incapable of lying about matters such as this. You had seen her in your sleep, sitting with you aboard a boat taking you both away far into the distance. When you told her about the dream, you didn't have the courage to mention how, in the end, the boat had capsized in a storm, how you had found yourselves tossed among the heaving waves – or how because you were a country boy, you didn't know how to swim, so you kept screaming for her to save you because you thought everyone in the city knew how to swim. You didn't tell her about your weakness and defeat in the dream, but rather offered an interpretation of the first part. You said that according to the books that explain dreams, the boat and the water meant happiness and bliss.

All she said was, "May the blessings of Allah come from it."

"But do you know how to swim?" you asked.

She responded laughing, "No, I do not. Why do you ask?"

You almost told her that you were both doomed, but her father entered the shop returning from the mosque, so you stopped talking. Haj al-Mahdy lifted the plate cover,but before inviting you to stop work and join him in his meal as was his custom, he said sighing, "Meat? Where did you get meat from when I have not bought any since last month?"

"From our neighbour Haja Najmiya. Her son finished his term in the army and returned home, and we received a portion of the sheep she slaughtered for the occasion."

Her father said, "Shouldn't someone have told us before-hand so we could prepare ourselves for a feast like this? The anticipation could have cheered us for a little while before we found a plate full of meat under our noses."

Before taking a piece of meat from the plate, he said, "Every person, my dear daughter, is accompanied by angels who receive the blessings that he receives, and these angels enjoy the wait that precedes happy occasions."

Then he turned to you, saying, "What harm if we had known about the meat two days before today? It would only increase the length of our happiness to three days instead of just the one minute when we put the meat to our mouths."

You and Thuraya exchanged laughter. Perhaps Haj al-Mahdy noticed this familiarity between you two, suggestive of an acquaintanceship that had developed behind his back, a more intimate relationship than that which he had seen pass between the two of you while he was present. The man had opened his heart to you from the first day he saw you, and he had begun to consider you like a second son, for the only son he had was still in his first year of Quranic studies, and his three oldest daughters were already married to distant relatives in Tajura. Thuraya, who still lived under his roof, was his youngest daughter.

What gave you cause for concern was that a girl of Thuraya's age and beauty would not stay trapped in her father's house for long. No doubt someone would come in the near future to ask her to marry him, and this groom-to-be would come in mere months, not years.

What were you going to do, oh son of al-Sheikh?

She was eighteen years old, the ideal age for girls to get married, especially if they were beautiful, virtuous, and from a good family. Maybe the suspicious glances your master shot at you and his daughter were a fitting opportunity to broach the subject and tell him plainly that you wanted the relationship of friendship between you and him to become the deeper relationship between son-in-law and father-in-law.

It would not be hard for you to prepare a room in one of the houses of the old city, and if there were none available near the home of Haj al-Mahdy, there were cheaper more modest houses outside the city walls. More than seven months had passed since you began work with Haj al-Mahdy, long enough for him to evaluate your character and know what sort of metal you were made of. Hardly a day passed without him talking about his theory of mankind, metals and fabrics. For example, he would say that one person was a genuine man like true gold, and another was lacking in character like fake gold. That person was made of silk fabric, another of cotton, and a third of sackcloth. Thus he had a definition for every customer who passed through his store.

The past Ramadan had been an excellent opportunity for him to wax lyrical about his ideas, for life in the city took on a different form during this holy month. The Haj opened his doors to guests, most of whom were strangers he invited after meeting them at sunset prayers, because he hated to break his fast without guests to share the food with. So he also invited you and some customers who came from outside the city, or from its suburbs, and added these guests to those from the mosque. In this the Haj was following an old tradition of the city's well-to-do families who held feasts for the poor, bringing the banquet to the mosque whenever transporting all the guests home proved impractical.

The Haj's guests remained until the time came for evening prayers, and sometimes he would bring them back home from the mosque a second time after the late nightly Ramadan prayers and they would stay up chatting and snacking. During these evening gatherings the Haj went to great lengths elaborating his thoughts about the metals of people and the kinds of fabric they came from, and he would reinforce his words with stories and tales from his interactions with people, or his journeys to foreign cities and other countries when he was still young, all of which endowed him with a special insight regarding the character and nature of mankind.

You were certain that Thuraya desired you as much as you desired her, but what did it matter if she wanted you when the first and last of the matter lay squarely in her father's hands, and you couldn't open the topic of engagement to his daughter without a relative to act as your intermediary. Matters such as these had rules and customs that needed to be followed, you needed a family member to represent you and ask for his daughter's hand, otherwise you would look like a disowned castaway. And the only relative you had in the city was a wretched beggar, from whom it would be best to stay as far away as you could, lest he suddenly ruin your chances of marrying Thuraya.

It would have also been unacceptable to bring your parents in from Awlad Al Sheikh. In fact, perhaps it would be preferable if your prospective in-laws didn't know you ever had a mother or father. You couldn't even risk mention of the embarrassing relationship between you and them, after the scandal you had caused them. Even before the scandal, things hadn't gone according to the normal rules that governed most children's relationship with their parents. They were divorced, so each of them lived independently with the families they had started after the divorce. You would move back and forth between the two houses. You always felt like an unwanted guest in your mother's house, so you had to go to your father's. But his wife considered you little more than a parasite in her house and tried to get you kicked out. Thus, years before you left the village, you had already preferred to live relying on your own wits rather than on your family.

You had adopted the ruined remains of the abandoned well as a base to build a hut in which you could have some privacy among the remote palm trees. You had assisted the shepherds in your village ever since you had been a boy, grazing the sheep and sleeping beside them in the valleys near your village. So you grew up without developing any affection for your mother or father. You certainly didn't hate them, but neither had they ever given you any reason to love them, and you didn't know what their feelings would be towards you now that you had left the village due to scandal. Perhaps they felt relieved at your departure as you would no longer be an embarrassment to them.

In any case, you felt no desire to know their opinion of your surprise departure from the village. You were too busy preparing your life under conditions that didn't allow for you to depend on anyone other than yourself, as if you were living out the Day of Judgement when no soul can help another, and can only hope to come to God with a true heart. God knows the truth behind faces, because He is All-Knowing.

But as for Thuraya's father, what face could you put forth if you asked for his daughter's hand? How could he give his blessing without knowing who you were, what made you tick, whether or not you came from a good seed? Did you really think he would deviate from the pattern he'd previously followed of marrying his daughters to relatives of his in Tajura? And would he think you an appropriate match for his daughter while you were but a young assistant in his shop? Perhaps it would be best if you convinced yourself that Thuraya wasn't meant for you, that she was just a vision haunting your dreams. All you could hope for was to enjoy the dream.

Before you found time to test your dream and decide if it was really attainable, or if it would remain a dream suspended between delusion and imagination, soldiers raided the market district.

SIX

They came searching for young men to take to the training camps. The Italian campaign against Abyssinia would soon begin and General Balbo had promised his president to bolster his ranks with fighters from the African colony adept at climbing mountains and operating in rough terrains.

Their expectations differed from their previous attempts, as before the Fascists came to power in Italy, the army had already taken command of the ravines which had once witnessed their defeat at the hands of the Abyssinians. The situation was also different because a nation galvanized by a Fascist doctrine would not relent once it had decided to launch an assault, no matter the obstacles. The vehement message issued by the Italian propaganda machine was that the Italian sphere of influence on the dark continent had to be extended in order to revive the glory of the Roman Empire.

The campaign against Abyssinia came as no surprise, but the sallies into the markets of Tripoli to forcibly conscript people were. Before you could flee, the soldiers blocked your way in front of the shop's door. You tried to resist and slip from their grasp, but they dragged you over the ground and put you in a military transport at the end of the street alongside other poor boys they had plucked from the market. They were all screaming and arguing and fighting with the soldiers, but the transport's sides were covered with a thick waxy fabric and two armed soldiers guarded the only way out of the vehicle.

You peered into the faces of those around you, hoping to finding someone you knew so that you could plan a way to escape together. But they were all strangers. Even though you recognized some of their faces from the neighbouring shops, you had never talked to any of them.

You felt despair as the hope of an escape disappeared and you could find no way to hold off the sorrowful fate that awaited you. But suddenly a chance to escape presented itself. The car had reached the gates of the military base and stopped to allow the guard to open them, when a number of the angry boys seized the opportunity to push the guards who blocked the transport's exit onto the ground. They threw the guards' weapons away and several of the boys that leapt from the transport kicked them before running towards the forest next to the military base. You weren't going to miss this chance. You leapt after them, running towards the forest.

The soldiers blew their whistles and opened fire, the bullets whizzed overhead as you ran through the forest, taking cover as best you could behind tree trunks. A sortie of military trucks chased the escapees, but they couldn't get far into the forest before its dense vegetation barred their way, and in some places the uneven terrain prevented them from going on, so a party of soldiers dismounted to chase you on foot, brandishing their rifles and shooting at you.

You heard a bullet whizz past your ear and saw one of the youths in front of you fall stained with blood. You kept running. There was no time to save anyone but yourself and when you found yourself in the line of fire all, you could do was take cover behind a tree trunk, then climb the trunk to the thick foliage at its top, hiding there from the eyes and bullets of the soldiers.

From your hiding place. you could see the soldiers who crawled over this part of the forest. Many soldiers from inside the camp had joined up with the guards. You could hear the roar of their gunfire and the screams of those who had been caught. They dragged them towards the camp, kicking and hitting them. You could also hear the groans of your wounded companion, though you couldn't do anything to alleviate his pains until eventually an Italian soldier came to take him from the forest.

You were scared, shaking like the branches in which you hid. You prayed to God that none of the soldiers would raise their eyes and discover you. Gradually, the movement below dissipated, except for some distant, intermittent gunfire that rang out through the forest. It was quiet enough for you to hear the fall of a single soldier's footsteps as he raced back from the chase, to make sure he returned to the camp before nightfall.

Darkness had begun to descend over the trees and added a layer of shadow to the layer of leaves that hid you from the eyes of those returning soldiers. Then the sounds of the soldier's booted footsteps stopped, as did the sound of gunfire and the clamour of cries. All that remained were the sounds of grasshoppers, the buzzing of insects and the croaking of frogs in some nearby ponds.

You keptstill for some time until you could be certain

that you were safely out of the soldier's grasp. You climbed down from the tree, feeling some scratches that you hadn't noticed when you climbed the tree in the heat of the chase. You ran away from the camp through the forest in the middle of the night, until you came out near the suburb of Qirqarish, after which you went back to the city by way of side streets. You reached the Shushan Agency just before dawn. A truck was parked there, loaded with boxes of fruit and vegetables and sacks of flour, and waiting for the beginning of daylight to set off towards Awlad Al Sheikh. You hid amongst the sacks of flour, inhaling their white dust, while you waited to return to the village from which you had fled, hidden amongst sacks of coal. You stayed low until the truck was past the city gate and took the desert route that led to the Western Mountain and Awlad Al Sheikh.

You thanked God that you had escaped before anyone had learned your name or address or had assigned you a number in the army, because deserters at the time were severely punished. Now there was no way for them to know who you were or where you lived for the deserters' law to apply to you.

It would have been difficult to return to the shoe shop to fetch your belongings and your Arab clothes, and you looked very odd as you returned to your village wearing a foreign suit. No one in Awlad Al Sheikh would dare to enter the village bare-headed as you were doing, and wearing the attire of the foreign infidels, especially because the suit was torn and tattered, and your hands, face and arms were scratched from the chase and from hiding in the tree branches.

You had been cautious and asked the driver to drop you off before entering the village so you could avoid the large crowd that always gathered to look at vehicles entering the village. Nevertheless, one of the children from your family saw you sneaking around the back roads towards your father's house. He started to call the other children, running to fetch them with his long white shirt billowing in the wind like the sail of a boat struck by a storm. The other children came and they all escorted you in a procession to the house shouting "Othman is back! Othman is back!"

In order not to turn the children's happiness at seeing you into disappointment, you took a detour to the grocer's store and bought a box of sweets and distributed them. You arrived at your father's house apprehensive about how he would receive you. There he was, angry with you, but for reasons that differed from those you had expected. He was angry because you hadn't told him you were leaving, because you had fled from false accusations directed at you by Sheikh Baraka, even though the medical clinic had proven that Aziza's honour remained intact and that nothing disgraceful had happened between the two of you. He told you he had tried to reach you in the city to tell you about the results of the examination and ask you to come home, but he hadn't been able to reach you. He reproached you for not having sent word of your whereabouts since you had left the village.

You made excuses, saying that you had been too busy looking for work and that once things had begun to settle down, the Italian soldiers had come and tried to conscript you. You told him how you had fled back to Awlad Al Sheikh, looking for a place to hide until the conscription drive was over.

Thus, you returned to living in the village that you

used to hate, staying in a small room on the house's roof. Half of the room your family used as storage for barley and wheat grain, which was the main source of nutrition for your family, and the other half they left for you to live in with the most modest of furnishings, a woollen mattress, a pillow, a blanket, and three nails to hang your clothes. You seldom left the house because Awlad Al Sheikh was also not exempt from the conscription campaigns. When you did leave, it was only to visit your mother, who complained of rheumatic ailments.

You spent most of your time sitting on the stone bench outside the room, enjoying the winter sun and reading reference books, and books of prayer and praise of God, among which "Signs of Blessings" was the dearest to you, because its prayers of salvation and relief from crisis made you optimistic and hopeful that you would find an answer to your prayers from the Creator. In addition, you recited the Quran and perused the Sayings of the Prophet.

During the holidays, when you prayed with the villagers in the courtyard of the Sunni Mosque, you spotted Abdel Mowlah the beggar. He had returned from Tripoli to spend the holiday with his family. He was wearing sleek new clothes that only the well-off wore. He approached you, welcoming you, his eyes shining with gratitude because you hadn't divulged the secret you had learned when you saw him begging in front of Mizran Mosque. He insisted that you visit him in his hut when you were back in Tripoli. Despite your aversion, you saw no harm in giving in to his insistence and promising him you would.

After the prayers, you encountered one of the sheikhs of the mosque, who told you the rumour that had sullied your name with the sin of adultery was now confirmed to be untrue, which made it possible for you to return and teach the Quran to the village children if you so desired. You informed him that you had moved past that stage of your life and would not return to it, for you had better opportunities in your work in the capital.

Three months passed. According to the news coming from Tripoli, the conscription drives for the Abyssinian offensive had diminished in the markets and streets of Tripoli. The time had come for you to return. April arrived. It was the same month you had left the village exactly a year ago. You decided to view this month as a good omen for travelling, and this time you asked your mother and father's permission. You asked them not to forget you in their prayers, and then you left the village for Tripoli once again on one of the trucks, but this time without hiding yourself between any dusty sacks, either black or white. Instead, you sat on a comfortable seat beside the driver, who hummed popular Libyan songs all the way.

SEVEN

As soon as the truck arrived at the Shushan Agency, you ran as quickly as you could to Haj al-Mahdy's shop. He welcomed you with an embrace, cursing the Italians who had spread terror throughout the country, debased its people, and robbed them of their youth. He told you he had been obliged to replace you, but that he had also been taken away. Despite his lame foot, this second assistant had been among the last to be conscripted in one of the raids. The Haj asked you how the army training was going, so you told him that you hadn't fled on the very first day, hiding in your family's house in Awlad Al Sheikh until the danger passed, and that now you wanted to come back to work.

You watched the Haj poke his head out of the shop, craning his neck, looking worriedly left and right at the passers-by. He told you that if he gave you your job back, he feared the Italians would take their revenge, because they reserved a grave punishment for those who fled from the army, and the punishment would also fall upon whoever aided or concealed them. He tried to excuse himself saying he was an old man in his twilight, too weak to defy the

Italians or endure the cruelty of imprisonment. He asked you to forgive him for not taking the risk.

You explained to the Haj that his fears were groundless, because your situation was different from that of a deserter. You weren't assigned a number, nor had your name been entered in any of their lists, and consequently they didn't consider you a soldier and no law could punish you. But the Haj smiled sadly, unable to believe you. He said that the Italians abided by no law. They were like demons, nothing could be hidden from them. No doubt they knew you had fled from their training camp and were in pursuit. They would remember that they had taken you from the shop, and if they didn't, then there were many spies that could fill in the blanks for them.

Haj al-Mahdy sighed, adding that the Italian conscription drives were still ongoing, as were raids on houses, shops and market places. He told you they had come to Kushat Al Safar more than once in the past few days, taking many young men, and how one of them had been the Haj's relative Fathy, who had been his helper in the shop before you. They had closed Fathy's store and taken him to the military base even though he was a newly married man. He told you how no more than a week had passed since his marriage, and that his wife was none other than the Haj's daughter Thuraya, who had now had to return to her father's house, with the henna of a bride still fresh on her fingers.

The Haj moved on to another subject, advising you to return to the village and hide there again, for the raids would not cease for another few months. But you weren't listening to him, nor did you comprehend what he said. Your mind and heart – all your senses – had stopped upon hearing that Thuraya was married. She was lost to you forever!

You wanted to scream, but your voice was trapped in your throat. How was the Haj supposed to have known you wanted to marry his daughter when you had never broached the subject? And Thuraya, would she have been able to do anything or tell her father anything about your intentions? Did she even have a clear idea as to your vision of a future life together? Then how could you expect her to wait for a man who had been taken away to fight in the Italians' war against the Abyssinians, when no one knew what would happen to him but God? Perhaps if she had known that you would definitely propose to her, she might have tried to delay the marriage. Maybe she had even done that.

You couldn't be sure about anything. All you knew was that you were lost. No work, no shelter, no Thuraya. Life itself no longer had meaning. You stood naked, with no present, no tomorrow. It didn't matter whether you stayed or went, lived or died.

You abruptly left Haj al-Mahdy while he was still mid-sentence and headed towards the Italian's base in Bumalyana. One of the guardsmen led you to the officer on duty. You told him that you had come to enlist in the army for the Abyssinian campaign. You must have been the first Libyan he had ever seen join this army voluntarily, and with a wide fake smile, he hid his astonishment at the stupidity of someone who would walk through the Gates of Hell on his own two feet.

He personally led you to where the new recruits were gathered, commending you to the supervisors' care because you were different from the rest, who had come dragged in chains and beaten by canes. So, he said, you were to be given special treatment.

The Italian officers and Libyan conscripts saw you as different, unique, for how could anyone willingly face degradation and torture? You saw incredulity in the eyes of the enlistees, and you heard them whispering in astonishment about the man who had happily walked into the snakes' den, flinging himself onto the path of certain death.

In the years following the end of the resistance, some people had came forward to work for the Italian military as spies or guards, but after the conscription drives had begun for the campaign against the Abyssinian lands, everyone avoided entering the Italian military, because wasn't an Arab Muslim couldn't willingly fight and die in a war the Italians were waging against an African people, half of whom were Muslims. As for you, you considered coming to them as an alternative to suicide. In fact, it was just another way of committing suicide, where you would be both murderer and victim.

It was the beginning of something you were sure would take you to the forests of death and the valleys of butchery.

You didn't know the slightest about the language these Italians spoke. You had lived to be twenty-five years old and yet never come into close contact with them. You had followed your family's example and the custom of the people in your village and rejected anything that might make you seem like them. You avoided their food and clothes, and mingling with them. You had attended the Italian school for a year, before your father pulled you out after one of the Quranic teachers decreed it was a sin to send the children there because the school would try to force them to abandon Islam and embrace Christianity.

Instead, you began to frequent the house of that scholar who set aside a room in his house to teach the Quran to children in exchange for eggs, dates, and dried figs, for in his view it simply would not do to accept monetary compensation for teaching the Quran. You didn't learn until later that the Italian schools weren't trying to get anyone to abandon their religion, or force a new one upon them. But that the teached had been solely motivated by his need for food at a time of scarcity, may God have mercy on his soul, for he would need it when he went to meet his Lord stained with the sin of depriving the village children of a modern education.

You had always worn your skullcap, your long white shirt, and your Arab coat, and all you knew of the Italians was their tricoloured flag that hung on the flagpole atop the governor's residence, which you had to salute whenever you heard the trumpet blare. You could only pick up the few words of their speech, enough for your limited needs. You tried to recall what you had absorbed in that year you spent in their school when you were six. Things were different now that you had become an Italian soldier, sworn into loyalty to their king, and with your life in their hands. You would have to master this language like a native speaker if you wanted to guarantee yourself any measure of success.

They gave you a blanket, a military uniform, a canteen, and a pouch of waxy cloth that contained the equipment and tools you would need when you went on manoeuvres and missions outside the base, like a plate, a spoon, a lantern and other utensils. They asked you to spend the night with a number of other recruits in a long rectangular barracks, which some soldiers called the Noah's tomb, since tradition had it that he had been a giant. One hundred and fifty grumpy soldiers were housed in this legendary tomb, and you had no protection from the cold of the tiles except a threadbare blanket. Your body shook with fright when you saw the walls of the barracks were splattered with blood. You relaxed a little when you asked your barracks mates and learned that it was just the blood of the bedbugs that they crushed against the walls.

This feeling of reassurance quickly left you when you found yourself the prey of countless bedbugs on your first night. No matter how many you killed and squashed, they didn't relent. You would ask yourself where all the bedbugs came from, and before you could reach an answer, you found yourself facing another insect army, more advanced in its techniques of camouflage and evasion: lice. They colonized your head on your very first night on the base. That's when you realized recruits shaved their heads to protect themselves from those pitiless creatures.

The following morning, you expressed your irritation to those who had come to the base before you, and asked how they could live with these pests. They replied sarcastically that it was part of the training to face the enemy, as these bedbugs, lice, and fleas were no less powerful than the mightiest of armies.

You shaved your head too, but the lice migrated to your clothes and took to sleeping in their every fold. Somehow you weren't surprised when the bugle call sounded an hour before the official wake-up time. They spent that hour scratching and rubbing their skin. You saw the barracks supervisor Sergeant Antar hitting them with his cane and telling them, "Come on, get up, scratch your skin."

On the fourth or fifth night you noticed one of the

recruits, who was sleeping beside you, sneak over in the darkness. He slipped over to your bed and pressed himself up against you hard. Realizing his intent, you got up from your bed furious at having found yourself the clear target of sexual molestation. You turned on the lights and tried to strangle the man. He pushed you away and tried to hide beneath his blanket, but you dragged him out for everyone to see. Instead, they buried their heads in their pillows, grumbling words of protest, demanding you turn off the lights and go back to sleep.

You realized that you had broken the law of collusion that governed the barracks. No one had the right to disgrace anyone else, and while you could refuse someone's sexual advances, you were to do it in silence, and without betraying their actions.

Naturally, the noise this caused reached Sergeant Antar's ears, who came with two aides asking what all the hubbub was about. When the sergeant learned that a fight had broken out between two recruits, one of whom was you, without even asking who had started it, he ordered you both to stand with your backs to him so he could flog you with a whip, five lashes on the back. That was the least severe of Sergeant Antar's punishments.

With every passing day you became increasingly angry and disgusted, experiencing the intense desire to leave both the barracks and the base. You transformed the hate inside you into a ball that swelled larger and larger, increasing until it exploded in the face of an Italian corporal who was in charge of the dining hall.

You had found a piece of a beetle in the bean stew, which was what was served every day. You hadn't wanted to complain to any of the Arab supervisors who were almost as wretched as you and who couldn't have done anything anyway, so you decided to take the fight to the Italian representative in that hall.

You got up, carrying your plate, and went over to where he stood at the head of the eating area with his arms akimbo, his head held high, as though he possessed a divine mandate from the Creator Himself. You knew you would be punished if you argued, but what were you afraid of? The most they could do was put you in solitary confinement for a day or two. You would consider it a break from training. So you advanced towards him confidently.

You asked him to see for himself the remains of the big black beetle that had been chopped into two, half of which landed in your plate, while the other half was lurking in one of your comrades' plates, or maybe even their stomachs. He told you to go back to your place so as not to cause a commotion in the mess. He had taken note of the matter and would instruct the cooks to pay more attention to cleanliness.

You threw the contents of the plate onto the floor to make a show of your disgust and outrage. Such food was unfit for people to eat, and you welcomed solitary confinement after being able to vent the anger and frustration that had been bottled up inside you. But as if the corporal had understood the intention behind your theatrical gesture, rather than ordering you to solitary, he ordered the cooks to prepare beetle soup for your dinner.

You didn't know how they were able to gather so many beetles in less than half an hour, but they made a soup and brought it to you. The corporal stood behind you, whip in hand, and ordered you to drink the soup and eat what was in front of you. You couldn't, until he ordered two of his soldiers to hold you while he whipped you across your back. When you refused a second time, he ordered the soldiers to tie you down and spoon the beetles into your mouth. You fainted, and when you came to the next day you spent forty-eight hours vomiting, and didn't dare eat a single bite. Every time you vomited, you felt like you were throwing up your intestines, because your stomach was already emptied. You spent the entire day in pain, pressing your hands against where it hurt the most.

You realized you were suffering the effects of your own anger, and that you had to find some other way to deal with this new world, one which you had entered recklessly, and without any knowledge of its rules and rituals. You couldn't be for it and against it at the same time, because then you would find only pain mixed with degradation. There was no compromise solution. You either stayed far away from the base, as you did the first time when you escaped beneath a hail of bullets, returning to the country-side and the walls of your house, a hundred miles away from the camp, or you stayed inside the base and integrated completely, giving it your heart and mind, and paying due subservience and loyalty to its leaders and laws.

You decided you would learn who the master of this place was and gain his approval. You would learn when to keep silent and look the other way, you would learn what was required of you and you would do it with a zealot's love and enthusiasm.

These were the fundamentals of the game in this new world in which you had neither family nor friend. You had frequently fended off injustice and tyranny in the village when you used to move back and forth between your mother's house and your father's. Now that you were living inside the walls of an Italian base, you had to familiarize yourself with it and play by its rules. You understood that obedience and submission were your only protection from oppression and tyranny, otherwise your back would break like a dry, inflexible stick.

You looked up to your countryman Sergeant Antar as your example. He had even forgotten how to pronounce his name correctly in the Arabic manner since he had joined the Italians and begun pronouncing it as they did, "Sergeant Intaar". He did the same thing with the names of others, as happened with you when he called you "Usman" in front of his Italian superior. He whipped his dark-skinned compatriots harder and more cruelly than any Italian, and he spoke harshly with them as if they were personal enemies. Not content to work only on-duty, he stole time from sleep. You would therefore see him in full uniform ready for a state of emergency in the middle of the night, at dawn and dusk, before and after he was on-duty. If order was disturbed even slightly in one of the barracks during the night, no one came to address the fracas and return matters to their rightful state except for Sergeant Antar, who would come out of nowhere, cracking his whip in the air and shouting gibberish in Italian, roaring and raving as if he had been possessed by the spirit of the Duce himself.

Despite his dark complexion, which betrayed his Bedouin origins, his nose had taken on a distinctly Italian colour, its dark colour changing into a shade of red like the Italians' skin colour. His nose became the one part of him that responded to his strong desire to shed his Arab-African Bedouin physiognomy and trade it for one of Italian origin.

You hated Sergeant Antar's personality, which had

melted into the character of the invaders, but you were truly impressed at the power he had attained and the mastery he enjoyed over these people who had mastered nothing but scratching their own skins. They rubbed and scratched constantly with their nails, sometimes using a stick to reach the areas of their back that they couldn't reach with their fingernails.

Once a week, Sergeant Antar came to the barracks carrying a disinfectant that smelled of gasoline. He sprinkled the recruits with it while they were in their beds, after asking them to close their eyes. He drenched their bodies, clothes, blankets, and the walls around them with this loathsome substance. Despite that the lice, fleas and bedbugs didn't die and the next round of scratching began as always at its customary hour in the morning.

The misery you experienced in the camp was enough to make you forget every other sorrow, including the great grief that had settled in your soul ever since they had snatched your precious Thuraya away. You only remembered her in those rare moments of tranquility you snatched between your training in military protocol and weapons use.

The drills and training usually ended in an hour of punishment. You usually spent it standing in the sun on one foot, hands raised up high like a crucified person without a cross until you felt your body fall apart piece by piece. Or you would spend it crawling across the ground until your knees burned from scrapes. No one volunteered to treat your wounds, which only worsened the aggravation caused by the fleas, lice, and bedbugs and the annoyance of the flies that made a colony of your body to hide and shelter in during the day. You began to suspect that this

wasn't about military conditioning, but was instead the
Italian military's way of exacting revenge for the heavy
losses it had incurred at the hands of the Libyan resistance,
and thus wished to degrade and debase every Libyan they
could get their hands on. This was not training as they
claimed, but torture.

You forgot your family for days on end. When you
remembered them and wrote to them, you quickly tore
the letter up, for you realized it would pass through the
military censor and you feared whatever punishment they
would subject you to if they read the curses and profanities
you had directed at them in the letter.

You learned they paid each recruit a few francs as
month, and that the amount was held until the end of the
first three months of training. You waited until those months
had elapsed, then sent what you had earned to your father
with a message that contained only a few lines, in which
you told him to give half to your mother and tell him that
you were in the Italian base by the Bumalyana region. No
sooner did the soldiers of the base learn that you were
fluent in reading and writing than your moments of leisure
were reserved every day for writing their letters to their
families.

The letter you had sent left you with a clear conscience
with regard to your family, but you couldn't do anything
to relieve the suffering of thinking about Thuraya. You tried
in vain to tear her image from your imagination and tell
yourself that she was none of your business so long as she
was married to another man. But it wasn't over, not at all.
She was the one woman you had opened your heart to,
like a sunflower opens to the rays of the sun, and there
was no other woman in your life, not even the ghost of

another woman, only her ghost, whom you called out in sleepless moments of loneliness. How could you possibly forget her?

The truth was that you needed her badly. You needed a face like hers, one that shone like stars in the darkness of life. If Thuraya hadn't been in your life, no doubt the camp, which resembled life in a prison, would have made you invent a face like hers to keep you company and make you burn with longing. You went to this spectre with your violent youthful passions, you spoke to her, slept with her, and in your dreams and daydreams alike you lived with her. You would not forget Thuraya, not as long as you were captive to this military lifestyle. Her memory was a necessity for your physical and psychological health, and although you had reconciled yourself to the impossibility of ever meeting with her in this world, you were certain you would meet her and realize your heart's ardent wish to rendezvous with her in a better life, and a better abode, in the next world.

What better blessing could there be than realizing dreams and hopes in heaven that you had been unable to fulfill in the mortal world? And here you had chosen the shortest path to that better world by joining the Italian campaign against the Abyssinians, knowing that the odds of dying in this war were more than a million times higher than the odds of surviving. You hadn't deceived yourself when you decided joining the army was a form of suicide.

EIGHT

When the bugle-cry rang out, commanding sleep, sleep would come as quickly as if it were the last sleep. A soldier began to obey the orders of the bugle even if he had been a sultan outside the walls. Then the dawn glowed on the horizon and the bugle-cry rose up once more, ordering wakefulness, and the day would start. The torture of training would begin, followed by the torture of punishments, until the bugle-cy sounded to order you back to sleep again. A daily repetitive routine without free time or relaxation. The only time you had to yourself was the brief period of quiet at the end of the day when you wandered through the parts of the forest that lay inside the base's walls. Time you spent looking at the pine trees, enjoying their sweet scent, feeling a kind of joy at their smooth, almost feminine trunks.

Throughout the months you spent at the base, you were unable to forget that its walls separated you from the outside world, and that there were watch towers surveyed every movement, and soldiers armed with rifles, ready to open fire at anyone who came near the wall. Despite your invocations to God and the Quranic verses you recited, apprehensions plagued you, because you knew that they were preparing you for a death unlike any other. It would be a death stripped of all honour and dignity. It would take place in a strange land, as you fought an innocent people beneath a banner that your people cursed every day for the atrocities and massacres perpetrated in its name. It was something every Libyan in the camp knew and felt, no matter how enthusiastically he worked, or how loyal he seemed to his Italian masters. It was the one thing that bound all the recruits together, even you, regardless of the fact you'd enlisted and that they had been forced to undertake this hateful humiliating mission. That you were all being herded to the field of death made such petty differences irrelevant. Surely, you were no more cowardly or frightened than they were simply because you had chosen this fate on your own terms. You shared their terror, a feeling that accompanied you everywhere, even when you looked up at the sky and saw tufts of clouds suspended in the sky as though they were thousands of scaffolds erected on the ceiling of the world to hang you and your fellow soldiers.

You had always been proud of two of your uncles who were martyred together as resistance fighters against the Italians. At that time, everyone had flown to confront the Italians during the first days of their advance. Three brothers left your village with a large number of men. They travelled northwards to the shore, answering the call to resist the Italian invaders. None returned – apart from your father, who had been assigned rearguard duties due to his young age, which had saved him from the death that took the souls of so many others.

"The gallant warriors died in Al-Hany" says the folk proverb of that day in the past when individuals of courage gave their blood for their nation until the earth itself was drenched with it.

You were barely old enough to understand all this when the resistance was defeated and General Badoglio, the governor of Libya, announced that every region of the country had fully submitted to Italian authority, meaning therefore that peace had come. But what kind of peace had they achieved when they had built it on forced conscription and concentration camps?

Every Libyan had to look for his daily wages as a labourer on the farms the Italians established, on the ground stolen for grazing. No work, no resources, and no livelihood remained to native countrymen except in the Italian settlements, where it was generally the lowliest jobs available such as porters, janitors or night-watch-men. If that failed, a Libyan was forced to work as a policeman or soldier in the army, so long as the possibility of facing one of his own family on the battlefield no longer existed.

Preparations for the Italian campaign against Abyssinia had begun. Despite the fact that the campaign itself hadn't begun, forces were being gathered and transported to the regions under Italian occupation, like Eritrea and Somalia, which bordered Abyssinia. The news was flying thick and fast that the invasion was near. There were important leaders who had previously led the war against Libya, like Graziani, Di Bono, and Badoglio, preparing the theatre of Italian military operations. In much the same way that they had brought soldiers from the lands of Abyssinia to fight Libyans, now they had conscripted Libyans to battle against the Abyssinians according to the principles of colonial equality, justice, and balance.

The bugles at the Bumalyana training base continued

to blare day and night, signalling the time to sleep and wake, a bugle for morning assembly, a bugle to raise the flag, and another for mealtimes. The bugle had its own power and sacredness, as though it were, God forbid, the voice of a divine power ruling the world.

"Rejoice! Rejoice!" said Sergeant Antar, the human bugle, when he came to the barracks during the scratching time. He yelled, "Rejoice boys!"

It was unusual for this man to issue an order so contradictory to his perpetually knitted brow and his ashen complexion. He seemed to wear an angry scowl constantly. "Today is a fieshta, an official holiday. Why? Because today is the thirteenth anniversary of the fascist party's ascent to power."

The camp and its like weren't permitted any holidays, religious or secular, due to the ongoing state of emergency. Nevertheless, for reasons related to the importance of this year, a decision was issued at the last minute that everyone was to enjoy the holiday, even those living in a state of emergency.

Sergeant Antar laughed, revealing his yellow teeth, which were hardly ever seen due to the scarcity of moments when he had occasion to smile, and after taking a long pull from his cigar, he added, "Today you can scratch your skins all day if you like."

But what was a "fieshta"? you asked one another, concluding that it meant no training and no punishment for today. Indeed the holiday and celebrations were continuous from the beginning of the day until the onset of night. You all spent the morning organizing football matches inside the base, and a brass band came and circled among the recruits, playing Italian military tunes and anthems that glorified the party and its leader. You were given a few sheep, which a group of you slaughtered and roasted on the edges of the forest.

Truly you all rejoiced, not because of the Fascist holiday, and not because Sergeant Antar ordered you to rejoice, but because the whip would not crack above your heads today as though you were horses hitched to carriages or carts. No one would hurl curses or profanities at you today.

People left the barracks and went to the forest. They lit fires and gathered round after they were too exhausted to run around any more. They sat in circles among the black smoke and some began to clap on boxes and wooden crates, beating the rhythm of a song popular at weddings in the city, which evoked a rich and beautiful world, bursting with luxurious feasts and gorgeous women with dark kohl around their eyes. Let that be a replacement for the poor wretched reality empty of banquets and women. You summoned the image of Thuraya from beyond these walls of silence. Thuraya, the absent one. You persisted in your passion, despite knowing it was hopeless.

You wondered where they had taken her husband Fathy, whose good luck at having won Thuraya had been tainted with misfortune when the Italians raided his shop and took him from her arms and led him to the camps of war and death. You didn't know if you would be able to recognize him, having only seen caught a fleeting glimpse of him when he had passed by al-Mahdy's shop to say a quick hello. You tried to be on the lookout for him, though you hadn't come across him so far, despite your conviction that he was also one of the recruits in that base.

Perhaps a day of celebration like today in which all the recruits were gathered in one place was the most appropriate of times to look for him. So you began to circulate among the groups of people spread out among the pine trees, scanning their faces hopefully but without finding him. Instead, you found another companion from your village, Salem.

He saw you before you saw him and appeared suddenly, embracing you warmly. It was a wonderful surprise to learn that your friend from the Quranic school had also become your peer on the base. You asked Salem how on earth he had come to the camp, and how long he had been there. He told you the Italian forces had only taken him a week earlier because the training camp they had established in his area, Abu Gheelan, had long ago been filled to capacity. Salem and other new recruits had therefore been transferred to the Bumalyana camp.

It truly gladdened you to find an old companion with whom to share the experiences of military life. It was the first time since you had arrived you had spoken with someone you knew from your days outside the walls of the base. All of Awlad Al Sheikh loved Salem for his trustworthiness, integrity and sensible nature.

With a playful note he said sarcastically, "If not for Mussolini's victory, which was the cause of this holiday, we would not have been able to meet. Here's to Fascist holidays!"

You replied, "Yes, we could have spent an entire year inside this camp and not seen each other."

You stopped looking for Fathy and spent the rest of the day in Salem's company, recalling the world of Awlad Al Sheikh.

Salem said, "When news of your whereabouts stopped, some people started to console your family, telling them the Italians must have killed you after you tried to escape. This rumour only stopped when your letter reached your family."

You said, "Maybe that rumour can serve as useful training for families before the real news reaches them."

"Don't talk like that, try to be optimistic."

You walked together among the groups of celebrating soldiers until you found yourself where you started, near the circle of soldiers who had now finished cooking a large amount of the lamb and had begun snatching pieces of the meat from the fire. You took one piece for yourself and gave another to your friend. They began to sing, moving from one song to the next, forming into dancing circles and swaying to the rhythm.

Whips cracked over your heads. The guards had come, ordering the singing recruits to return to barracks. They were now forbidden to participate in the celebrations. An Italian officer who knew Arabic had recognized the lyrics of their song, and it incensed him to hear these Arab recruits singing about Italian women in an insulting manner. He had ordered the group of singers to be stopped.

As the guards had started pushing and herding everyone like goats into the barracks, Salem said, "This is what happens to those who celebrate the victory of Fascists."

That evening guests from outside the military complex flocked to the Italian Officers' Club on the base. Among the arrivals were women in evening clothes, men carrying musical instruments, and cars bringing plates of food and crates of drinks. The party went on for most of the night, and its noisy hubbub reached as far as the barracks, chasing sleep away from soldiers' eyes and filling their hearts with sorrow and self-pity for the life of deprivation they led.

You met with Salem every evening. You had found a partner to share the moments you used to spend alone on the edges of the forests at sunset. The first day, he came laughing cheerfully.

"Today they ordered me to stand on one foot for an entire hour, so I tricked them and stood on one foot for two hours."

"I don't know when these humiliations will end," you said.

Salem's presence made you happy, for you were certain his company in this place was necessary for your mental health, just as your company was good for his. With the ability to talk to someone you could trust, each of you helped the other endure his suffering better. You could finally vent the angry burdens that weighed down on your chests, and you could pose the suffocating questions that oppressed you, not only about why you were in this place, but also about why you existed in this world.

Salem listened to you question the meaning of life, and then posed an even more perplexing question, which shouldn't have confused you, because you were older than him and thus supposedly wiser.

Of all the countries in the world, why did God choose our country to be tested in continuous cycles of rule by invaders ever since the dawn of history? Invader had followed invader, one after another without a moment of peace. No doubt God is Just, so how could this tyranny please Him? Why did he not answer the prayers sent from the depths of so many ardent hearts, from the simple, pure hearts of mothers and fathers asking for Him to ease His anger from them. In every prayer, they asked Him to keep these oppressors away from them, to save them from this evil so that they might lead sound, secure lives, so that they could worship him with humble, faithful hearts, content with the modest livelihood He provided. Then they went to sleep, waiting for His mercy and justice to rise with the dawn, but found nothing the following day save more oppression, torture, and tyranny.

"Tell me, where do you think all those prayers went?" asked Salem.

It was a question you had asked yourself many times as well, when you recited your prayers and read your hymn books every morning, searching for some meaning in them. But here, in front of this young man who trusted your knowledge and believed that you had answers for the confounding questions that turned in his head, you had no choice but to answer with something to remedy his confusion. You struggled to come up with an explanation that would satisfy him, hoping it might satisfy you too. "How can God remove them and answer our prayers when they are part of His Will?"

You saw Salem look at you with eyes full of confusion. You tried to arrive at a clearer response.

"Wasn't it God who created Satan? So can we ask God to destroy Satan? And if we did, would He answer our prayers? He would not, because His Will decreed that our mortal lives be a conflict between good and evil for all eternity. There is no alternative to the existence of good and evil, just like you need death in order to have life. You cannot say that the earthquakes, volcanoes, floods, and epidemics that kill people are not a part of Divine Will."

Salem couldn't let it go any further than that, for fear of being led down a misguided path, so he found a way of terminating the discussion by saying cynically, "An earthquake lasts no more than a minute or two, floods come for a day and leave the next, plagues last a week or maybe a month, let them take however many souls He wills. But the latest trial, which God has chosen to test us with, Italian colonization, is now more than a quarter of a century long, and it only becomes increasingly violent, powerful, and intractable. We resisted it until half our people died. Do you think we will find answers by going to fight beneath the banner of the occupier rather than against it?" You heard the sound of the bugle indicating mealtime, which would be followed by sleep. It also signalled the end of free time, but you didn't want the conversation to end on this note, so you consoled Salem as well as yourself, "Religious scholars have ridiculed this transient world. Our presence in this camp is merely the practical embodiment of that ridicule."

You turned the subject to the afterlife, which would be more just and fair. Your coming to this camp and joining an army bound for war in the unknown regions of Africa only hastened your journey to the afterlife, or so you tried to justify your decision to yourself.

The barracks enveloped you like the belly of the whale that had swallowed Jonah. Dark, damp, warm, and foul-smelling. According to the Quran, while Jonah had been in the belly of the whale, he had been neither alive nor dead. Let Jonah be a lesson to you, for God had bestowed upon him Prophethood, but not spared him any suffering.

Yes, yes. Whether you had come to the world of bedbugs, fleas and lice of your own will or a higher will that guides mortals to their inevitable fate, now you were here, in this camp surrounded by guards and watchtowers. This was your world, there was no other. So why did you talk about your desire to integrate into it, but do nothing to realize your goal? Why did you only grumble and complain? Would grumbling and complaining put an end to your tribulations? You fool.

You were unlike the others who came here dragged in chains with bayonets pointed against their backs. The Italians also considered you different and accorded you a higher status because you had come by choice. So you should play up to their expectations. Let your adaptation begin. You would spare no effort to harmonize your spirit with its spirit. From this moment on, you would belong to the institution of fear and death this base represented.

One day, a fight broke out in the dormitory between one of the recruits and a barracks supervisor. Sergeant Antar came with one of his aides to enforce the regulations that stipulated thirty lashes on the feet for anyone who rebelled against officers. The Sergeant shouted for two volunteers to hold the culprit down so his aide could mete out the punishment. You immediately stepped forward. The aide began to whip him, but he was a dull-witted man who was so incompetent at handling the whip that during one of the lashes he raised the whip too high and struck Sergeant Antar's face, who exploded in a fit of rage, snatched the whip from his hand and flogged him instead. Then he stepped up to resume punishing the troublemaker. That was your chance, and you seized the opportunity to offer your services to him, begging him to let you take over. You took the whip from him and finished flogging your barracks mate, whispering to him that you only did it to spare him Sergeant Antar's heavier lashes. Yet you actually hit him harder so as to please Sergeant Antar. You looked at him after every blow to see the extent of his satisfaction, and it didn't matter to you whether your barracks mate believed you or not.

You had decided to rise above your fellow recruits, to aim for a little higher than the absolute bottom where the rest of them clung. You wanted to be as important as Sergeant Antar, that was how you would save yourself from being trampled underfoot, and ingratiate yourself to the world of authority and power.

He smiled at your skilful use of the whip.

The following day, Sergeant Antar met you with greetings and took you by the arm to introduce you to his Italian superior during the morning assembly, saying you were of the type that could be relied on. He also reminded him that you were the soldier who had joined the army out of his own free will.

How quickly the results produced themselves. That very night, your straw mattress turned into a bed and comforter, and you slept by yourself near the door, away from the crowded bodies on the floor of the barracks. Sergeant Antar had selected you to be a corporal for the barracks and a supervisor to keep order there after he had moved the previous supervisor to a different barracks. Your word and your authority were now the highest in this barracks of one hundred and fifty soldiers. Moreover you gained a right to a larger share of cleaning supplies, including disinfectant to kill the fleas, lice, bedbugs and cockroaches.

NINE

You had taken the first steps towards being accepted by the authorities. The instances when you were punished gradually diminished before disappearing altogether. The hours of training also lessened after Sergeant Antar elected you to accompany him on his rounds. You alone had shown such skill with the whip and cane, a skill many of the aides envied. As a reward, you were given your own whip, which you could carry wherever you went, ready for use whenever Sergeant Antar gave the order.

You were even given the right to use it without Sergeant Antar's permission on a few occasions, such as when one of the recruits took too long to wake up at the appropriate time to scratch himself. You would go over and crack the whip over his head, or lash him across his back until he got up. That whip never left your side during the day, and at night you hung it on the wall above your head as though it were a medal or a badge. like those the guards wore. It was unquestionable evidence of your distinguished status on the base.

Salem once said to you jokingly, "Your star is on the rise. Congratulations, cousin."

You replied, "One has to choose between being the victim and being the executioner, and you know how the people of Awlad Al Sheikh hate playing the victim's role. They chose a life of dryness and drought in that desert rather than remain oppressedin more fertile lands."

"Do not conflate your faults with those of the people of Awlad Al Sheikh," said Salem. "They are still human beings and have not transformed into beasts. Let me see if you have grown claws and fangs. Why are you deceiving yourself? Why not say that your soul has become of no importance to you, that you no longer know the limits of shame? I prefer to be a victim who accepts his beatings a thousand times more than the whip that beats his coun- trymen at the hands of the Italians." There was no recourse but to confront Salem's angry tone with an even angrier tone. You had to play up to your new role, even with those closest to you. You would have to continue wearing your colonized personality until the very end if you wanted to achieve the petty success you desired. You couldn't allow any weakness to show through the façade you had just begun to build. You said, "If there is any shame here, cousin, it is from those like you. A stifling oppressive shame that I can no longer bear. Yes, I will be the whip that flogs, and I will not be the mule, donkey or dog that never tires of enduring the whip."

Furious, you left Salem sitting beneath the pine trees and returned to the protection of your master, Sergeant Antar, who had selected you as an aide. When you were beside him, you felt like you were no longer part of this gelatinous heap of worms who had once been human beings. Power has its splendour and ecstasy, and a value that couldn't be understood by some simple Bedouin like Salem, who didn't want to shed his village swaddling.

You knew what was happening to you, your country, and the world around you, was part of a higher will, which couldn't be resisted. It was a cycle in the turnings of history along the path heading towards the end, and no matter what you did, you would not be able to change God's Will. So what was the shame in going where one was pushed, or being part of this paradigm? Surely Salem was just being stubborn and naive.

The following days, you missed your evening meetings with Salem, and you wandered among the pines waiting for him to come. But Salem didn't appear. Despite his avoiding you for days, you never suspected he might have a nasty surprise in store for you.

When Sergeant Antar asked you to leave the training class on weapons disassembly in order to punish a disobedient recruit, you discovered that the soldier who had revolted and awaited the whip was none other than Salem. He had made a point of quarrelling with one of his trainers and refused to obey when he was ordered to stand with his hand raised in line with the other punished recruits in the scorching noon heat. He thus deserved the more severe punishment, flogging, as prescribed by military regulations. Sergeant Antar's voice urged you to whip your friend's bare back, which shone in the midday sun.

"Let's go, thirty of those lashes of yours will bring him back to his senses."

You stood still, not sure what to do, whip in hand.

This time, the allure of power and authority contradicted the demands of honour and friendship. It would be a point of shame against your humanity and your manhood, for Salem was your friend and your relative, joined to you by ties that called on you to defend him from harm, not be the arm that slew him.

Sergeant Antar shouted, "What are you waiting for, Othman? Make him taste the woes of your whip until he knows that it's God's Will that he be punished."

How could he mention God, when he spoke with the tongue of Satan himself disguised in the form of a man! Salem's eyes turned to you, and they were full of challenge and power, as though he were saying, "Hurry up and hit me, you despicable man, so you'll know how far you've fallen."

You raised your hand, muttering a few words you hoped only Salem would hear, "It's better I do it than someone else."

The first time you cracked the whip in the air without it touching his back. When it did land on the second blow, it was weak and light.

Sergeant Antar was almost beside himself with rage. "What are you doing? You're playing with him, not whipping him. Give me the whip."

He took the whip from you and furiously ordered you to return to your class on weapons disassembly. You spent that night without your whip. The news spread among your barracks' residents who saw you coming back without your whip and started to laugh, darting you belittling and mocking looks. They knew you had fallen from your master's graces and that he would soon seize the bed and comforter out and return you to your straw mattress, humbled.

Sergeant Antar entered the barracks, expressing his admiration for the peace and order you kept in his most sarcastic tone. Chaos reigned in the barracks, making it a perfect example of the opposite of peace and order. You had truly failed to assert your authority over the recruits, and your shouts were lost in the clamour. Your biggest fear was that Sergeant Antar would order someone else to take over supervision of the barracks, and that you would have to meekly hand over your bed, your comforter and your position before returning to being just another worm like the rest of the recruits, or even worse.

If so, you would not blame him. Keeping order needed determination, and you were the first to admit your own shortcomings. But after such a shameful fall, you would no longer be able to remain in the base. The only honourable decision would be to scale the wall and pretend to escape so you could be shot. That would be better than thedisgraced life you would lead among these human insects who had bedded with lice, fleas and bedbugs for so long that they had begun to assume their characteristics.

You were surprised when Sergeant Antar did none of that and merely shouted at the recruits, ordering them back to bed and under their blankets as he cracked his whip. They immediately complied and silence returned to the barracks. Sergeant Antar left without saying a word to you.

The following day, you went to Sergeant Antar and kissed his hand, begging him to forgive you. You explained that the person you had begun to whip was your cousin.

He said to you sternly, "Duty knows neither brother nor friend. That is the first lesson you must learn in this profession of ours."

Sergeant Antar said he would forgive you this time because you were still young and inexperienced, and he told you that he would no longer speak in Arabic to you,

because one of the qualifications for success was mastering
the Italian language. To learn it, you would have to give it
every ounce of effort you had. Sergeant Antar would help
you as much as he could. You swore that your only ambition was to be a pupil under his tutelage and benefit from
his experience and knowledge. He gave you back the whip
and let you follow him on one of his rounds to chastise
renegade recruits.

You quickly regained your control over the dormitory.
The situation forced you to treat them even more harshly
and cruelly than before, so you deliberately flogged everyone
who had insulted or scorned you that day, abusing your
free licence to wake lazy recruits with the whip. You would
lash whoever you wanted under the pretext that you wanted
to wake them up weren't. You asked Sergeant Antar's permission to withhold their ration of pest killer for as long as
two weeks so they would come begging you for forgiveness.
You became even stricter in your application of the rules
to the point that you forbade them from speaking to one
another after the lights were off.

After Salem began spending time with you again, he
said, "I just wanted to show you how humiliating it is to
flog someone."

You replied, "In this camp, humiliation is not a choice,
it is a way of life, mandatory material in the syllabus of our
work, as you see."

"I don't know how you make yourself play a role so
foreign to the Othman I knew in the village."

"Let's not discuss this any more, so that it won't ruin
our friendship."

"I know it's against your nature and not a part of your
nature, otherwise I would not be your friend."

In the days that followed, you exaggerated your show of friendship and loyalty to Sergeant Antar, hoping he would sing your praises in his reports to his Italian supervisors. You later learned that he hadn't disappointed you and had informed them you were one of the very few recruits who could read and write, and that you were learning the Italian language.

TEN

At the end of June, they held a celebration to mark the end of basic training. It was an occasion for you to reap the rewards of what you had sown. This time, you gained Italian recognition of your skills, represented by a stripe they placed on your uniform sleeve, removing you to a more privileged world than the rest of the recruits, who didn't have stripes on their sleeves. The celebration coincided with a visit from Marshal Balbo, the Italian governor of Libya. You were lucky to shake his hand and have your picture taken with him as he handed you the stripe. Thus, your induction to the army was completed by the most important figure in the country, constituting veritable proof of your ascent.

From that day on, you became a member of the highest circle. It was no longer merely an issue of a bed with a comforter atop it beside the door, or a whip hung by a nail above your head, or temporary authority given to you by Sergeant Antar. It was a stripe that awarded you precedence and seniority over all these others who crawled on their hands and knees during hours of training and punishment. No one, not even Marshal Balbo, could rob you of your stripe unless military court issued a ruling.

Not until a few hours after the stripe was conferred upon you did you learn that it came with many other privileges. It opened the doors of a world that had before been closed to the likes of you, a world that only granted entrance to those with a stripe on their arm. This was the world of the Italian officers' club. You were able to enter, not as a member, for membership was restricted to Italians, but as one of their lucky servants who were permitted to enter places like this and enjoy the festive atmosphere, or eat from the same plates that members ate from. You could watch dance shows with them, or films, and you could take pleasure in listening to music and inhaling the perfume of the beautiful women who visited the club.

The stripe allowed you to leave on errands outside the base, to cross the great gates and see the wide open world behind those walls. Now, you were able to deliver letters, securing provisions, and participating in the excursions for new recruits.

On your first errand outside the base, you stopped and breathed in the fresh air, which you knew none of your fellow recruits had inhaled since they had disappeared behind these walls. A sense of happiness overcame you, as if you had achieved total liberation from the recruits' world. You were tempted to return to your village while you could and dreamt of seeing your sick mother, finally fleeing the nightmares of this camp.

It was a fleeting thought. Today you wanted to be the object of your masters' trust, because you knew there was no use in escaping. You remembered that one of the Libyan chiefs who had cooperated with the Italians while his tribe rebelled against them had said that the Italians were like the ground and they were like the birds, no matter how far their wings took them in the sky, they would always be forced to return to the earth. These were the facts of life. No matter how clever you were, even if you escaped, what good would it do to spend your days a prisoner inside the walls of your own home? What would be the point of swapping a collective prison for an individual one?

You chased the thought from your mind, acknowledging that you were already trapped in the military life from which there was no escape until the Abyssinian campaign was over. Those who were still alive after the war would have the right to return to their civilian lives. But until then, the best you could do was improve your living conditions. Now you were blessed with a better position, and received the sort of treatment from the Italians that few could dream of. Therefore, you decided not to waste any more time and set to your masters' errands so as to impress them even more.

Sergeant Antar was no longer your master, for you had also become a person of rank, and your Italian had improved so much it had begun to help you understand what you heard, and to respond in kind. You no longer needed him, and he was no longer entitled to anything from you except the respect due to any of your seniors.

You treated ythe first day you passed through the gates into the outside world as a holiday. The errand was to deliver a letter to the centre of town, so you quickly walked to the main street and found a horse-drawn carriage. You jumped into the carriage, which took off at a trot. You arrived early, gave the letter to an employee in the inquiries department of the Bank of Rome, and still had time to entertain yourself.

You turned down Corso Street with its Italian shops

and shop fronts adorned with lights and mirrors. You found a shop that sold gelato and didn't hesitate to pay twenty baras for a scoop of gelato that you licked while walking down the street in your military clothes, not caring if that was a violation of your orders. You stopped in front of Cinema Odeon, where an Italian film was showing, and the glass windows in front were full of pictures of beautiful women and romance scenes. So you decided to buy a ticket. At this hour, the base was usually quiet and dull. No one would notice your absence.

That was the first time you went to the cinema, which you had heard of, though never seen before. You went inside, but after sitting down, you almost fled screaming when you saw a fire burning in the middle of the screen and tongues of flame spreading to the curtains around the screen, reaching as high as the ceiling. Horrified, you feared the fire would engulf you where you sat in the front row and you would die an ugly death, burnt to embers along with the wooden chair you sat on.

You jumped up alarmed, then regained control of your senses. You nailed yourself down to the chair.

You could see the people beside you in the darkness, calmly eating their gelato or peanuts, unconcerned with the mad outbreak of flames or its crackling noise. They knew that they were just pictures on the screen.

What interested you more than the film was the news-reel that showed Il Duce in Rome: his heavy facial features, his cruel jaw that seemed chiselled out of granite. He stood in one of the wide squares of Rome addressing a throng of people that churned and crashed against itself like the waves of the sea. They yelled his name in a state of hysteria, and responded to every sentence with shouts.

After the segment about Il Duce was a piece on the governor Marshal Italo Balbo flying his little aeroplane, with a blonde woman seated beside him, to inspect the interior of Libya. The people of every district came out in crowds, welcoming him as he waved to them.

Then there was a celebration on the docks for the Italian ships carrying three thousand immigrants from Palermo. They disembarked from the steamboats, welcomed by a band playing anthems, Marshal Balbo, other notables, and several ladies from Tripolig's high society holding bouquets. The Italians were really building themselves a new world in this country.

As you watched the romance scenes that constituted much of the film, your thoughts turned to Thuraya, and you regretted wasting that time watching the moving pictures instead of going to see her. You left the cinema before the end, intending to go visit her when you discovered that you were already over an hour late. So you swore to yourself that you would spend a few minutes visiting Thuraya the next time you left the base.

One evening, while you were serving the Italians at the officers' club, you were surprised to find a Libyan woman among the attendees. Nothing in her appearance announced her Arab-Libyan identity. She wore a glittering dress that revealed her back, shoulders and chest down to the opening of her bosom. She was as elegant and free as any Italian woman. Her skin was fair, which was rare among Libyans except for a few living in the city. Her jet-black hair was arranged in a crown on her head like those of the kings of Rome, and on her neck she wore a gold necklace set with precious stones, which had no parallel among the traditional gold necklaces that most Libyan women wore. But what really made her unlike any other Libyan woman was that she brazenly sipped from a glass of wine and exchanged pleasantries with the officers around her, so that only her wide dark eastern eyes bore evidence of her Libyan identity.

The cooks and waiters were professionals who had been in the club's service for a while. They were the ones who served the guests and took their orders. Your tasks were a little less important than that, such as moving the tables from one place to another, bringing chairs from the closet and returning them, and maintaining the cleanliness of the place. You had gone to where the lady was sitting in order to place new candles in the big silver candelabrum that adorned one of the four corners of the room, near where the lady happened to be sitting.

Despite its electric lighting, the club resorted to candles to light some of the corners for two reasons. The first was to give the lighting in these corners a romantic touch, and the second was that in case the electricity cut out, which happened often in that region, the place would still be illuminated by candlelight and none of the guests would panic.

She looked at you and smiled radiantly, then said to you in Libyan Arabic dialect without any trace of an accent, "You're an Arab, aren't you?"

You replied, "Arab and from Awlad Al Sheikh. My name is Othman."

You almost thought she was an Italian who had mastered the Libyan dialect.

She drew deeply from the long cigarette-holder and exhaled the smoke, pursing her lips in an extremely provocative way. Gracefully tapping the ash into the ashtray, she said, "I'm Arab too, from Tripoli."

You examined her closely, raising your eyes then lowering them, as if you couldn't believe what this woman had said. From the plaits of gold at the top of her head, to the white gems that glimmered in the light, the bracelets on her wrists and the rings on her fingers, from the seductive skin of the naked parts of her chest, to the black shining dress hemmed with threads of silver, everything suggested a woman who belonged to the upper echelons of Italian society. How could a Libyan woman warrant the attentions of these officers, who competed among each other to light her cigarette, or the waiters who stood waiting for a gesture of her finger, then rushed to serve her as though she were a queen? How could any wretched Libyan, male or female, reach such a privileged status in Italian society? Or more accurately, it was clear that she looked down with contempt on all these officers, whom she broke off listening to in order to talk to you, as if she had wanted to send them a message by turning her attention to a lowly worker lighting candles.

You had removed the remains of the extinguished candles, replaced them and lit them. Intending to withdraw, you inclined your head and whispered, "I'm greatly honoured to meet you, my lady." The lady signalled with a gesture of her hand that she wanted you to stay. "This is a beautiful, elegant candelabrum. I want one like it for my house. Do you know how

I can acquire one?"

"From the storeroom of course, my lady."

"I'm talking about the marketplace. I want to purchase one like this. Could you help me with that?"

"Gladly."

"Well then, inform me of its price, and come to my

house so I can give you the money. I want one exactly like it. My house is number seven on La Posta Street. I will wait for you tomorrow morning."

You said, "I will need permission from the officer on duty."

"Just tell them that you're going to perform a service for Signora Houriya," she said.

When you returned to the kitchen, you told the other Arabs about your astonishing discovery. The topic of Signora Houriya wasn't new to them. They all knew her because she often attended the parties at the officers' club and frequently spoke at length to the Arab serving staff in the club, asking them how they were, and telling their Italian supervisors to treat them kindly. She also gave them generous gifts on holidays and special occasions, affirming the link that bound them as Libyans. Despite her life with the Italians and her elevated status among them, she never denied her origins or disavowed her family, which only increased the servants' affection for her.

The most consequential thing they told you was spoken to you in whispers: that Signora Houriya was none other than the favourite mistress of the country's governor Marshal Balbo. Thus, many considered her the second most powerful person in the country, since Marshal Balbo never refused her.

The Libyan servants began to congratulate you on having won Signora Houriya's approval to the extent that she had asked you to do her a favour and invited you to her house. Prominent Arabs and Italians alike were eager to be of service to her. If she had asked for this candelabrum from an Italian general, he would have gladly relinquished it to her.

In spite of all this wonderful talk, your heart felt troubled. You saw only a new dilemma in the mission that Signora Houriya had assigned to you, which might lead you to an even greater evil. Everything you had heard and read told you of the dangers of getting too close to powerful men's mistresses, especially if the relationship between the man and his woman was as intimate and influential as that between Signora Houriya and Balbo's seemed to be.

You had lived a whole year in the city before enlisting at the base, but you were still a villager at heart. Like most villagers, you despised any woman living in sin with men. How could a woman of your flesh and blood, a Libyan like you, sell her body so cheaply to the leader of the Italian invaders? After that, how could you possibly go to her house as a humble servant and act cordially and obediently?

When you asked the Italian officer on duty the following day for permission to leave, you hoped he would refuse you. To your disappointment, he granted you leave until six in the evening. He had just given you the whole day off to perform this trifling errand for Signora Houriya.

You left the base and went out into the open spaces of the outside world with twelve whole hours to kill until it was time for you to return. What could you do with all this time when Signora Houriya's business would take no more than an hour? You felt that this much freedom was worthless if you didn't use it to see Thuraya, so you decided to make her your priority. You didn't want to waste time passing by Haj al-Mahdy's shop to glean scraps of information about her beforehand. You were certain she was now staying at her father's house during her husband's absence.

You bought a basked of fruit from a nearby store, ascended the stairs and knocked on the door. A boy answered, and you asked for Thuraya, mentioning your name. He left and came back quickly informing you that Thuraya was coming. Wasn't this in itself cause for happiness? So why did you torture yourself with questions as to why you had come looking for her, what you wanted from her?

Why would you need answers to such questions? It was enough to see her, and appease this flame that burned your heart. She came to the door.

You could scarcely believe that the only woman you had ever loved was standing in front of you. Her graceful figure, her beautiful oval face, her two amber eyes. She was wearing a cotton robe that flowed over her body and suggestively revealed the rounded shape of her bosom. Despite her troubles, a smile lit up her wheat-coloured face. How could you silence the roar of blood rushing in your veins, the pounding of your heart beating in your chest? It was impossible that she hadn't noticed the trembling that was convulsing your entire body. You were ashamed of yourself, for nothing could conceal your raw emotions.

You had been absent for six months, during which time these emotions had been pent up, and they wanted to explode the instant you saw the world again, the instant you saw Thuraya. She was the brilliant essence of all happiness and comfort in the world, and at the same time of every sorrow, deprivation, and grief. You extended your hand to shake hers so that might magically connect with the elixir of life.

Thuraya stood slightly behind the door as she talked to you.

"Hello, Othman. Are you still alive?" she said lightly, erasing the gloom of death that hung on the sentence.

Despite your astonishment, which kept you tongue-tied as you looked at her, you heard yourself saying in the same manner, "Did the funeral men come with news of my death for you and your father?"

Alarmed, she said, "May God keep you from evil,"

then continued saying, "The people have been wailing as though everyone who had been recruited were dead. How did you get out? Did you escape?"

"No, I haven't. Sometimes I am charged with tasks outside the base."

"What do they do to you there? Do they truly beat you to the brink of death?"

You didn't tell her that you had moved from the category of people who were beaten to the category of people who held the whip to beat them. Instead, you ignored what she had said and asked, "Who told you such nonsense?"

"That's what people say."

And before you had a chance to refute what the people said, she anxiously asked you, "Have you seen Fathy?"

"I'ven't seen him," you said. "Have you not heard from him?"

"It's odd that you haven't seen him. All we know is that he is stuck in one of the camps that no one is allowed to visit."

"There is another base in Tajura. Maybe he's there."
"My father asked about him frequently without any
    results. They said that they will let them visit their families before leaving for Abyssinia."

You could see that she longed to learn her husband's whereabouts. Perhaps she did truly love him, but you were sure that she held special affection for you. And yet however strong this relationship had once been, perhaps it had become a thing of the past after fate had bound her to this man. One's husband is always one's husband. He was the man joined to her by fate and destiny through that legal bond blessed by the angels in heaven. Any other relationship fell into the shadows of oblivion after that, and if such an extra-marital connection went too far, it could only lead to a sinful relationship. Every honourable woman understood this.

In this society, marriage no longer left you a place in her life, and you had no right to blame her. Why had you tired yourself walking down dead-end streets? What was the point of chasing after the funeral procession for your love? All it would lead to was more pain.

You asked her if you could be of any service to her. She made no answer, for what could you possibly do for a woman waiting for her husband's return from the camps of war? You thrust the basket of fruits towards her and descended down the stairs quickly.

Was this the last time you would see Thuraya? The question filled you with dread, but a voice told you not to fear, for every tribulation, no matter how large, is always compensated. Perhaps the compensation would be equal to the tribulation. The voice told you that Thuraya was yours alone, she couldn't be anyone else's wife, no matter what the marriage contract said. It couldn't be the final word. Such contracts were often nullified or retracted so that two lovers could be united after having been prevented from what was rightfully theirs by some spurious marriage.

The problem, you told yourself, was that Thuraya hadn't given you any sign, no matter how small, to suggest she would be favourable to such a proposal. She was Fathy's wife, and it was her duty to him and to herself to be true to him and to safeguard herself against any libertine tendencies. You would not ask her to disobey her husband and break her vows, but you had hoped to see a sign of the old love you'd shared. Nevertheless, the voice continued to insist, saying that this wasn't the end of your story with Thuraya. Perhaps it said that only to console and give hope. Oh! If only you could be sure of that, you would have made it your purpose to stay alive during the war until you could return to her. No, you were sure of it, that unfailing sixth sense of yours told you you were made for one another, and you thanked God for bringing Thuraya into this world.

ELEVEN

You left Thuraya's house in the old city and hastened to Signora Houriya's house in the new quarter, as if throwing yourself into mortal peril. You quickly passed by the shop of a Jewish silverware merchant on Corso Street to learn the price of the candelabrum Signora Houriya wanted. Then, without slowing down, you went to her apartment on La Posta Street, where you found a military vehicle and Italian soldiers stationed outside the front door, one of whom asked you what you wanted when he saw you trying to enter the building. When you told him, he led you to the apartment door.

A black youth in his mid teens opened the door. He spoke Arabic with an African accent. When he heard your name, he ushered you into the spacious sitting room. Your feet sank into thick carpets and there were sofas and armchairs upholstered with rich blue, gilded fabrics. Covering much of the walls were mirrors in wooden frames with fanciful designs engraved into them, and flower pots exuding fragrant aromas were placed in the corners. There was a large portrait of Marshal Balbo hung on the parlour wall, who with his small elegant pointed beard, looked as though he had been painted in Chinese ink. Beside that hung another picture of him shaking hands with the Duce. A large ostrich egg hung from the middle of the ceiling, dangling from red leather straps. When you sat down, you saw pictures of Houriya and Marshal Balbo in intimate poses, in one of which she had put her head on his shoulder, and in another she was sitting beside him in the cockpit of the little plane that he always piloted himself whenever he flew between his many houses in various Libyan cities. A collection of animal hides, consisting of tiger, lion, zebra and antelope skins, was arranged beautifully between the mirrors and the pictures. Above that was a board of ivory hung with necklaces of blue and red gems.

The smell of incense overpowered the fragrance of flowers. It smelled like musk and added an air of familiarity to the surroundings, for you had loved this scent ever since you were a child and the sheikh of the Sunni Mosque would perfume worshippers with it during religious celebrations. Nevertheless, this beloved scent and the African and Oriental décor didn't assuage your couldn'tapprehension.

Houriya came without delay, wearing coloured leather sandals that showed the henna on her toes. She had wrapped herself in a white robe and was drying her hair with a bath towel. A few drops of water dripped onto her flushed face like drops of dew on a rose. You got up the moment she appeared, standing to attention. She laughed, leaning her head back and arching her body with the clear ringing laugh. The movement made her breasts more prominent, and the robe slackened somewhat, revealing more of her shining marble neck. You realized you had fallen into a trap of your own making, and that you were at that moment in a predicament similar to Adam's when he stood before the Tree of Forbidden Knowledge. It was clear that Balbo hadn't chosen this woman over Italians for nothing. He had chosen the most beautiful gem the desert sun and the red sands could produce.

After she stopped laughing, Houriya said, "I'm not a general, so don't stand so stiff like that. Relax and tear that military mask off your face."

She sat down and playfully invited you to sit beside her. This was a woman on intimate terms with a seasoned military man who had participated in the March on Rome, which had culminated in the Fascist takeover of Italy. She knew how to captivate the hearts of men, big and small.

You sat on the edge of your seat and tried to form saliva in your mouth to ease the dryness in your throat, as if you were in the presence of one of the sorceresses of legend who could turn a person into stone.

There wasn'thing to fear, you told yourself. You had known what awaited you in this house. But the difference between the extent of your expectations and reality was huge. In spite of everything, she was one of your people, a Libyan who lived in sin with an infidel, which according to custom and tradition made her a woman of ill-repute deserving of the people's scorn. Moreover, the man she slept with was none other than the scourge of the nation. The Libyans would always see him as their executioner and hangman, even if he came clothed in the garb of reform and progress. All this meant she was lower than the prostitutes who sold their love in huts outside the city walls.

The only difference was that this fallen woman, whom you had come to serve in a show of loyalty and obedience, had through her sinful relationship become the most powerful Libyan person in the country. Some of the waiters and cooks in the club had even praised her, relating all manner of stories about her generosity to the poor.

"So your name is Othman and you say you're from . . ."

"Awlad Al Sheikh, near the Qibla region and Hamada Al-Hamra."

"Italo is very fond of the oases, and he's got me to love them too. We often spend our weekends in Ghadames. We have a house there that overlooks Ain Al-Farras. The most beautiful time of day is the early morning. The Sunrise there is absolutely wicked and terrifying."

She also told you that travelling back and forth between the desert and the sea gave a person the opportunity to appreciate the variety and beauty of the natural scenery in Libya. She didn't make any mention of the candelabrum for which you had come to the house, as though she had forgotten all about it. Although the Governor's residences in Tripoli had electricity, candles hadn't yet lost their importance, even in these grand mansions.

Finally you said, "I would have liked to buy the candelabrum and present it to you as a gift, but the shop owner does not sell on credit."

She asked you the price, and you stood ready to leave. But she told you to stay until you had drunk a cup of coffee, which the servant boy brought, while she remained sitting languidly in her chair. The robe had slipped from her thigh, which shone like crystal in the light from the window. A beautiful tabby cat sauntered up to her and rubbed itself up against her. Houriya bent down to pick it up and put it in her lap to stroke it while you looked on enviously.

"So you will be one of those deployed to Abyssinia at the end of the month," she said.

You were surprised. It was the first time you had heard the departure to Abyssinia would be at the end of this month, which was twenty days away, and you were sure that no one on the base knew about it, including the Italian officers themselves. Otherwise, no one would have been able to prevent this news from spreading to the entire camp. As of that moment, all you cared about was returning as quickly as possible in order to be the first person break the news to everyone. That was bound to increase the importance and status you had recently attained. You couldn't wait until it was time for you to go back, so you could see how the news would affect Sergeant Antar. He would be so preoccupied with figuring out how you had come across such vital information before him, that he would forget the excitement of the news itself.

Houriya noticed your surprise and took it for fear and dread of the campaign.

"God willing, you will finish your mission with success and return swiftly and safely to your family." she said gently.

She thought the war would be swift and successful. Perhaps you really would come back safe and sound. Life was worth living so long as there were beautiful women in the world like Houriya.

But what a shame that a precious gem like Houriya should be placed in such depraved conditions, you told yourself as you left to fetch the candelabrum and closed the door behind you.

In less than an hour, you returned accompanied by one of the boys from the shop, who carried the candelabrum for you in a box of reinforced cardboard. You had been eager to have him come with you so that he could carry the box instead of you, making you seem less servile and lowly in front of Signora Houriya.

The boy quickly assembled the candelabrum and put it in its intended place in the dining hall. Then he left. You took the coloured candles the merchant had given you and, completing your task, fixed them in place so that the silver candelabrum seemed even more splendid. All Houriya had to do was hold a match and light all the candles. The twisting flames flickered and danced, making a merry scene, and Houriya laughed with delight.

Realizing you had completed your task, you asked permission to leave, but she told you to wait and headed to the corridor that led to the bedrooms. You heard her speaking to someone in Italian, and then she came back. It hadn't occurred to you that the person who would be coming out from the apartment's sleeping quarters would be none other than Marshal Italo Balbo himself. You heard his footsteps before he appeared in his full military attire, wearing the Marshal's uniform, holding his cap in his hand, and his baton beneath his arm. His trousers were loose and his boots were knee-length. His face seemed to shine, an appearance heightened by the sharp contrast between his ruddy fairness and the darkness of his elegant goatee, which was slicked with pomade and thus gave off a dark light. His eyes glowed with a wily, cunning gleam. You stood to attention, stiff as a pillar. He approached you and scrutinized you from top to bottom. Then he stretched out a hand with a smile, saying, "Bravo! I heard that you enlisted in the army as a volunteer."

You tried to make your lips move in the words of thanks appropriate for such a situation, but he went on to say, "As I understand, you know how to read and write, which is unfortunately rare among our Libyan soldiers."

Houriya wanted to help you to understand what he

was saying and started to translate, but he stopped her saying, "Don't underestimate his Italian. I'm sure it's constantly getting better."

He waited for you to say something, but you remained unable to speak. He resumed speaking.

"Perfecting the Italian language is essential for the future of your military career."

You realized the man had taken an interest in you and requested a report. You considered his interest a cause for joy, because it was clear evidence of your success, but your happiness was diminished by the fact it meant further entanglement in a tainted world, a world of Fascists and colonizers.

"Was it love of adventure that led you to enlist?" He then left general speech aside and began to ask you more pointed questions. You didn't know what to say, and had you known what to say, you would not have had the strength to say it, so you just nodded your head and he went on talking.

"You have a daring spirit, such is the willpower of youth. No doubt you are looking forward to seeing the jungles and plateaus of Abyssinia."

A second of silence passed before he spoke again in a more serious tone.

"You will leave after a few weeks with your fellow soldiers to support the front in Ethiopia. It would be useful if you sent a report every now and then to my office to inform me of the condition and morale of the Libyan soldiers. I want to be sure you are treated well by the officers on the front. This is a matter of the utmost impor-tance. As long as I'm in charge of this country, I must be able to get a picture of the situation through the viewpoint of an Arab soldier. Reports from the Italian officers are not enough. I've chosen you specifically because I trust your devotion to duty."

You realized the candelabrum had been a pretext. The real reason was to recruit you to carry out a secret mission, which Marshal Balbo himself had entrusted you with. He had undoubtedly had his eye on you ever since the graduation ceremony and selected you to be one of his eyes to watch the Abyssinian battlefront.

Marshal Balbo finished what he had wanted to tell you, then turned to the mirror to check if his appearance. He put his cap on and made for the door, turning to you as he put his hand on the doorknob.

"Of course you will write your reports in Arabic." You bowed your head. "It is a great honour, my lord Marshal," you said in a voice that sounded strange to you.

All you could comprehend at that moment was your urgent desire to get out of that place as fast as possible. Something clenched in your chest, and the air in the house was not suited to alleviate that suffocating feeling. You wanted to be under open skies and breathe deeply and freely.

Houriya's quiet gentle voice soothed your choked throat like a balm.

"Is it really such a difficult a mission? One would think so judging by how blue-faced you've become. Take it easy on yourself, Othman. If you don't want to write the reports, don't write them."

She placed a cup of orange juice in your hands, adding, "What the Marshal wanted to say is that you are a source of admiration to him, and he does not want you to be shy about writing to him about whatever you wish to say. You might not know that he didn't want to send any Libyans to Abyssinia, especially because one of the leaders of the campaign is General Graziani, whom Balbo does not like because of his brutal treatment of the Libyans. Badoglio and his deputy in the Abyssinia campaign Di Bono promised him they would treat the Libyans well, so he agreed to it. Still, he wants to be assured by the Libyan soldiers themselves of the reality of the situation over there. I'll tell you something else, Othman. If you don't want to fight in the war, I can ask Italo to attach you to a military unit stationed in Libya."

You assured her you weren't afraid of going to war, and that you held only the greatest respect and esteem for Marshal Balbo. You made for the door intending to take your leave, when Houriya put some money in your hand. You tried to refuse, but she insisted. As you closed the door behind you, the feeling of suffocation began anew. You unbuttoned your shirt and welcomed the fresh air, hoping it would relieve some of this worry.

What the governor-general of Libya had said to you was too important to keep to yourself.

You had to find someone with whom you could unburden yourself. Your arrival at the base coincided with break time, which occupied the end of daylight hours, so you went directly to your meeting place with Salem beneath the pine trees and postponed informing the rest of the recruits about the date of departure to the lands of Abyssinia until the following morning.

As soon as you saw Salem, you said, "Believe it or not, I've just come from meeting Marshal Italo Balbo, the governor of the country."

Salem said, "And how did you pass up the chance to stick a dagger in his chest?"

"Quiet you fool! In case some spy hears your stupid joke and takes us both to prison on charges of plotting to assassinate the governor-general."

"I'm not joking. If I ever had a chance to kill him, I would do it, and welcome death after that."

"Don't forget it's Balbo and not Graziani. There is a big difference between the two."

"They're all criminal colonialists," said Salem. "May I know what brought you to this?"

"What could possibly lead me to something like this except chance?" you said.

You told your friend about meeting Houriya at the club and going to her apartment where you met the military governor of Libya. Salem was beside himself with anger. He ground his teeth and called Houriya the ugliest of names because the honour of any Libyan woman was the honour of Libya itself.

You laughed at this idea, for if he considered her a prostitute, prostitutes had always existed in every country, including under the Caliphs, and in your opinion their resence did no harm to anyone but themselves. You made light of his frenzied state, which almost prevented you from completing your story as yo uwere afraid of further upsetting his sensibilities. He thought you had acted immorally because you had tolerated the sight of this disgrace and willingly interacted as though it were perfectly natural. That was how he talked before hearing the rest of the story and learning what was even more outrageous.

"Save your anger until you hear what the Marshal told me," you said.

"Was he overcome with pride and did he start to brag about his soldiers' victories against us?"

"Marshal Balbo doesn't distinguish between us and them," you said. "He is more open-minded than that. We are all his soldiers: Italians and Libyans alike. That's how he sees things. The Marshal's conversation with me was personal, friendly, and full of praise for my daring spirit and the loyalty and dedication I've shown. That's why he chose me to carry out a special mission. I'm to report to him about what happens on the Ethiopian front as soon as we arrive."

You and Salem had been sitting on some chopped tree trunks scattered around the ground. Salem leapt up and shouted, "The criminal wants you to be a spy, does he? Why didn't you spit in his face?"

"Don't shout, and stop distorting what I'm saying. I wasn't talking with a nobody like you and me. I was talking to the most important person in the country. So I only uttered words of gratitude and respect."

"What a despicable scoundrel you are! I wouldn't be surprised if you took the initiative and started sending him your reports right now, beginning with the profanities I've just called him."

"Why don't you understand? He doesn't want me to do anything wrong. He just wants to reassure himself about the treatment of the Libyan soldiers because they're under his care."

"Oh Ladies and Gentlemen! Come and hear the truth of the matter. The underlying motive is the love that Balbo bears for his Libyan brothers! Isn't that right?"

"He didn't try to force me to take this mission. He left it up to me, so I will forget everything you've just said."

When you returned to the barracks, you saw Sergeant Antar on his routine inspection, and you couldn't wait until morning to reveal your secret about the date of the trip to Abyssinia. You took him aside and asked him if he had any idea about when the journey to Abyssinia would be. He showed surprise at the unexpected question, then, speaking loudly enough for all the recruits in the barracks to hear, and in the voice of someone who was certain of their information, he said, "No earlier than six months from now at the very least. Why do you ask?" You answered him in the same loud voice, "Because I've different information." "Different? How? We have new recruits who need this period to train on the basics, to say nothing of more advanced training for the other soldiers. The departure date can be any time after a number of months which, certainly, will be more than six. Where did you get different information and what exactly is the difference?"

You replied in an even louder voice than before, "I know for a fact, Sergeant Antar, that we will set out in exactly twenty days."

Sergeant Antar looked sharply at you with a look of derision that took in everything from the tips of your toes to the top of your head.

You spoke to him in a confidential whisper, making an exaggerated show of your victory over him, "Keep what I've told you to yourself. It's still a military secret."

Before leaving, he smiled and looked at you with pity as if he were looking at a dimwit.

The following day he came to you on the shooting range, where you were in a training session. He asked your instructor's permission to speak to you privately for a moment. As soon as you were alone, he exploded in your face saying, "What's the point of spreading the false rumours you were talking about last night?"

"How do you know they're not true?"

"I asked the base commander himself, who said that the date for deployment still has not yet been set."

"It has been set, and everything's been decided already." "Who are you to say anything about the matter? Do you know more than the base commander?"

You didn't want to expose your relationship to the highest authority in the land, so you contented yourself with saying he would see what you said was true soon enough.

You unabashedly announced the departure date to everyone you saw. By no later than midday, it had become official currency, as it was confirmed by the Italian officers who received an official communication from Central Headquarters. The communication informed them that this was the official date for their deployment, and that three steamships would arrive from Italy to the shores of Libya at the beginning of the month to transport them from Tripoli, Misrata and Benghazi south to Abyssinia.

You had scored a crucial victory over your biggest competitor for power in the camp, Sergeant Antar, whose attitude towards you changed from then on. He began to avoid speaking to you, as if he was afraid you would throw a scorpion in his face. He seemed to resent the order to deploy because it included the new recruits as well. He would say to himself aloud, "What will we do with them? If they don't have enough time to train, how will they cope after they arrive on the battlefield? They will die without firing a single shot."

He would talk like that to himself, and upon hearing

him, you felt for the first time that he was a man with a conscience and a heart that trembled in fear for the fates of those new recruits.

TWELVE

There was a steady flow of errands that required you to leave the base, and you always had plenty of time to spare, during which you thought only of Thuraya. She was the centre of your life, and your heart beat with yearning and desire for her. You wondered what pretext you could use to visit her and check on her welfare. Going without a good reason would be an intrusion and arouse suspicions, and you wanted her and her family's opinion of you to remain spotless.

As for news of your family in Awlad Al Sheikh, you could always talk to Abdel Mowlah the beggar, but you felt no desire to visit the tin hut he lived in, for the sight of it only upset and exhausted you, and it would have been unwise to waste valuable moments looking for a wretched man like Abdel Mowlah.

Instead, you strolled through the city gazing at shop windows, chewing on sweets you bought from a tiny shop in front of Cinema Alhambra, until you found yourself on La Posta Street, where Signora Houriya's building was located. Unlike the previous time, there were no military vehicles parked out front and no Italian guards with pistols hanging from their belts. Only an elderly civilian guard sat on a bench outside the building.

You stood near the entrance, uncertain, wondering if it was appropriate for you to knock on her door now that you didn't have a convincing reason to visit. You shook the thought from your mind and continued walking, but before taking more than a few steps, you saw her servant Morgan appear carrying a bundle of magazines in one hand, and a basket of fruits and vegetables in the other. You hurried over, reminding him who you were, and took the basket to help him carry his load to the door, where he tried to take it back from you, but you refused to give it back and went up the stairs to the first floor with him following behind you. As he opened the door, you told him to ask his mistress's permission for you to enter. You stood in front of the door until it opened again and Morgan asked you to come in. Even though it was noon, Houriya had only woken up a few minutes earlier, so you waited in the same hall you had previously sat in.

You had prepared a reason to save yourself embarrassment and justify this visit, although you had to ask yourself why you needed to invent reasons to see her. What had really prompted you to make this visit? Was it because she was a woman of stunning beauty and you wanted to feast your eyes on her? Was that enough of a reason for you to take such a risk? You knew the danger of getting too close to such matters, or of touching the beloved playthings of powerful men.

Hurry, flee now, get out, and tell the servant you apologize for coming so early, before the lady of the house has awakened. Leave before you cause yourself harm.

Yet despite these thoughts, you remained nailed to your

seat, unable to move. You had come and that was that. You couldn't fix the mistake of having come by making the mistake of leaving now.

"You did well to come, for I wanted to see you." Houriya's voice washed away the regret and worry you felt. You stood up to greet her as she entered. A full grey suit lined with white stripes lent her slender build even more elegance. She held her bag in one hand as if she were about to go on an outing.

"Did you happen to come here by coincidence?" she asked.

"I didn't want to intrude on you for no reason, but seeing Morgan in the street encouraged me to come." And without delay you plunged into the topic you had fabricated as a reason for your visit.

"As you know, the time of our departure is drawing close and I found myself confused, how do I send these reports the Marshal wants?"

She responded laughing, "You know, if you wrote 'Marshal Balbo, Libya' on the envelope, it would find its way here."

Still she agreed that it was an important detail that you should have been told from the beginning because of the confidential nature of these letters. She told you that you wouldn't have to send your reports to any address because Marshal Balbo would send an officer from his staff to the front to act as a link between him and the army. It was that person who would contact you and receive whatever reports you wrote.

Houriya was quick to talk to you about the Balbo whom people didn't know as she did. She wanted you to convey an accurate portrayal of him to your Libyan peers.

"All Libyans should know that Balbo is not like Caneva, or Folby, or Di Bono, or Badoglio, or Graziani. He really loves Libya and wants it to be like Ferrara, the Italian city he is from. He was responsible for making it a beautiful and prosperous city. He wants Libya to be a place where both Libyans and Italians can live happily, that's why he deserves the cooperation of Libyans in building and reviving this country."

The woman puzzled you more than ever. She spoke with love and zeal about the man who had chosen to live with her. She didn't consider him, as other Libyans did from afar, as a Fascist leader come to apply his party's and country's policies, or consolidate the Italian Occupation in Libya and settle Italy's unemployed on Libyan lands.

Perhaps the matter needed to be re-examined. Houriya wasn't the only one who felt this way. Other Libyans, some of whom were former leaders of the resistance, had learned to live with the reality of the occupation given that it was inescapable. They worked with the leader of the Italian Occupation's forces by neither refusing nor accepting the occupation. Instead, they tried to appease them and asked for their mercy so that no harm would come to the Libyan people.

A number of nationalistic poets had written poems of praise that sounded more like petitions for clemency from Balbo. "O God! We do not ask you to change fate, but we ask that it be kind to us."

They had acted according to this mentality, and you couldn't claim to be any better. So you didn't blame them or yourself if you had all renounced dreams and illusions in order to deal with unquestionable realities, and naturally that meant you could not blame Signora Houriya for talking about her lover through the image she had developed of him in the mirrors of that house rather than in the context of the country he had come to occupy.

You left Signora Houriya's house and saw Marshal Balbo's aesthetic touch everywhere you turned in Tripoli. Italian governors before him had built up certain new parts of the city, but he had come with a more advanced understanding of beautification, a finer tuned understanding of the local conditions and idiosyncrasies, so that Tripoli would remain a Libyan city with an Arab and eastern character, not merely a replica of Italian cities.

Marshal Balbo had taken a special interest in public spaces, putting statues in parks and public squares. He had seen to it that most of the statues had some relationship to nature, like the statue of the gazelle, or the statue of horses connected to a water fountain. Building façades had been illuminated with the colours that Tripoli was famous for, blue and white. He had placed oriental lanterns in the streets and courtyards, and rapidly built government buildings. And the palace had been nearly finished when he assumed the governorship, so he had put the final touches on it and made it his official residence.

Houriya wasn't just a pretty doll, but a woman with a powerful presence and her own opinions and points of view. She was only trying to raise her lowly position, as if she were saying that she wasn't some cheap commodity for sale and purchase, and that she was here in this house, and with this man, because she loved him.

After returning to the base you tried, with great circumspection, to slip into the officers' club to learn more about this fascinating woman. Marshal Balbo couldn't possibly have picked her up from the red light district, and no normal Libyan family, with their rigid traditions, could possibly have raised her with such a personality even if conditions had forced them to sell their daughter to a life of sin. Where had Houriya come from? From what soil had she sprouted?

As you learned from the servants in the officers' club, her story began nine years ago when then governor Di Bono had sent his bulldozers to demolish the huts and shacks on Makeena Street in the heart of Tripoli in order to make room for the construction of what would be the largest cathedral in the country. Houriya and her mother were living in one of the huts. Out of pity, the governor ordered them to be re-housed at the nurses' residence at Catania Military Hospital, which would later become Caneva Hospital. There, the mother swept and cleaned the wards while her daughter became a trainee nurse with the Italian nuns. A year and a half after assuming the governorship, Balbo was hospitalized for minor injuries caused by an emergency landing in the countryside. It was during his stay in the hospital that he met Houriya, who was one of the members of the medical crew assigned to him. Her femininity had blossomed and her beauty and charm, which had been hidden behind poverty, had come out as a consequence of her comfortable life in the hospital. Balbo was instantly captivated by her and would not leave the hospital without her. He gave her a house near the Governor's Palace, and despite having a wife in Italy, and many mistresses outside of the country, it was Houriya who became his constant companion, who attended dance parties, Italian clubs, and private and public celebrations with him.

Why, you asked yourself, were you so interested in a woman totally unconnected to you, and with whom you couldn't possibly develop a relationship of any kind? What did it matter if you knew or didn't know the life story of a woman whom you might never meet again ? You loved her and you hated her, you praised her and despised her. What was the benefit of living out such a futile inner conflict?

You couldn't find a single motive. Perhaps it was because you had lost Thuraya and the only other woman you knew in the city was Houriya, so you had gone to her with your repressed emotions, wanting a woman who was unattainable, who would not be a burden on your thoughts and emotions because clinging to her would be no different than a moviegoer clinging to the picture of an actress he sees on screen, or on an advertisement.

Perhaps thinking about a woman like Houriya would help you partly forget Thuraya, or at least give you a different woman to worry about so that you would not be tortured by images of Thuraya. You could ill afford such emotional turmoil when on the threshold of a new chapter in your life, preparing for a journey from which you were didn't know whether you would return. But as fate would have it, an opportunity would present itself that would allow you to visit Thuraya.

THIRTEEN

With all the new errands you had been assigned, you had forgotten about looking for Fathy, Thuraya's husband, and finding out if he was one of the recruits stationed on your base. Moreover, you were still unsure as to whether you would be able to recognize him, even if he were standing right in front of you, for you had no memory of your one brief encounter except a hazy impression.

When the departure date was definitively fixed, the recruits signed an urgent petition asking to be allowed to see their families before leaving. The base authorities responded to their request with a clever ploy. They decided that instead of permitting the recruits to leave and visit their families, they would open the camp gates to let the recruits' families visit them. This way, they could keep the recruits under their thumb until their units were shipped to Abyssinia.

They knew the hate the Libyans had for the war and didn't trust any of them to return to the base once they had been let out, no matter the penalty for desertion. Every recruit had family in the deserts, where it would be hard to find anyone. Rather than make a formal announcement, the recruits were informed of the matter personally to avoid all the city residents from crowding in front of the base at the same time. Despite the secrecy surrounding the decision, people began to come in droves to the camp, creating a traffic jam by the main gates.

You saw an opportunity to render Thuraya and her family a service by informing them about the visits so they could hurry to see Fathy before the Italians decided to close the gates. As soon as the time came for you to leave the base, you went to the old city and Bint Al Pasha Alley where Thuraya lived and knocked on her door. She opened the door herself this time. She didn't seem reserved this time as she had before, she didn't try to hide behind the door or conceal her face from you. She greeted you, uttering your name and invited you to come in as if you were one of the family. You didn't understand this unusual invitation to enter until she told you that her father, Haj al-Mahdy, was home.

You immediately thought the man must be suffering from some ailment, otherwise he would never be far from his shop at this hour in the morning. You asked her if her father was well, and she only said, "Please, in here."

She walked in front of you leading you to her father's room and then disappeared. Would your contact with her end at this? Were these meagre words all the reward you would reap from this visit?

Haj al-Mahdy was alone in the room. The floor was covered with mats and he was stretched out on a mattress near the wall. There were decorative plates hanging over his head. On the opposite wall, little baskets woven of coloured palms sat on several shelves, and a golden frame displayed a Quranic verse of al-Falaq written in calligraphy.

There was a pitcher of water and a large jar of olives not far from him, and a curtain screened off the part of the room where he slept.

The man struggled from his place on the floor into a sitting position, leaning his back against the wall. In a feeble voice, he asked you to sit beside him on the cushion he had placed on the mat. He looked extremely tired, his face was slack and dull, and sickness had added ten years to his life since the last time you had seen him. You somberly asked about his condition and the nature of the illness that kept him from his shop.

He said, "Is there any disease other than these Italians?"

"What do the Italians want with an old man like you?"

"Do they leave anyone alone, old or young?" he said.

He fell silent from weakness, so you urged him to speak more plainly about what had happened.

"Did something happen to the shop?" you asked. "Not the shop. It's my land in Tajura that my father and grand-fathers left me."

"Where you used to plant watermelon after the valley flooded?"

"That land and the fields and pastures around it have become property of the settlement projects for Italian emigrants. They erected a wire fence around it and placed sentries."

"That's outrageous," you said.

"They took it on the basis that we don't farm it all year long, and they said they compensate us, but it's all lies. By God, if I were strong enough to fight them, I would do. But every age comes with its own set of rules and limitations."

"Have you seen a doctor?"

"My wife gives me a mixture of herbs that brings blessings to whomever drinks it."

"I can go now and bring an Arab nurse I know."

"No, don't bother, I've never complained about any disease except for this vexing anger, for which physicians have no cure. I just need to rest for a few days until it passes."

A moment's silence passed before he added sorrowfully, "That land is all I had saved up for hard times."

The time for consolation was over and your eyes were on the clock as you told him how the departure to Abyssinia was imminent and how the base commanders were permitting recruits' families to visit them inside the base. They could visit their son-in-law Fathy if they wanted. The sick old man cheered up on hearing the news. This would allow him to learn about the son-in-law who had been absent for more than nine months without his family knowing anything about his whereabouts.

The Haj called his daughter and wife to discuss how they could arrange the visit. They agreed to visit Fathy tomorrow, and then find someone to carry a message to his family in Tajura, so that they could accompany his family on a second visit.

Haj al-Mahdy said, "I wish I could go, but God has willed otherwise. I'm depending upon you, Othman my son, to accompany the family to the base."

You had no difficulty finding time the following day to hire a horse-drawn carriage in front of the Castle. You brought the carriage up to Haj al-Mahdy's door on Bint al-Pasha Alley. Thuraya was wearing a white cloak over her embroidered clothes. Her younger brother was also dressed in a traditional Arab suit, while the mother would remain behind so as not to leave the ailing old man alone in the house.

Many thoughts passed through your mind as you sat beside Thuraya in the carriage while the deputized man of the family had his back turned to you from his seat next to the driver. Wrapped in her cloak, Thuraya silently watched the street go by.

This woman should have been yours because ou had known her and loved her before the other man had come and whisked her away. So you saw nothing wrong with trying to rightfully regain what they had taken from you by force. But you would not. You didn't want to frighten her or do anything she would not want.

However, you would not waste the chance to express what was in your heart and find answers to all the questions that burned in your breast. Why had she forsaken you when she knew with certainty that you loved her? Yes, you had made your love clear to her since the minute you felt it pierce your chest like an arrow of fire, and she had made you believe it was reciprocated. Had she truly loved you? Had you misread the signs? Perhaps you had mistakenly convinced yourself that she loved you back, when in fact your love for her was unrequited.

In a hushed voice, you told her that you wanted to ask her a personal question, if she didn't mind, and before she could answer, you whispered into her ear that you had always had strong feelings for her, that you had made a special place for her in your heart ever since the first time you had seen her.

All she said was that she considered you like a second brother now, but that wasn't what you wanted to hear from her, so you continued talking in what quickly became a one-sided conversation because she didn't once utter a single word in reply.

You said, "I had just one hope around which my life revolved ever since I met you. That was to win you over and marry you. Do you know that?

"I was sure that you returned my feelings in kind. Am I mistaken?

"You probably don't know, but it was your marriage that pushed me into enlisting in the Italian army."

"I had escaped from the soldiers that had seized me and taken me to the base, and they would have never found me, but after you got married, I discovered that my life had no meaning."

"I thought of killing myself, but I feared the punishment of God, who considers suicide a grievous sin against Him, so as an alternative to suicide I took myself to the Italians' military base in order to die in the war."

"Can you understand now how much I love you? How the shock of your marriage tore me apart?"

"I'm not blaming you or asking you to apologize or explain why you got married, because I know how these things happen. All I want is to explain myself and tell you that I still love you, even though you are married to another man. All I can say to you is that I will fight against this love that resides deep in my heart and soul. I will fight it with all the strength I've, knowing that it will defeat me and not the other way around."

Thuraya was silent.

The carriage arrived at the base where the Italian soldiers were doing their utmost to control the chaos that the visitors had created and turn it back into order. They gave numbers to people according to precedence of their arrival and let people enter the reception hall in small groups of five or six families at a time.

You left Thuraya and her brother waiting outside while you entered the base to search for some way to spare them a long wait in the sun. The Italian officer in charge of the visitors was unresponsive and considered it a violation of the rules. You had no other choice but to resort to mentioning Signora Houriya's name in the officer's ear. Signs of interest appeared on his face, so you told him that a relative of Signora Houriya was here to see her husband. The trick worked and the magic word of Signora Houriya's name opened the gates.

Thuraya entered the reception hall accompanied by her brother and an officer's assistant looked for Fathy's name among the lists of soldiers until he found it and wrote down his regiment, barracks, and identification number on a piece of paper, which he gave to a soldier whom you followed inside.

The scene inside was brimming with emotions, for the warm-hearted meetings lasted no more than a few minutes and were followed by painful farewells when each family had to face the reality that this was the last time they would see their son before he departed for a war in far-off lands from which he might never return.

The most heartbreaking scene was of a mother who threw herself into her son's arms, embracing him, weeping, and refusing to leave him when the time came for her to go. The guard had to tear her away from her son's arms.

While Thuraya and you were waiting for Fathy to arrive, she asked you how you hadn't happened to see Fathy the entire time you were living together on the same base. Her voice gladdened you, for it was clear and steady, without any traces of anger after everything you had said to her during the ride to the base. So she didn't dislike what you had confessed to her, perhaps she still had feelings for you that she didn't reveal.

You looked into her almond eyes searching for affirmation of these thoughts, but all you saw in them was a beauty reminiscent of the splendour of fields, and the pureness of skies touched with gold as they welcomed the rays of the rising sun. You were certain now that the emotions which loaded your heart with big dreams weren't born in a vacuum, but were shaped by the impassioned feelings that this young, beautiful, desirable woman had held for you, before tradition, custom and blind chance had married her to someone other than the man she loved. This marriage forced loyalties and obligations upon her that were contrary to what her heart wanted. That was all that mattered to you now, finding Fathy or not was of no consequence, rather you hoped he really did live on another base to spare you the pain of seeing him and suffering jealousy and envy.

Fathy came and stood at the entrance of the hall, scanning the crowd for his wife. You couldn't be sure that it was him until you saw Thuraya call him and head in his direction. You stepped aside to give them a chance to talk freely. The most appropriate thing was for you to keep out of sight until the visit was over. There was no need for him to know that you had brought Thuraya and her brother here, or to know of the relationship that tied you to her family.

You stood at a distance and watched Fathy rush towards Thuraya and take her hands in his. Then he realized that her brother was there as well, so he took him in his arms and kissed him on the forehead. His smile lit up his face. His handsomeness set him apart from the rest of the soldiers. His teeth were white, he had a clear complexion, and he shone with happiness and vitality at seeing his wife with whom he had lived only a scant few days.

You had never imagined that Fathy would be so handsome, and the glow that radiated from his face made it seem as if he hadn't just spent nine months beneath the whip of life on the base.

The instant her time with her husband was over, Thuraya burst into tears, weeping until after she had left the base. When you were both sitting inside the carriage, you asked her why she had cried so bitterly. She must have known since the first day they took him that Fathy would be sent to Abyssinia, so what had changed to evoke such powerful emotions?

She was still drying her eyes when she answered, "Is there any woman in the world who deserves to cry more than me? I'm crying because of a sick father, a husband going to war, and because misfortune follows me wherever I go."

She paused awhile before saying, "You spoke about our marriage which never happened. Suppose it had. What use would that be as long as you are going to war? And look at me now. I may never see my husband again, and after all that you ask me why I'm crying?"

Thuraya started to cry again and you kept silent all the way home.

When you returned to the base at the end of the day you went to meet your friend Salem. You found him sitting alone reclining against the trunk of a cypress tree with traces of tears in his eyes. It seemed that you were destined to be pursued by tears. What had made your friend cry?

You asked him if one of the soldiers or supervisors had hurt him and he silently shook his head. You insisted on knowing what was the matter with him.

He hesitated before admitting his weakness. He had been overcome with grief when he saw the recruits from the city and countryside bidding farewell to their families because he might die in the war in Abyssinia without ever having had the chance to see his mother or father like the rest of the soldiers.

With the accent of Awlad Al Sheikh, he said, "Forgive me, cousin. The world is too hard, and I don't know what to do except cry. Isn't that unjust? Wasn't the injustice of being forced into the army enough without the injustice of not being able to see our loved ones before going on this journey of death?"

"Don't say death, dear cousin, and stay away from such pessimism. Find refuge in God."

It suddenly struck you that Salem's situation was similar to your own. You too would be unable to see anyone from your family before going to war, although you didn't assign as much importance to the matter as Salem did. Otherwise you would have made an effort to arrange something by bringing the matter to Signora Houriya's attention and asking her to give recruits from the countryside permission to visit their families, if only briefly, because it wasn't easy for entire families to come from distant regions to visit their sons in the city. Perhaps the Libyan soldiers could have been escorted by guards so as to guarantee they would not try to escape. But now it was too late to undertake preparations for such an enterprise.

You assured Salem that you would look for a way to inform your families in Awlad Al Sheikh about your imminent departure to Abyssinia. They might find the means to come to Tripoli, and if they didn't, at least they would be kept informed.

The nature of the relationship between Salem and his family differed greatly from the relationship that joined you to yours. You didn't miss anyone, and no one missed you. It had always been that way ever since your parents had separated, so you didn't care that you were far from Awlad Al Sheikh. This wasn't the case with Salem, who had lived his entire life beside his mother and father. Your own ailing mother, who cried more than she spoke every time you saw her, had become accustomed to being apart from you, as had you become accustomed to living far from her despite your love for her and hers for you.

But travelling to Abyssinia to wage war in the jungles and on the plateaus was a new and unfamiliar degree of separation. An unknown fate awaited you in places tens of thousands of miles away from your country. You would battle warriors who personified cruelty and wickedness. They had previously annihilated the enormous armies the Italians had sent against them since the beginning of the century. The situation was unlike any of the previous trips you had made outside of your village to Tripoli or to the ravines and steppes with shepherds before that. It made you look back with fondness and love for everyone in your family, young and old, whom you had left behind in Awlad Al Sheikh.

The next day, you went to the city of tin huts very early in the morning searching for Abdel Mowlah, hoping to catch him before he woke up and began on his daily rounds. When you found his hut, all you said to him was to take the first truck travelling to Awlad Al Sheikh and tell your family and Salem's family that you were leaving for Abyssinia in a week. You provided him with money for the trip, and you gave him some money for your family and Salem's, to help cover the costs of travelling to Tripoli. You promised him a sum of money for himself once he completed the task, because you had used up all your savings for now.

You waited until he had donned the fine clothes he wore only to visit his family, then you headed towards the city centre with him in the first carriage you came across. He went to the Shushan Agency while you returned hastening to the base because you hadn't received permission to be gone for more than an hour. As soon as you arrived, you found a report waiting for you with the gate guardsman ordering you to head to base headquarters immediately upon your return. Your heart quailed when you heard the news. What could headquarters want with a local recruit of little rank or importance like you? It would not be for something good of course.

The most likely explanation was that one of the recruits had overheard you and Salem say something against the occupation forces and had reported it to curry favour with the Italians. You weren't a novice to the despicable measures these human insects could sink to. It didn't surprise you and only confirmed your contempt for these petty Libyan scum, for whom disgrace and dishonour had become a way of life. The only way you could have checked your suspicions before going to headquarters, was looking for Salem to see if he had been summoned as well, but unfortunately the order didn't allow you that luxury and obliged you to present yourself to the administrative coordinator as soon as you arrived at the gates.

With slow dragging feet you ascended the few marble steps that led to the building's door, where the guard led you to the first floor and ushered you into an Italian lieutenant's office. You were extremely surprised when the Italian officer welcomed you with a smiling face that bore no sign of anger or accusation and briefly informed you that starting tomorrow, you would begin a course in driving automobiles. He gave you a piece of paper to take to the department of transportation and mechanics.

As you left the building, you began to think about the significance of this assignment. Usually only Italians were given this job and they had never before entrusted any Libyan soldiers with the responsibility of driving cars or military vehicles. Was there a need for more drivers in the upcoming war that forced them to make use of local soldiers? But the remaining time before the departure for Abyssinia would not suffice for you to qualify for such difficult and technical work. The lieutenant who had given you the paper hadn't neglected to mention the skill, effort and perseverance it would demand of you.

The whole affair seemed very strange, especially because it happened so suddenly without any warning from the officers. No one had even mentioned the topic before, and you wondered who had issued the order and for what reason. Before you went to the training workshop the following day, you tried to find out more, but no one was willing to listen to your queries. It was a military matter, and you were expected to obey unquestioningly.

FOURTEEN

Mario was a tall cheerful man a little past his forties, and he
had been assigned to be your driving instructor. His teeth
were as big and white as a donkey's, and his upper lip had
a small cleft that made him look like he was always half-
smiling. He wore civilian clothes because he wasn't a military
man. He was an automobile technician whom the base
employed for his skills.Mario told you there were many
technicians like him who worked in the military bases as
civilians. During his spare time and holidays, he worked as
a driver to earn extra income because, he explained, his wife,
Signora Franca, was so demanding he was always out of
money,forcing him to sacrifice his leisure hours to guarantee
a higher standard of living for her than the wives of other
techniciansenjoyed..

When he saw you were apprehensive about this new
job, he patted you on the back reassuringly, saying that he
would teach you to drive in a single day. But, he said, you
were not to tell anyone since it was considered an important task that required four or five weeks at least, and Mario
wanted to take advantage of their ignorance to draw out

the training period for as long as possible so that the two of you would have time for fun, games and flirting.

To that last, Mario added with a laugh, "Cars have a magnetic power over women they can't resist. The timeless dream every woman has of the knight riding in on a white stallion has been transformed now into a knight mounted on this shining metal steed called the automobile. With this there are many avenues I can take my revenge on Franca, so don't be sad for my sake, friend!" He had a rapid manner of speaking, accompanied by constant hand gestures and movements of his head and shoulders. His entire body seemed in a state of agitation.

The only thing that caught your attention from Mario's chattering was the fact that four or five weeks were considered the minimum amount of time needed to learn how to drive, which conflicted with the fact that only a week remained before you and the other trainees would leave for Abyssinia. Mario laughed when you told him this.

"You can rejoice, because you will not be in the first wave going to Abyssinia. Otherwise they would not have sent you here to learn how to drive."

With quick steps he walked over to the small military car that was used specially for driving lessons. He hopped into the driver's seat and ordered you to ride beside him where there was an additional steering wheel. He warned you not to touch the wheel or anything else in the car before hearing the explanation he was about to give you. "Just as this metal beast is an ingenious method of transportation, it is also an efficient killing machine. Never forget that. If you use it incorrectly, you can kill yourself with it, or others, or you might get even luckier and kill both yourself and others. It's happened to many. Since its creation, this metallic innovation has been able to rival the most destructive wars and the most horrendous plagues. So take care and stay alert. You are the first Arab I've taught, so I beg you, do not ruin my opinion of Arabs."

Before you could say anything, Mario had shot out of the camp and was driving down a paved road through the forests, heading towards the city centre.

"Whatever pertains to driving this car pertains to driving any other car. If you learn how to drive this little four-gear automobile, you will have learned how to drive every car, even giant trucks and lorries."

He drove faster.

"I want you to feel the freedom the automobile allows you. She gives you wings to fly to any place you want. I can take you through all of Tripoli from the fortress of Gargaresh to Ain Zara and then to Bab Tajura and back to King Vittorio Emanuel Street in the city centre. All that would take no more than a single hour, thanks to Marshal Balbo who paved these streets with asphalt in record time and provided jobs for thousands of unemployed workers from your people."

"When will we begin the lesson?" you asked him.

"It has already begun, Signor Othman. What we're doing now is the lesson. Observe what I do closely. I want there to be an understanding between you and the car. I want you to feel her so that she can feel you and work with you. That's what I'm trying to do now. You would not ride a woman before getting to know her, without a familiarity between you and her. The same is true of the automobile. You have to know her and have a feel for her before you can enjoy the ride. The car, Signor Othman, wants a man who understands her and loves her so she can give herself to him with ease. This is your introduction to her, and her introduction to you. So don't worry and bear with me a little while. Here, have a biscuit."

"Thank you."

"Marshal Balbo's great project is the Strada Litoranea, a road from Tripoli to Benghazi. Preparations have already begun. It will be an achievement on an international scale. Grande. Molto, molto grande."

You wished he would stop talking for a while to give you a chance to ask him what he knew about his fellow Italians' arrangements for the Abyssinian campaign. It was the first time you had heard that the deployment would be in waves. That would solve the problem of insufficient training for the new recruits, which had infuriated Sergeant Antar so much.

Mario suddenly said, "Now watch closely as I decelerate. I put my foot on the brake and my hand on the gear shift without taking my eyes off the road . . ."

There was a surprise waiting for you when you returned to base after the lesson. The recruits had been informed during training hours that the departure for Abyssinia had been delayed until further notice. At first, rumours circulated that the complications the campaign faced were owed to the success of the Abyssinian Emperor Haile Selassie, aided by Great Britain, had met in arousing global public opinion against Italy and threatening Italy with an economic boycott if it invaded Abyssinia. However, it quickly became clear that the delay had happened for internal reasons.

A resistance movement had appeared in the Green Mountain following in the footsteps of Omar Al Mukhtar. The Italians feared the resistance would spread, which was why they had postponed sending the Libyan forces to Abyssinia in case the situation made using them to crush the opposition a necessity.

The recruits gleaned this from the Italian officers and from a number of people who came from outside the base to visit their sons, whispering of the reappearance of the resistance in the east of the country. This turn of events created an angry atmosphere among the recruits in the camp, who found themselves suddenly transferred from the Abyssinian front to a war against resistance fighters from their own country. It was the only topic of conversation among the recruits. They spoke of it in whispers, and occasionally whispers might rise to a nervous shout from a few who feared the worst.

Such recklessness manifested itself in its most extreme form when you met your friend Salem before the sunset prayer. He arrived furious and had brought a friend from his barracks with him. His friend was in an extreme state of nervousness. He didn't just speak with his voice alone, but also used gestures and facial expressions. Before Salem had a chance to introduce him, words shot out of his mouth like bullets as he shook his fist in the air and ground his teeth together.

"They forced us to soldiery so we would fight a war against a people we do not know in a country we do not know, all for a cause that does not concern us. We submitted to this injustice, obeyed their orders, and endured this test because it was the rule of the strong over the weak.

But to be driven meekly to a war against our own families and open fire on fighters defending the soil of our land, to kill them or be killed by their hands as sinning disbelievers, that will never happen. The exact opposite will happen. Italian chests will be the targets of our rifles and we will welcome death after that."

He was almost screaming and the blood had rushed to his head, turning his tan face black. You begged him to control himself and shut up. You looked left and right, terrified that someone had overheard you. You didn't understand what had possessed Salem to bring this idiot, knowing full well that his agitated state could mean the end of all of you. If he wanted to die, why should it involve you or Salem? You wondered what Salem wanted. In any case, regardless of whether what he said was true or not, or whether he would go through with it, it needed to be treated with discretion, not this brazenness that would quickly land him in a mess with the Italians.

Salem spoke up, saying, "The others were forcibly conscripted. You are the only one in the camp who volunteered."

"Are you chastising me?"

"No. I'm just making a point. You didn't volunteer to fight your own countrymen."

"Of course not."

"Then you should be the first person to object." You said, "These are just rumours."

"And we all know they're true."

"Do you have a suggestion in mind?"

"Yes. The Italians must know that they will not be able to rely on Libyan recruits in this war because they would simply revolt against them on the battlefield."

"Do you really think they won't be able to find a way to prevent something like that? They know Libyans' true sentiments."

The other youth had deteriorated into a bundle of

nerves and shouted, "I can't stand to stay in this camp. We must escape. Maybe we'll find a chance to join the resistance fighters."

You tried to make him understand that escaping would not be easy and that it was far more likely he would die trying. But he was undeterred and Salem agreed. You wanted to respond to their stubbornness by telling them that the walls were right in front of them and all they had to do was jump over and escape if they thought they could, but you affected a calm rational attitude for their sakes.

You asked them to be patient, telling them that all of this talk was premature. You said that war between Italians and Libyans was over. The two sides had reached an understanding. Peace and stability prevailed in the country and the famines and pestilences that had accompanied times of war had disappeared. Any resistance now would be a pathetic and isolated movement that would die down in a few days. You said all this to try to cancel out everything Salem and his friend had said in case there was someone eavesdropping.

Yet everything you said only upset them further. They continued to speak heedlessly, threatening to kill Italians, refuting what you had told them about peace and mutual understanding. There was no place for anything but rancour, hate, and waiting for the day of vengeance. It would not take much to kindle the flame of malice in Libyan hearts and create a climate that would provoke armed resistance of the sort that had been waged for twenty years.

You saw a soldier walking among the trees, so you left your friends to their speeches and returned to where the rest of the recruits were waiting to enter the dining hall. You ate and returned quickly to the barracks. You tossed and turned on your bed until late at night. Sleep would not come, for fear of that soldier who might have been a spy, eavesdropping on others so as to report it to his superiors.

A question emerged out of your insomnia, taking shape among the shadows that enveloped you. What would you do if they forced you to fight the Libyan resistance? This would not be the first time the Italians had employed this tactic. The history of the Italian–Libyan war, which ended with the hanging of Omar Al Mukhtar, tells us the Italians went into battle against the resistance with an army of Libyan mercenaries, who were compelled to join their ranks by poverty. This painful, shameful route was the only way they could earn a loaf of bread.

Nevertheless, you would not eat bread dipped in the blood of your own countrymen. You prayed that God would not let the situation deteriorate to the point that Libyans would be used against Libyans. You were certain that the grudge in these soldiers' hearts against the Italians would reach its zenith, and it would not be unthinkable for them to do what Ramadan al-Suwayhli had done over twenty years ago. When he and his men had marched in Italian brigades against the resistance fighters at the battle of Al-Qardabiyah, as soon as the battle had begun, he and his soldiers had aimed their rifles at the chests of their Italian superiors.

Naturally, it hadn't ended there. As had happened long ago and would happen again, the Italians avenged themselves brutally immediately after that battle, which the Libyans counted as one of their greatest victories.

The conflict would explode with ferocity and violence once more. The conflagration would spread until it engulfed the whole country, and the era of peace and stability would be over. The Italians had to understand this. They simply had to know the extent of the grudge that filled Libyan soldiers' hearts ever since they'd heard they might be used to quell the rebels on Green Mountain.

News poured in about conflicts between the resistance and the occupation forces, about the state of emergency that had been proclaimed and the curfew that had been imposed in the mountain villages. Anger simmered inside the base and developed into discord, rebellion and insubordination.Punishments multiplied. You had long ago distanced yourself from whipping soldiers, expecting to be permanently exempted from carrying out this abhorrent task. Sergeant Antar had chosen a new subordinate to take your place, but the cases of disobedience increased and forced him to temporarily use you to punish them.

Flogging the soldiers was more difficult than it had ever been before. Previously, you had done it as part of the framework that deemed punishment a necessary part of military training. Now, with feelings boiling over events in the east of the country, floggings had become a means to subdue nationalist sentiments.

You couldn't refuse the job that had jump-started your climb up the military ladder and raised you a rank above your peers. You couldn't destroy everything you had built by fleeing from the task at hand. So you carried out your orders, though with a heavier heart.

The repercussions were severe. You felt it the very first second you raised the whip over your fellow soldiers. You felt more isolated than ever, and you saw the recruits shoot you looks of venom and contempt. They classed you with the Italians. There were some who called you worse than that. One of them called you the dog of Al–Hattia, which was the name some of the recruits had given to the part of the forest where you spent your free time. You had no doubt that the soldier who said that had meant you, and that he and his kind were human insects who were more scornful of you than the Italians.

The Italians didn't know the sacrifices you made for them, and would never see you as one of them. No matter how close you got, no matter how much you gave of yourself, you would always remain the "Indigeno", slightly less than human.

Thus you found yourselfisolated from both Libyans and Italians, living in that space where spiritual resources ran dry, friendships diminished, and human warmth went cold in the midst of this environment where relationships were built on the savage triangle of oppression, hate, and contempt.

Although the situation seemed forced upon you, you had to admit that you had met it halfway. You had always been alone. Even when you had been living with your family in Awlad Al Sheikh, you had never felt like you belonged, neither with your extended family, nor your immediate family, which was split in two. You had lived on your own in the space between.

The first time you left the village, the curses of its people had pursued you as you had fled, hidden between sacks of coal on a truck. That had been representative of your broken relationship with the people of the village and the disconnection between you and life in the village which, had always repulsed you. You had constantly yearned for the day when you would be free. Someone had aptly named you the black sheep. Indeed, when you raised yourself over the sacks of coal the moment you left the village, your appearance matched your nickname perfectly.

You stood in the liminal area between the Italians and Libyans, with no one beside you save your mentor Sergeant Antar, whom you looked to as your role model. But he couldn't be trusted and it would not surprise you if he got up and left you alone in this grey area. Eventually, that is exactly what he did.

Sergeant Antar had begun to abstain from administering punishments himself to avoid incurring their wrath. He even declared his own aversion to the idea of going to war against the resistance fighters in the Green Mountain, saying in his Bedouin accent, "They are protected there by Sidi Rafi, one of the Companions of The Messenger of God, peace be upon him. Woe to whoever goes near there, for he will be punished in this world and the next."

Had the Libyan resistance been fighting somewhere else, far from the shrine of the Prophet's Companion, Sergeant Antar would have certainly been more prepared to carry out the Italians' orders. It was all empty talk to spare himself the soldier's malice. He would follow his orders even if there were fighters taking sanctuary in the Kaaba itself.

Despite that, you admired him for his stance. Without a doubt, this was the first time in his life he had said something against the Italians, and he said it in the middle of the barracks where there were plenty of eyes, ears and tongues to report on what he said.

You could see the looks of contempt that followed you around, in particular after you flogged one of them for disobeying orders, but you could do nothing about it. One day, while you were sitting outside the dining hall, a soldier you didn't know expressed his contempt with more than just a look. He walked up to you and called you an ugly word followed by "dog of Al Hattia". Then he spat on your face. You wiped the saliva off your face with the end of your sleeve. You didn't respond because you didn't want to create a scene, which would have attracted a crowd most of whom would be Libyans that would approve of this soldier's actions and praise him as a hero.

As for the Italians, they would not let an offense like this go unpunished, and according to the base's tradition you would be the one ordered to flog him. As such, you didn't even think of filing a report against him with the base authorities. You would not have hesitated to make every lash a journey in hellish pain and suffering, but instead you let him walk on.

You followed him until he reached an area isolated from the camp where no one would see the two of you. You suddenly grabbed him by the arm, twisting it with all your strength. You put his face up against the wall, grabbed him violently by his hair and banged his head against the wall until blood began gushing from his forehead. You took him to the clinic with the excuse that he had fallen while rushing to get somewhere and knocked his head against the pavement.

As you dragged him by his arm to the clinic you told him that you loved your country no less than he did, that you didn't flog people because you liked it, you did it according to military orders and had you disobeyed orders, you would have been punished severely yourself.

You told him that you were all living here under conditions of someone else's making, so everyone had to be understanding of each other and appreciate everyone's individual situations. What the Italians had done to you was enough, so there was no need for Libyans to add to it. Then you left him in the care of the clinic's nurse and went back to your barracks.

FIFTEEN

That day you didn't attend your rendezvous with Salem, fearing that he would bring his friend with him again, or perhaps someone even more wretched and volatile. You weren't in the mood to hear more criticisms. You went to sleep early, and woke up to begin your daily driving lesson having come to a decision. If your superiors brought up the rumours of what you had said to Salem and his friend, you would claim that you had been compelled to say it out of concern for the relationship between Italians and Libyans.

Despite Mario's clowning around and his lust for affairs, which was his way of getting back at Franca, his wife, and despite his confession that he often took whores with him to a safe place in the forest during the day, and that he had no problem with you joining him so long as you paid your share, you told him that you would make do with just the driving lesson because you had been charged with an important errand. You didn't enter into discussion about your religious obligations, which forbade you from committing such sins. You took no heed of his prattling when he began to embellish descriptions of that day's adventure, the pleasure of lovemaking in the middle of the forest, in harmony with nature.

Then he jumped to another topic.

"Why are all you Arabs like that? What the hell is wrong with you?"

"What do you mean?"

"This locking up your women in houses. Why? What's the reasoning behind that? What a curse you Arab men and women have brought upon yourselves and what a blessing you have deprived yourselves of by creating a world without women. This matter was bewildering to me when I came to your country for the first time two years ago. I didn't think that a place like this existed in all the world. A society specially for women behind walls, and another society for men. This is contrary to nature, it's inhumane, it goes against life and God!"

You laughed at what he had said, because what he saw as strange was only the natural order of things as ordained by religion, values, and morality. There was no fault in preserving righteousness, keeping women from the hardships of working or mixing with men in offices and marketplaces so that they could maintain their dignity and respect. The fault, you told him, was with the Italians who made their women work in cafés, clubs, and markets, or selling their honour in taverns.

In keeping with his manner of jumping from one topic to the next, Mario said, "I'm extremely curious to become acquainted with the body of an Arab woman. A woman's body is the best route to get to know the character of her people and to understand its views on sex. I want to know how she behaves in bed. After many relationships with women of different nationalities, I can say without a doubt that there is a relationship between sex and nationality. And I didn't mean bed in the literal sense. God willed the planet to be a giant bed for men and women to get close to each other. I have known non-Italians. Jewesses and gypsies, women from Malta and Greece. I can arrange a meeting for you with whichever you want so that you too can spend pleasant moments in the forest. In exchange, I want you to bring me an Arab woman. She has to be beautiful, young, and sexy so as to not disappoint my expectations of Arab women. They have to be lusting, hankering for love and sex, because when desire is trapped behind doors and walls it must erupt like a volcano when it gets the chance."

You asked him to stop the car before he could finish talking, because you had decided to get out and escape from his boring prattle. Let him say what he wanted in his report about you. The day's lesson hadn't reached its conclusion, but you found yourself near the middle of the city from which it would only take a few minutes for you to arrive at Signora Houriya's house on La Posta Street.

You had decided to visit her and you knew that she would be just waking, as you had learned from your previous visits. When Morgan opened the door, you went in and sat waiting for her in the hall. After a few moments, Signora came to welcome you, her perfume and radiance preceding her. You did not want to leave her guessing about the reasons for your visit, so you told her straight away why you had come. You told her that you were honoured that his Lordship, Marshal Balbo had chosen you to provide him with regular reports on the conditions of the Libyan soldiers once they arrived at the battlefield in the Italian campaign on the Ethiopian plains. That was why you felt no embarrassment if you could begin your mission starting now and provide him a report on the state of the Libyans before their departure.

Then you explained that the soldiers' morale had reached a nadir, and their anger had reached its apex. This had happened once the date of departure was suddenly delayed and they learned the reason was due to the rebellion on the Green Mountain. The leadership's insistence on using them to quell the revolution had only aggravated their state of mind.

You found yourself telling her your honest opinion: how this strategy would create a state of crisis and stir sentiments of revenge, and return the relationship between Italians and Libyans to what it was during the days of Graziani, bringing the era of stability, peace and prosperity since Marshal Balbo had become governor to a end. The Libyans praised him, since not a single Libyan had been killed by Italians hands during his era.

"And who told you that there was a rebellion on the Green Mountain?"

"That's what everyone is saying," you replied.

"Everyone," she laughed. "If you consider me one of those people, then there is one exception. Me."

Surprised, you asked her if what they had said regarding this rebellion contradicted the facts as she knew them.

"No one who knows what Italo has done on Green Mountain could believe these rumours," she said definitively. "Since becoming governor, he has initiated a reconstruction effort that comprises every patch of the Green Mountain, including building mosques and Quranic schools, pulling down barbed wires, releasing all the members of the resistance who were still in jails and camps, giving the unemployed among them work excavating the monuments of Cyrene, building the Jabal Hotel, and laying new roads in the region. I saw it when I went with him months ago to visit the area. The people there welcomed him in large crowds, and he went out amongst them without any guards. He shook hands with everyone who stretched their hand out. He loves that area too. It's enchanting. Terrible and wicked. Wicked, very wicked.

"The hotel Italo is building there overlooks the most beautiful region in the world, where the sea, the desert, the mountain, and the monuments of Cyrene meet. There are the temples of Apollo, Isis, Amon and Zeus which belong to the greatest civilizations in history. Not far away is the resort of Ras Al-Hilal, Cleopatra's pool, and the Stone and Cave of Saint Marcus. It's out of this world. Fantastic, amazing, impossible."

The telephone rang, so Houriya got up to answer it, then took it into the interior wings of the house. When she returned, she said, "That was Italo. It's strange how small incidents become wars in the imaginations of people."

Then Houriya told you that a skirmish had taken place between a Bedouin caravan and the Maharista, who were Libyan boarder guards. The Maharista had carried out old instructions requiring everyone to have a permit from the military governor whenever they were passing through that region towards the Egyptian border. The Bedouin hadn't had such a permit, which had resulted in a misunderstanding and eventually ended with the Bedouin holing up in a cave in the mountain and opening fire on the patrol. The Marshal had issued an order cancelling the previous instructions that required the licence and granted freedom of movement to everyone in the area. He also ordered the Maharista to remain in the vicinity of the borders and never stray from their posts. So the crisis, which had only lasted a few days, was over.

You were quite aware that rulers and politicians often had their own reasons to skew reality or twist facts. Thus you could neither believe nor disbelieve what Houriya had said or what Marshal Balbo had said. The important thing was that you felt a great relief because you had come to this house and said your peace without coming to any harm, without getting Houriya into trouble, and without provoking her companion, the Italian governor.

Before you could ask her why the departure to Abyssinia had been delayed, she explained that the postponement hadn'thing to do with Libya. It was purely to do with the front, where due to bad weather, it had been decided to postpone the invasion until the end of the rainy season. That would give the Libyan recruits plenty of time to complete their training. Then she added something that aroused your suspicion about her denial of a resistance on Green Mountain. She mentioned that the war would be waged on mountainous terrain in Abyssinia, which would necessitate moving some soldiers for advanced drills in similarly mountainous areas so they could perform better in Abyssinia.

"How are you getting on with your driving lessons?" she asked as she took a glass of orange juice from a servant and handed it to you.

"I see that no news eludes Signora Houriya," you said. "How could I not know when I was the one who nominated you for the job?"

You were baffled. You had wondered who had chosen you and why. Everyone you had asked had merely said that orders were orders. Now you were face to face with the woman who had been behind it all. They had been commands from the women's quarters, not military quarters.

You wondered what Signora Houriya was preparing you for and how she would benefit from this when you had already been designated to be sacrificed in the Abyssinian war.

"I've a small problem with my chauffeur Ayyad," she said. "He wants to resign because he has not seen his family in Murzak for four years and he does not know what has happened to his farmland. Because I've got used to him and his trustworthiness, we have reached an agreement where he is to be absent three months out of the year so he can spend them with his family and see about his land, meaning that I will need a similarly trustworthy driver to take his place during his absence."

You said, "I will do my utmost to be worthy of that trust."

"A job like this will help you immensely in your military career."

"When do I start?"

"As soon as you receive your licence. Then we will let Ayyad go to his family and hand you the keys to the car."

You thanked her, but deep down you felt an unease that you decided not to probe.

SIXTEEN

The automobile! The automobile! The automobile! The steed of the modern era, made from wires and sheets of metal, a symbol of power, speed and a life of extravagant luxury. How could you not soar with joy once you learned you would have the honour of driving one of the most splendid and beautiful cars in Tripoli. You would ride around the city in it, go from place to place like the rich and powerful. When you had begun driver's training, you had thought it was one of the military assignments you would be charged with during the war. Now you knew different. The car you would drive after a few days would be a civilian car, one belonging to the governor of the country. It would not do for anyone to own a more magnificent car than his. You would run errands for Signora Houriya, and in the remaining time the car would be yours. You would wander where you pleased without anyone daring to stop you, ask you questions, or fine you for breaking traffic laws, as your car would bear the registration plate of the governor-general.

You did not tell anyone about this, including your friend Salem. You couldn't wait until evening to see him,

so you chose lunchtime to inform him that you had personally lodged a complaint on behalf of the Libyan recruits
with the highest authority in the country. You took him
outside the mess hall and told him that the new uprising
of the resistance was just toying with people's hearts. No
sooner had they heard about Bedouins shooting at other
Bedouins, who were working as guards in the borderlands,
than they had jumped to the conclusion that it was the
rebirth of Omar Al Mukhtar's brigades.

"So cheer up. The Italians aren't going to take you to
a war on the Green Mountain against imaginary resistance
fighters."

"And you believe what they told you?"

"What reason would the governor-general have to lie?"

"Aren't governors the biggest liars?"

"Shut up and don't get yourself killed. I'm sure he's
fully reliable. Maybe you're just angry because you lost the
chance to revive the heroic deeds of Ramadan al-Suwayhli
in Al-Qardabiya."

You wanted him to convey the gist of this to some of
the other recruits, as you would too, informing them as soon
as you joined them in the mess hall. But as soon as you had
sat down, you saw Sergeant Antar standing in the middle of
the hall, ordering everyone to keep quiet and listen to him.
He said that there was no truth to the rumours that said
they would be sent to the Green Mountain to fight the
rebels, because there were no such rebels except in the minds
of malicious or bloodthirsty people. Peace and security
prevailed in the country, and what was really going to happen
was that the base would choose a group of soldiers to go
on daily training excursions to Mount Gharyan."

Coming from an official source, this information sent

a wave of relief throughout the recruits, who uttered thanks and praises to God. While you and Salem were sitting eating lunch and dipping bread in bean stew, you heard one of the soldiers from the post room call your names over the microphone, ordering you both to head towards the main gate. You left your food and rushed towards the visitors' hall, surmising that visitors had come for you.

As soon as you arrived in the hall you found them crowded together. Your families were waiting for you both, more than ten men, women and children altogether, for your mother had come accompanied by her husband, and your father had come with his wife and two of their children, as had Salem's father, mother and a number of his brothers and uncles. They had been led by Abdel Mowlah the beggar, and outside the gate a truck was waiting for them. They had come crammed into its bed and would return to the village on the same truck once the visit was over.

Salem's father had always led the chants and songs of praise during the celebrations of the Prophet's birthday, and so he had memorized some Quranic verses and religious phrases. Once the embraces and greetings were over, he raised his hands in prayer asking God to watch over the two of you. Behind him, the rest of the family members repeated, "Amen, Amen" in voices tinged with emotion and mixed with sobbing. Soon, all the visitors in the hall were participating in the ritual, and the number of people included in Salem's father's prayer went from two to all the soldiers who would be going to war.

He finished the prayer and asked the two of you to stand next to him. He placed one hand on his son's head and another on yours and began to recite the incantation of Al Hassan and Al Hussein, saying to Salem's weeping mother that this incantation would ensure her son and his friend came back safely. His words seemed to comfort his wife and your own mother who wept even more bitterly than Salem's. Hope even began to appear on their faces and on the faces of the rest of the family members, as if the prayer he had spoken would be answered by the Divine Will that very moment.

The visit was over quickly and the family packed themselves back into the bed of the truck that took offtowards Awlad Al Sheikh. They left you with provisions for your journey to Abyssinia, a bag of sweet flour and barley mush, a jar of dried meat, and a box of holiday cakes. Despite the blissful feeling of embracing your mother, brothers and father, the visit didn't have any lasting effect on you, and didn't awaken the yearning for village life and the meadows of an innocent childhood as you had expected. Your family had conveyed to you the greetings of aunts, uncles and cousins who hadn't been able to come, but you felt as if they were talking about ghosts from a distant past. In your mind. the village seemed like a faraway place that you had left decades − rather than months − ago, and its image, memories of the life you had led there, and the pictures of people you had grown up with all faded away in your mind until they were almost completely gone.

With the end of daylight and the approach of sleeping hours, the visit all but disappeared from your mind and instead, Mario's words from earlier that morning took its place. He had promised you the adventure of a lifetime, and in his thick Sicilian accent, which sounded strange to your ears, he said grandly, "Domani, Signor Usman, domani." It wasn't the first time you had stood wavering before the temptation of sex. Something similar had happened during your time working at the shoe shop when a customer, one of the prostitutes of Sidi Umran Street, tried to seduce you. She told you what her profession was without any equivocation and proposed that you pay her a visit in her house on the infamous street. She admired the women's shoes displayed in the store and wanted to take a pair, for which she would pay in trade. You rejected her offer and took to your bed that night unable to sleep.

The woman had been a master of the art of temptation. She had come to the shop wrapped in her white cloak, a block of white that revealed nothing of her body. She sat in front of you on the low backless seat intended for customers to sit on while taking their measurements and trying on shoes. She revealed her face which she had painted with make-up and colourful mascara so that it looked like a bride's face. Then she undid the wrap around her chest and revealed her two plump round breasts. When she noticed you trembling from fear and amazement at what you saw, after looking left and right to make sure the place was empty of curious onlookers, she laughingly said you could touch them if you wanted. She told you that they would not bite. You turned your face away, refusing her offer. She was shocked that a young man your age could resist the temptation. She got up and left the shop angrily, convinced that you were afflicted with some disease that impaired your virility.

In that woman from Sidi Umran, you saw the image of Satan, who corrupts people's faith and leads them to the Gates of Hell. Before you left your village, you had suffered a bitter experience like this when you gave in to your weakness towards the allure of Aziza, the water-carrier girl.

God's punishment had come sooner, not later when your shameful secret was discovered and you fled your village in disgrace.

You didn't want to make that mistake again, nor did you want a punishment like that to befall you in the place where you had found a safe refuge after times of suffering and hardship. But for a long time, despite not having done anything wrong, you had remained a prisoner of those breasts and their magic. You hadn't known any ploy to forget the picture of that woman as she had been, bare-chested, her eyes boring into yours. Even to this day she hadn't left your memory, even though you never saw her again, and your strength to resist temptation hadn't been tested since.

And here was Mario, whose friends in the workshop nicknamed him Old Man Mario, presenting you with a very tempting offer. He had invited you to share in one of his feasts on white Italian flesh. What would you say this time? Your conservative values and your fear of God's wrath in this world and the next prevented you from going down this path. However, in your heart of hearts, you wished you could find an open-minded sheikh that would appreciate the circumstances of a youth your age who had reached puberty ten years earlier, a youth whose desires ran in his veins, burning like fire every time he saw the shadow of a woman in front of him and who was torn between his religious conscience and the pounding blood in his body. A sheikh like this would not fail to find a solution for something as pressing.

At the height of the Islamic state's prosperity, your righteous forefathers had dealt with the problem through slavery. In modern times. you had heard that if you unexpectedly came across a woman you wanted to have sex

with just for a day or two, all you had to do was place
your hand in hers, and recite the opening of the Quran
with the intention of entering into a marriage contract.
Then you gave her part of her wages in the form of an
advance dowry so that the sexual intercourse would be
lawful, and you could give her the rest of her dowry after
you were done with her, whereupon she would be considered divorced.

Was it possible that the solution was this simple?
Manipulation of religiosity seemed self-apparent in these
acts.

You woke up and went to your meeting with Mario
without having reached a decision. During training, he had
asked you to pay close attention to the lesson, because he
was going to teach you in one course what was normally
done in three so the remaining time could be devoted to
fun. He had made arrangements with two Italian gypsy
women whom he would pick up in two hours' time from
the Porta Benito district, which was near the forest or 'Il
Bosco' as they called it. Mario would be able to take them
to a thicket that he had previously gone to on an earlier
adventure and had found to be an ideal place for pleasur-
able diversions such as these. It was far from the roads and
paths that criss-crossed the forest, and only a four-cylinder
military vehicle like his would be able to reach the place.

You didn't speak a word of opposition or assent, nor
did you say anything when he ended the lesson and drove
quickly to where he had promised to meet the two women.
On the way, he stopped by a store to buy a bottle of red
wine. You saw no reason to object because you would
simply refrain from drinking it. He had his religion and
you had yours.

In an obscure corner of a back alley plunged in the
shadows of trees, you found the two women waiting. You
couldn't make out their features owing to the thickness of
shadows at first, and Mario immediately asked them to get
into the back seat and lower themselves between the seats
so no one would see them until they entered the forest.

You followed Mario's lead, letting yourself do whatever
the situation dictated. You weren't didn'texcited as Mario,
whose smile grew broader and broader, and his words faster
and faster as he drove the car into the forest, leaving tyre
marks along the dirt road until he turned onto another
road on which the tyres left no trace. Mario penetrated
deeper into the trees, advancing into a shady thicket where
the intertwined branches would shield you from prying
eyes.

He stopped the car and took out a folding table and
a set of wooden folding chairs. He began to set them up
and prepare a place for a session of congenial revelry in
the thicket. He brought out glasses of wine and plates with
slices of cheese and olives on them before inviting you all
to sit down with him. But the women's fear of the forest
guards spoiled his plans. They wanted to do the deed quickly
before anything unexpected could happen and turn merry-
making into worry. Afterwards, they would be able to spend
time eating, drinking and chatting.

This was contrary to Mario's theory that getting to
know each other first would create an atmosphere of friendship and familiarity to complement the transition to the
pleasure of lovemaking. The problem, asMario put it, was
that the women were new to life in Tripoli. They had only
arrived a few weeks ago, which wasn't enough time for
them to have established relationships with the police

officers as other women had done for their protection. They also spoke Italian with a gypsy, accent which Mario himself had difficulty understanding. Perhaps the two women consequently had trouble communicating with even their own countrymen which would have accentuated their cautious natures.

In the end, Mario had no other choice but to comply with their demand that sex come first, and he had to abandon his theory that sex should always come last. Mario stripped rapidly and stood naked, trying to undress one of the gypsies and telling you to do the same. You fled from the sight of the naked man into the depths of the thicket. The second woman followed behind you and you found yourself suddenly rolling around with her on a bed of green grass. You became engrossed in the game of sex without thinking about right or wrong, sin or righteousness, punishment or reward.

That was the first time you'd had sex, because all you had done with Aziza had been to fondle her naked body. You didn't understand the reason for the gypsy's astonishment when you finished having sex with her only to begin again and again until you had repeated it many times.

Afterwards you felt exhausted. You threw yourself onto your back, naked on the bare earth, which was covered with a thin layer of grass. Your limbs were flung every which way as if these legs, these feet, these arms and hands had come undone from your body and separated from one another.

The gypsy girl got up, wiping herself with a handkerchief she took from her bag. She put her bloude, skirt and jacket back on, then in her loudest voice called to her friend, relating the marvel she had just witnessed, as if she had just been subjected to an act of magic worked on her by some Eastern sorcerer. Even after you were back in the automobile on your way out of the forest, she continued to talk in amazement at what you had done with her, telling her companion that the number of times must have been a record, and that if she hadn't pulled out from under you, you would not have stopped having sex with her until you had reached a hundred times. She considered this something extraordinary, the likes of which she had never seen before, whereas you thought it was normal, something that had happened with no intention to be excessive or to show off your sexual virility.

You had thought this was what everyone did until you learned, as Mario and the gypsy women put it, that what had happened had been caused by the explosion of sexual energies that had been pent up for more than a decade ever since you hit puberty, as if you had wanted to make up for those years of deprivation in an hour.

As for Mario, it was impossible for such a talkative joker to allow an incident like this to pass without comment.

"I don't believe that any man can do what you did. Is it true what Maria said about this record number of times? Impossible. Even I, with all the lust I possess, need an entire month to do what you did in one hour. Are you a human of flesh and blood like me? No, no. You are certainly the Blue Djinn himself."

Trying to change the subject, which had become a source of embarrassment, you said, "Are Italian infidels so knowledgeable of the Djinn that they assign them colours, blue or otherwise?"

"Just as there is the Blue Angel, like myself, and which was also the topic of a famous opera of the same name, there is also the Blue Djinn, you. He comes calling for self-restraint and asceticism . . . no, no, you're not the Blue Djinn. You're the Red Devil. He is much more wicked."

You had given in to your weakness once, and now you had done it again, finding yourself falling down the abyss of forbidden pleasure after your animal instincts had overwhelmed you. You had lain awake long nights atop a bed of coals, fighting this weakness in yourself. You had heard Satan whispering in your breast like a snake. You would expel Satan and shut your ears to his whispers, defeating him time after time until you succumbed to cursed Mario and this sinful trip to the forest. Your power to resist Satan had collapsed, because Mario hadn't been content to merely whisper and rasp. He had placed the woman before you, armed with all her charms.

He had brought her made her available to you, like someone putting a shelled almond into your mouth.

Mario had closed the way back for you, but he hadn't closed the path to repentance. You had been able to extricate yourself from a state of weakness the previous time, so it would be within your ability to save yourself from the pit of ruin you had fallen into this time as well, even though the sin was much graver. The unrelenting feeling of guilt troubled you and spoiled the pleasure. It only became heavier and deeper, making you feel like you were marked with an indelible stain.

You were at a crossroads now. In one direction this feeling of guilt and sin could guarantee that you would repent and refrain from going down the path of error again. In another direction, the animal instincts that had violently stirred in you violently would no longer remain dormant. Your appetites would constantly need to be appeased.

Perhaps the best solution, one which united these two directions into a single path, was marriage. That would satisfy your animal desires, keep you away from unlawful sex, and perhaps address a third issue, which was your unhealthy fixation to other men's wives. However, your involvement with an army being prepared for war in Abyssinia made the option of marriage impossible for now.

Hurrying up, you returned to the base hoping to find some way to free yourself, if only for a while, from the burden of your guilt. As soon as you got there, you went into the shower, ritually purifying your body to remove the unclean residue of your forest adventure. You stayed a long time under the water until you had washed off the dirt left behind from rolling around on the forest floor, but you didn't feel truly clean. You finished your ablutions and put on your jilbab and began to perform your prayers, during which you begged for forgiveness, praised your Creator, and recited verses from the Quran.

SEVENTEEN

The one blessing you saw in Mario's lessons was that they exempted you from morning assembly. Then, a new benefit gradually appeared. When Mario received new instructions to increase the number and intensity of the lessons in order to save time, you were freed from the task of whipping disobedient recruits, in part because the news that the recruits would not be going to war against their own countrymen had decreased the cases of disobedience.

They got used to your absences and consequently stopped assigning you any at the base. Then came a third blessing, when the recruits began to wake up just before dawn to travel to Mount Gharyan where they spent all day training in mountain warfare while you idled blissfully in bed.

Offsetting these blessings, Mario's lessons also took you to a land of sinful morasses that couldn't easily be escaped. Despite your oppressive sense of wrongdoing and the strength of your religious restraint, the power of desire and animal instinct had won that round and made you long to repeat the experience. You implored Mario to arrange a second adventure for you, which gave him incentive to blackmail you and a means to realize his dream of acquainting himself with an Arab woman.

Mario asked you to fulfil your side of the deal later, and he agreed to arrange another visit to the heart of the forest with two prostitutes he knew in order to make you even more indebted to him, and to give you time to follow through with your promise, which wasn't really a promise. You had merely given him a nod of your head in agreement with his chattering and he took that as a promise that you would bring him an Arab prostitute.

To hell with all these vulgar acts. If you hadn't been in the position of a soldier bound for war, you would have found a solution that allowed you to forego all this. Was it not true that you had been on your way back to the city to ask for Thuraya's hand in marriage after fleeing from the army? Back then you had truly been following a path that would have saved you from sin. That was before you discovered that she had disappeared into the house of another man, and so you too had disappeared, down this tunnel that would stretch on for a long time before the light appeared at its end, if it ever would.

Despite the shock you had experienced when you learned Thuraya was married and the violent reaction that led you to enlist at the base, you still had this feeling, which you couldn't explain, that this woman had been created to be your wife and no one else's. Inasmuch as it happened that she had gone to this man who had wedded her, the coming days would surely correct that mistake. This premonition was what made you keep all paths to her house open and all the strings taut between you and her, and perhaps one of the reasons behind your happiness at learning to drive was that it would provide you with a way to reach Thuraya.

You would go to invite her to ride beside you, and once she saw you sitting in front of the steering wheel, she would be dazzled by the sight, and proud of you. She would sit beside you and with this magical form of transportation you would take her on a ride that only the most fortunate and privileged women could enjoy.

The words of a beautiful, tremendously popular, song Lilian the Jewess used to sing at weddings in Tripoli came to mind:

> Coming in your best attire
> Looking sweet and beautiful
> If only we could take a spin
> I'd give my whole life for it!
> I'd give me whole life for it!

The 'spin' you intended to take with Thuraya would be much better than the one in the song because it would be in the most modern elegant model with the registration plate of Libya's governor. You remembered that you hadn't told her the trip to Abyssinia had been postponed. She probably still thought your and her husband's departure had happened as scheduled, and that you were both battling the Abyssinians on behalf of the Italians in the unknown regions of the dark continent. This was unfair and you decided that you would go to her at the first opportunity to reassure her and inform her of what had happened.

When she saw you standing at her door, her face lit up with surprise. She asked you if this was really you or the image of the ghost that appears after one dies, because she had thought you were now plunged deep into the war with the Abyssinians. You informed her that you were a peaceful ghost who didn't want to harm or frighten anyone. She invited you to come in and sit with her sick father.

Instead of disappearing into the back rooms as before, she remained standing near the door, asking about what had happened to delay the departure and whether her husband was still in Tripoli. You assured her that the entire army was still in Tripoli now that the journey had been postponed for several weeks, and that they were still allowing the soldiers to receive visitors, but only on Thursday and Friday. You proclaimed your willingness to accompany the family the following Thursday if they so desired.

As you spoke, your eyes took their fill of the splendour of Thuraya's eyes, the beauty of her moon-round face, which she left uncovered despite her father's presence. It had become natural for the family to see you as an older brother to her, and so nothing about her baring her face in front of you caused the slightest sense of breaking tradition and the rules of modesty.

You loved Thuraya. This kind of love made those powerful animal urges seem insignificant. Love's living domain became wider than those magnetic fields made by the allures of the female body, the masculine drive, and the push and pull between them.

You were in a state of perpetual longing that burned brighter every time you saw her. You wanted to place your head on her chest, wrap your arms around her, press your face into her hair, and mix your breath with hers. You couldn't imagine her as an object of the sexual escapades in the forest as you had been able to do with every beautiful woman you had ever met, and you didn't want to think of her the way you thought of Mario's women. Perhaps it was raising your feelings for her to their spiritual peak that led you to don the costume of the older brother on whom her family relied. You seemed well-suited to the role, convincing to even those who weren't members of the family, like the neighbours who saw you enter the house and accompany the family to see their son-in-law.

You expressed your sorrow regarding her father's illness and said you were always willing to do anything he might need. He asked you to take the keys to the shop and bring a few men's and women's shoes so his wife could try to sell them to the neighbours in order to cover household expenses. This further affirmed your image as a member of the family and an older brother to Thuraya and her brother.

Thuraya was the only person who knew the truth of your feelings and the extent of your love, which was by no means brotherly. Although she didn't see anything in your behaviour to disapprove of or fear for her chastity, meaning that even if your actions weren't without ulterior motive, they didn't pose any danger to her, rather perhaps in some way they appealed to the feminine desire to see a man like you adore her.

Thursday came, and the little brother was at the Quranic school, and the mother, who had readied herself to go with her daughter, found that her husband's fit of coughing had worsened so much that it would have been inexcusable for both the wife and her daughter to leave the man by himself. Postponing the visit would have been an unnecessary embarrassment after you had come with the carriage, as agreed upon, and were waiting in front of the house. The final decision was that the mother would not keep her daughter from visiting her husband when he could be sent to war any minute, especially when her older brother, meaning you, was there to accompany her.

Thus you found yourself alone with her in the carriage. You didn't want this opportunity to be limited to the road that led to the base. You wanted to make this time with Thuraya a little longer than that brief distance, so you asked her permission to not go straight to the base until the crowds of the first wave of visitors dispersed. You added that you could spend this time leisurely wandering through some Tripoli's most beautiful districts. Because you couldn't take her to the cinema, or get out of the carriage to stroll through the public parks, or sit at the Miramar Café, the two of you remained in the carriage. It was the only safe place you could sit together. passing the time before the visit without any unwanted intrusions in the relative privacy afforded by the canopy and curtains that covered the carriage.

The driver had his back turned to you, he was too busy guiding his carriage through the streets packed with cars, bicycles and other carriages. Maybe it would be better if you made her forget visiting the base for today and found a way to persuade her to refrain from visiting her husband by herself. He might be quick to question her about who brought her, which would open a door for troubles and suspicions that no one needed.

You didn't express any of these thoughts to Thuraya. All you did was order the driver to take you to modern Tripoli, which people had taken to calling Italian Tripoli. Among the most important landmarks there was the Governor's Palace, which had been completed a few months earlier, a marvel of modern architecture and a model of splendour and luxury with its high gates and its golden dome. It was surrounded by fountains, ponds and trees, where birds perched and nested adding their songs to the cacophony of voices created by the din of the city. These green grounds surrounding the palace provided a necessary space dictated by the eminence of authority, separating the palace from the rest of the district. The aesthetics of modern construction mixed with the spirituality and grandeur of Eastern architecture in this building, whose splendour outshone all the other buildings around it which, even if they were less pompous, were no less beautiful or important to the local architectural environment.

The colour green pervaded the district, and the predominant feature of the squares were their palm trees, that symbol of the Eastern Bedouin environment, which seemed more beautiful and elegant in the Italian quarter than it did in the suburbs inhabited by Arabs, as if here they washed the tree trunks and palm leaves with water and soap every morning like they did the streets.

You explained to Thuraya everything that Mario had told you about the philosophy of the Italian architects who had built these new districts so they would not be mere facsimiles of Italian architecture. They had turned to the realities of the Eastern Arab environment while benefiting from the techniques of modern Italian architecture to give Tripoli a different look from Italian cities and without repeating the flaws of the modern Arab cities, which had lost their identity. These architects had emphasized the necessity of starting a new school of architecture that would draw on both East and West to emphasize the pioneering spirit of those immigrants who established a new homeland for Italy, a fourth coastline.

The carriage took you along King Vittorio Emanuel Street to Cathedral Square, where visitors flocked to visit this important religious and architectural landmark. They snapped photographs of the church front replete with engravings and depictions of Jesus Christ, the Virgin Mary, and various saints. The square seemed like a miniature of Italian society, devoid of Libyans.

The pavements were packed with tables and seats put out by the many cafés and restaurants. The voices of their Italian patrons joined the noisy tumult of vendors, travelling salesmen, and photographers who carried their equipment and offered to photograph people. Some of them had brought props for whoever wanted to be photographed with a picture of a famous actress, or on a throne-like chair with a crown made of cardboard. The sounds of music and singing drifted from stores that sold records and restaurants that employed musicians to entertain their customers. Shops that sold clothing, antiques, flowers, newspapers and sweets occupied a side of the square covered by arches, and the shopkeepers had set up wooden shelves and benches on which to display their goods, creating a medley of shapes and colours that gave the place a special air that differed from most of the other districts.

This was all new to Thuraya who had never come to this part of the city before, since the Libyans from the Arab quarters of Tripoli didn't usually frequent these places, fearing harassment and mistreatment. There wasn'thing odd in a young woman spending her entire childhood inside her family's house in Bint Al Pasha Alley, limiting her outings to playing in the nearby alley. Once she started wearing the veil, she went out only to go to her father's shop or on seasonal trips with her parents to visit their home town in Tajura.

After the carriage had driven around Cathedral Square for the third or fourth time, the driver took you to Mazzini

Street, which wasn't as crowded. You asked him to stop by a kiosk that sold cold drinks and ice cream. You bought a few bars of chocolate and some gelato with almonds and pistachios for Thuraya, and two soft drinks for yourself and the driver.

You were happy and felt like rejoicing at Thuraya's presence in this carriage that whisked you along like in a dream. The world seemed a delightful place, governed by the beautiful rhythm of the horses' hooves on the asphalt, the tinkling of the decorative bells that hung from the carriage, and the clamour of life in the streets and squares, all mixing harmoniously with your heightened heartbeat. Everything before you wore the colour of happiness, and everything around you spoke the language of joy. Everything that had once worried you disappeared, all the sources of oppression and annoyance, including your life on the base, talk of war, the rituals of pain and punishment, everything that had come to pass and would yet come to pass. You didn't remember any of it, and you couldn't imagine anything at the present moment except this woman. There was neither past nor future. Only this moment of bliss.

Thuraya's contentment as she licked her ice cream was no less than your own as you watched her do it. Her lips and face were rose-coloured and framed beautifully in the white of her cloak. Her astonished happiness and excitement never left her face, which made her seem yet more sweet and innocent. The sight of her captivated your heart and evoked the most beautiful feelings in you, especially when you looked into her two honey-coloured eyes and beheld their radiance which pierced your chest and lit the depths of your heart with their blessed fire. With tender longing you listened to the comments that she made from

time to time, expressing in her sweet voice the astonishment on her face.

"Oh my God, my Lord! Is this really Tripoli or another
city that descended from heaven? Is this a dream or real?"
Her words settled in your ears like the notes of a flute.

The carriage was well-suited for a woman like Thuraya.
From within, she could see the city and views of life in its
modern districts. She could see the people, the streets, and
the squares and at the same time remain certain that no
one could see or approach her. It would not have done for
her to walk through this part of the city on foot, and other
forms of transportation would not have worked, like the
open carriages people from the Arab quarters used which
would not have provided such security and protection from
the eyes of the people.

The sights continued to amaze Thuraya. She burst into
laughter at the sight of an extremely fat Italian woman
with a tiny dog the size of a mouse that followed behind
her on a leash and a large hat that was decorated by feathers
and colourful ribbons. Thuraya pointed the woman out to
you, so that you could laugh with her. There was also a
Maltese boy selling balloons from his bicycle seat as he
rode alongside the carriage, calling out in the Maltese
language, that mix of corrupted Arabic and Italian. Clusters
of coloured balloons swayed above his head, tied to his
hand by string. He shouted out, offering his balloons for
sale, pushing them towards you until they brushed your
faces.

You were within sight of the fountain in the middle
of Italia Square. The water poured out from a huge bowl
held aloft by statues of mythical seahorses with wings that
stretched several metres into the square, and although you

passed by this square and its fountain every day – since it was at the crossroads between the old city and the new city – you nevertheless felt just as much wonder as Thuraya.

Somehow, the fountain seemed larger, more majestic and beautiful, and the stone seahorses seemed to possess a life of their own, ready to take off with their giant magical wings into the air. Perhaps it was because this time you saw everything in Thuraya's company and because you were looking at it from a higher vantage point than before, when you walked on the pavement with your head hung low so that the fountain water would not splash you. Now you could see a new image from a different angle with Thuraya beside you, happy at having made this spontaneous outing, laughing even when there wasn'thing to laugh about.

The original reason for this trip seemed to have slipped her mind, for she didn't mention it or bring it up. Instead, she was wholly engrossed in the sights and sounds as they unfolded, and at every opportunity expressed her happiness at the moments of freedom and liberty that the trip afforded her.

The walls of buildings along the streets were draped with large posters advertising commodities that couldn't be found in the old city, types of perfume, wine, cigarettes, and make-up, in addition to advertisements for musicals performed for Italians in the Miramari theatre and the Alhambra theatre. There were advertisements for films, automobile races, boating races, sports matches, and many other colourful attractive posters that advertised dance and music lessons at the Italian clubs, for the benefit of any interested Italian settlers.

All of it was written in Italian, but the accompanying pictures explained their meaning and spared the viewer from having to read the writing. Indeed, they tempted the viewer into wanting to become a part of this fortunate class of people who purchased, used or performed what these advertisements offered. Similarly all the men and women who appeared in these posters had attained the highest form of human perfection in terms of beauty, elegance and health.

Suddenly, an advertisement appeared. Spanningthe length of the wall above the façade of the Odeon Cinema, it advertised an Italian film with a picture of a young hand-some hero, his long flowing hair almost covering his eyes, as he leaned over the face of a beautiful heroine, intending to plant a kiss on her pursed lips. Both of you stared at the suggestive picture while the carriage stopped at a turning point that would take you back to the Corniche. Previous governors had begun the construction of the Corniche, but it hadn't been completed until Marshal Balbo had come, accompanied by the huge budget that the Duce had given him. He had finished it in record time so that he could brag to his visitors from the European coastal cities about the Corniche, its graceful balustrade, its night-time lighting, and the palm seedlings he had planted along the beach.

A moist refreshing breeze washed over your faces, bringing with it the scent of the sea whose waves broke against the walls of the Corniche, sending foam flying into the air, before they receded in sinuous white lines. In this expanse, nothing appeared in the field of vision except a few distant sail boats appearing like white dots above a blue carpet that stretched as far as the horizon.

The driver cracked his whip over the horse's head when he found himself in the middle of the wide newly-paved road that seemed like a strip of black mirrors reflecting the rays of the sun. The horse galloped like a stallion on a racetrack even though there was no reason for haste. As you understood it from a conversation with one of these carriage drivers, they were in the habit of galloping down wide empty paved streets to create a sort of excitement that would please the customers. This was especially the case with your driver, who hadn't received any orders from you to go anywhere specific, so he figured you were out on a pleasure ride for sightseeing and leisure.

Because of the jolt that shook the carriage when the horse started its gallop, Thuraya lost her balance and the next thing you knew she was thrown into your arms. Taken by surprise, you wrapped her body in your arms unintentionally and drew her chest to yours for a brief moment, during which you inhaled the aroma wafting between her breasts before she realized what had happened and regained her balance, tearing her body away and returning to her place. In that brief moment, which had been like a flash of lightning, you felt as you held the world's treasures in your hands, as if you had drawn a draught of its magic and beauty. You felt intoxicated and fulfilled, as though you had attained all you could ever want from life, so much so that you closed your eyes trying to hold onto this fleeting moment as long as you could.

The horse quickened its pace, pulling the carriage along the Corniche until the built-up areas ended and the horizon opened up over the green spaces of farms and parks alongside the sea at Al-Hanishir Point. The path wasn't paved, but it was levelled in such a way that it didn't hinder the carriage from running as smoothly as it had before. The place was devoid of farmers and passers-by at this early hour of the morning. A quiet stillness reigned, broken only by the rustling of the grass and the chirping of birds hopping on the tree branches. Butterflies spread their colourful wings and swam in the sunlight. It was now possible to emerge out from under the carriage's canopy, and after you ordered the driver to stop, you and Thuraya stood in the open space behind the driver's seat and looked around at the landscape, which emanated a majestic peacefulness.

Thuraya, who had always covered her face and kept a firm grip on her cloak, now revealed her face in broad daylight. Because of the stinging cold wind coming in from the sea, her face had begun to glow a bright red that spread across her wheat coloured-skin like flames, whose sparks singed your heart. A lock of her night-black hair had slipped out from under her headdress and fluttered above her forehead in the winds, which added yet another colour to her face.

She continued to gaze at the fields while you gazed at her, trying to preserve this picture in your memory to take it with you whenever you departed for those distant lands in the near future. Let that image nourish you in the days or years of famine and spiritual barrenness you would endure on the front.

A man pushing a cart of vegetables passed by on his way to the city. Neither of you noticed his presence until he approached the carriage and greeted the driver. As soon as Thuraya saw him, she threw herself back into her seat, lowered her cloak over her face and hunched beneath the canopy saying in ragged breaths, "That's my uncle Ashur al-Aqel, our neighbour in Bint al-Pasha. He must have seen me. Oh no! What will become of me?"

You were sure the man hadn't noticed either of you because he had been occupied with pushing his heavy cart and greeting his friend the driver. Moreover, even if he had seen her, he would not have been able to recognize her with just a passing glance, because she never walked in the streets with her face bared and he would not recognize the little girl he had seen playing in the alleys more than ten years ago in this grown woman riding a carriage by the seashore. Even in the unlikelihood that he had recognized her, that didn't pose any danger because she had gone out with her family's permission to visit her husband.

Thuraya wasn't convinced and none of your reassurances revived the cheerful mood that Ashur al-Aqel's appearance had dispelled. She insisted on going home and postponing the visit until another day.

EIGHTEEN

After taking Thuraya home, you returned to the base without allowing what had happened at the end of the outing to ruin the beauty of this experience or diminish the feeling of just having eaten from the tree of happiness. Nothing could rob you of the delicious taste that lingered on your tongue.

You returned t the base in the same carriage so you would not be late in entering the mess hall when the roll was called. From your seat, you spotted her husband Fathy. You felt slightly irritated. What misery and ill-fortune had thrown this man between you and the only woman in the world whom you loved and who loved you? Was he wronged, or had he wronged you? Was he the victim or the executioner? He was the husband you envied for having taken Thuraya, but hadn't he also been deceived in his turn?

Just hours ago, you had been enjoying his wife's company. You had taken her from her family on the pretext that you would bring her to visit him, and then you had tricked her into staying with you instead of going to her husband. So had you stolen from this this man, or was he

the one who had stolen something precious that was rightfully yours alone?

Thuraya wasn't just a precious possession. She was much
more than that. She represented the life that was stolen
from you. Yes, *you* were the wronged party, and whatever
you did to lift the injustice that had fallen upon you, it
was an endeavour blessed by the angels charged with helping
the wronged and oppressed in this world.

You recalled the wonderful moments you had spent in
Thuraya's company. She had been very happy to go on this
outing with you and had been affectionate. She had done
away with formalities and she hadn't objected to the change
of plans, as if it didn't concern her whether she visited her
husband or not. She had seemed extremely grateful to you
for freeing her from the suffocating environment she inhabited within the walls of her house, where her bed-ridden
father slept and her mother wept out of sadness for her
husband and fear of the ghost of poverty that hovered over
the family.

You didn't want to fool yourself into thinking that you
were the source of this outpouring of happiness that had
almost leapt from every word Thuraya had said, every movement she had made. The essential reason had been that this
woman, almost twenty years old, had never lived a moment
of release and freedom in her life like the one she had
experienced this morning. Nevertheless, she couldn't have
enjoyed her time in your company if she didn't hold a
special place for you in her heart.

You couldn't ask her how she felt about her husband,
for you knew that no woman could ask herself such a
question when she belonged to a society so steeped in faith
and religiosity and governed by the strictest traditions

surrounding the preservation of proper relationships between a man and a woman. This was especially the case if that woman, like the vast majority of Libyan women, had never received an education and never read anything that developed her faculties of thought, or enabled her to discuss the rigid matrices that society had prepared for its virtuous women.

Perhaps there was no point in a woman like her receiving an education, because it would simply cast a harsh light on the degradation in her life without giving her the power to change it. For how could an educated woman respond to the prevailing ideas about how women were treated? How could she accept her father marrying her off to a man she had never seen or known before? And after she was married, how would this woman, whom they had kept from displaying barely a finger of her hands in front of a man, then place her naked body at the disposal of a stranger who might be repulsive to her? Despite all that, she had to accept him and sleep in his bed every night, and thus become his lawful wife, just as Thuraya was now Fathy's wife.

Husbands and wives were tied together by the sacred bond of marriage. Laughing, you found yourself mouthing aloud the word "sacred".

No one around you in the dining hall understood what your laughter meant. The attribute of sacredness here was a lie. The truth was that it was a contract of duress, deception, and servility and it was false in the eyes of the law as well, because it wasn't agreed upon consensually. This specious quality of sacredness had granted marriage inviolability, making any attempt to break away from it an act of deviance or betrayal.

You understood that what Thuraya had done with you

that morning hadn't been a sign of even the slightest incli-
nation to rebel against the ties of marriage. Even if she had
shown some concern for you beyond the concern of a
woman for a family friend, even if she had shown more
than just yearning for the fantasy of a lost love, it didn't
mean she had necessarily intended it that way. Your belief
that she favoured you was just your own exaggerating or
your raging desire to find in her an echo of the powerful
affection you felt for her.

You didn't didn'twant this outing to be the last however.
You intended it to be the beginning of several more trips,
especially when you were on the way to attaining a tool
to steal the hearts of women. The automobile. It would
open new horizons and close distances, among them the
distance to the heart of your beloved. Even if Thuraya's
actions towards you hadn't been motivated by love as you
wanted to believe, something akin to love would surely
happen once the car came into view. You would doubtlessly
seem bigger in her eyes and gain more admiration and
approval from her when she saw you riding the contraption, which only the elite of society could enjoy.

You really tried to lend your eyes and ears to what
Mario had taught you during the driving lesson, hoping
to gain as much trust from him as you had from Thuraya,
so that you could shorten the training period as much as
possible. You were in a rush to reach the day when you
would drive the car alone. But the magical effect of that
outing would not disappear and you couldn't wait to be
beside the woman who had ensnared your heart. It
continued even the following morning, when you returned
to your seat beside Mario in the military vehicle, listening
to his inane chattering full of sexual gestures and phrases.

If the time you had spent with Thuraya had awoken the loftier aspirations of your spiritual side, the filthy maw of your carnal lusts had also been blooded, and was now greedier and more eager than ever to feast on the cheap delights of sordid flesh. Fate saw to it that it would find no dearth of sustenance in the near future.

SINFUL PLEASURES

ONE

Mario was obsessed with prostitution was an expert at navigating its insidious and ensconcing labyrinths, but he kept refusing to arrange any more meetings, arguing that he was still waiting for you to keep your end of the bargain and bring him an Arab whore. As you weren't a native of Tripoli however, you didn't didn't know how to find a prostitute to satisfy Mario's curiosity.

You wished you knew where to find the woman who had tried to seduce you in the shoemaker's shop when you had still been young and callow, but you didn't. You even contemplated the risk of going to Sidi Umran to search for a woman who would agree to venture outside the official brothels with you, but you didn't even know where that street was situated. You had never gone there, nor did you have any experience of the etiquette there.

The only solution was to go to Abdel Mowlah, the beggar, to ask him to help you find such a woman, since he had previously told you of his experience with a prostitute. He was the only one among your acquaintances who would be able to guide you to a fallen Arab woman.

After making up your mind to consult Abdel Mowlah,

you asked Mario to drive you to the cluster of huts in the Porta Akkara district where Abdel Mowlah lived. You were certain he would still be in, as the early morning was not a suitable time for begging, as people were less sympathetic to deformity and stench this early in the day.

The motor car passed through the Sidi Khalifa district with its squat houses and narrow dusty roads crowded with children. You passed in front of al-Kattani's shrine, whereupon you recited the opening of the Quran for the sheikh of the shrine, but immediately felt disgusted with yourself, for you were on an errand of sin without the slightest consideration for the pious Sheikh Sidi al-Kattani.

Had you been on foot, the domes and the minaret of the shrine would have shamed you. However, the car moved faster than your thoughts, as Sidi al-Kattani meant absolutely nothing to Mario, whereas to you he represented the piety and righteousness from which you were fleeing with both metaphorical and physical speed.

Mario drove the car jerkily along the dusty paths kicking up clouds of dust. You were soon assaulted by the smell of the tannery that separated the Arab residential areas from the huts. The odour was nauseating and made you forget about abandoning this errand, since all you could think about at that moment was escaping from the abominable odour. After passing the tannery, the smell became even more pungent thanks to the heaps of rubbish piled up outside the huts. No one ever bothered to collect or burn them, and swarms of rats leapt away as the car drove by, heading towards the huts where they lived amongst human beings.

There were no drains for the filthy water on the streets, so the car ploughed through puddles and streams of water, green water splashing onto its sides and windows. Curses and profanities flew from Mario's mouth, some of which targeted you for not having been able to find a better location to hunt for women other than this loathsome place.

You told Mario that only Libyans lived in neighborhoods like this, and if he couldn't bear these slums, he should return to his Italian women in the clean and decent districts of Tripoli. Mario said that it wasn't the poverty of the district or its tin huts that he objected to but the impoverishment of spirit that kept people from doing something about the filth around them.

Mario told you he had been born and raised in the poorest district of Palermo, but its inhabitants had at least planted rose trees in the vacant areas between the dilapidated buildings to assuage the degradation.

Everything in the district confirmed what Mario had said and you were unable to defend your countrymen against the accusation of spiritual impoverishment. On either side of the road, among the piles of rubbish and the stagnant water, the residents of the quarter went about their daily lives as if they didn't see the squalor that surrounded them. Others sat in front of their huts without showing any sign of movement, especially the skeletal old men and women reclining in the shade of their huts, gazing at the piles of rubbish. Flies buzzed around them and landed on their faces as they stared stupidly at the military motor car that had intruded into their sanctuary of dunghills.

Only the children could compete with the energy of the flies. They ran barefoot in tattered clothes black with dirt. They tried to catch up with the motor car and held out their hands for money. Their Bedouin mothers must still be observing the desert tradition of rarely washing their children's clothes to avoid wasting water, even though water was abundant in Tripoli.

The shouts and pleas of the street urchins mixed with barking dogs from one direction and bleating goats on the other. Although you had visited this district many times before, you felt that you were seeing it for the very first time as you entered it sitting next to Signor Mario in the spotless Italian car. Mario's eyes were wide with shock and his face twisted with disgust as he made his harsh comments. You felt ashamed of belonging to the same race as the residents of this ugly, filthy world.

As you flew by these human skeletons, whose faces swarmed with flies from the rubbish heaps, you wondered whether Houriya had come from such an environment and tasted such misery. Before moving with her mother to live in Caneva Hospital, Houriya had lived on the edges of Makina Street in a slum similar to this one. Because of their proximity to the centre, the huts had been cleared in order to build a new Italian district around the great Cathedral, which subsequently became the finest district in Tripoli.

It was as if the transformation from backward wretchedness to a paragon of progress and civilization mirrored the parallel rise of a seedling named Houriya who had been planted in that district's soil. She had moved from the absolute bottom of society to its highest echelons. You could hardly believe that Houriya had the slightest connection to a place like this. Her beauty shone like the morning sun, full of haughty pride, and she was surrounded with the trappings of authority, and success, which gave off the impression she had been born in a royal palace.

Why, then, did Signor Mario grumble that he was too

disgusted to have any contact with a woman who lived in this filth? What would he say if he saw Marshal Balbo's mistress and learned that she had lived in similar huts? But was Houriya's path the only path out of this world of poverty and filth and into the clean ordered world of food, clothing and housing fit for human beings? Was there not a less sinful path one could take care to avoid leading a decadent life?

The motor car passed through the narrow muddy lanes, between the tin huts and shacks until you reached Abdel Mowlah's hut. Before getting out, you saw Abdel Mowlah's head peering out through a small slit in the door.

He looked puzzled, as if he was trying to learn the reason for all the commotion the children created as they ran screaming and shouting behind the automobile. He was undoubtedly terrified to see a military car parked at his door. You quickly called him before any wild thoughts might tempt him to flee. He raised his hand over his face to shield his eyes from the glare of the sun, trying to make out who had called to him.

"Who is it? Is that you, Othman?"

Many other inquisitive faces peered out from the neighbouring huts.

"Yes, it's me, Abdel Mowlah. I want to speak with you quickly."

Abdel Mowlah disappeared for a second before appearing with a broom made of palm tree branches which he waved in the faces of the urchins who had crowded around the motor car to beg. They moved a short distance away from the car, but continued to stretch out their hands, unwary of Abdel Mowlah's broom. Abdel Mowlah came up to the car and leaned against the window.

"Come in and have some tea."

You replied, "We don't want any tea."

"Then what do you and this foreigner want?"

"Mario is just a driver who works with us in the camp."
Abdel Mowlah said sarcastically, "What an honour! What
brings you to the huts in Porta Akkara?"

"To tell you the truth, we have come to look for a
woman."

"And who might that woman be?" asked Abdel Mowlah
suspiciously.

"Not any woman in particular, just a woman who is
willing."

Abdel Mowlah asked again, "What do I've to do with
such a matter or such a woman?"

"I mean a woman like the woman you told me you
had brought to your hut."

"Have you fallen so far?" "Don't misunderstand me."

"Everything you say is wrong. You have come to the
wrong place and to the wrong man, because I'm not a
pimp nor is Porta Akkara a district of brothels. Go away
before I beat you with this broom."

You were surprised by Abdel Mowlah's unexpected
outburst and you tried to explain the matter to him.
However, Old Man Mario felt that the situation had become
embarrassing and he saw the angry man threatening you
with the broom, so he started the car to drive back down
the way you had come.

"Porca Miseria!"

He swore, pressed his foot on the gas pedal, and drove
as fast as he could, taking no notice of the children that
ran and leapt into the rubbish heaps to avoid being caught
beneath the wheels, or the hens that for the first time used

their wings to escape certain death at the hands of that roaring metal beast.

Mario continued to swear and curse until you reached the camp gate, where he stopped the car so you could get out. The entire time he hadn't said a single word to you that wasn't some curse or profanity in Italian, and when you asked him whom he was swearing at, he curtly replied, "Just the swine in front of you. Myself."

The very same day, during the lunch break, Abdel Mowlah the beggar came to visit you in the camp. He said that he couldn't bear to see you leave him in such a temper, so he had come to make it up to you. He added that he had had no choice but to act that way when his neighbours were watching him from all sides and the children picked up everything he said.

Your request had caught him by surprise and he couldn't have answered you since the situation hadn't allowed him to speak freely or make his motives known to you. The presence of an Italian military car outside his hut was enough to create suspicion among his neighbours. He said that if anyone had heard a word of what you had said, that would have been disaster. There had been no other recourse but to chase you and your friend away to clear himself of suspicion. So Abdel Mowlah had come to visit you as soon as he could to ask you not to be angry and to explain to him in the calm atmosphere of the camp what you had been unable to convey to him outside his hut in the morning.

You told Abdel Mowlah that you weren't angry with him because you realized that what had happened had been a misunderstanding. You explained that the matter would not sully his honour or yours and that your need for the sort of woman you were looking for would not be the disgrace that he had imagined.

You told him about the working relationship you had with Mario and the adventures you'd had in the forest with Italian women. Mario had made the preparations to bring them and in return asked you to make your own contribution at a later date. That was why you had gone to Abdel Mowlah's hut, searching for a woman like the one he had previously told you about.

Abdel Mowlah swore that he had never been involved in arranging such a matter for anyone and that he had never allowed any person to even joke about such things with him. He added that since he was certain that what you had told him was the truth, he would give you the address of a woman who lived in Bahlool Alley, parallel to Sidi Umran Street along the western wall of the city. The houses in that street were public brothels and he advised you not to go there yourself, so as not to ruin your reputation. What was more, these women only offered their services within their homes and couldn't go out to visit customers since they were watched by the police.

The address he gave you was for a woman named Sherifa, who worked as an intermediary for this kind of business. Sherifa managed a group of female entertainers who sang and danced at weddings. Abdel Mowlah advised you not to go to that address in your military uniform lest you be considered a government official. He also suggested that you initially claim to have come to arrange a wedding party and then only reveal your true intentions after she had sized you up.

You waited until the time for your driving lessons. You carried your civilian clothes under your armpit, because you couldn't be seen leaving the base with them on, and hid them in Mario's car. As soon as the lesson was over, you looked for a safe place near the city walls for Mario to park the car while you changed into the Arab clothes in which you would meet Sherifa. You told Mario to wait in his car until you had concluded the deal.

The house was in the old city and had been built in the Arab style, consisting of two storeys and an open outer courtyard. From the outer door, you strolled down a covered passageway that led to the inner courtyard and then to a small room where the lady of the house greeted her guests.

Sherifa sat on a mat spread over the floor and her wide body took up almost half of the room. You quickly moved from talk about the imaginary wedding to the real reason for your visit after having noticed her willingness to offer you the service you had come for.

The high prices surprised you. She told you that there were three price ranges, one for quick in-calls, another for quick out-calls, and a third option that only the very rich could afford, a whole night, regardless of whether it was her house or yours.

You realized that with the money in your pocket all you could afford was to take a woman on a trip outside the house. Without bargaining, you took out the ten francs she had demanded and gave them to her. She admired your decisiveness and initiative, so she raised her voice and called Nuriya, Fawziya and Khadouja into the room in order to give you a chance to choose between them. You chose the first woman because she was taller and plumper than the others and wore less make-up. Nuriya went to her room to prepare herself to go out with you, after her mistress had told her that her outing would be for two hours.

You were going to continue sitting in the room until Nuriya was ready, but there was a knock at the front door. Sherifa asked you to wait for Nuriya in her room since she didn't know who the person at her door would be, and it would not be wise for her to greet him in your presence.

You went upstairs and were surprised to find that the room you entered was clean and spacious. It had a large bed, a wardrobe that spanned the breadth of the room, and a wooden dressing table with a large mirror. You suddenly understood why the brothel's services were so expensive.

You sat on the edge of the bed while Nuriya sat in front of the mirror combing her hair and putting the finishing touches to her make-up. She told you that she would provide you with a better service if you wanted to stay inside the house where it was warm, clean and safe, and the mattress was made with metal springs that went up and down during intercourse, turning the bed into a trampoline that doubled the pleasure of sex.

Nuriya didn't hesitate to use her body to convince you of the benefits of staying in the house, and you were unprepared to resist. All it took was that magical moment when her breast brushed against your shoulder unintention-ally as she took a handkerchief down from a hook on the wall behind you and you were convinced of the truth of her words. The only problem that stood between you and obeying Nuriya's orders was your obligation to Mario, whom you had promised to meet beside the wall after half an hour. You could have canceled your appointment with him had you not left your military uniform in his car, without which you couldn't re-enter the base.

An idea suddenly flashed through your mind, which

would enable you to keep your appointment with Mario and also fulfil your desire for Nuriya. All you had left in your pocket was five francs. You offered them to Nuriya in exchange for quick sex now on the bed, asking her to take them without telling her mistress and to also keep her share of the money you had already paid Sherifa for the agreed-upon excursion with Mario.

Nuriya hesitated a little before reaching for the money. Then she agreed, but only after extracting a promise from you not to prolong the sex lest her mistress began to suspect something and came to see what was keeping her and discovered their secret agreement. She didn't want problems with the mistress of the house.

You snatched her hand, pulled her towards the bed and flung her on top of it. You jumped on top of her fully clothed, and no more than a minute passed until you were done taking your fill of her. Then she put on her clothes and followed you out to meet up with your Italian friend who was yearning to devour a morsel of live female Arab flesh.

There was no common language between Mario and Nuriya, so you translated for them throughout the outing, except for the few moments when they disappeared into a thicket to converse in the language of the body. Mario's curiosity was satisfied, although the lack of a common language had ruined his pleasure since he could never enjoy anything without talking incessantly, and as such he told you that he didn't wish to repeat the experience.

However, for you the house of entertainment in Bahlool Alley was a real discovery and it saved you from more of Mario's forest adventures, which didn't appeal to your provincial shyness or your preference for cleanliness and washing yourself after any such experience. The bedroom was the natural environment for such an intimate and private ritual. Visits became even more appealing with the presence of this amazing invention, the springy, rolling bed that undulated like the sea. This invention had never reached the countryside and desert, and it was as if it had been made solely to increase the pleasure and bliss of lovemaking.

You reached an agreement with Nuriya to come to her for an hour every week for seven francs, which was the price that her mistress Sherifa had asked.

You had now come to the painful realization that you were unable to control the tyrannical force of your libido that pushed you on the road towards the district of debauchery every week. The only way you could combat desire when it lit its inextinguishable fires beneath your skin was by committing more sins. You would never be able to return to your former innocence. All you could do was keep praying, ask for forgiveness and to cleanse yourself after each visit to the house of worldly delights.

TWO

Your relationship with Mario became limited to your driving lessons, until one day he informed you he had set a date for your driving test with the Department of Roads and Transportation. Mario had commended you to a number of his acquaintances in the department, so your test only lasted an hour, after which you received a card with your picture on it, which gave you the right to drive a car.

Your barracks mates considered your acquisition of a driving licence an occasion for celebration, as no Libyan recruit had ever acquired one before. As soon as training hours ended, they brought you a plate full of oriental pastries and a pot of hot tea from the camp's kitchen. Sergeant Antar, who attended the celebration, congratulated you on your success, as he considered you his star pupil. He made no pretenses about ingratiating himself with you and told the rest of the recruits that they should rejoice as you had become their representative in higher society.

Feigning modesty, you replied that you didn't belong to higher circles and that your place would always be in this barracks under Sergeant Antar's authority. Although you had returned his compliment, his words had fanned

the embers of ambition in your heart and had heightened
your self-importance. You knew Sergeant Antar could sniff
out centres of power and authority and he hadn't been
speaking without ulterior motive. His sixth sense must have
predicted you were bound to ascend the ladder of success
and authority.

The following day, you were on your way to Signora
Houriya's house to present yourself and inform her that
you were ready to take the job, when it occurred to you
that you could take a day off without anyone in the camp
realizing and spend it by yourself or with the person you
loved. And since Thuraya was the only person you loved
and by whom you were loved in this city, you decided to
visit her and her family, after dilly-dallying in the streets a
while to relish in the victory you had won by passing the
driving test and acquiring a driving licence.

As you walked towards Thuraya's house, you passed by
a confectioner's shop and bought a plate of sweets and
pastries to celebrate your success with Thuraya and her
family. You were consumed with yearning to see her eyes
and her smile, the totality of all beauty.

You knocked at the door and expected that she would
open it as she had always opened it every time you had
visited them in the morning when her brother was at
school.

No one opened the door, so you knocked again louder
and continued knocking until it became clear that no one
was home. You were seized with worry that something
bad might have happened to Thuraya and her family.
Thuraya's father might have died and his family taken him
to Tajura, his village, to bury him beside his ancestors. Dark
thoughts raced through your head, but you would not

knock on the neighbours' doors so as not to worry them
or invite gossip about the stranger who had come to Haj
al-Mahdy's house.

You left the door and returned to the main road. You
decided you would have to ask someone, so it was best to
ask the shopkeepers who worked next to the Haj's shop.
They were all friends of his and since you had worked in
his shop, they all knew you, and your questions would not
arouse any suspicions.

As it turned out, there was no need to ask anyone
because when you arrived you were surprised to find Haj
al-Mahdy sitting in his shop, engrossed in his work, hammer
in hand, a box of nails beside him. Pieces of red leather lay
scattered around him. He took a piece of leather and put
it on the small anvil and hammered it gently in order to
soften the leather.

You felt both happy and sad. You were happy that the
man had recovered from his illness after you thought he
might have died. He was able to work in his shop once
more and stave off the hardship that might have befallen
him and his kind family, who had opened their doors to
you and treated you like one of their own. On the other
hand, you were sad because the father's return to his shop
meant there was no chance you would be able to go to
his home to sit and chat with him, his wife and his daughter
as you had done during his illness.

You entered the shop and congratulated Haj al-Mahdy
on his recovery before sitting down across from him on
the small stool that customers used. The man had not
recovered completely but considered himself well enough
to drag himself to work, reopen his shop and earn whatever
he could until he was his old self again.

Without your having to ask him why no one had been home, he informed you that his wife and daughter had gone with Fathy's family to visit Fathy in the military camp. The old man added that had you arrived earlier, you could have helped accompany them to the camp.

You felt no regret at not having accompanied them, for you were certain that you would never have been able to get anywhere near Thuraya in that crowd. Also, why would you want to take her to her husband in that cursed base, after you had accompanied her around the most romantic sights of the city? You had discovered alleys that had only been wide enough for her and you. You would revisit those places together in the car that you would begin to drive the following day.

Seeming overworked, Haj al-Mahdy put down the hammer to catch his breath and chat with you. Moved by concern, you suggested he content himself with selling the shoes he had already made and not exhaust himself by making new shoes until he had recovered completely. He waved his hand dismissively, as if to indicate that neither he nor you should talk about the matter.

He asked you how you had managed to live under the injustice and oppression of the Italian infidels. You thanked God that his son-in-law Fathy didn't know you or your relationship with his in-laws, or else he would have informed them and his family of the true nature of your work on the base. You were the whip of those Italian infidels, the tool with which they oppressed your countrymen. You were glad that you had become a qualified driver for that would open a new path for you and exempt you from flogging the wretched recruits. Your work in the camp had become a source of embarrassment, which you felt even now as you sat chatting with an old man who knew nothing about what happened inside the camp.

Thuraya's father continued to curse the Libyans who volunteered to work for the Italians in jobs that disgraced their people and their country. He cited the example of some who had informed on the Libyan youths who had fled from the recruiting campaigns by guiding the Italian authorities to their houses and wrenching them from their mothers' arms.

Haj al-Mahdy said, "The Italians forget that our country's land is hot and the graves of God's saints are in every corner of the country. The hot earth shall scorch them and they will receive their punishment in this world before the Hereafter. Woe betide any Libyan who wrongs his fellow countrymen and harms his homeland."

You felt a cold shiver running through your body as if the man had been talking about you. You wanted to escape, but the man had a lot to get off his chest that could only be said to people he trusted. He considered you such a person, so he continued to curse those who cooperated with the Italians.

"Every bone in the graves of our dead countrymen will curse them before the living curse them."

He then blamed himself and everyone else who remained in the country, accepting life in the shadow of an infidel governor instead of emigrating and leaving the land according to the Book of God which says, "Was not the earth of Allah spacious enough for you to emigrate therein?"

The old man said that had he been in a position to leave Libya and go to another country, he and his family would not have swallowed their pride and subjected themselves to such servility for even a single day.

He added in a tone of grief, "But God is He Who prevails. We can do little, though we see much."

All you could say was to repeat "God prevails."

You took a breath of relief when Haj al-Mahdy changed the subject and began talking about the war in Abyssinia. This war was further proof of the depravity of these treacherous, tyrannical Italians who drove Libyans to invade a peaceful land. It was a crime against the Libyan and Abyssinian peoples. He then asked you about the date of your departure.

You told him that you didn't know, and that none of your superiors deigned to tell you, perhaps because they themselves didn't know, or perhaps because they considered it a military secret. You added that your departure would most likely be in the near future since the Abyssinian plateau's rainy season would soon end and the weather would be suitable for military operations.

Haj al-Mahdy, like many others, thought that the postponement was due to what had happened on the Barqa Plateau and not on the Abyssinian Plateau. It must have been a shock for him to learn news of the conflict breaking out in Green Mountain was just wishful thinking, and that there was no longer anyone who could turn such wishes into reality. The Italians had complete control of the country and its resources, and the Libyans had to accept the facts, however painful they may be.

You didn't want to wait until Haj al-Mahdy could complete his thoughts concerning the oppression that the country suffered at the hands of the occupiers, for you had heard the same thing from him more than once before. You also knew his theories about the stars that continually turned in the heavens where nothing was fixed, and how no human being could depend on the heavens to always shift in his favour. So if the Italians were victorious today, the stars would not be in their favour tomorrow. Their injustice would have to come to an end and the homeland would return to its rightful owners, thanks to the will of God.

It was the talk of a man consoling himself as he watched his life falling apart, his world collapsing and his land confiscated.

You didn't want to return directly to the camp and let your day off slip through your fingers. You needed to find someone close to you who could celebrate your success with you. You didn't need to think long since your options were very limited. Accordingly, you quickly made your way to Bahlool Alley even though it was not the scheduled day for your visit and Nuriya didn't receive any of her customers. She always reserved this day to spend with her seven-year-old daughter Warda.

Nuriya wasn't at home when arrived. She had hired a carriage in which to take her daughter on an outing, to buy her toys and sweets. You had left her house and were about to head back when you saw her and her daughter getting out of the carriage in front of the house. That was the first time you had seen Warda, after having heard much about her.

In the red-light district, a woman who found herself pregnant customarily tried to register her newborn child under the name of one of the youths who worked in the area. There were four of them who always went around the brothels working for the prostitutes in exchange for fixed wages. They lived in the district, spending days and nights preparing tea, taking the rubbish to the dump, carrying water to the houses, and protecting the women from violent or drunk customers, amongst other things. Each one had at least ten children registered under his name. The standard routine was to have a marriage contract drawn up between the man and the pregnant woman, then annul it once the child's relationship to this spurious father was established.

You gave Nuriya the box of sweets you had bought for Thuraya and you praised her pretty daughter, asking God to bless her. You wanted to return to the camp since there was no place for you in the intimate atmosphere between a mother and her daughter, but Nuriya insisted you join them in the celebration by cutting the chocolate cake that her daughter loved so much. You tried to excuse yourself, but Nuriya laughingly said that one person by himself couldn't make a party, and two people would still not be enough. As for three, it was the necessary minimum to have a pleasant party.

You certainly would not be happy if you deprived her and her daughter of the quorum necessary for a party. You liked Nuriya's cheerful easygoing spirit, so you agreed to stay. After you all entered her room, you confessed that you had come to celebrate successfully passing your driving test. You promised you would take Nuriya and her daughter for a ride along the promenade from Tajura to Janzour and they were thrilled.

It wasn't an appropriate time to talk to Nuriya about anything else, or to think about being alone with Nuriya, who didn't want to appear before her daughter in any role other than that of a loving mother. She seemed to transform into a little girl who played, sang, and joked with the other little girl. Even you sang along with them to the words of a well-known children's song:

O little kitty,
you're naughty by nature,
Naughty by nature.
O little kitty,
You stole a mouse from our room,
You're naughty by nature,
Naughty by nature.

Before sunset, a middle-aged Negress came to take the little girl to the house where she lived in the Belkheir district. It was the prostitutes' custom to entrust their children to such women. In exchange for a meagre wage, the children could grow up far from their mothers' professional work, as was the case with Warda, who would grow up considering this woman as her a second mother.

Warda left the house and the innocent games came to an end, clearing the air for you to play a different kind of game with Nuriya.

Afterwards, you returned to the camp more prepared than ever to give the whip a rest, and welcome the sunrise tomorrow as the herald of a new life.

THREE

Your first day was full of excitement, beginning with registering your name at the drivers' department at the governor's palace. You received the uniform worn only by drivers in the service of the Governor-General's palace. The uniform had silver hemming that brought out its navy blue colour and the cap was similar to an officers' cap.

You were given a four-door Alfa Romeo with a shining grey frame and a convertible top. They gave it to you brand new, "at the zero", as they said in drivers' jargon. Mario remained with you the entire time, helping you to complete all the necessary procedures, and spending hours teaching you how to drive that particular car.

The bigger source of excitement was that from now on you would be close to a woman whom God had blessed with such beauty that she indeed deserved her name, Houriya, which means nymph. Providence had put her in your life and made you one of her servants instead of remaining Sergeant Antar's servile subordinate. You thanked God for exchanging the tarnished farthing for a golden dinar.

Houriya lived on the first floor of a building on La

Posta Street. She had a private entrance to the building on a side street called Michelangelo Street where you parked your car when it wasn't in the underground garage, and where you spent most of your time inside the car waiting for your mistress's orders.

At first, you were delighted at the complete comfort of your new job, which was a welcome change from life on the base with its arduous training and difficult combat drills, in addition to the minor errands related to supervising the barracks, helping keep discipline, and delivering the base's mail to the government postal centre. But after three days, you began to feel restless when all you did was sit every day staring into space, without anything to do and anyone to talk to.

During these first days, you didn't dare to ask Signora Houriya's permission to use the car for any personal errand. You came every morning by bus or carriage, and returned at the end of the day by the same means after parking the car in the garage. All you did on the fourth day was to move the car from its place in the quiet side street to another spot in the main street that bustled with life and movement.

Across the street was a large store that sold women's, men's and children's clothing. The customers who frequented the shop were of all ages, and were mostly Italian, although a few were Arabs, Jews, Maltese or Greek people too.

Since Marshal Balbo had assumed power, Tripoli had become a centre of tourism, and so from time to time a wave of camera-carrying tourists would pass by. Beside the big clothing store were two smaller shops that sold antiques and local food, and a table set up on the pavement to sell newspapers and magazines. Add to that the customers who visited the centre of commerce and you had a pleasantly diverting scene before you to watch in order to fight off the boredom.

You watched everything from the driver's seat and it wasn't rare for the sight of the new elegant car and the driver in his official uniform to draw looks of curiosity from women crossing the street. Yet the most interesting thing you saw happen was a customer trying to sneak a piece of clothing under his jacket and slink out of the store while the shopkeepers were busy with other customers. As he went out, he was startled by the sound of the door alarm, after which the owners of the shop grabbed hold of him and dragged him to the police station. You were a little surprised to learn this thief was Italian, which contrasted with your impression that all Italians were affluent.

You passed a week in Houriya's service without seeing the Governor-General visit his mistress in her flat, or even seeing visitors of any kind. The only people you saw were the postman and two nurses who had worked with Houriya at the Caneva Hospital. One of the nurses was an Italian who wore a nurse's uniform. The other nurse was a gaunt Jewish woman who wore a Star of David necklace and was so skinny that she seemed to be all bones.

Houriya's outings were short. She went to a dressmaker on Cathedral Square, and to Caneva Hospital, where she used to work as a nurse. You once drove her to the old city and to the entrance of Shaib Al Ain Alley, whereupon she headed towards the home of the venerable Sheikh al-Balbal, who lived with his mother. You waited for Houriya until she left his home after a few minutes. You had no idea why she had visited him. She told you that it wasn't the first time she had visited him and she appeared to be in a state of serenity thanks to the blessings of the pious Sheikh al-Balbal.

Contrary to her habit of sitting silently in the back, this time Houriya told you that before she had knocked at the door of his home, his mother had opened it and said, "Please, come in Houriya," even though she hadn't informed the sheikh of her visit. When she asked the Sheikh's mother how she had known that she was coming to visit them, the woman said that her son had told her that Houriya was coming to visit them and had asked her to open the door.

Signora Houriya's remarks about the Sheikh's miraculous premonitions reminded you of what Haj al-Mahdy had told you about the pious men of this land, about its scorching earth and about the penalty that pious saints had in store for every person who had committed sins against people of the land.

Although your job as Houriya's driver took up most of your day, it still allowed for a part of your old routine to endure. You returned to the camp just before darkness fell over the base and spent some time with your friend Salem before going to the dining hall to join the rest of the recruits. You went amongst them in your distinguished uniform which had made you a minor celebrity to everyone in the camp, Libyans and Italians alike, both officers and soldiers.

You had become an employee in the GovernorGeneral's palace. It was a temporary assignment, as everyone knew, but it would provide you with invaluable experience and connections to high-ranking officers, and guarantee you special treatment when the time came for the journey to

Abyssinia. Also, because your work as a driver was temporary, you still retained your military status on the base. You still had your bed and you were still responsible for the nightly supervision of the barracks, in addition to being subjected to Sergeant Antar's inspection every night.

Sunday was still your weekly holiday, even though you were now working for Houriya, and you spent it however you wished, on condition that you always kept an hour free in the afternoon for Nuriya, the woman who had become the focus of all your sexual energies. You hadn't sought any other woman ever since you first found her. Even when you chanced across Mario on your way in and out of the base and he reminded you of your adventures in the woods, mentioning the possibility of repeating them, you always told him that your new job didn't leave you any spare time.

You kept the secret of your relationship to Nuriya to yourself. You never mentioned her or did anything to allude to her around anyone, even Salem, letting him believe that you were as pure and pious as you had been since you had come to the city. You made a point of praying at sunset prayer with him, after which you would sit on the grass, chat together and pray to God to protect you both, provide for you, and bless you in this world and in the Hereafter.

Despite Salem's reservations about your new job, he no longer criticized and mocked your behaviour as he had previously, because he viewed your new job, in spite of its lowliness, as having saved you from the evil deeds you had been committing as one of the base's disciplinarians. You brought some pastries stuffed with honey and almonds and wrapped in silver paper from Signora Houriya's kitchen.

Offering some to him, you said, "I wanted you to taste some of the Signora's food so you could see the value of living among the upper class. You have never tasted anything like it in your life."

Salem took the pastry, put it in his mouth and said, "This is a blessing that cannot be refused."

"It's a reward for your good conduct during the last few days."

"I didn't want to add to your worries."

You said, "Free your eyes of this black gauze that hides the light of the sun from you. Can't you ever see anything other than worry and sadness? Was I complaining to you about worries or suffering? I'm living the best days of my life, so why do you say that I'm burdened with misery? From where did these worries you speak of come?"

Salem replied, "Do you consider living under Italian rule, and being driven like flocks of sheep to the massacres of war, a happy life?"

"You are still harping on the same old story. The trouble with you is that you're always looking at the bigger picture, whereas I take it day by day, bit by bit. I'm happy with the new uniform I wear, the incredible car I drive and the delicious food that I eat at Signora Houriya's house. I'm also happy to look upon the most beautiful woman in the world every morning."

What you said was true, you really did enjoy your new life as Signora Houriya's driver. You were thrilled to be able to be close to her and every morning this yearning led you to her doorstep. You started your shift at eight o'clock, and Hawaa, her housekeeper and cook, always opened the door for you and asked you to have your breakfast in the kitchen.

The breakfast you always found waiting for you was unlike any other you had enjoyed in your life. At its most basic, breakfast was a cup of tea and a little piece of bread, just like the breakfasts in your village. But in Signora Houriya's home, breakfast consisted of many kinds of cheese, butter, jam, honey, hot or cold milk, yoghurt and seasonal fruits. In addition to tea, there was coffee and hot chocolate, the breads and pastries stuffed with grated coconuts, almonds and hazel nuts, and as much fruit juice as you could drink.

After breakfast you would take the car keys and go down to the garage where you would find the car shining and spotlessly clean, thanks to Mukhtar the garage guard, who always washed and dried it overnight. You would then drive out of the garage, park it in front of the building, and sit in the driver's seat waiting for Signora Houriya's orders.

No matter how many errands were required of you, whether they were driving Signora Houriya wherever she wanted to go, or performing Houriya's errands on your own, you were nearly always back in time for lunch. There was always at least one meat dish waiting for you in addition to three or four other courses, which you either ate in the kitchen, or in the garage, in which case you would share it with old Mukhtar and sometimes with Morgan.

So how could Salem want you to not be happy with a life such as only the most distinguished members of society could enjoy? Maybe he had wanted to express his own feelings of misery and the misery of the other Libyans in the camp, forgetting that you had fought tooth and nail to forge your own path differently.

You hadn't handed yourself over to blind fate, letting

it do what it willed with you. You had made a planned your own fate and shaped events in order to make life less miserable, even if you couldn't make it happy.

To some of the recruits, your behaviour probably seemed like abandoning the duties of loyalty and camaraderie that bound you. But in your view, it was a miserable camaraderie that wasn't worth saving. You felt entitled to be free from them like a songbird from a flock of wretched pigeons.

You were very happy being in Signora Houriya's service and the only thing that could upset your happiness was when a day passed without seeing her. She remained asleep throughout the morning until after you had already come, had your breakfast, and gone below to take up your position in the driver's seat of the car. You would hunt for reasons to go inside the apartment again, so you would be able to see her. If opportunities didn't present themselves, weren't your only hope was to see her open the door of the car, get into the back seat and ask you to take her on some of her errands. You would immediately adjust the rear view mirror so that it only reflected Houriya's face, so you could let your eyes wander between the road in front of you and the image of her face in the mirror. When she broke the silence and spoke to you, the sound of her voice filled your senses as if it were an intoxicating, celestial wine.

Barely a day passed without your finding an excuse to go back to the apartment in the hope of feasting your eyes upon her. You might not see her despite your efforts, but you were compelled to go up even for the most fabricated of reasons. Morgan always went to buy the Italian magazines that Houriya loved to read, so you took steps to procure that task. Let Morgan move on to some other job, like fetching the apartment's food, drinks and household appliances.

Every morning you went to the newspaper seller, who had set up a stall above which he displayed Italian newspapers and magazines, and every morning he had at the ready the daily mix of publications that Houriya ordered. Most of them were magazines with satirical cartoons or illustrated short stories, but also some women's magazines displaying the latest fashions. Houriya didn't care for the political newspapers that came from Italy, and the only newspaper she bought was the local *Tripoli Journal* issued by the publishing office affiliated with the Governor-General's office. As such, the Marshal's photograph invariably covered the first page along with news about him and his most recent movements and statements. Houriya filled her free time by reading these magazines and listening to Italian songs. Although you knew there was an invention called "the radio" and another one called "the gramophone", which together produced the loud music that issued from Italian cafés and restaurants, you had never seen either a radio or a gramophone with your own eyes until you worked for Houriya. You looked at these new inventions and touched them. They had a magical air to them, and the most incredible part was that you heard Arabic words and Arab songs issuing from these inventions.

Houriya laughed when she saw your astonishment and ignorance of how the devices worked. If the gramophone relayed a voice recorded on this black disc they called a record, then where did all the voices, singing, and music on the radio come from?

Houriya tried to test your intelligence by asking you to guess, but you failed to come up with any idea, because the closest comparable invention was the telephone which had a wire to connect the speaker to the listener. But this invention sang, spoke, and played music without wires or connections.

You didn't take Houriya seriously when she said that the answer had to do with a djinn called Electricity whom modern science could capture and bend to its will. She added that electricity existed everywhere, even in human beings, and it was sheer chance that had led an inventor to make electricity flow from a positive end to a negative end, and that when they met that was the magic recipe by which the djinn was captured and produced light, like in electric lamps.

Houriya continued to explain to you that the djinn was what foreigners called energy, which was what the radio ran on. The people who produced these programmes in broadcasting stations sent them through this djinn in electric currents, who then put the programmes on the radio.

As Houriya talked, you realized she wasn't joking about the djinn. She said, "Let the foreigners call it science, or magnetic fields, or electric currents, or moving particles. None of that explains how a wire connects to a wire and creates light or how particles transform themselves into speech."

She explained to you how the broadcasting stations in Italy transmitted programmes from a company called the RAI. Then she got up and stood near the window, pointing towards the site of the trade fair on Corso Di Sicilia where a big antenna rose above the roof of the fair. She said that Marshal Balbo had brought the broadcasting station to Libya as part of his programme of modernizing the country and the Arabic-language service was broadcast from that building.

Another day, she made you listen to Arabic songs on the gramophone. The first record began with a song by Mohammed Abdel Wahab, who sang "Tell me, train, where you are going to?" The second song was "Take me back to my beloved homeland" by the "Star of the East", Um Kalthum.

Houriya's surprise to you, Hawaa and her servant Morgan was a Libyan song produced by the Libyan company Fahmyphone. The song was composed, set to music and sung by Basher Fahmy, who sang "How beautiful you are, O my cousin". Then she put on another song, also sung by Basher Fahmy, about a romance between a Libyan and a black woman of African origin, which delighted both Hawaa and Morgan. Both songs were short and beautiful, with a quick rhythm to the melody and simple colloquial lyrics.

During the two weeks you worked as Houriya's driver, you felt you had learned so many things you would never have learned if not for this woman, whom you began to know through daily co-existence after knowing her only through fleeting visits before. Your love and admiration for her grew daily. There was something charming about this woman that you couldn't pin down. It was more than just beauty. Something gave her an enchanting presence and surrounded her with a brilliant halo of contentment. Just the sight of her was enough to eliminate any annoyance that clung to you, as if seeing her were like going on permanent holiday.

Whenever she was busy browsing the illustrated magazines you brought for her, you would gaze at her face, with its constant smile, trying to discover the secret of this resplendence. Perhaps the secret was the sparkle in her eyes, the sweetness of her smile, her shining forehead, her perfect complexion or the femininity her body exuded. But you decided it was deeper than these external features, no matter how alluring they were. It had to do with another beauty, the indefinable beauty of the soul which was more similar to a scent, or a light, or the spark of electricity running through a wire. Who knew if it was possible to attribute this beauty and light to the same elusive hidden forces Houriya had attributed to electricity?

This was a beauty nurtured by the milk of the mother who nursed her and the night of lovemaking she spent with the man who planted the seed for this beautiful child's creation in her mother's womb. This was a beauty rooted in a childhood that despite its poverty must have been full of love and tenderness, and in the rays of the moon that kissed her face as a child in her swaddling clothes, and in the years growing up in Caneva Hospital that spared her the anaemia that afflicted so many others who were born and raised in poor Libyan districts.

Houriya suddenly looked up from the magazine she had been reading and caught you staring at her. You looked away in embarrassment and lowered your eyes to the floor, regretting such a sin. She understood you had been staring at her in admiration, so she smiled, as if to say she had forgiven you. You quickly withdrew and went to sit in the car.

You remained oblivious to everything around you, still under the influence of the magnetic force that surrounded Houriya and drew everyone into orbit around her, spellbound, unable to break free of her. According to what you had read in Jalaluddin al-Suyuti's book, attraction in its most common form was something the lover saw in the face of his beloved that others couldn't see. That was exactly the case with you and Thuraya. You were attracted to her by something that spoke to you in a language that no one but you could discern.

Houriya's attractiveness was something else, and her beauty spoke a language everyone knew, words that reached every heart. That was why she enjoyed the admiration of everyone who came into contact with her, even if that contact was brief as had been the case with you at the beginning of your acquaintanceship. There was no doubt these open conduits between her beauty and people were what made Houriya a difficult catch. Every man who saw her must have been enticed by the desire to win her, but no matter how many men courted her, she would only be able to choose one man. In order to be deserving of her and capable of winning her love, this man had to be of such calibre that he excelled above all others who saw her and fell in love with her, and who else could win the heart of the foremost lady of love and beauty but the foremost man of the country, namely Italo Balbo? He wasn't just rich and powerful, although these were important qualities to be sure, but weren't enough on the scales of love. He tipped the balance of these though with his youth, good looks, and charming personality. Everyone agreed that it was only natural that such a person should pick the most beautiful flower from the gardens of Tripoli and clip it to his lapel.

Marshal Balbo had women in every corner of the world, because all limits vanished before his airplane, which he piloted himself, crossing oceans and continents, and partic-ipating in international competitions. He also attended ceremonies that honoured this pioneer of the airplane, Italy's darling. He stood among spotlights, surrounded by beautiful women and the hands of kings, princes, and presidents stretched to adorn his neck with garlands.

In Tripoli, the capital of his private fief, he held festivals to which he invited princes, princesses, movie stars and singers from around the world. The festival lights were always kept on and and all of the young, beautiful female guests dreamed of hearing their handsome host whisper a word of love in their ears, in the middle of a desert night redolent with the aromas of the East.

The fact that he had chosen Houriya, a Libyan girl, to be his permanent mistress over these women wasn't coincidental. It had happened for one very specific reason.

Houriya possessed something that elevated her above all those other beauties hailing from the four corners of the globe. She possessed that other kind of loveliness that few could sense except those who became close to her and interacted with her. This kind of beauty didn't offer itself up to others all at once, because it was deeper, wider, and richer than the physical beauty that petered out hadn'tafter the first glance. It was that sort of loveliness that, every time you gave it another look, sent back even more from its inexhaustible reserves. couldn'tEvery new thing you learned about it and each subsequent moment you spent with it repaid you with a constant flood of generous gifts.

Houriya could have taken advantage of her special relationship with the Governor-General and surrounded herself with the pomp of rule, gained power and authority over people, and lived in a palace surrounded by gardens. Instead. she chose to live in this small elegant flat, which better agreed with the spirit of simplicity in her nature which shied away from complications and affected airs. She wanted to live a quiet peaceful life in this comfortable nest, far from the trappings of power, and in the shadow of the man who loved her and had chosen her to be the second woman in his life after Donna Manu, his wife and the mother of his three children, who lived most of the year in Rome.

Everything in her life indicated that Houriya was quite happy being with an exciting man like Balbo and living in a house with him. She seemed satisfied with her status as the shadow woman of a married man, whose wife bore his name and appeared beside him at parties as his equal. And although there were manyoccasions when Houriya accompanied Balbo, one had to wonder what she thought about his many relationships with other women. People gossiped about it and newspapers hinted at it in articles, publishing pictures of him with the beauties of the world, who came panting to the new luxurious hotels his predecessors had begun constructing and that he had completed.

The same happened with other projects that had come to a standstill because of the financial crisis the country had suffered. The crisis was not resolved until Balbo came to the helm, having been granted extensive powers, bolstered by an exorbitant budget from Mussolini. Balbo set out to make Tripoli into a civilization to rival the European civilizations, and he made the grand openings of these tourist hotels and cultural projects into an occasion to invite the beauties of the silver screen and theatre from around the world. Houriya had obviously distanced herself from anything that might disturb her happiness with the Marshal. So the gossip articles and photographs in star-studded magazines all talked about affairs that didn't exist as far as Houriya was concerned. She simply didn't read such magazines or allow them into her house. As for the rumours, Houriya's relationships with the general public were as limited as possible, to the point that there was no way for any of these rumours to reach her house, despite their prevalence. And whenever a word or newspaper slipped into her house suggesting a link between the Marshal and the women he invited to Tripoli, Houriya thought of them as random, fleeting women in his life who didn't challenge her standing, equal only to that of Balbo's wife.

Or perhaps like many of Balbo's friends and allies, Houriya saw his relationships with the celebrities of the world as a necessary part of his position and a natural extension of his policies, which sought to give Libya the appearance of glamour. In a number of Libyan picture magazines, below a picture of a cruise ship visiting the country, you had personally read that Marshal Balbo intended to make Libya a land of mirth, entertainment, and stability, a place where the rich and famous, actors and actresses, came to vacation.

Naturally, it saddened you that she was living with him in sin. You expected better from a Muslim Arab woman with such a noble spirit and refined gregariousness. If only her life with the man had been built on the Law of God, which made polygamous marriage lawful and adultery unlawful. But such a solution was impossible for her when the man's religious beliefs didn't permit him to marry a second wife, and it wasn't in his power to deny his religious beliefs.

You wondered how she felt about a relationship for which her society condemned her. She was not like the girls of Rome, for whom marriage or lack thereof made no difference. If she had convinced herself that a marriage-less life with Balbo was better than married life with a Libyan, how had she been able to forget her maternal instincts, to silence in her depths the feminine longing for a child? Had she forced herself to make this sacrifice? Was it her reserves of love and affection for Balbo that allowed her to ignore these debts owed to herself, or the calls coming from her sensitive refined self?

The sensibilities that Houriya wrapped in a modern Italian perspective didn't heed the instructions of religion. But her apparent faith in spirituality and the miracles of saints revealed the depth of her character's religious dimension. You caught yourself once again, as you sat in the motor car, wondering about matters that didn't concern you. This was the private life of a woman with no connection to you, a woman who hadn't asked you to worry on her behalf. She hadn't appointed you her guardian, nor were you responsible for the lifestyle she had chosen for herself. She lived happily with her lover, and you weren'thing but one of her little helpers.

Your status was even inferior to that of her servants, as you were only a temporary driver whose employment would end with the return of the permanent driver. Why then did you behave so disrespectfully towards her? You were fretting for the sake of a woman like her while you were the miserable, weaker party, under constant threat of being thrown from this car and onto a steamship to meet a disgraceful death in Italy' wars.

It was you who deserved pity, not Houriya, so save your concerns for yourself and try to think of a way to escape from the dead-end path before you. Your proximity to the highest military and civil authority in the country afforded you an opportunity that no other Libyan recruit had attained. Why shouldn't you make use of this position, which was surely the gift of angels, to create a path to salvation from the dreaded fate that threatened you? Why shouldn't this temporary job become a permanent one with the Will of God and the decree of the Governor-General?

You could be guaranteed to stay in Tripoli and be spared the trip to Abyssinia. Common sense told you the Italian government in Libya would not send all its soldiers to war, because it would always need some to keep the peace, guard the borders, and serve Italian officers. Why not take steps so you too could be fortunate enough to stay behind? Who was more entitled to such treatment than you? Whoever the stars of calamity willed to go, let him go. As for you, there wasn't thing to do but remain in Tripoli and leave only as far as Tripoli's outskirts or for a vacation with your family in Awlad Al Sheikh, far from the horrors of the war.

You made up your mind to do your utmost to convince the Governor-General of the value of your services to him and his mistress, being a dependable and capable chauffeur. There didn't seem to be a clear, passable road that led to this intended result without problems and obstacles along the way, but you had to try to find it. It was possible so long as you didn't trouble your mind with anything except your own personal deliverance.

Houriya was your golden ticket to convince the Governor-General. You decided to stop concerning yourself with delusions of Houriya's life being wretched. She was blessed with a level of comfort that was unequalled by any other woman in Libya. You couldn't claim to have seen her upset or troubled for even a moment since you had entered her employ.

You would focus your efforts on winning her approval

so that in her eyes you would seem better than the driver Ayyad al-Fezzany, and she would insist on you remaining after his return. Her approval would hopefully lead to the Governor-General's himself, and your future would be secure.

FOUR

One sultry afternoon, you were waiting for Houriya to
return to the car during an outing, when a policeman
ordered a two-horse cart to leave the main street immediately, as horse-carts there was expressly forbidden. As it
quickly turned onto the side street, the cart emitting a
choking gust of dust from its open load of coal. The dust
clouded the car windows and you swore at the cart driver
who went obliviously on his way.

The coal dust had also infiltrated through the half-
open window onto the back seat of the car. The profanities and insults you flung at the driver were fruitless, and
didn't prevent you from needing to clean and polish the
car as quickly as possible before Signora Houriya could
arrive with one of her friends. She had invited this friend
to accompany her to an important celebration near the
Red Castle, held under the auspices of the Governor-
General.

At first, you hadn't known why this celebration was
being held, but on your way to your work from the camp,
you hadn'ticed that the streets were decorated with flags
and that the walls were covered with huge posters of the

Duce. As you approached Baladiya Street, bands of musicians appeared. After reaching the house, you learned that Marshal Balbo was going to receive and welcome a passenger ship coming from Syracuse.

You also learned that aboard that steamer were four hundred Italian families, new settlers who would find four hundred modern farms waiting for them southeast of Tripoli. Public facilities had also been built for them in the Italian style, including a market, a school, a medical centre, a church, a sports and social club and a cinema. This was one of the many settlements that were being built near the capital on land confiscated from Libyans, who had used it for pasture and sheep herding.

Signora Houriya and her friend got into the car. She was wearing a hat with white ribbons and a pink dress with white dots. A gold necklace adorned her graceful neck and she wore sunglasses with ivory frames. She carried a silver-coloured handbag and wore white shoes decorated with a cloth flower on each shoe. Her friend was an Italian nun and wore her habit. She carried a bouquet of red roses with which she intended to shower the newcomers.

You set off with them down the main street, which was crowded on both sides with people going to the celebration. When you reached Citadel Square, where the celebration was to be held, the two ladies got out of the car beside the dais that was reserved for the guests. The traffic officers guided you to a place where the guests' cars were parked, away from the crowds.

After parking the car, you came back and stood with the guards near the dais in order to remain close to Houriya and her friend. That way when the celebration ended, you could lead them to where the motor car was parked. Not far from you, an honour guard was lined up, and the military band played music to welcome the attendees.

The seats reserved for the guests were placed in an area that extended from the Miramari Theatre to the walls of the Corniche. Across from the seats was the raised dais for the Marshal and his assistants, and both sides of the street leading up to the dais were lined with soldiers on horseback. They wore white flowing robes brocaded with gold and silver threads over their military uniforms, and stood at attention with their swords in their belts.

A picture of the Duce, freshly painted on cloth, covered the entire length of the ancient citadel's walls. He was wearing a grey metal helmet and multicoloured medals covered his jacket. He held his head up proudly, looking over the crowded square from on high, and his right arm was raised in a salute, but one that gave the impression of a threat because his hand was clenched in a fist.

To everyone's surprise, the picture on the wall suddenly moved as if it had transformed into a real person and shouts of astonishment broke from the crowds. He waved to the people with his fist, that sign of determination. His eyes shone and his mouth moved with speech as he conveyed his greetings to the people, welcomed the new settlers, and congratulated them on their safe arrival. He expressed his confidence that they would be messengers of the Roman civilization to create life in this wasteland.

The whole act had been a theatrical device perfected and prepared by the technicians and had only lasted a few minutes, yet it had been enough to stir up enthusiasm and patriotism among the crowds of Italians who shouted, "Long live Italy! Long live Mussolini!"

The high and imposing steamship hailing from Sicily

had anchored near the citadel and seemed to be yet another citadel blocking the horizon. Its four decks were crowded with immigrants who clapped and waved their hands to the crowds on the shore and repeated with them, "Long live Mussolini!" after hearing their welcoming words. They were waiting to land in the Promised Land and weren't the first settlers to come to populate the 'fourth shore', as they called the shores of Libya.

These settlers were the fourth or the fifth group of settlers that had arrived during the rule of Marshal Balbo and he always made a point of making the arrival of new settlers a cause for great celebration, as if he were inaugurating a new era for Italy, which revived the glory of the Roman Empire by occupying the old colonies that had once been the symbol of its power and might.

The brass band played their instruments and sounded the cymbals, and at the same time the steamboat's horn greeted Marshal Balbo, who had arrived in a grand procession preceded by a number of motor cycles. He stood in an open car and raised his arm in the Fascist salute to the crowds that hailed him, Italy and their leader Mussolini.

Marshal Balbo got out of the car and walked along the red carpet surrounded by his aides and camera flashes. He made for the ship in order to receive the first group of passengers who had descended from the steamer, in order to welcome them to the new land. Then he and a number of his guests moved to the dais for the opening ceremony of the celebrations. He began by delivering an enthusiastic speech about the new Libya that embodied the dream of the Fascist Party and its leader Mussolini. He declared that past glories would be regained and that a Greater Italy would rise and lead the world in the march to progress and civilization.

He welcomed the Italian settlers to their new homeland and promised them a life full of prosperity. He commended the efforts of the companies that had made the land arable, built modern villages, and established farms for the settlers. He urged them to do their utmost to populate the land and build a prosperous future for themselves, their children and grandchildren. He added that their success would bolster Italy's pride and confirm their great leader's confidence in them, after he had granted them the opportunity to live and work in this land over which the Italian flag fluttered.

Marshal Balbo didn't forget to mention the Libyans, whom he referred to as the original sons of Libya, and who would reap the fruits of civilization and the renaissance projects that would guarantee them prosperity and happiness after their country had been annexed.

An ageing Italian poet came after Balbo's speech, and recited a poem about the Italian pioneers who had come from Mother Italy and left their homes and families to establish a cultural extension of Italy in Libya. He said that they had come to build modern buildings on the fourth coast, and to loosen the soil and extract its hidden treasures, fulfilling the summons of their inspired leader, who would always remain an "unsetting sun".

Marshal Balbo told the newcomers to go out among the people, to acquaint themselves with the streets and squares in Tripoli, where kiosks that distributed drinks and snacks had been installed, courtesy of the local Italian community to their newly arrived brethren. A number of pretty Italian school girls waited upon the newcomers and upon every person who attended the celebration. Balbo then asked one of the priests to lead the crowds in a short prayer for Italy to close the celebration's ceremonies.

Houriya left the celebration in a state of extreme delight and spoke to her friend enthusiastically about the atmosphere of friendship the Marshal had created between Italians and Libyans. She then addressed you in Arabic as you drove her back home saying, "Did you hear the Marshal when he addressed the Libyans and declared that he wished that Libya be a place of happiness that would be shared by the original Libyans and the new Libyans, so that all would benefit from the fruits of progress and civilization?"

You allowed yourself a smile that Houriya couldn't see from the back seat and said to yourself that you would like her to be a witness to the promises that Balbo had made to the Libyans, because you would ask for your share of the happiness and benefits of the fruits of progress and civilization. You didn't want to find yourself cast away and imprisoned on one of the ships that would take you to your death in Abyssinia.

You told her, aloud this time, that you would do your best to fulfil the Marshal's wish to achieve your share of happiness that he had invited the original inhabitants of the land to enjoy. And as she had done many times before, Houriya opened her silver-coloured handbag and gave you ten francs to spend in the festive atmosphere that enveloped the town. She also told you that she would not didn'tneed you for the rest of the day.

You loitered in the noisy streets where Italian music was playing, and where young men and women were dancing. However, you felt no joy, because you didn't belong to this worldwasn't. You couldn't even partake of the food or the drinks that were offered, since three quarters of the drinks were alcoholic and the meat wasn't halal and was hadn'tmostly ham and bacon.

You had no place here. This was the world of the Italians who had come to settle your land. They alone would reap the happiness and pleasure, and in spite of what Balbo had said, there could be no shared happiness between the Libyans and the Italians. It didn't surprise you that no Libyans participated in these celebrations, despite the fact that they were open to the public, and despite the dire need of the poor and hungry for the drinks, sweets, and snacks that were distributed free of charge. They understood that it was not their celebration, but the celebrations of another people that had come from across the sea in successive waves to pull the earth from under their feet.

Your eyes hoped to recognize a familiar face, Italian or Libyan, anyone to lighten your feelings of alienation, but there was no one. You stopped in front of a circle of Italian men and women dancing in the streets, though you weren't bold enough to join them. As the women danced, their breasts swayed, enticing and challenging the men. You would not have minded dancing. But you imagined there was an invisible wall preventing you from joining in, so you just watched them, isolated and alone, apprehensive that someone might come forward and ask you why you were there as you hadn't been weren't invited.

In order to escape these misgivings, you walked through the main streets and squares in the direction of the road that would lead you to the camp of Bumalyana. You were sure that the recruits would be busy with their training exercises after lunch. You longed to rest on your bed all alone in your dormitory, so that you would be able to think of a way that would enable you to stay in Marshal Balbo's service.

A little before reaching the dormitory, Sergeant Antar

met you and said, "Welcome Othman, our representative in higher circles! What's the news?"

"News?"

"News about the forthcoming war in Abyssinia."

"Who said that?"

"The *Tripoli Post* in today's issue, according to the watch guard."

"I'm not at all worried about this war. Let those who are going go. As for me, I'm staying in Tripoli."

"I wish you could get me an exemption from going to this war as well. But how far-fetched! There is no hope for me or for you, since your name comes immediately after my name in the lists of the soldiers going there."

"Thank you for these glad tidings. But I'm going to try forcibly and successfully to exempt myself by any means. You should do the same."

"Save your strength. Such a matter requires the High Commander himself to make an exception, and such an exemption has never been granted to any Italian, so naturally it would never be granted to Libyans. The members of the Fascist Party are the only people who are above the law, as you well know. Are you by any chance Balbo's colleague in the party?"

Sergeant Antar laughed loudly as he made his last remark, but the idea rang loudly in your mind. Membership of the Fascist Party. How had it not occurred to you before to join the party? What Sergeant Antar had said about the extreme difficulty of joining the Fascist Party applied only to the Italians because the examination and selection period was over for them. For whoever had been passed over for membership during his time in Italy, it was impossible for him to become a member after his emigration to Libya.

Perhaps in Italy itself, joining would have been difficult owing to the rigorous testing one had to pass in order to benefit from the authority of the party.

It was a completely different story though for Libyans, because Balbo's policy towards them was based on inclusion and attracting as many as he could. One of his priorities was creating a Libyan cadre for the Party. You had recently read an advertisement in a magazine inviting Libyans to join.

You realized an illiterate person like Sergeant Antar had no idea about these things and although you knew nothing about the party's principles, you didn't need to, because while you had certainly resolved to join the party, you would not do so out of conviction for its aims or beliefs. You intended to join it for one purpose only: to serve your personal interests and to increase your chances of success in work and life.

From what you saw in both the civilian and the military world, a Party member enjoyed a privileged position that made him even more important than his superiors at work. That was what you would also have if you succeeded in joining.

Your efforts to crystallize these thoughts went on for morethan two days. You bought the Arabic newspaper, and listened to the radio during the broadcast in Arabic. You learned that there was a song by the Libyan Fascist Youths that was broadcast along with information about the history and achievements of the Fascist Party. You listened to it from the speaker phones hung from certain buildings in the town, one of which was the clock tower.

You contemplated discussing the matter with Signora Houriya, then decided not to, so that the decision would be your own free will, and not the result of anyone's opinion or encouragement. You found out that the headquarters of the Arab branch of the Party were situated in the Trade Fair next to the RAI broadcasting station, where they interviewed applicants every evening after five o'clock. So the next evening, you finished work early and decided to go to the Party headquarters.

FIVE

You felt hesitant and sceptical about the rationality of what you were about to do, realizing that it was essentially a leap in the dark. Although you were aware of the many advantages you stood to gain, you didn't know what services you would be obliged to perform in exchange.

You passed through an open gate and into a courtyard that resembled a school playground. Above the gate a sign read: "Libyan Fascist Youths". You had begun to have second thoughts when you saw a group of ten-year-old boys in the middle of the courtyard. They were playing and they wore the shorts and black shirt of the Party faithful. You watched them as they stopped playing to assemble in a row and swear the oath of allegiance to Mussolini. They then sang a chant in Arabic about the glory of the Fascist Party and the honour of belonging to it.

You turned your back upon the boys, retracing your steps, abandoning the dreams of the power and glory that could have been yours. From what you had just seen, you realized that you had passed the appropriate age to nurse on Fascist milk.

Suddenly you saw an Italian youth about your age

wearing the Party's black shirt. He asked you if he could be of service. Encouraged by his friendliness, you asked if membership in the Libyan Fascist Youth Party was limited to children, as you'd only seen children in the yard.

The youth replied, "Our hope is that these children's presence will erase the widespread impression in people's minds that we as a party rely on severity and cruelty to carry out our work."

"Yes . . ."

"You work as a driver for the government, as it seems from the uniform you're wearing."

"Yes."

"Have you come to pick up one of the children of a Libyan official?"

The words "Libyan official" rang strangely in your ear. Was there a Libyan within the Italian administration who could be called an important official? Was there truly someone who had penetrated the circles of power and authority, as you dreamed of doing?

You had fancied yourself a pioneer. But you were no longer the first, and all that remained was the dream of being an imitator and a follower of whoever had beaten you to winning the approval of your masters. The Italian youth's statement proved to you that there were in fact Libyans who held high posts in the government, and that it wasn't just a dream. What was even more significant was that they sent their children at a tender age to the centres of power and influence, for they believed that the future of the land would remain in the hands of the Italians. So they had arranged their lives and the lives of their children on this basis. Such people were the epitome of cunning and craftiness and you realized that you should imitate them and follow in their footsteps in order to achieve the same success.

You wanted to ask if these high-ranking Libyan officials were members of the Fascist Party like their children. However, the Italian youth resumed talking about the party and you didn't want to interrupt him. He said that in addition to these "cubs" there was an excellent group of Libyan youths who formed the core of the party in Libya.

As he led you to his office, he explained that joining the Fascist Party was exactly like joining a sports club because here they also trained their members in swimming, horse riding, running, and archery. There were also obviously courses on weapons training for whoever hadn't been previously trained. He gave you a number of pamphlets, some of which were in Arabic and contained facts about the Fascist Party's history and aims. Other booklets contained the Duce's speeches and his analyses of world politics. He also helped you fill in a membership form and told you it would be submitted to the secretariat.

When he learned that, in addition to your work as a driver at the Governor-General's palace, you served in the army and had completed basic military training, he assured you that acceptance of your application would be guaranteed. It would not take as long as other applications that necessitated further investigations. In your case, it was a matter of routine and would only take two or three days. He added that you could consider yourself from that very moment a member of the Libyan Fascist Youths.

As he bade you farewell, the Italian youth didn't forget to congratulate you on the sound decision that had led you to serve the three important spheres in the life of any citizen living in this country: Italy, the great motherland,

Libya the little motherland, and finally one self because of the opportunities for success that being a member would offer. He also informed you of the very good news that Marshal Balbo, in his capacity as the Party's highest official, had exempted all Libyan members of the Party from the membership fees at this stage, in order to encourage Libyans to join the Party.

As you shook hands and bade him farewell you said, "May God reward the Marshal for his kindness to his Libyan brothers."

You weren't naive enough to believe a word about the three issues that the Italian youth had mentioned. You had gone to join the Party knowing full well what you were doing. You hadn't needed anyone to entice or dissuade you, nor did you need this noble pretence of serving the home-lands. All that concerned you were your own interests and ensuring your personal safety.

Joining the Fascist Party would not serve the homeland to which you belonged. All that could be said in such circumstances was what the Prophet Muhammad's grand-father said to Abraha the Abyssinian about the Ka'ba. The homeland was like the Ka'ba, it had a God to protect it. In fact, joining the Fascist Party was condemned from the nationalistic point of view, but who was noble enough these days to serve the cause of the homeland after the whole country had been crushed beneath the heels of the Italian occupation?

Abdel Muttalib, the Prophet's grandfather, had sought to regain his camels and had abandoned the Ka'ba to the Creator's protection. However, the most any Libyan like you could strive for under these conditions was something even more lowly than that. It was to remain alive, merely to survive, so that the Italian Abraha would neither kill him nor drive him to his death, since he could find no food, no medicine if he was ill, and nowhere to hide. You only intended to wear the Fascist badge in order to escape certain death in Abyssinia. That was your only aim.

Your only goal was to remain a driver and have your name stricken off the list of soldiers going to war. Nevertheless, you couldn't be certain that joining the Fascist Party would achieve your hopes. It was a gamble.

You knew the next step you had to take, one that was much more important, although it didn't carry as much heavy political significance as joining the Fascist Party. The next step was to find a way to keep Ayyad al-Fezzany away from his job. That meant you had to find some way to pressure him into staying in Mirzaq. You thought about spreading a rumour that would strike terror in his heart until he thought it unsafe to return to Tripoli. He would be forced to excuse himself from resuming work for Houriya because of critical circumstances that had forced him to remain in his home town.

As soon as this idea flashed through your mind, you went to Abdel Mowlah, whom you found in front of Mizran Mosque. You arranged to meet him the next day at noon in the municipal park. He knew where the people who came from Fezzan gathered and where their travel agency was situated.

He proposed to take you to the travel agency that was near the Tuesday Market where you could find someone who knew al-Fezzany and deliver your message to. You told Abdel Mowlah that such a mission needed someone like him who wasn't connected to your official work. You explained what you wanted him to do.

The message was of the utmost importance and must reach Ayyad al-Fezzany as quickly as possible. As such, he must wait until he found a man who was ready to travel at once to the capital of the south in order to deliver the message to al-Fezzany in person. You suggested that one emissary would not be sufficient, and that he should strive to find many men, so that if one of them failed to give al-Fezzany the message, he would receive it from someone else.

You urged Abdel Mowlah to impress upon the messengers that he would send that the message was extremely confidential and that it must be delivered to Ayyad in secrecy. The contents of the message stated that, owing to the size of the forces mustered by the Abyssinian army to confront the Italian army, the Italians had decided to double the number of military vehicles they would need in the war. The military authorities had issued a command to gather all experienced drivers, especially those who worked in the government, in order to send them to Abyssinia. So in order to save himself from certain death in that far country, Ayyad should remain with his family. He should also think of a good excuse to prevent him from returning and working for the Supreme Commander.

You divided the ten francs that Houriya had given you with Abdel Mowlah and you urged him strongly to leave immediately to carry out this humanitarian mission. You naturally didn't tell him your true motives or the fact that you had fabricated this story to keep Ayyad al-Fezzany away from his work so you could take it. You pretended you were helping a friend whose children faced the possibility of orphanhood or homelessness if he came back to Tripoli. However, by virtue of the ongoing communication and cooperation between you since you had come to the city, the beggar had become attuned to the violent tendencies that wrestled behind your meek appearance, so it wasn't hard for him to discern the nature of the motives hidden behind your humanitarian mission.

The beggar smiled wickedly as he took the five francs and narrowed his small eyes, which had no eyelashes, and said, drawing close to you as though he were examining the look in your eyes, "I want something more important than these measly francs. I want you to find me to work as a doorman or watchman in the Lady's household after you become the permanent driver."

You replied saying, "Go now and remove these suspicions from your mind before they turn into flames and burn you, God willing."

When you laid your head on your pillow that night, you felt pleased with the steps you had taken to ensure your plan's success. Hopes are not fulfilled just by raising two hands in prayer and supplicating God. The prayer has to be supported with the efforts of the supplicant, to prove to God that one deserves His succour. The Prophet Muhammad explained this matter to a Bedouin Arab who wanted to depend upon God to keep his camel safe for him. The prophet had said, "Mind your camel first, then trust in God."

Ever since you entered the crucible of city life, you had learned not to leave matters to chance alone, but that you must do something to turn chance in your favour. Ayyad al-Fezzany's resignation would arrive very soon and your membership of the Fascist Party would become official in the very near future, thus moving you up from the the lower classes to a more fortunate demographic. Reaching such heights was only achieved by a minority of Libyans.

Let your friend Salem say what he pleased in his big, blustering, empty speeches. Everything he said couldn't, in your present conditions, make you feel guilty as you had felt a few hours earlier, when he had approached you in the forest in a fit of rage as if he had been bitten by ten snakes all at once. He had shouted at you without caring if anyone heard what he said about snitches and spies, "Have you really become a member of the Fascist Party?"

You denied having anything to do with that party and had asked him who had told him such a lie.

He answered saying, "There is not a single Libyan who has not heard about the matter. Sergeant Antar told everybody, one by one, to prove how much slime you've covered yourself in."

You had met his rage with cool nerves and tried to extract some laughter from the middle of this storm of fury by saying, "I don't think that joining the Fascist Party in Sergeant Antar's opinion is contemptible, but rather the summit he dreams of reaching. I swear to you that I personally didn't know that I had become a member of the Fascist Party, so how could Sergeant Antar know something about me that I don't know about myself?"

Salem replied, "Don't try to cover the eye of the sun with a sieve. You made an application to join the Fascist Party and they have begun their investigation of you. They asked Sergeant Antar about your obedience to military rules and regulations. They also asked about your loyalty to Italy. Maybe the official who wore the black shirt didn't explicitly say why he had come, but Sergeant Antar was able to sniff out the reason. Afterwards, he came and told us he had praised you for your unwavering loyalty to Italy."

You said, "It's not surprising for Sergeant Antar to say such things about me."

Salem replied slowly in a voice choked with grief, "And I'm no longer surprised by you when you do such shameful things."

He added, "I'm not here to reproach or blame you. I just came to make sure that what I had heard was the truth and I've done that."

He began to walk away but you stopped him and said, "Wait a minute and hear what I've to say."

"I don't want to hear anything and you will never hear another word from me. If you ever happen to see me anywhere, don't greet me because I will not respond."

You stood in his way, but when he refused to stop, you walked beside him and when he quickened his pace, you kept up with him and said, "Be as patriotic and moralistic as you want, it won't change the realities of life that prevent you from being anything other than what they want you to be. You are going with God's Will to Abyssinia. What will you do there? You are going to kill people, whom you have never met, between whom and yourself there is no cause and no hatred. Their only crime is that they are defending their homes and villages against the invaders. You will kill as many of them as you can because if you don't, they will kill *you* and you will die a filthy, undignified death. You have no choice, O honourable man, to kill innocent people like a criminal! What do morality and patriotism say about this? It is true that you are being forced into this war but that does not cancel out the immorality of your actions. That is why I insist that anything a person like me does to avoid going to the war, however disgraceful that may be, is not as disgraceful or as sinful as participating in the war. Can you understand now why I applied to join the Fascist Party? I don't know anything about Fascism and its cursed Party that could tempt me to join. All I know is its ugly side, the side that wiped out half our country. The only reason I want to join is because it is the lesser evil. I've accepted miring myself in a bog that reaches up to my neck, so that I would not drown in a bog that would reach past my head and kill me, burying me in its stench and filth. Now do you understand why I behaved as I did?"

Salem replied, "I only know one thing. That there is no hope for you and that there will be no end to the path you have chosen."

After Salem left, you weren't angry with him for what he had said, nor were you angry with yourself. You knew that Salem was a pure, naive boy who had come from Awlad Al Sheikh without abandoning his village morals. It would not be long before he would run up against the hard facts of reality, that like rocks would draw blood and convince him the world he lived in hadn'thing to do with the ideals he had learned at the village mosque.

SIX

When you returned to the dormitory that night, all the recruits refused to talk to you, avoiding you with their noses in the air. You would greet them and they would ignore you. Despite how unusual it was, you thought it was unintentional. So you repeated your greetings and asked if anyone had seen Sergeant Antar, not because you wanted to know where he was, but because you wanted to ascertain what had made them all decide to shun you.

When you were sure that Sergeant Antar had told them about your application for membership of the Fascist Party, you were amazed at the behaviour from such a group of wretches subjected to a life of misery and oppression. Every last one of them presumed to be noble and patriotic, forgetting the muddy ground they walked, sat, and slept on. They had taken this rumour from Sergeant Antar as an opportunity to demonstrate that they were more honourable and more patriotic than you. You wanted to curse them: curse the land upon which they stood, the roofs of the houses that had sheltered them and the parents that had begotten them.

However, you controlled yourself so as not to validate

their actions. You switched off the dormitory lights and stretched out on your bed. You decided that the best reaction would be to laugh mockingly. Yes, the difference between you and them was very wide, they warranted only laughter, so you chuckled loudly to make them understand that their behaviour was a mere joke as far as you were concerned.

In fact that is exactly what they were. They had all mocked something that none of them had the power or daring to attempt. They were all pusillanimous cowards, and on top of that, they turned their cowardice into a source of pride. They shunned you to prove that they were gallant and noble, when the truth was quite to the contrary. You had refused to be one of the herd to which they belonged and chosen a different path to save yourself from a dreadful fate.

You laughed loud and long and your laughter reverberated in the dark dormitory. There was no response to your laughter, but it seemed to lift the heaviness in your heart caused by Salem's stinging rebukes and your barracks-mates' silent treatment. You placed your head upon the pillow and felt a deep tranquility, like you had felt when you had decided to join the Party of the strong. You did what you did of your own free will and for your own well-being with justifiable motives. It had been a plan blessed by the angels of God, because you wanted to put yourself beyond the reaches of harm.

You were still in charge of the dormitory and you could easily have found an excuse to punish your barracks-mates, but any report would go through Sergeant Antar first, and they might have conspired with him against you. You decided to leave matters as they were until a better opportunity presented itself.

The following morning, the chain of events unfolded so quickly it robbed you of all assurances and brought everything to the brink of collapse. Orders were issued to your base to prepare for deployment to Abyssinia in three days, and steps had been immediately taken to carry out the order. When you tried to leave the camp, you were prevented from passing through the gates since no one was permitted to leave before having been examined and vaccinated. There was a medical committee that had begun its work inside the base, wanting to finish quickly so it could move on to the other military camp at Tajura.

You could do nothing apart from submit to your orders and you told those responsible to vaccinate you quickly because you had work to do at the Governor-General's palace, realizing that every hour that passed weakened your chances of finding a way out. Half the day passed before you were able to leave, which meant that one of the three days was almost over without your having done anything.

You went quickly to work hoping to make use of the rest of the day. You rushed up the steps of Houriya's house and knocked on the door. Hawaa hesitated before allowing you to enter as Signora Houriya was still taking her bath. You pushed her aside and told her that you had some very important news that couldn't wait. You sat in the hall, wracked with worry, unable to steel your nerves or stop fidgeting. You suddenly jumped to your feet as you heard the voice of the lady of the house asking you about the nature of the breaking news you had come to give her.

Shock kept you tongue-tied when you saw her standing in the hall like this. For the first time she had done away with formality between you two and had come straight from the bathroom wrapped only in a bath towel that covered part of her body and left other parts of her body bare, glistening with light that overwhelmed your heart, blinded your eyes and paralysed your faculty of thought. She realized that you were unable to utter a word so she asked you to be seated and took a seat opposite you. The towel slipped off one of her thighs. It stopped only a short distance above the knee but the sight of it stunned you, and all you could see was irresistible temptation.

Houriya repeated her question about the nature of this urgent news, but what news could be more significant than this awesome power? Was it possible for the naked thigh of a beautiful woman to induce someone to faint? That was what you felt like as you tried to get hold of yourself. You turned your face from her glowing body and the seductiveness of her shapely thigh, and in panting breaths you told her about the preparations being made for the army's departure within three days. You added that you were among those who had been vaccinated against the diseases endemic to Abyssinia, because your name was on the roster of those scheduled to depart.

You couldn't understand why she smiled when she heard the news, or why nothing changed in her relaxed appearance. You reminded her again of the causes for distress.

"No more than three days remain. Only three days." You fixed your eyes on her, begging, pleading. All she said was, "Three days is a very long time, if you didn't know."

Houriya stood up, dried her hair with the towel and walked away. You couldn't understand her last sentence. Did she mean she wanted you to remain in her service as her driver and would postpone your departure? Did that also mean any postponement would only be for as long as she needed you as her driver, or did it mean that you had been exempted from the war as you had hoped?

You wondered about the strong emotion that had violently shaken your very being when you had seen her coming out of the bathroom. Before her, you had felt like a piece of paper in a storm. You were certain that it wasn't just a natural male reaction to her beauty, nor the effect of the elements of seduction that had been present in the scene. It wasn't because of your admiration for the woman, whose beauty had always dazzled you. It wasn't just that as soon as you had seen a naked part of her body, your senses had been aroused and your admiration had increased, transforming into lust for the body itself. What had happened was more than that, something that could only be compared to a state of illness. The sweat that poured from your body, the trembling that shook it, in addition to a feeling of dizziness, were but symptoms of a disease.

Four weeks had passed since you had begun to work as Houriya's driver, during which time the duties of your new job distracted you from sexual sustenance, despite the agreement you had made with Nuriya to visit her every week. You were now among the soldiers going to war, unless you were to be exempted, and that meant that you had to behave accordingly and pay farewell visits to all your friends, whom you might never see again.

Because your meeting with Houriya had happened in such a provocative manner, it had put you in a state of sexual arousal, so you decided that Nuriya be the first person you should visit, not only to satisfy your passions, but also because she – more then anyone else in the city – symbolized pleasant times for you. Her room was the only place where you could find pleasure without any disturbances, and so she deserved to be the first person on your list. You would say goodbye and thank her for her kindness.

The next important person on the list was Thuraya, not because she meant less to you than Nuriya. On the contrary, she was far more exquisite, more beautiful, and the dearest to your heart. But your sexual urges were more pressing. As for the calls of love, they were more enduring and everlasting. Thuraya was a source of hope and happiness in your life, but a terrible sense of deprivation gripped you every time the vision of this woman appeared and occupied the corners of your memory. Would all this have happened if Fathy hadn't beaten you to her?

Only a day before, Signora Houriya had asked you why you hadn't married at an early age according to the custom. The occasion for the question had been when you were taking her to attend her Italian friend's engagement party that had been held at an Italian club close to the Ghazala Theatre.

"People from the countryside usually marry early. What caused your break with custom?"

"It wasn't meant to be," you said.

"What about in the future?"

"It's in God's hands. Going to war does not give one the opportunity to think about things like this."

"So everything is put off until you return from the Abyssinia campaign."

"That is, if there is a return."

Houriya said, "The military estimates it will only go on for two or three weeks because there is no comparison whatsoever between the might of the Italian and Abyssinian forces."

You were alone in the car with Signora Houriya on

the way to the party. She wore a black glittering evening dress that hung loosely over her body down to her feet. She wore one large pearl on a necklace against her throat, and her hair was gathered up like a crown which was studded with a gold brooch with shining gems that augmented Houriya's glowing beauty. When one of the club attendants invited you and other drivers to have a cold drink to celebrate the engagement, you even felt proud that this woman, who shone like a jewel among the cream of Italian society, was Libyan like you.

On your way home, Houriya asked you to drive slowly on the promenade so she could smell the sea breeze on that beautiful Spring night. Although she had only exchanged a few words with you about the subject of marriage, you felt that there was something else to it, that she had wanted to say something, but felt unable to do so. Perhaps it might have had to do with her affair with Marshal Balbo and she had felt the urge to confide to someone of her own nationality, someone she could trust. Perhaps she hadn't found anyone but you, and when she thought about it, she remembered that your relationship did not permit her to confide in you so intimately.

That had happened just the previous day and now she appeared before you today, wearing only a bath towel and baring areas of her translucent, glass-like skin to tell you another line of this mysterious message that she had decided to reveal to you in instalments. The question had taken you by surprise, coming from a charming, refined woman like Houriya. If you had a chance to marry a woman like her you would marry her today, even if the departure to Abyssinia were tomorrow. One night in her embrace would be worth a lifetime.

But, be careful, take care, beware of letting your eyes stray to the possessions of the high and mighty. You would have no one to blame but yourself if they pitilessly crushed you under their heels. After a while, the time would come for you to go and see Nuriya. That blessed woman who slept with you like lovers would, as though you weren't just another customer. Let Nuriya be the highest pleasure you aspired to in these dark times.

You hadn't imagined anyone would consider going to fight a war in Abyssinia cause for happiness, until you heard Mukhtar, the garage guard, say, "You should rejoice, Othman, because the day for which you have waited so long has arrived and going to war in Abyssinia has finally become a reality after being only a hope for so long. "

"What on earth are you talking about, old man? Has fighting in the war in Abyssinia suddenly become everybody's dream? For God's sake how does this make any sense?"

"My dear son Othman, how could it not make sense? God has opened wide the gates of prosperity for you and for the other lucky young men."

You had previously heard talk about raising the wages of soldiers once they reached the front, but you hadn't paid much attention to the matter, nor had you asked about the details. Did this rise truly warrant examination?

"What prosperity are you talking about?"

"During training, you only get thirty francs every month, right? Imagine that this amount will multiply not two times, or three times, but more than ten times over when you are at war. And if you prove your bravery, you will get pay rises and promotions, and you will be able to save up all the money you get because you will not have to spend any of it on food, clothes, or rent."

He concluded his enthusiastic speech with, "So what if the campaign continues for four or five years, imagine the fortune you stand to make. You will be richer than the countess herself."

The amount of money that Mukhtar had mentioned was a very great amount indeed, and you had been completely ignorant of its existence. Yet you wondered at the man's unbridled enthusiasm, so you said, "Don't forget, Uncle Mukhtar, we are talking about a war and the odds of dying in a war are often greater than the chances of surviving it."

Mukhtar didn't pay any attention to what you had said, nor to your disapproval. He considered what you said an appropriate opportunity to wax eloquent about the benefits of going to war.

"If you die in the war, your death will be a source of livelihood for your family for the rest of their lives. They will bid farewell to poverty forever, God Willing, because a monthly pension of half your salary will be sent to them for many years, according to the law."

The man continued to calculate the number of years during which the monthly pension would be paid, which differed between a man who had been single and a man who left behind a widow and children. If he were single, his father and mother would be the beneficiaries of the pension, except for a third that would support his brothers and sisters.

You interrupted him saying, "You seem to be quite an expert in the matter of pensions, as if they had put you in charge of dispensing these pensions. How exactly did you learn all this?"

"I learned all these facts from an Italian guard who

comes here with Marshal Balbo and became a good friend." He added that the advantages of fighting in the Abyssinia campaign had tempted him to join the army, and he asked the Italian guard to recommend him for civilian work in the army, as a construction worker or kitchen hand, or even in the warehouses where animal fodder was stored, for he had been brought up in a pastoral Bedouin society.

Even though the Italian guard had promised to help him, Mukhtar had, owing to his old age and aching bones, changed his mind and abandoned his dream of becoming rich, contenting himself with the sustenance that God had destined for him in his own land. He had said to his Italian friend the same thing that the mouse in the popular parable had said. The mouse, who lived in a barbershop, had come out of his hole tempted by a friend who led him to a food and supplies store filled with milk, olives, cheese, and butter. So he said to his friend, who was eventually caught in one of the traps set up in the store, "I happily lick the leather strap the barber wipes his razor on. Living in a barbershop is a thousand times better than being killed in a store of milk and cheese."

Mukhtar, the garage guard, was about sixty and had come to Tripoli six years ago. He had spent three years in the concentration camps, where he had lost his family: his mother, his wife, and three children. After he was released, he worked as a labourer for an Italian contracting company and had participated in the final stages of cthe building that housed Houriya's apartment. As he had no home and no family in Tripoli, he lingered on as the building's watchman. He lived all alone in the room in the garage and guarded the entrance of the building and the cars in the garage at night.

His eyes brimmed with tears every time he spoke about his internment in the camp and recalled its painful repercussions. He said in a bitter tone, "May God forgive Sidi Omar."

He meant the martyr Omar Al Mukhtar and when you first met him you had asked him questions, the answers to which had shocked you.

"Do you blame Sidi Omar for what happened to you?" "What befell us befell us during his leadership."

You were stunned by his answer and replied, "Curse Satan, man! Do you blame Sidi Omar for what the blood-thirsty Graziani did to you?"

"How can I blame an enemy who I know from the very start has come to torture the people of my land? I blame the person who should have been foremost in averting the hardships we suffered yet didn't care about us."

"Did Omar Al Mukhtar do anything other than defend our land and honour?"

"He was the source of all the suffering. All because he defended our land and honour. As you mentioned, Graziani's army confiscated our cattle, destroyed our homes and drove us all to concentration camps full of death, anguish and disease, keeping us as hostages until the rebellion ended. However, Omar Al Mukhtar refused to end his rebellion, so no hostages were released. We wrote him letters, begging him to save us from the camps and explain what suffering the women and children had endured. If he didn't want to sign a treaty with the Italians, we entreated him to flee Libya, just as the other leaders of the resistance had done, because there was no longer any gain to be had from his war, only more pain, oppression, and death for our people."

You defended the legendary freedom fighter by saying, "Don't forget he died a martyr."

"He wanted to be a martyr so he could be forgiven by God, while we paid the price through our families who perished, our houses that were destroyed and our lives that were ruined by the stubbornness of an old man of seventy." You enjoyed pestering a man of divided loyalties like Mukhtar the garage guard. Although the Italians had killed his family, he had accepted the fact and lived as their servant. You had found a copy of the elegy by Ahmed Shawqi on the martyr Omar Al Mukhtar. You had sat down to learn it by heart and could find no better place to recite it than Mukhtar's garage:

"O sword, unsheathed in the desert!
Over time swords wear their sharpness,
You had to choose, so you chose shelter rather than the mat.
You didn't win fame, nor gather riches."

Although he only understood a word or two of what you said, Mukhtar nodded his head in agreement saying, "God have mercy on Sidi Omar's soul! He was a man unlike any other."

"Don't you blame him for the tragedies that your family went through?"

"Yes, I blame him, and I'll continue to blame him, but that doesn't mean he wasn't our greatest champion."

Mukhtar liked to reminisce and you never tired of listening because his playful sense of humour melted the bitter sadness. Had it not been for his sense of humour, he would have made haste to re-unite with his family many years ago.

There had been no food in the concentration camp and each captive family had been forced to plan their lives around a handful of barley that was hardly enough to feed the children, let alone the adults. When you asked him how he had been able to survive in such circumstances and what he had eaten to stay alive, he said that the delicious plates full of rice he had eaten at night had kept him alive.

When you had stared at him dumbfounded and asked him where these plates full of rice had come from, he said laughing, "The divine mouthwatering rice that God's angels presented to the hungry in their dreams. That food alone kept me alive."

For there is an old Arabic proverb that says people who sleep soundly have eaten rice pudding with the angels.

SEVEN

You were relieved to learn Signora Houriya didn't require your services that evening, so you gave the car keys to Mukhtar and left. After all of Mukhtar's chattering about the riches those who fought in the war stood to gain, you still wanted to escape that fate by any and all means, even if that meant employing deceit, as you had attempted with Ayyad al-Fezzany, Houriya's permanent driver. Your last resort would be to seek assistance from Houriya, who could be of aid to you as the woman closest to the Governor-General.

It was time for you to bid farewell to those who needed sorrowful farewells, so that news of your departure for the battlefield didn't catch them unawares. You wished you could visit your family in Awlad Al Sheikh which, despite your dislike of it and your escape, still occupied a special niche in your heart that no other place could take.

Since there wasn't enough time for you to go to your village, you should at least bid farewell to the people you knew in Tripoli, the city where you had fled to seek refuge. It was in Tripoli where, despite all your suffering, you had found friends, a job, and compassionate hearts. You would bid farewell to everyone you had met in Tripoli, and through them you would be taking leave of your homeland, whose sun had withdrawn behind the dark clouds of the occupation, whose lands had been pulled out from under the feet of its true owners.

But despite the wounds, the dark clouds, and the stolen, scorched earth, it was still your homeland. You didn't have any other homeland, and more than being stone, tree and earth, it was people, hearts, and emotions. It was the ancestors who died and left their breath lingering in the air, and their blood and bones mixed in the earth.

In your mind, the sum of all this formed the outlines of this country called Libya. The homeland, in your moments of despair and frustration, seemed to have abandoned you. In such moments, you considered the interests of the smaller entity, the self, as independent and separated from the larger interests of the homeland, an entity you cared nothing for, using the justification that you hadn'thing to give it, and it hadn'thing to give you ever since it had fallen beneath the hooves of the invaders' horses. It had fallen, and with it the nationalist slogans disappeared, leaving in their wake only enough room for survival and guaranteeing oneself a loaf of bread.

You hadn't joined the Italian army out of faith in their policies, or conviction in the justice of the wars they waged in order to expand their empire. You had come to them hungry, looking for a crust of bread. You had come to them frightened, looking for safety, since all doors had been slammed in your face except two: suicide or joining the army. So you had chosen to join them as an alternative to suicide. How could a youth in your circumstances, who tottered under the burden of poverty and servility, ever have the luxury of being patriotic?

Here you were today, after discovering that what you had done wasn't to escape from suicide but to fall into its trap. In order to escape from the traps of death in the Abyssinia campaign, you had fallen into a more terrifying trap. To use a saying of your mother's, it was as if you had been enclosed within a bitter almond's shell. The whole land of Libya with its plains, deserts, mountains, sky and stars had become a narrow place overflowing with bitterness, just like the bitter almond shell in which Libyans were trapped.

Mukhtar the garage guard blamed the martyr Omar Al Mukhtar for the death of his family, because Omar Al Mukhtar had fought against the Italians until they slew him. Omar Al Mukhtar had died a nationalist hero but sacrificed its spirit. Could anyone blame Mukhtar, who had witnessed the slow death of his family at the hands of the Italians, and who, despite his criticisms, was as much a patriot as Omar Al Mukhtar?

Ramadan al-Suwayhli used Italian funds to recruit ten thousand impoverished Libyan youths to fight with the Italians against their Libyan countrymen. He led them to the battleground in the Al-Qardabiyah wells and waited until just before the attack to reveal his secret plan to join the Libyan resistance and attack the Italian army of which they were a regiment.

That Libyan, who had sold his soul to Satan and marched under the Italian banner, had become a true and loyal patriot despite everything, and had achieved the greatest victory in the history of the Libyan resistance. What kind of a man was he who entered the battle as a traitor to his homeland, but emerged a martyr and one of the most courageous heroes in Libyan history?

The total impotency that affected Libya might forgive a Libyan in your circumstances from having to make the difficult choice that people had had to make just a few years ago. They had had to choose between fighting against the Italians and fighting against their own people. They had all wound up the same, including the heroes who had fought the Italians, for they had been driven out of the country, and they had crossed the borders in order to escape execution.

These heroes of resistance had responded to the pardon that Mussolini issued. They had pushed and shoved to return and find work with the occupation authorities to feed their children.

Nation and country. Every person belongs to a place and a circle of friends and acquaintances. He was born and raised among them. That place and that circle of people are his homeland. At that very moment, two days before your departure for Abyssinia, Nuriya was that homeland. Nuriya, whose dearest hope was to obtain a licence in order to be able to pursue her profession officially, without being hounded and blackmailed, was a Libyan woman. Despite the degradation of her profession no one could deny her identity or her roots, nor her daughter Warda's or her mistress Sheifa's. They all belonged to this homeland.

As for Thuraya, who was the symbol of a thwarted love and an aborted dream, she would always remain, despite the anguish you suffered on her account, the window through which you looked out on the light of your homeland, its air and its happiness. You considered her father, Haj al-Mahdy, the shoemaker who had embraced you with paternal warmth, part of your family and homeland, and you would go take your leave of him as a proxy for bidding farewell to his whole family.

You also would not forget to call on all the people who had passed briefly through your life since your move to Tripoli whether they were in the Shushan Agency or Kushat al-Safar or your uncle al-Sharif who made and sold tea at Bab al-Jadeed. You intended to go and shake hands with every one of them before going to Abyssinia because each one was precious to you and part of your memories of Tripoli. Nor would you forget Abdel Mowlah the beggar, who had been your guide to all the unknown parts of the city, or your co-workers in Houriya's household.

There was Hawaa, who had always offered you delicious pastry and sweets that were unknown in your village and delicious food that not one of your family or your ancestors had even dreamt of. You remembered Morgan the negro boy, who spoke Arabic with an African accent and who had never refused any of your requests even when you had asked him to let you buy the magazines for Signora Houriya, thus giving you a chance to see her more often.

Even Mukhtar, whose burning hatred of Omar Al Mukhtar consumed his whole being, whose memories came out covered with the ash and coals of years past like dough from the ovens of Arab bakeries.

Last but not least was the beautiful, alluring Signora Houriya, a cut of lace that, with all the finery and grandeur around her, represented a part of the multicoloured national tapestry. Even though she lived in the Italian governor's home and slept in his bed, she couldn't be anything other than a Libyan woman as evidenced by the joy in her eyes whenever she heard Marshal Balbo speak of his promise to help the people of her country, to the point that she would repeat his words to others as if they were a song.

You went to Bab al-Jadeed, summoned by a mixture

of duty and desire, hoping that this visit would not be the last between you and this woman who had hosted you at the banquet of her femininity and given you moments of pleasure, the like of which you had never experienced with any other. You arrived at Sidi Umran Street and then branched off to Bahlool Alley and knocked on the blue door with its brass doorknob.

Dragging the weight of her corpulent body, Sherifa came to the door and led you to the room upstairs. She begged you to persuade Nuriya to remain in the house and give up her rash thoughts of leaving her profession. She would never find a more profitable profession especially as her official licence was about to be come through. Sherifa added that a doctor had come to the prostitutes' district and examined all the women in the house, and all of the other requirements for a woman to become official had already been met, one of which was that a woman had to be apprehended in the act with a man more than once. Sherifa said that fortunately, rather than the two required times stipulated by the government, all the women had been caught in indecent situations more than five or six times.

Sherifa added that Nuriya was the star of the house, who always attracted the wealthiest customers, so if she was so popular despite working secretly, she would be a thousand times more popular when she worked openly under the auspices of the government. You knew that Nuriya was the goose that laid the golden egg for the mistress of the house, but Sherifa had another motive behind this chatter besides pressuring Nuriya to stay. She wanted to distract you a while until Nuriya finished with the customer who was with her.

However, when news of your arrival was passed on to
Nuriya, she turned out her customer, who angrily protested,
demanding to be refunded the price he had paid in advance.

Nuriya came like a hurricane, dragged you away from
Sherifa and pushed you into her room. She shouted at you
for leaving her for over a month in spite of your agreement
to visit her once every week. As you went into her room,
you learned that she had gone looking for you at the Italian
military bases, even though she had known nothing about
you other than your first name, Othman. Everyone she
asked sneered at her saying they didn't know which Othman
she meant.

Nuriya had finally remembered your Italian friend
Mario, so she had gone to the government garages and had
only managed to find him the previous evening. He had
told her where your camp was and your barracks number,
so she had gone there and had been informed that visitors'
day was the following day.

You listened to this mad woman in astonishment, hardly
believing that she had actually looked for you in all those
places. You couldn't understand what was behind these
furious outbursts, which she directed at you simply for not
coming to visit her in the secret brothel for three or four
weeks. She continued to rebuke you, so you interrupted
her in a rage equal to her own and asked her why she had
done all this to find you, and what could she possibly want
by defaming you among your fellow soldiers.

The violent desire that had driven you to her house
dissipated and the only thing on your mind was the burning
question about what this woman could want from you
when all that connected you to her were the minutes of
pleasure that she sold to you for a fixed price. Once those

minutes were over and you gave her those dirhams, it put an end to any obligation you had towards her. There was no excuse for her to go all over the city looking for you.

You made the matter quite clear to her so as to dispel any delusions she might have, but that further kindled her emotions and she burst into tears, throwing herself into your arms. You kept her close until she calmed down, then pushed her away from you and sat her on the bed. You asked her to tell you what had happened. She pulled out a filled every corner of her heart. Her love for you increased after her daughter Warda had met you, for she too had loved you and grown attached to you like a girl to her father. Because she couldn't accept following this path or life in this district, she had felt that her love for you was a shining light in her heart, bringing her tidings of a life of purity. She had heard a call from the heavens, telling her to repent sincerely and move away, to live beside the man she loved in order to devote her life to him, to her daughter, and to the child she would bear him.

She had wanted to tell you all this, so she had waited for your next visit week after week, and with every day she had grown more distressed, because she hated living in this place. She wanted to leave as quickly as possible in order to live with the only man she had ever loved. This is what had compelled her to search for you however she could, because she had arranged everything for you and her future life, including the place you would live and the money that you would both need in your new life together.

You could hardly believe your ears, because during your meetings with Nuriya, you had never even hinted at any kind of commitment between you and her other than within the limits of her profession. She was just a woman who sold fun times to customers, and you didn't know what had planted such a notion in her head. She even spoke of the decision she had made to commit herself to you in a way that didn't leave you room for discussion, as if she expected your response to be one of happiness and joy that out of all the men in the world, she had chosen you to be the foremost and best man in her life, and the second father to her daughter.

You didn't want to shock her by telling her your true feelings, that you utterly refused such an arrangement, that you only made love to satisfy a physical, bodily need which you knew to be an unquestionable sin, and that afterwards you always prayed and asked for God's forgiveness, begging Him to guide and forgive you. Instead, you told her that you would have agreed to her proposal had you not been bound by the strictest military laws that neither left you time for marriage nor allowed you the luxury of living away from your base and its ironclad rules.

Nuriya thought you were just making excuses to save yourself the embarrassment of marrying a woman with a past like hers, so she quickly said a legal marriage wasn't necessary for she understood that such a marriage would cause you a lot of problems, with your family steeped in village values and traditions. She wasn't interested in marriage so much as she was interested in being with you and no other, enveloped together in a house filled with love. She said it as if she were presenting a magical solution that would nullify the excuses preventing you from accepting her offer. After this concession, there was no longer a reason to justify preventing this union of bodies and souls.

It was truly a generous offer from a woman in love. Any youth in your circumstances would have been delighted with it, but you had to be cruel to her, and to yourself, and refuse this kind offer.

You hadn't wanted to excuse yourself by telling her about your imminent departure to the war in Abyssinia two days from now, because if your efforts to remain in Tripoli succeeded, nothing would prevent her from reappearing and expecting a commitment from you. However, you were forced to use this excuse because the highly emotional way she treated the topic required an excuse convincing enough to close the discussion for good.

With Nuriya expressing her feelings in a flood of tears, the only way out of your predicament was to talk about war, death and the frightening journey to the unknown parts of Africa as the reason for separating and going different ways. It was a separation that you would insist on from now on, from this very moment, because with a woman like this there was no other option but to decide the matter conclusively, definitively, otherwise she would persist in pursuing you andeventually ruin your life.

You told her that your departure for Abyssinia in two days was the overriding reason preventing you from realizing the dream of spending your life with her. You insisted that she forget you from that moment on, because it would be useless to wait for your return. You hoped she would have the good fortune to find a better man than you, someone whom she could love and would love her, so they could build their future nest together.

The poor woman wept bitterly and kept repeating, "It's not possible, it's not possible." You didn't understand what she meant and wondered what she meant. She buried her head in the pillow and continued to cry.

You seized the opportunity to escape and left the house

as quickly as you could, pretending not to hear her calling you back. You truly wanted to escape from the tense atmosphere that Nuriya had created, even though you had come here burning with desire for her before you had seen the sad state she was in. You decided to end your relationship with her even if you remained in Tripoli. Sex would not be an issue, as you had discovered several other avenues.

EIGHT

You had reached a crossroads. You would either go to the war in Abyssinia to begin a new stage in your life, or you would get the exemption you wanted, at which point you would be able to think about settling down and starting your own family, like everyone else your age who had a steady income.

There was no problem about finding a girl you could marry because, as far as you were concerned, after having lost Thuraya, all women were alike. You had intended to visit her immediately, to bask in the sight of her eyes and bid her father farewell. But you were tense and grieved by what Nuriya had done, and you hoped that her madness would go no further. So you decided to visit Thuraya another time, perhaps the following day or the day after that, so that it would be at an unspoiled juncture suitable for experiencing the splendour and sweetness of a woman like Thuraya.

Perhaps it was best for you to go to her until your fate had been decided. You would either go to bid Thuraya and her family farewell if you were destined to go to Abyssinia, or you would celebrate your remaining hours in Tripoli with her. You didn't want to go back to the base early, because you hated finding yourself sitting inside it, facing a handful of the scoundrels ignoring you and circulating rumours about you. It would be best if you didn't return until they were all deep in a nightmarish slumber, for what sort of dreams could visit a person about to be driven to fields of death, blood, and gunpowder?

You would avoid getting into any conflicts with them since you would soon be separated, and the companionship of sharing residency in one barracks was near its end. You would look for any place to spend these two remaining hours before bedtime. It would not be hard to spend them loitering in the streets. As you left the narrow alleys of the old city, you saw the arches and domes of the Musheer Market and you remembered the Eastern café situated in the centre of the market.

You had driven Houriya to that café for a dinner party, but hadn't had a chance to see the café from the inside. You had passed it several times and had stood outside its doors looking at the photographs of the singers and the musicians featured in the café's programmes. You had been apprehensive of entering the café because it was a place for foreign tourists or Italian settlers wanting to experience an oriental evening, people with money and important positions. You didn't belong among these people.

The image of Musheer Market was incomplete without this café. It was an ancient market that had been rebuilt by the Italian authorities in the eastern style, giving it an architecture representative of the spirit of the city with its desert character and its Islamic heritage.

The shops in the market specialized in making local handwoven carpets and rugs, embroidering headscarves and tablecloths, engraving plates, bowls, and picture frames. There were horse saddles and bridles in traditional colours and souvenirs made from palm fronds and sugar cane stalks. There were also stores that made and decorated mock-rugs, pillows, and cushions. There were looms for weaving silk cloth for men's and women's clothing, and craft shops for making trinkets in gold, silver and ivory, or Arab musical instruments of all kinds.

So a tourist coming to Tripoli would not only see the modern Italian city and the old Arab quarters in all their poverty and abandon. Instead, that tourist would also see the new buildings that represented the East with their attractive colours and the distinct aroma of its traditional wares, all of which were ready to meet the tourist's needs and satisfy his curiosity.

Unlike the shops in King Victor Emanuel Street, Cathedral Square, or Italy Square, where wine was sold and Western music filled the air for exclusively Italian audiences, the Eastern café had been established with an unadulterated Eastern ambience. It presented the arts of the East through music, dancing and singing that didn't exist in any other place in Tripoli. In order to make this place popular, the colonial administration made a point of holding official banquets on its premises, which incited the owners of the café to employ attendants wearing the traditional uniform of cavalrymen consisting of a black robe brocaded with gold and silver thread.

You went up the few marble steps in Musheer Market that led to the picturesque hall, covered by domes pierced with small scattered stained-glass windows. You found your-self in a hall that resembled the halls of the palaces of Eastern kings. The floor was covered with white and green ornamental tiles, and also surrounded by a frieze of shining brown marble. The walls were decorated with small mosaic panels that had been brought from the ruins of ancient cities, and murals that bore the decorations and designs for which Islamic art was famous.

Electric lamps and chandeliers hung from the ceiling of the hall. Their light reflected off the ornamental tiles and the decorations on the walls, giving the place a dreamy atmosphere that made it seem thousands of miles away from the poor slums that were covered with the dust and rust of the years. To accentuate this lofty mythical atmosphere, a large fountain had been placed in the centre of the hall. A ring of flower pots surrounded the fountain, and the branches of the flowering plants added to the beauty of the dancing arcs of water. The water made a low, constant sound like the pushing and pulling of gentle Gulf Stream waves, which worked in strange harmony with the sound of hammers coming from the goldsmiths' workshops and craftsmen's stores that stayed open into the early hours of night.

Most of the closed shops had left their store windows lit to display their wares. Before doing anything else, you went to one of the small fountains in the four corners of the market, which aside from adding aesthetic value, also served a practical purpose for visitors to the market who wanted to quench their thirst with the sweet waters that came from the wells of Bumalyana. You drank your fill, and felt that your presence among these beautiful surroundings – and quenching your thirst with these pure waters – had washed away the irritation that had burdened you just a while earlier.

This particular spot in Tripoli made you proud of belonging to this city and brought to mind the glory of your country's Libyan, Arab, and Islamic heritage as embodied in the arts and crafts before you. It was the issue of the homeland once again, but from a different perspective. This was what you had come searching for, its hidden face behind the clouds of occupation, fumbling about for a clear vision of it through the mist and haze, looking for the people you knew, the places you were familiar with, even the prostitutes' district and one of its women.

Here it was, the face of the homeland, shining and sparkling, assuming a clearer and more beautiful form, taking on a scent, a colour and a voice. Perhaps the anxiety about your coming departure for Abyssinia had led you here unconsciously to fill your lungs with the spirit of your ancestors, who had ingeniously fashioned these methods and tools for their lives. Through their innovations in the arts of arabesques and ornamentation, you felt these artists had devoted an excessive amount of time to arts like these which had no immediate purpose, provided no sustenance, and met no vital needs.

You realized that in addition to time, talent, artistic temperament and mental capacity, certainly there had also been an abundance of food from the earth to meet everyone's needs before they could draw their attention to things besides earning a living. That had all been before people became so numerous that they crowded the face of the earth, and the first priority became the fight to survive at the expense of art and culture.

You stood in front of the shop windows for a long time, gazing at all the different kinds of beauty therein, relics of your people's heritage, hoping to hone from them the necessary resolve to face the momentous events that threatened your life.

You made a final decision to enter this place of

entertainment, which you had always considered above your social status. Yet when you asked about the price of the ticket, you found it was only five francs. You bought the ticket and entered the hall, which was neither a saloon nor a theatre, restaurant, or a café, as its name deceptively indicated, but rather it was a combination of all these things, with some additional element that was difficult to pin down. It was something in the atmosphere.

The place was not brightly lit, nor was it dark, but there was an even distribution of light and darkness such that the light cast a bright rectangle in the middle of the hall and the darkness withdrew to the many corners and nooks on the upper and lower levels, for the customers who sought out this darkness for the sake of privacy while they sat with one of the hostesses.

The place was neither wide nor narrow because its wide breadth was encircled by corners, screens, and curtains that gave every customer accompanied by one of the café's female artists a false sense of privacy and seclusion with the woman he wanted, despite the noisiness of their surroundings and the other customers. At the same time, these nooks and crannies gave the place a sense of spaciousness. It was neither crowded nor empty, and despite the fact that the tables were occupied, other tables were brought out whenever a new customer entered.

The walls of the café were lined with wooden arabesques with their rich traditional patterns, enhancing the locale's Eastern appearance. Most of the seats were in the form of wooden benches that rose a few inches above the floor, covered by cushions and throw rugs. The tables were of a similar height and resembled the low round tables where traditional sectors of society used to eat.

Under the circle of light in the place reserved for artistic shows seven musicians appeared. They comprised the Eastern orchestra and wore the Libyan national garb which consisted of a shirt, the embroidered trousers and a red headdress with black threads. A plump woman stood singing in front of the band. She wore a dress that revealed her shoulders and part of her chest. Perspiration trickled between her breasts, so she wiped it with the handkerchief she always held in her hand, despite the large fans spinning overhead and the small fan of coloured palm leaves that she continually waved. She sang:

> We passed by the date tree and the Dis herb,
> we went too far.
> Regret overtook us,
> oh, if only we had turned back.

The band members repeated the chorus with her, and the sweat, which neither fans of metal nor palm leaf could prevent, gave her breasts a sheen that made them appear more seductive. A waiter informed you she was the renowned wedding singer Masouda al-Rahily, the most famous Libyan singer to come from Jews' Alley.

> Pour your honey, well of Bumalyana.
> A little girl is sitting by our side.

Songs from the locale, dipped in the melancholy of days past. You sat down next to the bar, not too far from the band. You sipped a cold drink as you listened to the singing and looked at the mixed crowd of Italians, Jews, Maltese and a few tourists wearing the Libyan headdresses and red fezzes that were onm sale outside the café. The multiplicity of spoken tongues created an international clamour, and they repeated clips of the song in parroted Arabic because they didn't understand any of the words. Despite that, they were enjoying what they heard and it created a festive atmosphere that epitomized the meaning of fun and diversion, which was what this place was all about.

You recognized one of the musicians in the band, whom you had known and worked with during your time in Haj al-Mahdy's shop. He had worked in the store of an Italian merchant and had sold you the coloured thread with which the shoes were embroidered. You were delighted to see him because he made you feel more at home in this place. You racked your brain searching for his name until you found it. Numan. Yes, you were, by virtue of your oud-playing friend's presence, no longer a stranger in strange company inside this café, which was anything but a picture of the larger society you were familiar with in Tripoli.

The inhabitants of Tripoli never permitted the intermingling that you saw in this café. Tripoli was a city divided into two halves, each of which was also divided into another two halves, and perhaps these halves were divided further in successive divisions that never ended once they began. One half of society consisted of women imprisoned behind the walls of their homes, and men deprived of a natural life, prisoners themselves within the walls of oppression. Even before this, there was the old, poor, collapsing half hidden within the narrow lanes and muddy alleys. This was the Libyan half that lived in the old city with its guests from long-standing foreign communities of Jews, Maltese, Greeks, Armenians, and Circassians who were themselves separated into many subdivisions.

The other half of the society owned the illuminated shop fronts, the wide streets, and fashionable clothes. This was the Italian half, which also included other foreign minorities that followed their lead, abided by their policies and had chosen to be a part of their administration.

Within the Libyan section of society, one came up against the poverty line. Some were less impoverished than others, and some were more impoverished than others. The Italians knew only the line of luxury and riches, some of them were above the line, sitting atop the peaks of power, wealth, and authority, and others fell into the role of the servant at the feet of his masters, enjoying through them a life of ease.

Between all these categories existed psychological, social, economic, cultural and occasionally religious barriers that begat hatred, prejudice and social or historical grudges as some Libyans described their attitude towards the Italian occupiers. But this place was an island far removed from its surroundings. It was concerned only with its own clamour, which separated it from the noise of the outside world, with all its laws and divisions. In this island, all social classes, nationalities, sects and religions were integrated into one amorphous mess, united by the pleasant atmosphere of entertainment and relaxation.

The time came for the band to take a break, so you waved to Numan. As soon as he saw you, he changed places and quickly came over to welcome you with his glass still in hand. He anxiously asked you how you were, because all he knew about you was that the Italian soldiers had forcibly taken from the shoe shop and made you enlist. He too had been caught in the raid, but the café had managed to get him a postponement that could be renewed every few weeks.

You saw no need to give him a detailed account of what had happened to you after that raid, and instead informed him that you had been trained to drive motor cars and were currently assigned as a military driver, which was what gave you the freedom to go in and out of the base without having to adhere to the officially appointed times. Laughing, you said that if you'd known about the exemption granted to musicians, you would have done everything you could to learn how to play the tambourine or drums long ago, but alas, the chance had passed and the axe had fallen.

Numan beckoned to the waiter to bring you a glass of wine, but you told him that you didn't drink. However, the waiter had hurried off to fill the order before he could hear your objection.

You tried to apologize again, but the oud player stopped you, saying, "Don't be sorry. When that cup of goodness comes I'll drink it myself so long as you wish to deprive yourself of it. And I'll drink a third cup and a fourth. Intoxication is a pricey achievement reached only through diligence and hard work."

After drinking the glass of wine, he said, "These are things that you will understand soon, God Willing, because entering such a place as this is only the first station in a long journey with many stages."

"What is the second stage?"

"In your case, it will be submitting to the temptations of the cup and I'm sure that you will reach that stage in a very short time, God Willing."

"Then what?"

"There are many ranks of exaltedness, and the most sublime rank is attained only by he whose soul becomes pure and whose cup becomes see-through like this cup."

"What rank are you?"

"I'm still at a rank very close to the ground, I like to call it the rank of music. As for the higher ranks, take this example."

He gestured towards one of the café's corners with his hand. You turned your head to follow the gesture and saw an Arab man wearing a fez sitting at a table with a fair-skinned woman. Their table was set with glasses of wine, plates of appetizers, and a candle that lit the man's delicate features. The man seemed refined and in his late sixties. The woman's features were hidden behind a curtain of lustrous chestnut hair that flowed over her shoulders and enveloped the top half of her body. Strands of her hair strayed over her face and concealed it from view.couldn't

Numan continued, "That old man belongs to one of the wealthiest families in Tripoli. He has dedicated his life exclusively to wine and women. He does not work during the day because he stays out all night, then sleeps and does not get up until it is time for the next night's revelries. He has no wife and no children and no problems, because whenever he needs money, he sells some of his land and resumes his life of luxury. You can see him here every night; he is the first to come and the last to leave."

"A man like him should bless his ancestors every minute of his life."

"And we should hail the power and depth of his understanding of the game of existence, for there are people who have inherited wealth and were made miserable by it. Look at the candle on the table in front of him. Next to it you will see a pile of golden lire the same height as its flame. Do you know why?"

You said, "Please, enlighten me."

Numan said, "The time he spends with this woman is measured by how much of the candle has been spent. So the price of the session that lasts until the candle is burnt out equals the pile of gold lire that is as high as the candle. So the price increases or decreases according to the amount of the candle that is used up."

You felt that the price was, by any measure, exorbitant, especially if the man needed a second candle on the same night and even more so if a third candle was needed to light up his home where he and the lady would retire after their evening at the café as Numan told you. That man's life had turned into pure worship of the lord of pleasure and diversion, and Numan thought he had reached the highest rank, which he too hoped to ascend to one day.

The sole question that crossed your mind was, "Who is that woman whose company is worth so much money?" "That woman is Esther, Tripoli's star in the world of love and beauty. She is called the 'bride's bride' in the trade fair's advertisements, because Tripoli is said to be the bride of the Mediterranean, and Esther is the bride of Tripoli, so she is known as the bride's bride. Her star first rose in the city sky a year ago when she succeeded in becoming one of the poster girls for the trade fair and attracted the attention of the prince of the land himself." You asked him in a whisper, "Do you mean Marshal

Balbo?"

"Is there any other prince in the land? Esther is his most recent mistress and has become known as Queen Esther to the point that this name follows her wherever she goes and she herself does not respond to anyone who fails to address her as Queen."

You said, "Do you mean to say . . ."

Numan interrupted you in his clowning way and said, "Of course I mean to say everything that's on your mind, what you cannot say except in strictest confidence, and what you want to say but cannot."

"Then he has many mistresses."

"Maybe he wants to imitate the ancient Arab princes who kept as many slaves as there were days of the year. Balbo has a mistress in every place he visits, such as the island of Farwa, Mirzuq, Ghadames, Gharyan, Benghazi and Derna. As for Tripoli, which he sees as his kingdom's capital, he has more than one mistress and they belong to different nationalities so as to deal equitably with those under his care. There is Houriya the Libyan, Esther the Jewess, a third from Malta, a fourth from Greece or Armenia, and probably others."

You returned to watching the old man buying minutes with golden coins and measuring them by the melting candle. You tried to gauge the beauty of the woman with thick chestnut hair, but failed to couldn'tcatch a glimpse of her royal features.

"Are you sure she's the mistress of the governor himself?" "Do you really think that our Libyan friend sitting with her would pay all that money unless he felt like he was competing with the most important person in the land and going head to head with the Air Marshal himself? Well, the man also has a patriotic motive, for by means of his wealth, he can share in the Italian governor's harem."

"The Marshal is truly an honourable man. But how can he allow his mistress to become involved with other men?"

"Rest assured that Marshal Balbo is much more tolerant than the princes of Arab nations and he doesn't mind this kind of behaviour from his mistresses at all. It does him no harm if this mistress, whom he only sees a few times every year, meets with a rich man, for it will save him from having to spend on her himself."

There were so many questions you wanted your friend's opinion on, but the call of duty took him from you, for a new session had begun and he had to join the band with his oud. A young singer called Muhammad Selim sang a cheerful song to which the audience responded with applause and shouts.

> Nights of gaiety, nights have come
> Oh, the nights we're in.

And so that the gaiety being sung about became true gaiety in word and deed, a dancing girl appeared like a butterfly, wearing coloured clothes made of gossamer cloth that revealed more of her sensuous body than it concealed, and fluttered around her like wings as she flew from table to table. She dallied with and flattered the customers, receiving presents from them in the form of bills that they stuck between her breasts.

You left the café dazed after what you had heard and seen, but before leaving, you had stolen a glance at Queen Esther. All you could glimpse was her profile, which nevertheless gave you the impression she relied on make-up and embellishment to emphasize her beauty, whereas Houriya's beauty was naturally captivating.

You realized Houriya was only one of many mistresses that Marshal Balbo kept like canned food to satisfy his lustful cravings. He treated them as though they prostitutes, allowing them to sleep with other men so long as they were paid in golden lire. You couldn't imagine Houriya in such a humiliating role.

You had always considered Houriya as special, virtuous, generous, chosen by that man above all others because something about her conferred a distinction that was beyond them. However, matters seemed quite different, for surely she must be aware of these other mistresses, as a matter like this concerned her more than anyone else.

Balbo himself made a point of boasting about his relationships with women and never sought to conceal them. He would not have called his Jewish mistress Queen Esther had it not been to boast about his relationship with her and to imitate the Arab prince who had ruled the citadel of Tripoli before him and had a concubine called Esther, who had been known as Queen Esther owing to her power and influence over all affairs the land.

You felt the respect and veneration you had felt for Houriya begin to evaporate. She was just a woman who had meekly surrendered to her immoral life and placed over her face the mask of happiness in a kind of self-deception, even though she was miserable and wretched.

You recalled that you had personally seen Marshal Balbo make only one isolated visit to her during that month you started working for her. This confirmed what Numan had said about the many lovers, each of whom he could only visit a few times a year. But what about whether he really gave his mistresses the freedom to have relationships with other men? Did this apply to all his lovers, including Houriya? Or was it a special arrangement with Queen Esther, whom he had seen fit to match with a rich stupid man after he saw how much her monetary demands would exhaust him?

Only a man of wanton carelessness, unconcerned with all values, could permit his women such licence. Had Houriya taken advantage of this? You had seen nothing to suggest so during your time as her driver, but that couldn't be considered decisive proof, for you knew some things, while others remained hidden from you.

NINE

It was oddly provocative when Houriya appeared before you wearing a bath towel again the next morning, water dripping from her hair and head, the nakedness of her shoulders, arms was seductive. You wondered if this appearance was related to the licence Balbo allowed her, or if it was spontaneous.

Esther the Jewess had used her licence to gain larger quantities of gold, but what could Houriya ever gain from a man like you? What could she possibly say to the Marshal if he learned she had taken liberties with a recruit who worked as a temporary driver for her? You were amazed to catch yourself thinking about this at a time when your life and future hung in the balance. Your heart filled with ire because this behaviour didn't seem to embarrass the people involved, all the way from Balbo to his lovers and his lovers' lovers, who were all strung up like golden lire on one necklace, glittering with all the trappings of love, money, beauty and power.

But why should you be so concerned about a matter that didn't in any way affect your life, which had elected to soon bring your relationship with this city to an end and would probably meet its end in the jungles of Africa.

Perhaps the purpose behind this unnatural fixation on other people's imaginary woes was to escape from more pressing concerns that weighed more heavily on the heart because they were linked to whichever destiny lay in store for you. They were woes you had tried to escape from, and you thought you had succeeded, but your return to the barracks put your success to the test, because as soon as you placed your head on your pillow, all these worries would come to you like a bird of prey sinking its talons in your stomach, filling the night with sleeplessness.

The instant morning arrived, you hastily set out for Houriya's in the hopes of news about your exemption from going to war, even if that news was of Ayyad al-Fezzany's resignation, which would give Houriya a strong reason to ask you to stay in her service. As for your membership in the Fascist Party, you had left it too late for it to be of much use seeing as the ships that would take you to Abyssinia were already anchored in the harbour and would leave the day after tomorrow. Even if your membership in the Fascist Party were approved, there would not be enough time to enjoy the privileges it conferred or even wear the black shirt; and there would certainly not be enough time for you to scour the party's corridors for an exemption.

When you arrived at the garage, you were surprised to find it empty. You shouted to Mukhtar who was drinking his morning tea in his room and, running towards him, asked where the car was. He didn't seem at all worried and with calmly offered you a cup of tea, telling you not to worry and that the car was in safe hands. Ayyad al-Fezzany had come early to take the car's keys and saw that the oil needed changing, so had taken the car to the government garage.

You stood horrified, wondering what had brought this man back at such a critical time to ruin everything.

Where had you failed in keeping him out of your way? Was it Abdel Mowlah's fault? Had he made a mistake in relaying the message, or was whoever had delivered the message to blame?

There was also the possibility that Ayyad al-Fezzany hadn't been frightened by talk of war and instead viewed it the way Mukhtar did, as a chance for fast riches. The magic had backfired on the magician, and what you had thought to be a reason to keep him away had perhaps instead made him return all the sooner.

All this guessing was useless now and would not make the man return to the deserts of Mirzuq. The embargo had fallen and the original driver had returned in front of the driving wheel. The temporary role you had built such hopes on was over, as were the dreams that had transported you to fanciful worlds before you had been rudely awakened to reality.

You were still standing in the middle of the garage, ruing what your plans had come to and not knowing what your next step would be, when Ayyad al-Fezzany came driving into the garage like a rocket and would have run you over had you not jumped of the way. Such recklessness was out of keeping with his calm nature and his fifty-plus years of age. He parked the car and swiftly opened the door, getting out like a soldier on an urgent mission. It seemed to be his strange way of showing off his skills to prove he was more qualified. You needed no proof, because you knew the job was his better than anyone.

You approached al-Fezzany. welcoming him and congratulating him a safe return. He left your outstretched hand hanging in the air and then swore at you using the vilest pejoratives. But that wasn't enough. He also took advantage of your state of bewilderment to push you in your chest so roughly that you fell down after which he threw himself on you, kicking and punching.

Before you had a chance to do or say anything, Mukhtar the garage guard came and pulled him away from you, then helped you stand on your feet and tried to brush away the dust on your uniform. You didn't know what had made kind al-Fezzany so vicious and violent. Mukhtar asked what the reason was for this attack, and al-Fezzany, who was still worked up, said that you had sent him a fake message warning him against returning to Tripoli and advising him to send his resignation because the Governor-General had issued a decree that all drivers working with the government had to go to Abyssinia to participate in the campaign. Al-Fezzany said he had believed this message anddrafted his resignation, giving it to someone on their way to Tripoli. However, Marshal Balbo had flown to Mirzuq that same day and the people of the city had gathered to welcome him. Ayyad had been one of the men who had carried the plates of dates and the jugs of milk offered to the Marshal. As Balbo had recognized him, he had asked him what he was doing in Mirzuq. Ayyad had told him it was his home town and he had come to spend his holiday with his family, although now the vacation had turned into a request to resign because he couldn't go to war at his age.

Balbo had laughed, asking who had been responsible for this cunning jest about enlisting drivers in the war, since no such decree had been issued. It was then and only then al-Fezzany realized he had been the victim of a plot. So he had returned early and before his resignation reached the government offices, which would have been difficult for him to retract.

Still mad with fury, he grabbed a big wrench used to screw on the car's wheels, and rushed at you, but Mukhtar stepped between the two of you, asking him to take refuge from Satan in God, and asking you to leave the place for a few moments until the man calmed down.

You didn't have the strength to answer al-Fezzany, nor did you have the slightest desire to get into a fight with him. Perhaps because you knew you had after all tried to trick him and everything he said was true, except for one particular. He hadn't entirely understood when he said you had wanted to take his job, which you had only wanted in order to save yourself from going to war.

What you didn't understand was how he had known that you had sent the message unless it had been purely a guess, since you were the only person who would benefit from his resignation. It could also have been because Abdel Mowlah hadn't been careful enough to conceal the name of the person who had sent the message, although you had warned him against mentioning your name in connection with the message.

The end result was that al-Fezzany had learned what had happened and was here to replace you. All your efforts had come to naught, both those in accordance with principled behaviour, and those that weren't. Going to war was now inevitable. Oh, how Sergeant Antar would revel in your misery.

Looking for a way to blow off some steam, you left the garage and went up to the street with its din,, its light and the open blue sky above. They had assembled the soldiers in the camp and were informing them about their journey to Abyssinia, starting with how they were to conduct themselves on the ship, where they would spend two weeks before reaching their destination. They were being told about the routes they would take by sea and by land, as well as the weather conditions they should expect. They were also being taught a few basic phrases in Amharic that would be useful once they arrived.

You realized that you were missing out on all that, and that your knowledge would lag behind the others. Upon arrival you would be incapable of dealing with the new conditions that the others had trained for. You saw it as unjust considering you who had stood out amongst your comrades at the base.

You were still wondering how you would cope with al–Fezzany's return, when you caught sight of Gorgi, the old Maltese postman, coming towards you with a pencil behind his ear and several envelopes and parcels in his hands. He looked at the building to check the address and asked you if you knew Othman Al Sheikh. Even though he had met you more than once before and handed you the letters and magazines for Houriya, he didn't know your name. You hesitated before revealing your identity, fearing the unknown, then you remembered that you had given this address to the Fascist Party official and you guessed that the letter had to be from him. You took the letter from Gorgi after declaring you were Othman Al Sheikh and signed for it.

Before he left, you asked him to help you read the letter since your knowledge of Italian might prevent you from fully understanding it. To your great surprise, you found that part of the letter was written in Arabic. The letter congratulated you on being accepted as a member of the Fascist Party in the Libyan Youth Branch and informed you that, ass part of the admission protocol, you had to go to the Party's office to swear the oath in Arabic and Italian, which was as follows: "I swear by God and by Mother Italy that I will faithfully carry out the orders of the leader Mussolini and defend Italy and the principles of the Fascist State with my blood and soul. Long live Italy! Long live the Duce!"

After having read the first few lines to you, the old postman left, laughing into his sleeve, because he sensed the embarrassment you felt for the predicament this put you in, especially concerning the strange oath that made no mention of Libya at all even though it was the Libyan Youth Branch that had demanded you swear the oath. You realized any mention of Libya would not have been logical, since Libyan and Italian interests could be contrary to one other as they had been during the resistance.

You asked yourself which side a member of the Fascist Party should support. The answer was clearly Fascist Italy. This was the party you had thought would be a plank that would save you from war and death, but it was only more mud and filth in return for which you would receive nothing, because there wasn't enough time to procure the exemption you had hoped for.

In your despair, an idea came to you that would save you from your suffering and take you far from this dark corrupted world. You could flee to the desert. You would not be the first or last. You had begun in the desert, you had escaped it and now you would return to it. You would escape into the deepest depths where these Italians and their servants would never find you. They would not even think of following you because they knew they would be beaten back by the desert, which would inevitably favour you and would kill them all once you were in its protection.

You would find that the gazelles, antelopes, ibex, and goats you used to herd as a child would still be waiting for you. They would be your company and a generous source of sustenance. This was the only solution left now that the wings that had briefly allowed you to soar above reality were broken and the building that would have sheltered you from calamity was demolished.

You no longer hoped of satisfying your craving for advancement or recouping the sacrifices you had made for the Italians. So why continue? Your fate would be like that of any other man who made no concessions to them, who showed them only scorn and rancour. Go back to your desert. In those boundless expanses, you would not hear anything about Italians, Abyssinians, rulers, marshals, mistresses or whores. No law other than the law of the desert would apply. It was a law that granted its inhabitants a free heart and conscience, in addition to freedom. In the desert, a man was his own master and acted according to his free will. Nothing tied him down except the vault of the sky, the blue of the horizon, the rising and setting of the sun and the starlit night.

Here a man could be at peace with himself because there wasn't thing to disturb him. He could listen to his inner voice because there were no external interferences to confuse it and he could commune with his Creator thanks to the lack of barriers to obscure His purity and beauty.

TEN

No matter how certain you were that escaping to the desert was your only path to salvation, you didn't know if you possessed the courage and determination to follow through with it. The feeling of suffocation that had afflicted you in the garage now returned violently, as though someone had suddenly come and placed a giant boulder on your chest. Frustration and despair built up and hindered your breathing.

Hawaa was on her way back from the market with a basket full of fruit and vegetables when she saw you putting your hand to your chest, loosening your tie and the buttons of your shirt with nervous jerky movements to give your lungs room to inhale. Alarmed, she put the basket to one side and raced over, supporting you and helping you up the stairs to find something to relieve your condition.

You stopped before the stairs, telling her she didn't need to bother and that you would go back to the base to recover. However, you were exhausted and unable to move. You leaned against the wall, trying to normalize your breathing. You finally allowed her to help you up the steps of the building one by one until you reached the flat, and then after entering, you threw yourself onto a chair in the salon.

Hawaa brought you a glass of water followed by a cup of tea. Your breaths quickly calmed and your strength returned. You wanted to leave, but Hawaa stood in your way and told you Signora Houriya wanted to see you. You also wanted to see her and would not have travelled to Abyssinia without saying goodbye, but you knew she was still asleep and would not wake up for another three hours. Before you could express your surprise, she explained that the noise you had made when the two of you had entered the flat had woken Signora Houriya. When she had asked Hawaa what had happened, she had expressed her desire to see you and make sure you were well.

"Is she coming now?" you asked. "No. You will go to her."

"In her bedroom?"

Laughing, Hawaa said, "What of it? Believe me, you will see nothing but her head."

Under Hawaa's insistence, you walked to the bedroom door, confused and embarrassed. Hawaa opened the door and remained outside the room. You entered and suddenly saw you were in a hall of mirrors. Your feet sank into the carpet and your image was reflected by the many mirrors. You directed your greeting yo the luxurious bed that was covered with rumpled shining bed covers, all in different colours. When you heard no reply, you turned back towards the door, but then you heard Houriya's sleepy yawning voice asking you what had happened. You quickly answered that it was only a trifle: you just hadn't couldn'tgotten used to wearing this so-called neck tie. Your neck always twitched disobediently, refusing this tie until you yourself tore it off, which was what you had been doing when Hawaa had come and asked you to rest inside the house for a while.

Houriya rose a little, reclining on her elbow, still stretched out on the bed. She waved her hand at your appearance and your attire.

"Anyone who saw you looking like this would think you had slept on the pavement last night. Your clothes are in a state of dreadful neglect. Come closer."

You moved a few steps closer, then she asked to see your face so that she examine it. You leaned your head towards her. She reached out, caressing your checks and chin and a shiver ran up your spine. The velvety palm of her hand as it passed over your face was like a deadly radiating element that shook the entirety of your being. You used all the strength of will you had to remain rooted in your spot, otherwise you would have fallen, or succumbed to a psychological impediment that stopped your senses from functioning.

"Don't tell me you shaved this morning."

As if Houriya sensed the physical and psychological crisis she had caused you and wanted to give you a little respite, she removed her hand from your face and gave you time to regain your ability to speak by calling Hawaa, who was just outside the door. She entered and waited for her mistress's orders.

"Go and prepare Othman a bath. Give him everything he needs to shave including cologne so that he can regain his vitality."

In the meanwhile, you slowly and painfully managed to raise your head and recover your posture. Terribly embarrassed, you tried to apologize for not being able to use her bathroom and the Marshal's shaving brush and razor.

Houriya said, "You know I've always praised your industriousness and commitment to the Marshal and I don't

want him to get the wrong idea of you if he comes today
and sees you in this frightful state. Don't you know you
have a guardian angel is watching over you and whispers
your name in the ears of one of the rulers of the world?"

Even if such praise was of little consequence to you,
you could never forget that favour. Hawaa led you to a
different bathroom instead of the one next to Houriya's
bedroom. She handed you towels, robes, perfumes and all
you needed to shave. The bathtub was filled with hot water.
A white foamy mountain formed on top of the water,
which smelled like jasmine.

Hawaa shut the bathroom door and then returned after
a moment. From behind the bathroom door she asked you
to hand over your uniform so she could clean it and iron
it. She also asked you to give her your underwear. When
you hesitated, she reassured you, saying that she had brought
you fresh underwear. You were being led around like a
sleep-walker, responding to the temptation of the moment
and the instructions of the servant obeying her mistress.

You were unable to imagine what would happen if the
Marshal came and found you naked in his bathroom, using
his shaving brush, razor and perfumes, as well as his bathrobe. You quickly undressed, gave your clothes to Hawaa
through the crack between the door and its frame and then
jumped into the bath, enjoying the hot water scented with
jasmine nectar. Your pleasure at such luxury was marred by
the fact that, naturally, you didn't forget you were in a very
compromising situation.

You pricked up your ears trying to hear every movement
outside the bathroom so that events didn't catch you unawares.
You finished taking your bath, shaved hurriedly and waited
for Hawaa to bring your uniform and the underwear she

had mentioned. You busied yourself with putting cologne on your face, brushing your hair and putting pomade on it. You knocked on the door until Hawaa came. You asked her to hurry and bring your clothes because you were ready to get out. She said she hadn't expected you to be done so quickly, but that as you had the robe, you should put it on and come out.

You thought she must be a lunatic, first for leaving you naked in the bathroom, and now for wanting you to come out in this skimpy robe that was little more than a bath towel and would not cover your genitals unless you shrank yourself into it and pulled it downwards with both your hands. She probably didn't know that the bathrobe was too small for you, but the very idea of leaving the bathroom wearing only that robe was in itself improper.

Despite Hawaa insisting you come out because you couldn't, as she put it, stay in there forever, especially as she had prepared a cup of tea for you and didn't want to reheat it. Consenting to her request, you came out pulling the robe over your body and sat crosslegged on one of the chairs in the salon, praying to God that no one would see you.

Instead of bringing you the cup of tea, Hawaa told you that a complete breakfast was waiting for you in Houriya's bedroom. You sat in the chair, refusing to move, and told the woman that you couldn't possibly go to Signora Houriya's bedroom like this. You would not allow it. Signora Houriya was a chaste woman who didn't realize the consequences of such a situation and didn't know what sort of malice filled people's heads.

You explained to Hawaa that if anyone were to come and see you in a bathrobe in the lady's bedroom, even it were al-Fezzany or Mukhtar, rumours would be spread all over the city. What was worse, one of the Marshal's men or the Marshal himself might see you, which would in disaster for both you and Signora Houriya.

What if the man would be a messenger from the Marshal, or the Marshal himself were to arrive unannounced? Wouldn't that be catastrophic? Why did she have to put the both of you and such a compromising position?

You angrily yelled at Hawaa to bring you your clothes and threatened to look for them yourself, as you couldn't understand why she was taking so long. If she hadn't cleaned and ironed the suit yet, why didn't she just bring them to you as they were so you could get dressed before meeting the lady of the house?

But before you could carry out your threat, Houriya's voice rang out, asking you to come to her immediately. You had no other choice but to obey her alluring voice.

When you reached her door, Houriya was standing in the middle of the room surrounded by the mirrors. She was also wearing a bathrobe and as soon as you saw her, you realized she too had just taken a bath. The aroma of scented soap wafted from her, her hair was still wet, and her skin had turned rosier thanks to the hot water. She glowed like a bride on her wedding night, even though she hadn't put on any make-up. She surprised you by letting out a laugh like the tinkle of holiday bells.

"Is it really that cold?" "Cold?"

"The one that is making you shiver and shrink into your robe, clutching it with stiff fingers."

Unable to say anything, you produced an uncertain smile in response to what she had said. Your eyes roamed around the room searching for the breakfast Hawaa had

mentioned, hoping it would save you from the embarrassment of standing there hunched in your robe. But you
didn't see any breakfast in the room. All you saw was the
bed, on top of which lay rumpled sheets, and blankets glittering with the colour of flames.

You became aware that the door had been shut and
that you were alone in the room, except for Satan that is,
who no doubt had engineered the scene with characteristic
perfection. Religious texts confirmed that in every licen-
tious meeting between a man and woman, Satan was always
the third wheel.

Here you were: a man and a woman, wearing nothing
but robes in a locked bedroom. Let the purest, most chaste
of the angels in heaven come now if he wished. He would
find something bereft of all innocence and virtue, something
to arouse doubt and suspicions that deserved to be reported
to the Lord of Heaven.

You no longer needed to guess that everything that
had happened to you since you had entered this apartment
had been planned, including Hawaa taking your clothes
and leaving you naked except for this piece of cloth. What
did Houriya want? What could she possibly want from a
man like you? You weren't handsome and distinguished like
the Prophet Joseph, who had been tempted by the wife of
al-Aziz, the most beautiful seductress in history.

These questions spun in your head like leaves scattered
by a storm. You were overcome by fright, mixed with
curiosity and excitement, when she asked you to relax and
touched your hands with her fingers, which only increased
your nervousness.

You couldn't remove your hands from the edge of your
bathrobe. Had you done so, a small crack would have opened

up revealing your naked front. Houriya looked you over from the crown of your head, and back down again to the tips of your toes, gazing at every part of you as if she were seeing you for the first time. A brief silence ensued, giving you the calm you needed to bring your emotions to heel and adapt to the strange, exciting scene you suddenly found yourself in with the woman you had so often dreamed about.

Perhaps the dream had begun unfolding. You found yourself living in a hypnagogic state. You didn't know what the next step would be because you didn't dare take the initiative. Whatever needed to be done, you were the passive recipient. But that didn't matter; what mattered was that it happened.

Did she do it out of love? Or was it just a fleeting caprice? Perhaps she wanted to use you to make the Marshal jealous. Whatever her motives, you could do nothing but obey her wishes. You were but an atom floating in the flood of light radiating from her, a tiny speck in her sublime universe, intoxicated with the heavenly nectar of love. Had she beckoned from the farthest regions of the earth, you would have come flying.. You burned with desire to taste even a single drop of her saliva. Then you could die happy having realized your most cherished dream.

Bewildered, unable to believe what was happening, you watched her take the robe off her body until she was completely nude, freed from clothes that had veiled the magic and glory of her body. She had been created by divine providence, which had wanted this nymph to shine with the light of her beauty, wielding her lethal weapons: her breasts, waist, abdomen, navel, thighs and buttocks. All of these had been hidden from sight, buried beneath the most elegant clothes, and now were ready to be preyed upon. Nothing on earth or heaven could be more deadly and terrifying than her, and nothing could have prevented you from being crushed beneath her indomitable power.

You stood, watching her, silent, bewildered, like a wax statue as she tugged your robe until it fell to the floor, and drew near to you. She wrapped her fingers in your fingers, pressed her chest against your chest, her stomach to your stomach, her thighs to your thighs, and she placed her lips over yours. Her hair covered your face and obscured your vision of the things around you, opening instead windows to other worlds. You saw stars giving birth to stars, creating a new beautiful creature in the dome of the sky, and you saw rainbows multiplying until a riot of colours that exploded like a dazzling sunrise, filled with the most resplendent sights and a tumultuous music capable of stirring all the happiness and love in the universe. Everything was enraptured by music, dancing and singing, mountains, rivers, seas, planets, the creatures of God that swam, ran, crawled and flew.

Meanwhile, you emerged from your bewildered state to join Houriya in that sensual game. You embraced her more forcefully than she had embraced you, and you heard her bones knocking against each other as you squeezed with all your strength. The sighs of ecstasy mixed with moans of pain. You kneaded your mouth against hers, crushed her breasts against your chest, pouring out all the passion and fire in your body, and all the repression and deprivation stored up in your pores. Burning, scorching, you penetrated her body, awakening in it a thirst and yearning to be sated, a desire for revenge against the days of famine that the heart had lived.

You forgot there was anyone else in the world. The universe had placed all its creatures and all its phenomena under your commands. You played with stars and celestial bodies, burning the seas and oceans with them. You transferred the inhabitants of the forests to the bottom of the sea, and the residents of the sea you moved to the forests. You turned the earth into a mattress, and transformed the sky and the stars into a bedspread, remaking the world as you saw fit.

You forgot your misgivings about being interrupted by someone because no such person existed and there would be no way for him to pierce the incendiary energy that engulfed you. And if by some miracle he did happen to break the ring of fire around you and Houriya, you were capable of instantly turning him to stone, even if it were that very tyrant who claimed dominion over Houriya's body. Today, you were more powerful than Balbo himself, even if the latter should arrive armed to the teeth. There was a greater magic in you, and you would turn him into a marble statue.

This woman was yours, and you were hers. This union had imbued the two of you with new identities, making you forget who she had been to you, and vice versa. All you remembered now was her body melting into yours, as its intoxicating sweetness inebriated your soul and drowned your body in an ecstasy that could only have come from the gardens of Paradise.

Dormant sexual desires awoke in you like a volcano, and you couldn't bottle them up again. Your lovemaking became animalistic, which incited her to protest. It seemed as though she didn't want to see your lovemaking coming to its inevitable conclusion, or perhaps she wanted to allow more time for embraces, kisses and sweet foreplay. She didn't want you to climax too early, whereas you were ruled by your desire to climax so that you could make love to her again and again.

But she didn't understand, and pushed you away from her, pulled her body away. She was clearly displeased by your violent haste to ejaculate. But she wasn't the only one in charge anymore. You grabbed her and mounted her again, despite her resistance.

You used a technique that had been successful before in similar situations like this and pushed her against the wall when she tried to pull away again, hitting you weakly. But you were able to penetrate her again, so she surrendered to bliss, and continued moaning and sighing to express her delight.

Her body collapsed from the intensity. She inclined her body against yours, linking her arms around your neck, which was all you needed to arouse you a second time. After that second time, her body turned to butter and melted in the fires of lust. She was no longer able to keep her balance despite leaning on you, so she started to slip into a fall. Rather than stop her, you fell to the ground beside her, entangling your bodies. Then, clearly hungry for more, you pounced on top of her, pulling at her breasts, drinking the saliva from her lips, and relishing in the odour of her body as you pulled it towards you and pounded it with your own until you came for the third time.

Afterwards, you remained quiet for a few minutes, resting your head on her breasts, savouring the motion of their rise and fall before you carried Houriya to the bed and lay beside her, taking in her presence beside you on the softness of the covers, cushions and silken sheets. You listened to the cheerful music coming from the radio outside the room until you were aroused again and plucked a fourth petal from her glistening rose.

After the pleasure of the last lovemaking session, you saw Houriya close her eyes in a pleasant doze while still stretched out naked above the bed with the ghost of a smile on her lips. You were loath to wake her, despite your voracious desire to make love to her a fifth time, and a sixth, and a seventh. You let her sleep and sneaked outside to the bathroom, where you quickly washed yourself. You found your clothes clean and ironed, so you put them on and left the apartment, hurriedly descending the stairs.

ELEVEN

After leaving Houriya's flat, you walked towards the seashore. You felt you needed to be alone in an unfamiliar place, where no one would intrude upon your privacy. So you went to walk by the sea, where you had always felt at harmony with its eternal blueness.

You went up the plateau of Sidi al-Sha'ab and chose an isolated spot at the top. You lay down on a stone, which was surrounded by larger boulders whose shadows shielded you from the sun and the people going to the nearby mosque. The worshipers would come from every direction but the sea, which was all you cared about. You gazed out at the blue as far as the horizon. You watched the swaying waves and the coming and going of ships in the port. From a distance, you saw the arc of the sky that encompassed the planet, mixing its blue with that of the sea in a lovers' embrace.

You tried to regain your equilibrium after the volcanic experience and those hellish moments of blessed pleasure that had shaken your whole being. Time passed by imperceptibly. The sea was before you and you were surrounded by stones and a great emptiness. You felt exhausted and didn't want to move. What had happened in Houriya's bedroom had depleted your energy.

You would never go back to her. Never again would your feet cross her threshold. You were the male bee who had fertilized the queen and then must die. You had merely been her replacement driver and now he had returned. The temporary job was over and you had been given your severance pay, more than anyone like you could expect.

Recalling what had happened in that moment outside the scope of time, you could say that it hadn't been merely the whim of a rich, beautiful, influential woman. It had been meticulously planned. However, you were in no position to explain it, except to say that, as you thought back to the sequence of events, every moment had clearly been organized by the lady of the house.

That was as far as you could go, because there were other aspects you might never understand, and it might not matter whether you knew if they were connected with her relationship to Balbo or not. As for you, it was possible to consider what had happened as a violent and unusual farewell that had also granted you one of the happiest moments of your life. After having plucked this rare fruit from the tree of bliss that grows only in paradise, you felt as though you could willingly head to war. You ought to be extremely grateful to the angels for showering you with such favours that quenched your thirst, watered your devastated lands, and ended the drought of your days.

Who would dare say that what had happened had been an act of seduction attributable to the influence of Satan whispering in people's ears? You would not agree that this magnificent experience, which had been like sitting at one of the tables of heaven, could be ascribed to anything but divine blessing from above. And you didn't say that just to reconcile your religious conscience with your lurid lust. You considered your body's sexual energy as separate from the needs of the soul, because it derived from the raw materials, salts and metals that made up the body. You didn't say it for this reason.

What you had experienced in Houriya's bedroom had bridged the divide between body and soul, both of which had been ecstatic to join her body. The act of love with Houriya couldn't compare to your sexual escapades in the forest, or in the brothels of Sidi Umran Street. Houriya was a fitting name for this nymph, who was one of the creatures of divine paradise, and the time spent in her good graces could only be measured by the status nymphs occupied in religious and folk traditions.

Up to that point, you had always felt guilty after sex. You felt as though you had soiled your body and you begged God to forgive your sins. But things had been different this time. You didn't feel guilty in the slightest. wasn'tWhat you felt was a sense of exultation and an abundance of joy that made you unable to move and prolonged this state of relaxation. Perhaps you were simply deceiving yourself, or perhaps you were proud that exclusive property of the country's Italian governor.

You remained in your place until daylight began to fade. Then you gathered your strength until you could get up and stroll along the beach. The sun had started to set, putting its aesthetic touches on the horizon, drawing a mural in resplendent, melancholy colours that awoke the most beautiful qualities of the soul.

Cheered up, you walked on, humming a merry tune from a song that said:

> Leave me alone
> O my friends, leave me alone
> I'm busy with my wanton love.

You continued watching the sunset and all the beauty it had summoned into the sky, all the shapes it reflected onto the surface of the sea. It was like a magical world and you spent a long time on the shore without thought of food or drink despite the fact you had only had the tea Mukhtar had offered you earlier that morning, and the one Hawaa had brought you. The state of contentment you felt carried unchanged, as did your sense of satisfaction.

You returned to the camp as soon as darkness began to creep over the sea and earth. You were heading there early, since it would be your last night on dry land. By the following evening, everyone in the camp would be in the bowels of the five ships anchored in the harbour.

The first person you met upon your return to the camp was Sergeant Antar, who was standing alone next to the gate. You had the impression he was specifically awaiting your return, perhaps so as to tell you to quickly get ready to leave – his petty way of avenging himself and letting you know that all your efforts had come to naught. You truly hated seeing him at this moment, and you turned your head left and right looking for any excuse to avoid talking to him.

Sergeant Antar saluted you first, although it was usually up to the lower ranked officers to salute their superiors.

"What's this, Sergeant Antar? You outrank me. Why the mockery?"

"You truly deserve this salute, because you've outsmarted me. You are more cunning and clever, even if you are lower in rank."

"Tonight is the last night we'll spend together in this camp, so let's behave properly for God's sake."

"Is there anything improper, Brother Othman? Your devilish plan was fruitful and has brought phenomenal results. Congratulations!"

"What are you talking about?"

"I'm talking about the secret of membership in the Fascist Party. It's true whoever said only iron can dent iron."

"Please, stop spreading these rumours. They just aggravate the other soldiers' resentment of me."

"I don't blame you and I don't envy you. I'm happy for you. As for the rest of those you speak of, every one of them wishes they were a hog like you," he said laughing, and still shaking your hand.

You snatched your hand away angrily and were about to object to the reprehensible description of you as a hog, but Sergeant Antar pre-empted you saying, "Don't be angry, Othman. Be happy, trill with joy if you have a woman's tongue fit for trilling like they do, for just two hours ago the decision came to exempt you from going to Abyssinia. They're calling it a postponement, but it's really an exemption and the decree has been issued only for you, bearing only your name and signed by the Governor-General himself. Now have you realized what kind of magic that membership card can achieve?"

A crowd of soldiers had gathered around the two of you, some whom you knew, others you didn't. All had heard what Sergeant Antar had said about your exemption, so you braced yourself and prepared to retaliate.

However, their reactions were the opposite of what you had expected, and they all shook hands with you, congratulating you, expressing their happiness. They thought that

joining the Fascist Party in order to save yourself from
going to war had outwitted the wily Italians and defeated
their plan to kill Libyans. You had saved yourself, and they
all admired your successful planning, because in the depths
of their souls, all of them wished they had done the same.
For life was better than death, remaining far from war was
better than burning in its hell-fire, and a live hog was better
than a dead lion as Sergeant Antar jokingly said. As soon
as you were sure that he meant what he had said about
having escaped the sad fate that no one else had been able
to avert, you laughed along with him too. In your mind,
you reviewed all the past times you had heard the word
hog used in the form of praise for patience and perseverance. You saw no reason to correct his mistaken ideas about
the magical effect of the membership card, nor was there
any need to tell him you hadn't yet received it.

The support you received from your fellow soldiers
encouraged you to look for Salem. You hoped he would
be less angry and more understanding of your actions in
light of their results, especially as it was the last night you
would be able to spend together. You didn't go to him
seeking to be exonerated for what you had done, he would
not validate your actions, nor would you ask him to because
your thoughts differed from his and could not be reconciled.
However, there was always room for a personal reconcili-
ation so that at least you wouldn't part on an angry note.

You couldn't find him. so you returned to your barracks.
You found it half empty because most of the soldiers had
been given extra work loading military equipment from
the warehouses onto trucks. They were told they would
make up for the lost sleep with days of sleeping on board
the ships bound for Abyssinia.

You didn't have enough time to look for Salem next morning, since according to the order of exemption, you had to go in the small hours of the morning to renew your status as a driver at the Department of Transportation. Your dream of remaining in Tripoli had finally come true without knowing who was responsible for it. It was definitely not the Fascist Party as Sergeant Antar had thought, since in addition to not having become an official member of the Party yet, you hadn't expressed your desire to be exempted to anyone there.

No person other than Houriya could have taken an interest in fulfilling your wish, especially because you didn't have any other powerful acquaintances to whom you could have conveyed your desire. Naturally, it was unlikely that Marshal Balbo, who had wanted you to send him reports from Abyssinia, would have taken the initiative to grant you such an exemption in order to assign you some other unknown task. The only possible explanation was that his dearly beloved had convinced him such an exemption would be useful. But what reasons had she used to convince him? Regardless, the last few months in Tripoli had taught you that no one in this city did anyone a favour without wanting something in return.

Whoever had kept you in Tripoli hadn't done so for your sake, for his or her own motives. Your presence in Tripoli would serve him or her more than your departure from Tripoli. It was one of those rules society was governed by and it didn't bother you. This was what you had wanted, and this was what you had received, and you were ready to pay the price.

The time came for you to meet Houriya in your capacity as a driver in her service, despite that the car was in the hands of her original chauffeur. You went up to her flat to coincide with the end of her breakfast. She welcomed you in the salon, assuming a cold serious manner without a trace or echo of what had happened between the two of you in her bedroom the previous morning. She seemed to want to impress on you the necessity of separating your work as her driver from that personal moment you had shared. She greeted you sitting down while you stood before her in your official uniform, expressing your utmost gratitude for the trouble she had gone through to get you exempted and keep you on in her household. You voiced your readiness to be an obedient servant to her as well as to Marshal Italo Balbo, who had issued the decree.

After you had finished, she asked you to sit and ordered Hawaa to bring you a cup of tea. Then she said exemptions were only issued for very serious reasons, like a sudden illness, or an accident that prevented a person from working, however a postponement could also mean you might be needed for a different task.

"Regardless, the end result is the same. You're staying in Tripoli."

Then, she suddenly moved onto what had happened between the two of you the previous morning, as if she had tired of this subterfuge.

"You no doubt know – perhaps you had already guessed so – that I hold a special place for you in my heart."

The trivial talk had come to an end. It had only been a cover for this topic which touched upon the essence of what joined you together and was related to what the lady of the house wanted from you; perhaps it was even the reason for keeping you in Tripoli. You felt a trembling in your limbs that you managed to subdue just as you managed to subdue the sexual arousal that Houriya awoke in your body.

A thought came to you, one that you had heard from your teacher Mario while he had been talking about the women he had slept with. He had said that every time he encountered a woman, he felt as though they communicated with their reproductive organs rather than with their voices and minds. For, after becoming sexually acquainted, dialogue acquired another layer, one that more truthfully conveyed sentiments than say tongues, words, and minds.

You kept silent, listening to what the Signora had said with her tongue. She obviously hadn't finished what she wanted to say and you continued listening to those hidden messages being relayed between your bodies.

"I don't want things to reach the point that they did yesterday, and after it happened, I wished that they had happened lawfully according to the Path of God and His Messenger."

You couldn't rectify the thoughts evoked by her words about Islamic law and the Path of God and Messenger, with all the sacredness they represented in these matters. Despite the difference between her relationship with the Marshal and the fleeting fling with you, you didn't understand how Houriya could possibly speak of it in terms lawfulness and sinfulness. Nor did you understand why lawfulness was necessary in one case, and not in the other. Was it because your common religion and homeland stipulated that this kind of relationships be lawfully concluded, whereas foreigners enjoyed an exemption? Was that what she really thought? Or was she also hinting at something else ?

Houriya waited until Hawaa had brought the tea and left to continue.

"Please understand my position. I'm a woman who yearns

for motherhood, to have a child of my own to carry for nine months inside me. A child to hold and nurse and raise. To see him grow older before my eyes. That child has to come from a lawful relationship, and from the loins of a man I love, a man of my religion and people. Do you understand?"

Of course you understood. She left nothing to guess at, just as she left you no opportunity to object or reply, for she continued talking before you could collect your thoughts.

"The Marshal understands that completely. He and I cannot be married for obvious reasons, which I think you know, and I will not commit a crime against my future child by having him out of wedlock. The Marshal, out of the kindness of heart, understands the needs of a woman who has seen years of her life go by without enjoying her maternal right."

You were no less civilized or kind than the Marshal and you understood the maternal yearning a woman like her must feel. You also knew that womanhood was incomplete without this desire to be a mother. What you still didn't understand, or perhaps you did understand but needed more concise clarification, was what exactly she wanted from you.

Your exemption from the Abyssinian campaign wasn't divorced from Signora Houriya's ulterior motives, and she had just mentioned one of those motives, which perhaps was the most important one. This mission was just as dangerous. Instead of fighting atop the Abyssinian plateau, you had been selected to invade the honeyed plateaus of this beautiful female sitting in front of you, on a gilded chair, upholstered in red plush.

Houriya kept silent, filled with sadness, so you couldn't

keep silent as well. You ventured to say, "You are in the prime of your youth, with many years ahead of you before you have to worry about bearing children and nursing."

"I hope I've not become a mother since yesterday morning, because what happened between us happened without preparation so I didn't take any precautions."Before you could wonder what she had meant, she got up and said, "We will continue this conversation later. You must have friends who are leaving and whom you need to see off at the harbour."

By which she meant the information she had given today sufficed, and she didn't want to ruin it by revealing more, which she would leave for the next round. It just went to show her work as a nurse hadn't gone to waste. She knew how to administer doses in a timely fashion.

Throughout the short span of time the meeting had taken, you had felt the excited by how communicating via your sexual organs was more beautiful and sincere than the speech of mouths and minds. Therein was a harmony that you didn't think materialized in other types of communications that dealt in the languages of deceit as they probed for weak spots in the clash of wills.

You would not go to the harbour to say farewell, but simply to check that they had indeed left, and that you really were to remain in Tripoli. You gripped the doorknob, preparing to go, but Houriya stopped to tell you that you would share your duties with Ayyad al-Fezzany. She would leave the two of you to work out a schedule starting tomorrow.

TWELVE

By the time you reached the harbour, the ships had been loaded with equipment and weapons, and loudspeakers had been set up in the streets and squares, which relayed the words of one of the speakers, who had come to bid farewell to the first wave of Libyan soldiers leaving to take part in the Abyssinian campaign.

The orator spoke in classical Arabic, expressing the pride he felt, on behalf of the families of the soldiers, for the civilized message these brave soldiers would convey to the friendly Abyssinians. For they were currently living in slavery, bought and sold at the will of the Abyssinian royal family and their slave merchants. Fascist Italy and her intrepid soldiers – which included these brave Libyan heroes – would rescue those people from their suffering and their arrival would herald peace, justice, and security beneath the tri-coloured banner.

You were unbothered by weren'tall these lies and false-hoods now that you had been saved from delivering this particular Fascist message. You weren't eager to step into the crowd, which was made up of men and women in Libyan dress, the families of the departing soldiers.

But then you remembered something that suddenly sparked the zeal in your heart and prompted you to dive into the crowd. Thuraya and her family, along with her in-laws, had to be there, so as to get a last look at Fathy before he left. God willing it would be the last time they would ever see him before calamitous fate led him to the land of the Abyssinians.

It would be wonderful if you could find her in the midst of this crowd. You would not greet her only by clasping her hands alone, but also her body. Thanks to the jostling masses, you would be able to press your body against hers intimately and bask in its provocative warmth. It was a bold and yet depraved idea, but no one could claim to be noble in the sort of environment to which you had been subjected.

Your surroundings were depraved. Nothing embodied this more than this charade of a wedding ceremony, which was for the benefit of ignorant youths being paraded like a flock of sheep to the slaughterhouse. The voice booming out of the loudspeakers also sounded depraved as it talked about the happy occasion amidst the wails of the soldiers' mothers. He spoke as though he belonged to one of the soldiers' families, but was he really a soldier's father? Was he so proud of the civilization of bombs that would liberate the Abyssinians from bondage by hastening their deaths?

So why not swim in the ocean of depravity like the other swimmers? Why would someone who commits grave depravities shy away from committing such a minor one?

Thuraya, who was perfectly innocent in your mind, didn't deserve to be treated like this, no matter how despicable you were with others. The mere thought of treating her in this vulgar fashion was an insult to the affection you claimed to have for her. You wondered if you were any longer capable of interacting with anyone according to the rules of love, after you had seen everything – including bodies, emotions, consciences, and hearts – put up for sale and bartered in the market.Houriya had plans for you, which she had wrapped in silver wrapping paper and was now revealing one by one. To play this game, you would have to be even more depraved. In the beginning, you would play the rule of the dimwit who didn't know what was happening around him or what was wanted of him. Yet when a harsh, revealing light was cast on all the dimensions of the gameyou would begin a concerted bid to win it.

The crowd had an odour you recognized all too well: the smell of poverty. It was the smell of the shirt that remained until it stuck to its owner's skin because of all the accumulated sweat that the owner could afford to wash off with soap. The stench would make you dizzy if you didn't leave this suffocating place and attend the pressing business that would take up the rest of your day.You would abandon the idea of seeing Thuraya for another occasion, when you would be ready to face her.

The most urgent of these affairs was to prepare a place for you to live after the Italian army had lifted the covering that had been protecting you from the viciousness of the market, saving you from having to think about the problems of food, lodgings and clothing. You were now temporarily out of the army, or more precisely, you were a soldier on non-military missions and the army could recall you whenever it wished. As for now, during your temporary exemption, you had to take charge of looking after yourself.

The base that had sheltered you was to undergo

maintenance starting tomorrow to prepare its transformation into a real Italian military base that would fulfill other functions besides recruitment and training. This meant that there wouldn't be any waves of troops going to Abyssinia that would surpass the scale of this current wave, which comprised fifteen thousand soldiers from training facilities across the country. This first wave would Fascist Libya's contribution to the Italian war effort in Abyssinia. There was nevertheless the possibility of sending small numbers of soldiers who had been trained in local recruitment camps.

Once more, you wished you could take a short holiday and visit your family in Awlad Al Sheikh. They must have believed you were on your way to the battlefields in Abyssinia, but you realized that such a holiday was out of the question since Houriya had fought for the postponement on the pretext that she needed you for work. It would not do to grant a vacation under the circumstances.

You didn't know what had suddenly made you feel so sentimental about Awlad Al Sheikh when you had escaped it, hating the wretched life there, the idleness and apathy the villagers, your parents included, lived in. You resented what they had done to you and the misery they had inflicted on you from your childhood up to the very last day when you fled.

So where did this nostalgia for Awlad Al Sheikh come from? It was a form of childish weakness that ill suited wasn'ta man like you. You owed it to yourself to rid yourself of it in order to go back strong and powerful, so you could repay those people in kind. You would be doing yourself an injustice if you didn't treat them with the exact cruelty they had used with you. That was what this environment of neglect, apathy and wretchedness deserved, so leave Awlad Al Sheikh to neglect and forgetfulness, as it had left you in its turn.

You decided to stop thinking about your parents since they deserved to be treated in the same way they had treated you. You should attend to yourself and your future, for a new life was waiting for you. You would need to employ your heart, mind, and body to benefit from the broader horizons before you and to establish yourself in this new civilian life, where you were just another ordinary person.

The only place left you could go now was the old city and its ancient bazaars, to Bab al-Bahr, where hotels once welcomed caravans and their cattle. The district had under- gone some development and renewal in recent years, so it had stopped houring cattle and the stables had been trans- formed into cafés, cheap restaurants, ware-houses and shops. After the war had come to an end, people had drifted back from the outskirts and countryside in large numbers to find work until it had become difficult to find a vacant room to let.

What you really hoped for was finding an available room right away. Even if you managed to get permission to stay on the base for two or three days, you would not be able to bear staying there alone in the middle of that maze, which was no longer fit for anyone but ghosts to live in.

After looking around for several hours, you found a hotel that hadn't been modernized. It still retained its small courtyard for anyone who might arrive on camels, horses, or donkeys loaded with goods, and where a stable boy would tend to the beasts. This was the last hotel in Tripoli that provided these services and it had once stood out above the abodes, corrals, and markets at the end of the long caravan road. Nothing remained of them now except their names, like the current livestock market which, despite changes in the nature of its business, was still called the Slave Market, because that's what it had been in the past.

In spite of its primitiveness, you considered yourself lucky to have found a vacant room in it because it was located at the foot of the hill of Bab al-Bahr, not far from the port and midway between two buildings that had become cultural symbols of the old city. One of them, the ancient Mosque of Gorgi, was a religious, historical and archaeological landmark. Its minaret was unlike any other because of its multiple floors. The other was the Arch of the Emperor Marcus Aurelius, a Roman monument said to be the oldest edifice in the city. The Italians had assigned a task force to renovate the arch, pave the courtyard beside it, and plant rose bushes around it to turn it into a tourist attraction.

Consequently, you didn't hesitate to take the room on the second floor that overlooked the portico, which in turn gave out on the inner courtyard.

It so happened that the hotel was situated in your favourite part of Tripoli. You thought of it as the link between the desert and the sea, the old and the new, the villagers and the urbanites and between the era of Tripoli that went back to the dawn of time, the Tripoli of the Islamic Middle Ages, and modern Tripoli.

You paid cant attention to the room. Humidity had eaten at the lime coating on the walls and peeled the green paint that covered the wooden door and window. The room was completely bare except for an old wardrobe and a bed. Before the stores could close, you quickly bought insecticide to fight the fleas and bedbugs that had left their marks on the walls. You also bought a gas burner to cook your food, as well as several cooking utensils and a kerosene lamp. You would wait until the following day to purchase some food. You had hired a bicycle to facilitate your errands, which included going to the camp to fetch your clothes.

The hotel owner impressed you as a jolly fellow. As he was very fat, people called him al-Kubran because he had been a foreman for a work gang at the harbour before devoting himself to his hotel. He was nevertheless still involved in freight and shipping.

Al-Kubran had turned a ground floor room into an office, from which he could manage the hotel and his other interests. You spent the first hours of the evening exploring the area that was to be your home. Al-Kubran invited you into his office, which in the evening became a place for nightly entertainment where his friends met, played cards, sipped tea, ate peanuts and listened to al-Kubran talk, for he was an inveterate talker. He made up stories on the hoof and was always full of ideas about how to fix the world, begging God to keep him alive long enough to achieve his mission.

THIRTEEN

You went to bed late that night. You had walked a lot during the search for a hotel, and ridden the bicycle across town. The ensuing exhaustion lowered you into a deep sleep from which you didn't wake until some time after your customary hour. You went to Houriya's half an hour later than usual.

As soon as you arrived, you found Mukhtar and Ayyad al-Fezzany both waiting for you outside the building. Al-Fezzany told you that he had gone to the camp the day before looking for you, but had learned you had moved to a new residence. He hadn't known what to do as he had been sent to inform you to come early the following morning because you had been chosen for an important mission.

From the instant you reached the building, even before hearing what al-Fezzany had said, you knew that Marshal Balbo was inside the apartment. You could tell by the presence of three military cars lurking around the corner, and the conspicuous number of military guards scattered around the front. You imagined that there must have been hordes of secret police who must also have been stationed in the vicinity. Balbo must have spent the night with her, since he would not have come to visit her so early in the morning.

You learned from al-Fezzany that Marshal Balbo would need an Arab driver today as he planned to attend the Spring Festival at the Janzour Oasis, and you had been selected for the task. You told al-Fezzany you believed he was more deserving of this mission by virtue of seniority.

He said the decision wasn't his or yours to make, but rather that it was Marshal Balbo's, and he had set the parameters for the job, one of which was that the driver should be from the people of the region as a tribute to the Tripolitanian attendees at the celebration. As someone from the larger Tripoli area, you were closer than someone like al-Fezzany, who came from distant Mirzuq. There was also the fact that the Marshal preferred having a trained military driver in the event of any emergency.

Your delight was mixed with doubt and suspicion, although you didn't want to worry yourself by looking for the hidden motives behind these preparations. It was best if you just appreciated this decision and took your lead from the famous saying that Sergeant Antar always repeated, "Relax and you will float." Because, as he would say to the recruits, nothing causes a person to drown more than resisting the current.

One of the Italian guards came to ask you to prepare the car, which Mukhtar had taken care to wash, dry, and spray inside with perfume scented with musk. No sooner had you brought the car out and stopped outside the building than three Italian guards came and inspected it thoroughly to make sure it was absolutely safe. One of the guards searched you personally, which vexed you somewhat although you hid your resentment and tried to understand the reasons for the guard's conduct.

You went back to sitting behind the steering wheel, with an armed guard in the passenger seat. The military vehicles moved, one of them stopping in front of your car and the other two military cars stopped behind you. You recited the opening of the Quran, then the surah of Sincere Faith, and the Throne verse. You also asked the pious Sheikh Sidi Abdelsalam al-Asmar to lend you his support so that you didn't lose your nerve while you transported the Pharaoh of your times. If you were to err now, you would surely be slain by these myrmidons.

After half an hour, Marshal Balbo appeared laughing loudly, his white teeth shining out from his dark black beard. He was wearing his military uniform and held a cigar in one hand and pulled Houriya along with the other. She was trying to keep up with his quick strides in graceful bounds.

She wore a dress with pleats that fanned down from the neck to the hem. The dress was tight across her body and was patterned with blue and white circles that inter-sected like waves. Her belt was fastened so tightly around her waist that the dress almost disappeared before spreading out once more in the multifold pleats that swayed around her legs. The sound of her high-heeled shoes tapped in perfect timing with the Marshal's powerful strides. Meanwhile, her black locks swung over her laughing, smiling face as she walked in tune to this melodic rhythm. She seemed like a creature made of light and air.

The couple descended the marble steps from the door of the building and crossed the small portico that formed part of the pavement. One of the guards quickly opened the back doors of the car for them. The procession drove through Caneva Street then Corso Sicilia in the direction of the village of Janzour. You had turned your head when the Marshal got into the car and your eyes met his deep eyes that shone like fire. A shiver ran through your body as an electric current ran from his gaze.

He spoke to Houriya continuously in his powerful and strident voice. All you understood were his references to Rome and the names of Fascist leaders who angered and opposed him because they didn't understand this country, for instance how vast it was and the budget that was needed to develop it.

Meanwhile, you drove the car so nervously that you almost crashed into the car ahead of you when it slowed down to make a turn. Houriya noticed how nervous you were in the presence of the Governor-General, so she tried to put you at ease by reminding you that the Marshal had wanted you to carry out an extremely sensitive mission in Abyssinia, but that she had convinced him you would be more use to them as a safe and loyal driver in Tripoli.

You wanted to thank her and Marshal Balbo but the words refused to come out of your mouth. Houriya then asked you where you were living after having left the camp. With some effort you were able to mention the old city.

When Houriya translated your words for Marshal Balbo, his voice rang out with the thoughts and associations that the old city evoked in his mind, saying that every stone in the old city had a historic value that made any architectural achievement in the new city pale by comparison. He added that he and his predecessors Folby, Di Bono and Badoglio had all made a point of keeping the modern districts of the city in conformity with the venerable antiquity of the old city.

He also expressed his regret that despite his many journeys, during which he had covered almost every inch of Libya, even to its most distant regions, he hadn't yet gone to the old city. He had gone no further than the Musheer Market and the Red Castle, as the narrow alleyways weren't wide enough to allow his car to pass through. The officers responsible for his personal safety always postponed his visit to the old city.

The only solution left was to escape from these officers and enter the old city, relying on the experience of a local guide to visit the ancient consulates in the old city, and to see the roofed markets where traditional arts and crafts were sold. He wanted to see the houses of worship there, the oldest of which was the renowned Naqah Mosque and the Jewish Synagogue that was famously housed in a peculiarly narrow lane. He had been entranced by the houses with towers and domes, which he had spotted when flying over Tripoli in his aeroplane.

As you listened, you understood most of it because he was talking about a topic familiar to you, and you recalled that all Italians avoided entering the old city. During the months you had lived in Kushat al-Safar, you hadn't seen a single Italian soldier or policeman. Even the responsibility for keeping the peace had been left to the Libyans.

The only time you had seen Italian soldiers in the old city was when they came in droves of armed bands to pluck youths from the streets and force them to join the army. Other than that, the old city was monopolized by the Libyans and those who had made it their home for centuries, such as the Maltese and Greek sailors and fishermen, as well as the Jews who had come during the days of the Roman Empire.

The motorcade headed towards the tent prepared for the Marshal, passing through the throngs of Libyans wearing their traditional flowing white robes, standing on both sides of the street to hail the Governor-General and the Duce. The tent was enormous, luxurious carpets covered the ground, and couches and armchairs were placed in its corners as if it were a hall in a palace. Gigantic bouquets of flowers were placed at the entrance. In a corner by the entrance was a large table where there were a great number of carafes filled with a wonderful variety of juices, as well as baskets of fruit.

You stopped the car in front of the tent where a number of Marshal Balbo's aids were waiting. Some of them were in uniform, while others were in civilian clothes and accompanied by their wives. When the Marshal arrived, they rushed forward to greet him and his companion, after which they all entered the tent.

The security escorts showed you where you should park the car. You left the car where it would remain in the guards' sight, which gave you a chance to watch the celebration, though you didn't stray too far as you had to be ready at any moment if the Marshal wished to leave the celebration.

In the centre of the square where the celebration was being held, there were a number of cavalrymen on horseback wearing black cloaks with hems brocaded in gold and silver threads. They had lined up and were standing to attention, ready to begin a demonstration of their horsemanship in front of the raised dais. A canopy of coloured mats had been set up to shield the guests from the sun on the dais, as well as in the other places, where important guests were sat in comfy leather armchairs. The Italian flag fluttered high atop a flagpole, which was symbolically taller than the palm trees scattered around the square.

Marshal Balbo didn't remain in the tent for long since the celebration would not commence until he had taken his place on the dais. A number of aides accompanied him, while Houriya remained in the tent with the Italian ladies who had brought their children along.

As Marshal Balbo approached the dais, a number of sheikhs and officials from the local government welcomed him. Some of them were wearing suits and fezzes, while others were wearing traditional Libyan clothes. They led him among the many tents that had been set up in a crescent around the racecourse.

Crowds of Libyans who had come to attend the Spring Festival surrounded the tents within which singers sang and beat their drums. The organizers had brought in flocks of sheep and enough butchers to slaughter them. The slaughter was accompanied by singing to herald the coming of Spring.

Troupes of dancers danced, and bands of musicians sang and played their tambourines, small conical drums, and other musical instruments, filling the air with a cheerful clamour while the Governor-General was passing by and smiling graciously at them. He beckoned one of his aides over, who stepped forward and gave the singers, dancers and musicians some money.

The time came for the cavalrymen's show, so Marshal Balbo returned to his raised seat on the dais, while his aides and guards sat on seats at a lower level. Houriya and the Italian ladies were seated directly behind the Governor-General, and a distance separated them from the racecourse, so that the clouds of dust caused by the horses' hooves would not trouble them, even though the racecourse had been sprayed with water.

The horsemen had taken their cloaks off and began their skilful exhibition, which the Marshal watched through his binoculars whenever their tricks took them far from the dais. One of the horsemen stood up on his saddle while the horse continued to gallop at the same speed. The horseman held the reins in his hands and remained standing without losing his balance.

Five other horsemen galloped in close formation, then linked their arms together in the middle of the gallop and broke into a song about horsemanship, whose melody harmonized with the rhythm of the hooves of their horses, which continued galloping as if they were a single horse with five heads and twenty legs. Two other horsemen rode with their hands interlocked and then stood up on their saddles and with their interlocked hands saluted the Marshal, whose hand waved in answer whose lips moved with exclamations of wonder that were lost in the din.

When the performance came to an end, the Marshal invited the horsemen onto the dais to congratulate them on their skill and to be photographed with him as a memento of the exhibition. They joined him in drinking soft drinks and milk and eating the dates that had been brought by the festival organizers for the guests of honour.

Everyone was waiting for the next performance on the programme, which would consist of Sufi chants and prayers performed by a troupe that stood at the side of the square holding their drums and cymbals, preparing to perform as they passed in front of the dais. The Marshal's laughter resounded in the midst of the festive atmosphere, which agreed with the Marshal's cheerful disposition, and his renowned love of parties.

Suddenly, the sound of a gunshot rang out from one of the Marshal's guards, quietening the tumult of voices and the music. A Libyan wearing a white cloak splattered in blood dropped dead at the Marshal's feet. The guards had spotted him breaking through the circle that surrounded the Governor-General with his hand in his waistcoat pocket to draw the weapon that would assassinate Marshal Balbo. They had finished him off before he could carry out the deed.

As you were near the dais, you heard and saw the whole thing. The gunshot terrified the people who had been standing close by and they pushed one another in the attempt to flee. The Italian military guards and police encircled Marshal Balbo in order to protect him. He put himself in the hands of his personal bodyguards, who hurried towards him with one of their military vehicles without waiting for the car that had brought him.

The car shot off with incredible speed to get him away. Several motorcars followed behind it, some of them military vehicles, while others were police cars or those of his Italian aides who had been shaken by the assassination attempt and feared a plan to target them too. They hurried to their cars, shouting to their women to get in, and then accelerated as quickly as possible, heedless of the people in front, who had to make way in order not to be run over.

The hungry and poor, on the other hand, considered it an opportunity to rush to the tables laden with drinks, fruits, sweets and other food to fill their stomachs as much as they could. Some of them even carried off the chairs, mats, and carpets that had been part of the dais.

You weren't sure what you were supposed to do except take Houriya, if she was there, and catch up with the Marshal. You went to the tent reserved for the guests of honour to look for her, but the tent had been invaded by hordes of barefoot children in tattered clothes who were rolling up the table cloths, dragging away the chairs, and emptying the plates of fruit into their laps. You didn't try to stop them, because all you were concerned about was finding Houriya.

You feared that if any of the instigators who had attempted to assassinate Marshal Balbo saw her, they would consider her a traitor who deserved to be killed. All the automobiles had left the place and all that remained were a few horse-drawn carriages that had brought the sheikhs and prominent Libyans. Your car was the only one left bearing an Italian government plate the flag of the occupiers and it would be a tempting target for the rioters. And although those wretched troublemakers were too busy looting, they would notice the car before too long. This was especially true in the absence of policemen or troops, who had all disappeared to protect the Governor-General.

You couldn't possibly leave the place without making sure that Houriya had left safely as well. You were certain you hadn't seen her leave, so you would have to search for her in the neighbouring tents. But you couldn't leave the car at the mercy of these gangs of hooligans.

At that moment, you saw one of the sheikhs, who lived in the district, attempting to calm the people down and telling them to stop stealing. Suddenly an idea occurred to you, by which you could protect both yourself and the car while still searching for Houriya. You grabbed the Sheikh's hand, pulling him towards the car, and asked him to get in and ride with you so he could move quickly among the crowd and persuade them to remain calm. He consented.

You ripped the Italian flag off and bundled the sheikh into the car, putting the roof down for him. You started to cut through the crowds while the sheikh stood up in the car and loudly called upon the people to remain calm and stop looting.

As you drove the car, you looked for Houriya everywhere and stopped outside every tent where people had sought protection from the chaos until the panic subsided. The sheikh tried to raise his voice over the shouting and yelling, advising everyone he saw to return to their homes lest they anger the authorities and force them to send a police force to arrest them.

Every once in a while, the sheikh slapped his palms to his cheeks, mourning for the man who had been wrongly shot. When you asked him what he meant, he told you that the man hadn't intended to assassinate Marshal Balbo as the guards had thought. The assassin in question was simply an unemployed man named Matouq whom the Janzour primary school sometimes employed to clean the school and its grounds. He had applied for a permanent position as a messenger at the school, but they had refused to appoint him.

Some people had told Matouq that the Governor-General was coming to Janzour, so he had written a petition asking to be appointed at the school. And after he had been shot, his hand still clutched the petition the guards had presumed had been a weapon.

You kept on driving uneasily, your hands gripping the steering wheel stiffly. You sensed the anger and sorrow of what had happened. Then, in the midst of all the confusion,

you heard Houriya calling you from one of the tents you
had passed. You stopped the car, looked in the direction of
her voice, and found her surrounded by a group of female
singers. She later told you she had hidden among them and
pretended to be one of them in order to hide from a
number of angry men who had been threatening to kill
her.

You drove the car to the entrance, so she could jump
directly into the back, where she crouched between the
seats so that the men who had threatened her would not
notice her. Without notifying the sheikh about what you
were about to do, you jammed on the accelerator. The car
roared and jumped forward, frightening the people in front
of you who darted left and right to avoid standing in your
way. The sheikh angrily began to shout, demanding to be
let out, but you didn't stop until after the car was more
than a mile away from the festival site.

The streets were empty, so you looked behind you in
order to tell Houriya she could sit up, but you found her
face turned away, weeping silently. As soon as the sheikh
got out, the silent crying turned to wailing and sobbing.
You drove the car away from the main street, got out of
the car and helped her to stretch on the back seat. You
found a bottle of water in the trunk and advised her to
sprinkle some water on her face to freshen up.

After she sast up, she took a small bottle of perfume
out of her bag that sent a pure scent throughout the car
and helped her return to her normal self. She knew that
Balbo was unharmed and had also heard what people were
saying about the dreadful mistake the Italian guards had
made by killing an innocent man and causing all that chaos.

What had terrified Houriya the most had been a man

carrying an axe who had threatened to kill her as vengeance for the honour of the Libyan people, which she had
sullied by being Balbo's mistress and accompanying him to
the festival. The man had taken advantage of the absence
of Italian soldiers and policemen to come looking for her
in the tent where the guests of honour had sat. If not for
one of the women singers who had pitied her plight and
hidden her among her troupe, this man would have seen
Houriya and she would have been caught beneath the
blows of the axe.

When you arrived at her house, Houriya asked you
not to mention what you had seen. Blowing this accident
up and spreading word of it among the people was out of
keeping with the humanistic relationship built on mutual
understanding and friendship the Marshal had tried to build
between the Libyans and Italians.

"We must not let a stupid guard ruin everything," she
said.

Obeying her instructions, you didn't utter a single word
about the incident, not even to Mukhtar or Ayyad al-Fezzany.
They asked you why Marshal Balbo hadn't returned with
you as expected, and why Houriya was so ill she had had
to lean on you as she left the car and climbed the steps to
her flat. You ignored them and hurried back to your hotel
in a quiet, pensive mood.

FOURTEEN

When you reached the hotel, you decided not to meet with anyone that evening so you would not have to be part of any conversation where the topic might arise. Your desire to conceal the incident aggravated your emotional turmoil, to the point that your sleep was ridden with nightmares.

The slain man was the protagonist of your dreams. He had put on a clean cloak for the festival and had come with a heart full of hope in the Italian governor's chivalry. Marshal Balbo would help him achieve his dream of becoming a full-time worker at the Janzour primary school. Then the guard's bullets murdered his simple dream, and that poor old man fell onto the carpets, a stiff corpse, his gaunt face peering out with frightened bulging eyes, his baffled mouth open in a scream that was frozen in time. That was the last detail you remembered before waking up.

You immediately went to buy the local Arabic and Italian newspapers only to see that what Houriya had told you last night had become an official policy, and a cloak of silence had been dropped over the incident, for none of

these newspapers even mentioned it. Then you went and
sat in a café to listen to the

RAI's morning broadcast and also heard nothing about
it.

You went to Houriya's house to ask after her health
and found an urgent order waiting for you with Hawaa.
You were to go to Sheikh al-Balbal's house in the Sha'ib
al-Ain Alley and to bring him back to her home as quickly
as possible.

In spite of Houriya's work as a nurse in the Italian
hospitals, she was a firm believer in the spiritual therapy
that was practised by pious men such as Sheikh al-Balbal.
The sheikh's house wasn't far away and the alley where he
lived was too narrow for the motor car to pass through.
Nevertheless, you took the car for those were Houriya's
orders, as had happened before when you went to collect
her dressmaker or the boy who fixed the curtains, amongst
others, whom you could have easily fetched from nearby
places that didn't require the use of a car.

Houriya ordered you to go with the car as an expression of her respect for these people. Most of them were
thrilled to find an automobile waiting for them, some loved
to be seen riding in this sleek car, and Houriya delighted
in making people happy. But Sheikh al-Balbal wasn't one
of the people who boasted of material pleasures. It made
no difference to him if he went on foot or rode the most
luxurious car in the world.

You left the car nearby and went down the alley only
to find him waiting for you outside his home. He was
wearing his white jalabiya and his white skullcap. He
thanked you for your punctuality. You knew that Houriya
hadn't sent him an advance message asking him to visit

her, and he didn't own a telephone on which she was able to call him. The sheikh however was aware of many matters that became known to him via his own spiritual channels and mystical knowledge.

After settling into the seat beside you, he said, "The murder of poor Matouq at the hands of the Marshal's guard has saddened you. What great ignorance this Italian governor had displayed. While he fears being killed by Libyans, he will die at the hands of his Italian soldiers. They and only they will shoot and kill him."

The Sheikh's remarks sent shivers up and down your body. No one had dared mention the catastrophe, so you didn't know what to make of the idea of the ghastly fate that awaited the Marshal at the hands of his own men. You wished that he hadn't mentioned such a matter, because you would be forced to keep the burden of the secret to yourself and not breathe a word about it to anyone.

You knew that holy men had their own way of expressing themselves that differed from the ways of ordinary people, and that they had their own reasons for matters no one else could predict. You wondered why he had chosen to reveal this dangerous prophecy. Was it because you seemed to be very upset about the death of the innocent man, and he had wanted to assure you that a suitably just revenge awaited the governor who caused it?

You didn't dare utter a single word and couldn't find the strength to ask him when the prophecy would be fulfilled. For his part, he didn't say another word, but immersed himself in praying and invoking God silently, and the only words he uttered – in what resembled a shriek – were, "God is Everlasting. Help us and protect us, O Sidi al-Shanshan who lies buried in Dahman.

Help us and protect us O Sidi Mansour, whose light is the brightest."

After you had brought him to her apartment, the sheikh spent more than two hours inside with Houriya, and after his work was done. he preferred to return home on foot and so you left him to his own devices.

Houriya sent Morgan to inform you that she wanted to see you. She didn't want to dwell on what had happened the day before and only referred to it casually, as she conveyed to you the gratitude of the Governor-General for refusing to flee from the rabblerousers and for looking for her until you found her, saving her from life-threatening danger.She had obviously got over the psychological crisis caused by the previous day's fright. Thanks to Sheikh al-Balbal, she had managed to regain her cheerful nature. Sheikh al-Balbal's herbs still enveloped the whole house with their scent and calmed one's nerves, so much so you almost felt compelled to lounge on one of those cosy chairs. You were giving in to a forced state of mental languor under the influence of this aroma, when you realized Houriya had handed you an envelope full of money. The edges of paper currency were sticking out from the envelope and the sight of it returned you instantly to a state of wakefulness.

You stared at the envelope in surprise, for you couldn't imagine at first why it was being handed to you. No doubt you were meant to deliver it to someone. Houriya however confirmed it was for you, saying it was symbolic compensation from the Marshal for your courageous action yesterday.

You told her you couldn't accept the money and returned the envelope, saying you had only done your

duty, which you were paid to do; thatand the kind treatment you received from her was more than enough
compensation.

You had spoken sincerely, but you knew that she would
never take the envelope and would insist that you accept
it, which is what happened. When you finally opened the
envelope, you couldn't believe your eyes. The amount was
equal to more than two years of wages.

At first, you didn't know what to do with all this money,
or how to spend it. You decided to be practical and save
half of it and enjoy spending the other half. It was noon
and the only person around was Mukhtar the garage guard.
You went into his room and found him taking his noon-
time nap, so you woke him up and put a pile of more than
a hundred and fifty francs in his lap. He opened his eyes
and, still in a hazy state between slumber and wakefulness,
asked you what had happened. With your head bent low
in the darkness of the room, you whispered that the angels
who feed people rice in their sleep had changed their tactics
once they discovered that money brought people more
happiness than rice. Then you told him to continue sleeping
so that the angels might bring him more francs.

As you left the garage, you saw Ayyad al-Fezzany coming
towards you and you were about to stick your hand in
your pocket to give him a handful of money when you
remembered the beating he had given you two days earlier,
so you decided not to give him any money at all. There
were more deserving people nearer to your heart with
whom you wished to share this reward.

Ayyad al-Fezzany and you instead decided how to divide
your duties between the two of you. He chose the morning
shift, leaving you with evenings and nights. You agreed to

this arrangement although it deprived you of delicious free breakfasts and lunches at Houriya's house. You agreed to begin the following day, so you gave al-Fezzany the car keys to finish today's work on his own.

Before leaving the building, you saw Hawaa returning from the vegetable market with her baskets, so you took the money you had contemplated giving to al-Fezzany and gave it to her. You walked down Caneva Street in ecstasy. You turned down King Victor Emmanuel Street and looked in the shop windows, thinking about the best ways to spend the obscene amount of money you had been rewarded with.

You had decided to send most of the money to your family in Awlad Al Sheikh in order to lighten the misery of the children. And in order for the money to truly reach those children, you would not send money that the adults could hoard for themselves. You would send it in the form of clothes, toys, sweets and food instead, so that these deprived children might enjoy a few days of what you had yearned for as a child, when you had seen toys, sweets or apples in the hands of other children, but had been unable to have them yourself.

When you went to the Shushan Agency the following morning, everyone who knew you was amazed that you were still in Tripoli for they, like your family in Awlad Al Sheikh, had all believed that you were now in the middle of the ocean on your way to Abyssinia. You told them that an order had been issued at the last minute postponing your departure since you were needed as a government driver.

You asked the people who were going to your village to inform your parents of the postponement of your departure. You then learnt that a freight truck was going to your village that evening, so you took a porter with a wheel barrow and headed to a grocer's shop where you filled the wheel barrow with flour, tea, oil, biscuits, and sweets. You also filled a big basket with bananas, apples and grapes and bought a bag of Italian bread that was only sold in Tripoli.

Next, you bought a large number of children's clothes of all sizes for boys and girls, in addition to an equal number of traditional Arab clothes worn by people in the village and suited their taste in colours. From the vending carts on the street that sold toys, you bought a collection of dolls, toy cars, balloons and whistles. You divided everything you had bought into two equal shares, one of which was to be sent to you father's home, while the other share was to be sent to your mother's.

Satisfaction enveloped your whole being as you imagined the surprise your brothers and sisters would feel when they received your gifts. Now you could rest at ease about what you had done for your big family in the village, you decided you should look after your small adopted family in the city as well.

You waited until the shops reopened after the midday break and then went to Kushat al-Safar, where you hired a man to carry the goods you intended to buy. He went with you to the butcher's shop, where you found a small lamb for sale. You thought it would be a good idea to buy a whole lamb, so the surprise would be even greater than if you had just bought a cut of lamb, no matter how big.

After putting the lamb in the porter's basket, you bought items that would be useful for cooking the lamb. You added oil, fat, tomato paste and several packets of macaroni. You also bought tea, sugar and peanuts and filled another basket with fruits and vegetables. With that basket in one hand, you filled another with goods from a merchant that sold traditional Libyan clothes, a fine dress for Thuraya, a cloak for her mother and a jalabiya for her father.

Carrying all this you set course for Bint al-Pasha Alley, followed by the porter who thought you were bringing all this to propose to someone, though you didn't respond to his question or his congratulations on what he supposed to be a happy occasion. When you brought him to the house of Haj al-Mahdy, the man's face betrayed his surprise, for he knew the owner of the house and knew his youngest daughter had been married the previous year. Then his eyes lit up as though he had guessed what was going on and wondered out loud whether this girl had gotten divorced and you had come to marry her. Your only response was to mutter under your breath and from the bottom of your heart, "I wish."

You expected Thuraya's family to be overcome with shock once they saw all the expensive gifts you had bought. People were only accustomed to giving and receiving such extravagant gifts for engagements or weddings, so you readied yourself to say you had merely wanted to celebrate your deliverance from the horrors of war with a feast.

You put your trust in God and knocked on the door. You had expected Thuraya's face to be the first thing you saw, but her younger brother had got to the door before her. You ordered the porter to leave the baskets in the roofed passage where he stood and then dismissed him.

Overjoyed by what he saw, Thuraya's brother ran to tell his family you were waiting at the front door, then quickly returned in order to take you where his father was sitting.

After sitting with Haj al-Mahdy, you learned he could only walk with great difficulty because of complications from a bone disease. He was sitting with a pillow between his back and the wall and tried to appear well, saying that what had happened to him was the will of God. A broken note of anguish infiltrated his voice. Of course, nothing was above the will of God, but how could he find a new source of income for the family?

All the family could do was have their son leave school and start working at the shop. But he couldn't make shoes or mend them like his father He could only try to sell the remaining shoes and those his father's friends, also shoe-makers, had placed in the shop, in exchange for a paltry commission.

Thuraya and her mother came to greet you, surprised that you hadn't sailed with the army to Abyssinia like Fathy had. They asked if the ships carrying the soldiers had turned back. Before they could be taken in by false hopes that Fathy had been spared from going to war, you quickly told them that you had been the only one exempted from going to war. The mother said how odd that was, inasmuch as you had also been the only one to be able to leave the base every day. You didn't want to elaborate on the circumstances, nor did explain the gifts you had brought for them, for they accepted them grate-fully and without any objections.

It was obvious that their circumstances didn't allow them the luxury of declining the gifts. They didn't even ask about the occasion that had called for such generosity. They felt that the father's illness was reason enough for such aid. All you heard was a reproachful word from Thuraya's mother, who scolded you for troubling yourself so much every time you came to visit them. She followed that by thanking you and invoking God to bless you and open the gates of prosperity for you.

The mother sat down in a corner of the room to make tea while Thuraya brought a plate of peanuts, which she shelled and roasted beside her mother. Her brother couldn't wait till his family inspected the gifts you had brought, so he rummaged in the baskets until he found the apples, took one and started to eat it.

It was clear you had been heartily welcomed by the family and it seemed natural you should act as one of them. But the great joy you felt at the reception you received contrasted with the air of gloom that prevailed over the household and covered the faces of the family. Thuraya had become thinner, her face paler, and her beautiful eyes brimmed with sorrow.

You didn't want the conversation to be tainted by the their worries about the father's illness, the absence of the girl's husband, the end of the boy's education, and the floundering shop. You started talking to them about the miracles of Sheikh al-Balbal, his ability to predict the future, and how he knew secrets about this world no one else knew. You advised the ailing fathe to make use of the pious sheikh's blessings since he lived in an adjacent district and would not hesitate to pay a quick visit to their home.

You moved on to talking about the new models of cars that scaled hills, and traversed rough terrain. You also mentioned the foreigners' latest inventions, modern contraptions that spoke and sang, like the radio and the gramophone that you had seen in Italian shops.

Thuraya's face suddenly glowed with delight as she said, "Everyone is talking about the gramophone that sings, and every time a new song is sung at a wedding, they say that it has been sung on the gramophone. How I wish I could listen to a gramophone and see what it looks like."

You told her that life with a gramophone was so much more pleasant because she could order every singer of the East to sing for her. All of their songs were recorded onto black discs called records. No sooner did you place one on the gramophone than it began to turn and sing.

The third round of tea had come to an end, which signalled the end of the visit, but you couldn't stop thinking about the revolving record under the needle of that gramophone, which changed the shape of life, making it more beautiful and less morose.

Thuraya's mother invited you to have lunch with them the following day so you could share in eating some of the meat you had so generously brought. You asked them if they could make lunch slightly earlier than usual, as you had to be on duty in the evening. You also asked them to postpone the visit for a day, as you intended to come back in two days with a special new gift, the gramophone that Thuraya had dreamed of seeing and hearing.

FIFTEEN

Lovers in stories crossed the seven seas, climbed mountains and towering walls, and risked their lives merely to win a smile or approving glance from their beloved. So how could you be miserly about money – especially over an amount which you possessed several times over – when it came to buying a gift for the woman you loved? Especially when she needed something like this gramophone more than any other woman in the world.

Thuraya sat all day long at home without work to do, without a husband and without children. All she had was a sick father in the constant care of her mother, and a younger brother who spent all day long in his father's shop. There wasn'thing for a lonely woman trapped within four walls to do except endure boredom and depression.

The gramophone would be the magic solution to Thuraya's problems. It would turn her life around and nullify her cruel reality with its cheery songs. Buying Thuraya a gramophone was a humane deed for which God would reward you on the Day of Judgment. Thuraya would not only cherish the gramophone her whole life, but it would be a token she could remember you by. You loved her hopelessly, and you each knew that your love for her, like any other in the world, made claims that ultimately had to be met without expecting anything in return.

What encouraged you to buy the gramophone even more was that a Libyan merchant named al-Musheeriqy had recently opened a shop beside the Italian stores on Corso Sicilia that specialized in modern appliances like radios, gramophones, sewing machines, and the necessary accessories that went with these, such as transformers, batteries and records. Many of his customers were Libyan, which meant these appliances were no longer the exclusive domain of Italians and wealthy Jews.

You had previously made the acquaintance of al-Hady, one of al-Musheeriqy's sons, and he had told you they had a special discount for Libyan customers, so you decided to buy the gramophone from his shop.

The main shelves in this shop were filled with Italian records, whereas the Arabic records occupied a small corner. The owner of the shop informed you that most of them contained the works of Egyptian singers. He was astonished when he found that you had never heard of singers like Salama Hijazy, Sayed Darweesh, Fathiya Ahmed, Saleh Abdel Hayy, Munira al-Mahdiya, Um Kulthum, Muhammed Abdel Wahab, Najat Ali and Zakariya Ahmed. They were all famous singers or composers of music and he knew many of them personally since many Egyptian singers had come to give concerts in Tripoli's theatres and he had met them there, or else had met them when he had visited Egypt and seen their concerts there.

He showed you pictures, hung on one of the store walls, of him with some of these people who all had songs and music on the records he sold in the store. He also expressed his disappointment because Libyan singers couldn't find anyone to record their songs, with the exception of the Jewish singer Masouda all-Rahily and her partner Sahyoun Mahloula. The only Libyan recordings were by Sheikh Ali Hanka in Germany and a number of musical sketches that had been recorded by Basheer Fahmy, the singer and composer who had emigrated to Tunisia.

Hady told you he intended to persuade his father to establish a recording company for Libyan singers like Othman Najeem, Kamel al-Qady, Shakir al-Murabet, Muhammed Selim and Ahmed Shaheen. He said that was the way the Arab world would learn about Libya's artistic ingenuity.

Hady then helped you to choose records, recommeding Masouda al-Rahily's songs, which had been recorded in Tunis, and one of Sahyoun Mohloula's famous tunes. You also bought Sheikh Ali Hanka's song "Girls of Berlin" and other records recorded by RAI, which included Sufi chants and solo performances geaturing traditional musical instruments like the maqrouna, the ghita and indigenous percussion.

You also bought Basheer Famy's records, among which were his songs, "My cousin, my angel" and "The bird sings and his wing sings back". Before venturing to finish the transaction, you wanted to make sure you had enough money. You asked Hady how much it would cost. After calculating the prices, and applying the discount, you found you still had enough to buy another gramophone.

You handed over the money and were pleased that you could bring Thuraya such a wonderful gift so cheaply. As a token of his appreciation, Hady added a recording of a recitation of the Holy Quran by the Egyptian Quranic reader, Sheikh Muhammed Rifat.

When you arrived at Haj al-Mahdy's home at the

appointed time, you weren't in a rush to open the cardboard box with the gramophone inside. You brought it with
you and left it closed, hinting you had bought it for yourself, but hadn't yet had the chance to take it back to your
hotel before lunch.

You and Haj al-Mahdy sat down around a large bowl
of soup, with enough meat in it to feed ten people. You
ate heartily and thought of your presence in that house as
a holiday. When it was time for tea, you stretched your
hand towards the cardboard box and opened it. Hady had
taught you how to use it and had prepared it. All you had
to do was put a record on, slide the needle over it and
switch it on.

You had chosen to begin with the recitation of the
al-Rahman from the Holy Quran. No one noticed anything
until this moving voice, which seemed to come from the
sky, reverberated throughout the room.

"God Most Gracious! It is He who has taught the
Quran. He has created man. He has taught him speech and
endowed him with intelligence. The sun and moon follow
predestined courses and the stars and trees both bow in
adoration. And He has raised the Firmament high and He
has set up the Balance of justice."

The family was far more surprised than you'd expected.
At first they were struck dumb in bewilderment, then
everyone let out shouts of surprise. Haj al-Mahdy suddenly
stood up as if he were no longer lame and then he praised
God as though he had just witnessed a miracle. Thuraya's
mother's reaction was mixed with fear and she continued
to invoke God to protect them as though she were in the
presence of djinns.

The reaction of Thuraya's mother and father didn't

surprise you, since they knew nothing about these modern inventions, except for what you had casually mentioned a couple of days earlier, so you let their daughter explain how the gramophone worked.

The recitation of the Quran had come to an end, and instead of playing the other side, you moved to another record featuring quick tempoed Andalusian songs. People in Tripoli sang them at weddings and celebrations, songs like "O Crescent Moon, veil yourself from me", "Gazelle of the valley" and various others.

The feeling of surprise faded and transformed intp great joy as Thuraya's family began to understand what was going on. They expressed their delight at this amazing invention you had brought that allowed them to hear the voices of the greatest singers and Quranic reciters in the comfort of their own home.

You led them through several kinds of religious and popular songs, leaving aside the songs that spoke of love so that Thuraya could enjoy them when she was alone with the gramophone.

You were pleased with the air of mirth the gramophone had stirred in a house where the father's illness had cast a gloomy atmosphere. The price you had paid for the gramophone and the records paled in comparison to the joy it had brought. You felt you had done a good deed and repented for your sins.

After your third cup of tea, you stood up and asked the family's permission to leave. On your way out, several voices reminded you you had forgotten to put the gramophone back in its box and take it with you. They all thought one of your bosses at work had lent it to you for a few hours and that you would have to return it.

Instead of correcting them, you bent down and took the gramophone in your hands, then rather than putting it in its cardboard box you took it to a small closet in a corner of the room, which would be a good place for it. You asked Thuraya to bring a piece of cloth to spread under the gramophone, saying that it would not be fair to bring the gramophone from its original home in Rome and not give it a fine reception.

When you realized nobody had understood, you explained that you hadn't brought it to the house only to take it away again, but that it was a gift. As if an electric current had shocked each family member at the same time, they rose up shouting, refusing the gift in one breath. Unexpectedly, even the young boy refused. And for the first time, the father's voice, which had been weak and tired, loudly demanded you take the gramophone with you as you were most deserving of it and its music.

The gramophone remained in your hands as you stared at them, astonished by their refusal. Thuraya came forward picking up the cardboard box and begged you to put the gramophone in it and to take it with you. The refusal was unanimous, in contrast to what had happened with the meat, groceries and clothes, which they had gracefully accepted.

They either thought the gift was going too far and would arouse suspicions, or they viewed gifts related to the necessities of life, like food and clothes, as a chivalrous gesture done out of friendship. On the other hand, they couldn't accept this device, which belonged to the world of luxuries. Perhaps they thought that purchasing something like this was beyond your means, or that you had bought it for yourself but felt too ashamed to take it with you.

Nevertheless, you were absolutely determined the gramophone should stay in Haj al-Mahdy's house. They could use it to dispel the gloom and depression. So you refused and walked briskly towards the door, leaving the gramophone behind and saying, "I've no right to take this gift back after it has found its owners."

You ran down the steps in leaps until you reached the street. You hurried away, certain you had achieved your aim, but the sound of the front door forced you to turn around. The door had opened and a hand extended out to place the box with the gramophone on the doorstep. You remained standing in your spot, not knowing what to do. Then you watched yourself walk towards the front door, and bend over to pick it up.

Their insistence struck you as strange. There was no point in knocking on the door and trying to persuade them. They wouldn't consent and you found no other alternative to taking the gramophone back to your hotel. Their refusal had threatened the foundations of your relationship with them. You couldn't possibly have foreseen their reaction would be so adamant, nor that Thuraya and her family would treat you with so much suspicion.

You reconciled yourself to reality and contented yourself with loving Thuraya in these moments when you were close to the splendour of her eyes and your soul could glean some joy from her sweet smile. It was an unrequited love, and you remembered hearing a phrase from a song that glorified the love of the soul as eternal, and scorned physical love for being fleeting.

Such a song seemed fitting for your love for Thuraya. Having lost all hope of seeing your affections fulfilled in this world, you wanted to elevate your love to a sublime status. She too could love you in her soul without causing herself shame or guilt.

Whatever the extent of her love for you had been before her marriage, her subsequent attitude had always remained familiar and accepting, which suggested she had found some way to not burden her conscience, whenever she felt happy at seeing you might conflict with her lawfully bound to another.

As for your relationship with Thuraya's family, you had been a friend of their even before her marriage, and your work in her father's shop had brought you much closer to him, so much so that he had looked upon you as a second son. Thus, there was no harm in Thuraya considering her relationship with you as fraternal if that made her happy. It didn't put any restraints on your feelings, and didn't hinder your freedom to view this love in any light you pleased. Regardless of how you perceived Thuraya's feelings for you, or what her father and the rest of her family felt about you, you still couldn't rationalize their unjust refusal.

SIXTEEN

Returning to your hotel with a gramophone wasn't easy. These objects were associated with riches and luxury and it would be a source of worry and suspicion in such a cheap hotel. You would not be able to hide it, because it was a talking metal contraption that would cause a hubbub. So the only solution was to advertise it instead of hiding it, to tell the hotel owner and his companions about how this gramophone had come to you in a way that made your possession of it seem natural and not worth bothering over.

As you were still in a bad mood after your visit to Haj al-Mahdy's house, you felt like stirring up the hotel owner's playful sense of humour. Perhaps it would cheer you up. As usual, al-Kubran's wide girth took up most of his office, which faced the entrance so he could see everyone who went in and out.

You went straight to him and said, "Guess what I've got in this box."

They replied, "Why does it matter if we know or not? Are we going to divvy up what's inside ?"

"Yes, we'll all benefit from it, even though I own it." One of the men said, "I wish it were full of sweets.

You own it all and we eat it all. What do you say to that?" Al-Kubran disagreed, saying, "It must be something else, and I think I know what it is. If we take into account its large size, and you say that we shall all benefit from it, and there's scribbling on the box, so I'm going to say it's one of these foreign-made grills."

Another friend laughed and said, "Al-Kubran thinks only with his meat-craving stomach."

You said, "It is neither a grill, nor a box of sweets. Look and see."

You took the device out and placed it atop the table. One of the men said, "Its still difficult to say what it is. I've never seen anything like it."

You didn't say a word and al-Kubran fingered the gramophone and asked you, "Isn't this what they call a gramophone?" One of the men added, "Then this is the thing whose voice we hear coming from the Italian restaurants, cafés and hotels."

"How did you get it?"

Al-Kubran said, in a suspicious tone, "It must have been a deal. Some rich man gave it as a present to one of his poor relatives who then put it on sale for half its price when you bought it."

One of the others said, "Good for them and good for you, but wouldn't it have been better for the wealthy man to give his poor relatives a sewing machine, which they could have made use of when times got hard?"

"Don't you think this gramophone is more capable of combating hard times than a sewing machine?"

Another man said, "If that had been the case he wouldn't have sold it to you."

You replied, "He sold it because he didn't know its value."

"Show us its value then."

"You'll see in a second."

You put a record on and switched the gramophone on. Um Kulthum's voice rang out, singing a cheerful song that said, "Take me back to my beloved homeland."

A new atmosphere awoke in the sleepy hotel and people from came from everywhere to gather around it until the office became too narrow for them all, so they began to crowd around outside.

A Maltese fisherman called Tony formed a circle with two Libyans and danced to the rhythm of the song inside the hotel courtyard. More people joined in and the circle grew. Even al-Kubran, with his hulking limbs, swayed and danced to the tune, and repeated the words of the song in his gruff voice.

One of his friends said al-Kubran should be called al-Karawan, which means a curlew, the sweet-voiced song-bird. The dance circle combined several ethnicities, races and religions. You could see Muslim Libyans, Maltese and Italian Christians, a Jewish merchant and a Negro fisherman.

You suddenly realized it was time to go to work. You didn't want to interrupt everyone's fun, so you left the gramophone in al-Kubran's care and went to your room to change into your uniform.

When you reached your destination and were sat in the car, you were torn between waiting for instructions and going up to the apartment to enquire after Signora Houriya's health and ensure she had fully recovered. Or maybe it would be better if you were honest with yourself and admitted you yearned for her, and wanted to feast your eyes.

You were unable to make up your mind, so you decided to ask Mukhtar. Mukhtar was more experienced than you in such matters because he had served these people for a long time. Even though the garage wasn't restricted to Houriya's use, as it was open to four or five other cars owned by businessmen with shops in the same building, and even though Mukhtar was officially answerable to the real estate company, he only really answered to Houriya. He was charged with serving her, guarding her car, and took his orders from her. Mukhtar never left the garage and was either inside his room in the garage, or sitting on the wooden bench in front of his room wearing his Arab white clothes with a blue and brown vest and a red skull cap, holding one of the cigarettes that he rolled himself and had perfected inhaling its delicious flavour.

Mukhtar cleared a place for you beside him on the wooden bench and when you sat down, he looked right and left conspiratorially and then whispered`, "'My only ailments are the house of al-Aqila, the tribe's imprisonment and the distance from my origins.' Do you know who said these lines which describe the life we led inside al-Aqila camp?"

"I don't."

"Our master, Sheikh Rajab Abu Huweesh, a pious man and one of God's saints. He wrote this poem. He was with us in al-Aqila camp and used his spare time to teach people to read and write. He strongly insisted I learn, but I made light of his invitation saying, 'Writing is beyond grey hairs'. So here I am today, regretting I didn't listen to him. If I had studied, I may have had a different fate than working as a garage guard."

"Do not regret anything, Uncle Mukhtar, I've studied the Quran and I know how to read and write but I work a job that does not require that."

"I would have at least been able to read the Quran and

filled the emptiness of my days by reading it. I mocked Sheikh Rajab's offer because I wasn't capable of understanding anything in that hell-hole. My job there was to carry the dead bodies and bury them in the wilderness. I was not alone. Ten other men worked with me all day long because the dead were many and burying them required a lot of people. We would carry an average of one hundred and fifty corpses a day. There wasn't enough time didn't to dig graves for them, so we looked for depressions in the land, stuck them in and heaped dirt over them. The coyotes, hyenas and vultures took care of the rest."

"Your whole family died in that camp, didn't they? Did you bury them?"

"At first I couldn't bury my sister Mariam, who was the first to go to the embrace of God. My punishment was a hundred lashes of the whip and being tied to a stake under the sun because I refused to do my job. When my father followed her a few weeks later, I decided to participate in burying him, not because I was afraid of the punishment, but because I wanted to dig him a real grave that would protect him from desert beasts. I recited a few verses from the Quran and invocations for the dead and turned his face towards Mecca.

"After that, I buried the rest of my family: my mother, my brothers and sisters, my wife and my three children and then my second wife and my daughter."

"And here you are, Uncle Mukhtar, recalling those sad events."

"Give me happy events and I will recall them instead. The guard's profession is cruel. Because you are left alone with yourself most of the time and with loneliness, memories like these come pouring down."

"You need some distraction instead of staying in the garage twenty-four hours a day."

"Where do you want me to go?"

"Let's agree on a day to take you on an outing. Either to the seashore, a stroll through the countryside or to see a film at Alhambra Cinema. Leave it to me."

"I went to the cinema once, and when I found they were showing a film about the new villages for the Italian settlers, I couldn't bear to watch it, so I left."

"That wasn't a film, it was just the propaganda reels they show before the film."

"This is what happened . . ."

The old man's eyes brimmed over with tears as he talked about his family members whom he had buried in the al-Aqila camp. He was still a prisoner of these moments and was unable to break their spell. When you tried to change the subject and asked him about Houriya, all he said was that she had gone to visit the hospital that morning and had returned in a good mood. Then he immediately reverted to his painful memories, and you resumed listening. These stories touched you as well and put you in a mood that didn't allow you to go anywhere other than sitting beside him outside the garage.

The incidents that he narrated had happened only a short while ago, their protagonists were still alive, whether it was the executioners, or those who had cheated death. The conditions that created these tragedies could recur at any time.

"God forbid."

As you watched him revisit memories of these disasters, you wondered if there was a kind of pleasure in recalling pain.

There was another question you were unable to understand, which was how could he find it in his heart to reconcile these disasters with their perpetrators? He was delighted to work for the Italians and had wanted to join their army, as he had once confided.

He suddenly said, "Do you know who informed me that I had been discharged from the camp?"

"Who?"

"Sidi Rajab Abu Huweesh. He was a pious man and had dreamed I would be set free a week before they told me. 'Rejoice, Mukhtar, liberation has come.' He asked me to go to a merchant in Zalam Market with a secret sign from him so that the merchant would give me five gold lire with which I was to start my life over, because I would leave the camp barefoot, naked, with only a single bara and nothing on my back except a torn shirt. How I wish I could visit him in Benghazi so that he would bless me."

The quietness of the side street and the dreamlike atmosphere these emotional reveries had evoked were suddenly shattered by a military car that stopped outside the building. Four soldiers from Marshal Balbo's guard jumped out of the car, with the heels of their shoes striking the tiles on the street so hard the earth shook. They spread out in all directions and one of them came up to you and told you to clear the street and go inside the garage. You chose to sit in the driver's seat, realizing that Marshal Balbo was visiting his mistress that evening.

A sleek white car pulled up. It had black windows, which concealed the person inside and was followed by another military car. Marshal Balbo got out wearing his military uniform. Surrounded by his guards, he entered the building, while the others remained outside.

You stayed in your seat in a state of readiness, prepared to carry out any order. Before an hour had passed, the Marshal appeared preceded by his guards, descending the building's stairs and striking the pavement with his heavy steps. He then got in the white car which sped off, preceded and followed by the two military cars, which drove away as noisily as they had come.

Quiet returned to the street. Darkness began to creep over the world and the street lamps gave the buildings a different look than they had during the day, sowing a sense of melancholy in the heart. You thanked God that Marshal Balbo's visit had passed without you being assigned any new tasks that might revive painful memories in your mind or create new ones.

Morgan came running up to you and told you that Signora Houriya had called for you. You leapt up the steps and caught up with Morgan as he opened the door of the flat.

As soon as she saw you, Houriya said, "The Marshal only came to check I was all right because I've not yet regained my health since the accident."

"Whoever sees your beauty can only praise God for His Grace."

"Thanks to Sheikh al-Balbal. His spiritual treatment, and his use of herbs have helped lift me out of depression."

"Don't forget the doctors at the Caneva Hospital."

"I didn't go there for treatment. I went to make sure the mistake we made the other day – I don't know how I could let it happen – didn't leave the seed of a child in my womb."

"I'm very sorry to have caused you any embarrassment."

"That's not what I meant. I want our relationship to

be built upon a sound religious basis in order to close a chapter of my life and begin a new one with you, God Willing. I want to have a child, or children, but I want their father to be of my people and my religion and to marry me according to the Path of God and the Prophet. Do you understand what I mean?"

"Of course I understand."

"You know, Sheikh al-Balbal himself told me that satisfying the natural needs of motherhood and childbirth are a guaranteed way to psychological, spiritual and physical health. We'll have to make a point of bringing him to the marriage ceremony as one of the witnesses, because he always makes me feel happy and optimistic."

You started to ask yourself if she had summoned you to her house from the very beginning for this relationship and if your role in the process had already been decided upon, perhaps without any need for your opinion on the matter.

Houriya said, "The best thing about the whole situation is that Italo has been very understanding of the fact that I can't go on living like this forever, and that I must fulfil my dream of becoming a mother before it is too late."

"And will the Marshal be able to stand separating from the woman he favoured over all the women in the world?"

"Don't forget he has a wife and three children whom he should pay more attention to and they will compensate for my absence. We shall just remain friends." A moment passed in complete silence before she beckoned you to sit next to her. Laughingly, she passed her hand over your forehead and asked, "What is the meaning of this furrowed brow?"

She then held your face between her hands and leaned towards you until you were very close together.

"What's the matter? Are you really this stupid or are you pretending to be stupid? You're the child I really want and I also want to satisfy the call of motherhood by having your child. I really do want to turn a new leaf with the Marshal and lead a normal married life that will be blessed by angels in heaven and acknowledged by everyone on earth. Am I not entitled to that? Is it too much for a woman like me to ask for?"

"No, not at all, but it is too much for a man like me to win a woman like you."

She pressed herself against you and touched her lips to yours. Tongues of red fire sprang up in your body. You felt like you were burning and your bones had turned to firewood. You stayed in this position for several moments before the gap between her breasts caught your eyes, and you impatiently reached to touch her there, while your other arm encircled her waist to draw her body to yours. She stopped you, freed herself from your grasp and moved away to sit on the chair opposite you.

All your senses had been aroused and you wanted to get close to her, but she motioned you to remain seated and said, "We must wait until we are married." You forced yourself to remain seated, and in order to conceal your frustration, looked upwards at the ostrich egg swaying from the ceiling.

Houriya arranged her hair and sat up in her chair. She wore a serious expression as she said, "Such things can wait a while, for there are more pressing matters and I want you to listen very carefully to what I'm going to say."

She spoke slowly and raised her eyebrows as she always

did whenever she wanted to show an interest. You gradually began to emerge from your lustful state and tried to focus on the new topic at hand.

"The Marshal has chosen you for a mission which is extremely confidential and dangerous, because it concerns his personal safety. Had you not deserved his complete confidence, he would never have chosen you."

Remembering the incident in Janzour and taking advantage of the informality of the conversation, you whispered, "Whatever the mission may be, I would be happier if he chose someone else." Her answer was quick and decisive. "Don't ever say that again, because to gain the Marshal's confidence is the dream of every person in the world. Soon you will understand the value of his trust and the efforts I made in order to assure the Marshal you deserved it."

"Tell me then and give me some peace of mind. What is this mission?"

"In brief, Marshal Balbo has decided to visit the old city incognito and no one outside the immediate circle of his closest aides knows anything about the visit. You will be his only companion so he can move about freely.

"He wants to visit the important places where Libyans and foreigners live, such as Kushat al-Safar, Qus al-Sariya, and al-Arba Arasat, the small Hara and the large Hara, in addition to Bab al-Bahr, al-Turk Market and other markets. He also wants to see the Naqah Mosque, the Gorgi Mosque, the Church of the Virgin, the Synagogue and the old French, British, Venetian and American consulates. He also wishes to visit the home of an ordinary Libyan family.

"This is just a preliminary idea for you to go and plan the visit so the Marshal puts every available minute to good use. The trip has two purposes. The first is that the Marshal wants to spend some time away from the routine of his official life in a place where no one knows him. The second is that he wants to complete his knowledge of the capital, and of the rulers and history of this part of the city."

You were terrified at the thought of being charged with such a tremendous responsibility, which could very well be incredibly burdensome, given the international importance of a man like Balbo. But then you remembered something that cleared your fears. Sheikh Al Balbal had foretold that the Marshal would be assassinated by Italian soldiers and that meant you would not have to worry about him dying at the hands of Libyans during the tour.

Houriya noticed your relief after your face had been clouded in dismay, so she cheerfully said, "You seem happy with your mission."

"What's more important is securing the Governor-General's safety."

"Don't worry about that, there will be security precautions in the event of any emergency."

"And what date will the visit be?"

"He wants it to be on Sunday, a holiday for all government offices, yet is an ordinary working day in the markets and the places he wishes to visit."

"You know all the markets close for an hour during midday, so he'll have to start early if he wants to see it in the morning."

"Yes, the visit will take place in the morning, because the evening turns to night, and it would become more dangerous."

You wanted to ask her about the exact time of the meeting on Sunday and the details pertaining to it, but she interrupted you saying, "Today is Thursday so we only have tomorrow and the day after tomorrow to arrange the details. But beware you don't leak a single word about this to anyone. You have enough time to visit the important sites before the visit and plot a precise path."

As you left Houriya's apartment, your mind was torn. One half was preoccupied with the offer Houriya had made you, while the other half was concerned with the Marshal's visit to the old city and how you had been selected to guide him through that small maze of lanes and interlocking alleys.

The first of the two topics would have to be put off. You hadn't even had time to think it through, because a quick answer would be of no help, and it was better that Houriya's proposal not occupy a lot of space in your mind, which would have to be wholly dedicated to the Marshal's visit. There was also the fact that Houriya was a very different woman from Nuriya, whose marriage proposal you refused without hesitation as soon as it was offered.

It was more complicated with Houriya. Any miscalculation would come at an exorbitant cost, which was why it warranted your full attention as soon as you had completed this urgent mission.

You didn't know three quarters of the places Houriya said the Marshal wanted to visit. That meant the remaining time would be best used by conducting preliminary research for the visit, getting acquainted with these places, and plotting the shortest route you could take and win the Governor-General's approval.

The most difficult part would be finding an ordinary Libyan family the Marshal could visit. You would need to familiarize yourself with their life. The only house you knew was Sherifa's secret brothel on Sidi Umran Street which, considering the Governor liked a good time, was probably more fitting than an ordinary house like Haj al-Mahdy's. His house couldn't be considered one of the traditional houses of the old city because it was on the upper floor of one of the houses with a patched-up entrance and stairs that weren't wide enough for a man of the Governor-General's girth.

SEVENTEEN

You returned to al-Kubran's hotel after buying a loaf of bread, as well as some onions, cucumbers, tomatoes and green peppers from a nearby grocer's, enough to prepare a plate of sharmoula, to which you would add salt and oil. You decided to cook a hot meal some other day and ate your light dinner quickly, then placed a kettle on top of the burner to make some tea. You started to read verses of the Holy Quran in order to regain your peace of mind, after it had been exhausted by the thought of love, politics, and the governor's security.

"And for the God-fearing, He always prepares a way out. And He provides for him from sources he could never imagine. And whoever puts his trust in God, sufficient is God for him. For God will surely accomplish His purpose. God has appointed a fate for all things."

You had completely forgotten about the gramophone, which was in the hotel owner's possession. You hadn't remembered it when you entered the silent hotel, because the door to al-Kubran's office was ajar and you hadn't been in the mood for socializing, because you had come home to be alone in your room.

Had the sound of women trilling to the rhythms of tambourines and drums suddenly brought it to mind? At first, you thought it was a wedding procession passing in front of the hotel that would quickly move on, but when the clamour continued you realized the noise was coming from the gramophone. One of the records had a recording of a Bedouin wedding. You had bought the very instrument that had disturbed your sleep and dispelled the calm of night.

There was no other solution except go back to the ground floor and regain possession of it so you would be the only one in charge of it during curfew hours.

The commotion would quiet down while you drank a cup of tea, which you suddenly felt the craving for. Then you went down to put a stop to this wedding, although before you left your room, the wedding had turned into a small musical band with traditional instruments. The band sounded almost real rather than just noise produced by a record, because everyone in al-Kubran's gang joined in singing parts of the song. They were famous words everyone in the city knew by heart and which were sung on religious and social occasions: words that moved the hidden depths of sorrow and stirred up sad romantic passions.

Nevertheless, everyone was singing along with much laughter and mirth when you got there, which contrasted with the words.

"My tear run like rain down the plate of my cheek." Al-Kubran was sitting on the floor surrounded by his companions. A flask of a drink extracted from palm pith was placed before him and he poured some of it into a small glass from which everyone sipped.

"I see something is flowing other than the tears that are mentioned in the song."

Al-Kubran replied, "This is a sweet drink that is not prohibited by God or His prophet. Come and take a sip of it if you don't believe me."

He offered you the glass containing the palm nectar, and you put it to your lips to test the truth of the man's words. You discovered that what he had said was a boldfaced lie, because it wasn't sweet like most harmless drinks made from palm pith. It had been fermented and become a sour intoxicant that would burn the chest, heart and brain.

"It's more sour than vinegar."

Al-Kubran pretended to be surprised and laughed, "O my God! Why does it taste sweet in my mouth then? Perhaps I've been transformed into one of the pious men of God who turn alcohol into honey in their mouths."

For the first time you realized that al-Kubran liked to drink. You had seen him playing cards before, but without anything to drink other than his three rounds of tea. He understood what was going through your mind and so, as he swayed to the melody with his corpulent frame and echoed the lyrics with the others, he smiled and said, "I'm a tea drinker just like you, but tea doesn't suit these songs. It's just a glass we sip in honour of this wonderful gramophone."

One of al-Kubran's companions raised his gruff voice over the sound of the gramophone as he sang a popular song that made excuses for people who drank wine. You had left your room in order to take your gramophone, but weren't so brazen as to ruin al-Kubran's revelry with his companions, so you left it and went back to your room.

The following morning, al-Kubran stopped you on your way out of the hotel, saying with a strange mixture of contrition and gratitude, "About the gramophone." However, all you were able to think about was the Supreme Commander's visit to the old city and the arrangements you needed to make for it, so you answered him saying, "We'll talk about it this later." Al-Kubran, on the other hand, could think of nothing other than the gramophone, so he said, "I just wanted to thank you for showing me this wonderful invention, and I've seen for myself how it has changed the atmosphere of the hotel."

"Leave these things to modern hotels. Al-Kubran's Arab hotel does not need such a gramophone; it represents a piece of Libyan history when caravans came in from the desert. What your hotel needs is not this gramophone, but a poet who recites the adventures of Abu Zeid al-Hilaly and the Ghoul."

"Believe me, your gramophone has inspired new ideas I intend to soon put into practice. However, the whole matter depends upon your approval."

"My approval?" you asked with surprise.

"I shall change the corner where the mounts are kept into a parking lot and I'll transform the roof into a modern café that overlooks the harbour. Tourists will come here to listen to the music of the East and dance to its rhythm."

"You still haven't told me what I've got to approve of."
"Leaving me this gramophone while I pay you its price in installments."

"I've got a very important appointment, so let us discuss the matter when I return this evening." It was yet another predicament, one you would not be responsible for, except for the white lie you had told him about the way you had acquired the gramophone. Ever since the arrival of Balbo and his rhetoric, the concept of renewal and modernization had caused a sort of hysteria in the city's inhabitants. People were tempted by success stories like that of al-Musheeriqy, who had gone from selling perfumes on al-Nakhly Street to selling radios, sewing machines and other household appliances.

Al-Kubran envisioned new buildings and pavements being built around the harbour and new modern boats for tourist guides. He believed the piles of dirt under the Arch of Marcus Aurelius, or the marble depot as people called it, should be planted with a rose garden surrounded by ornamental tiles. He had heard the propaganda that said tourists were on their way to visit Tripoli, and so the devil of modernization took hold of him. As soon as he had seen the gramophone, he thought that divine providence had been sent him the means to transform his hotel.

After leaving, you asked the people in the nearby shops where the French, British, Austrian and Venetian Consulates were situated. You also asked them about the Synagogue, the Church of the Virgin Mary, al-Naqah Mosque, Yousef al-Qaramanli's palace and the other places the Marshal had requested.

You hadn't imagined all these landmarks were so far apart from each other, or that the old city covered such a large area that no one could fathom it unless they specifically had had to learn it inside and out like you did. You rushed here and there, drenched in sweat, trying to save time, sometimes getting lost and sometimes returning to the very same spot from which you had started.

You began to feel out how the visit could be mapped out, but after spending half the day exploring and asking about the most important landmarks, you returned exhausted and dizzy, feeling like the most unsuitable person Marshal

Balbo could have chosen for such a mission. You should admit you were unfit to carry out the mission so the Marshal could choose someone else and you could avoid being punished for your inevitable failure.

Your pessimism increased when you finished your tour by attending the Friday prayer in al-Naqah Mosque, where the sermon was anti-Italian, and the Imam condemned all Libyans who submitted to the occupation and its atheist rule. The Imam urged the people to resist the colonists or emigrate, because it was wrong for Muslims to live like servants in a Muslim country under the rule of foreigners. He finished his fiery speech by quoting the Quranic verse that urges Muslims to emigrate when they are oppressed.

You remembered having heard thoughts like these frequently discussed by Haj al-Mahdy, who must have been attending Friday prayers with this Imam and listened to his sermons, falling under the spell of his ideas. The problem was, of course, that this Imam was usually arrested the night after his sermons as retribution for expressing his inflammatory opinions. If they arrested him tonight, tomorrow the Governor-General would find the streets mobilized against the Italians when he came to visit.

You had become acquainted with all the important landmarks Balbo wished to visit, but you still had to discover the shortest route you could use. That would require the help of someone who knew the old city and could spend the bulk of the day plotting the route until you had memorized it street by street. The best person for the job would be a porter who bore baskets on their backs and carried vegetables, fruits, and household supplies from the market to all the houses in the city. It was in his interest to master the shortest routes that would save him time and effort.

That was the specialist whose services you would hire tomorrow for the task at hand.

When you met with Signora Houriya that evening, she didn't have anything to say about the forthcoming trip other than that the Governor-General, would not eat or drink anything during the tour for security reasons, since he would not be accompanied by the guards who also acted as his tasters.

You had to share your confusion with her, since she knew how hospitable Libyans were, so how could the situation be dealt with? Houriya suggested the Governor-General pretend to eat and drink what he was offered in the shops. It would be up to you to help him out. For instance, he might be given a cup of tea, and it would be your job to take it from him to return it empty to the host, either by drinking it yourself or emptying it without their noticing. You laughed because she wanted you to perfect in one day the skills of prestidigitation magicians spent years perfecting.

But what about the family he would visit? You wished the old consulates had still been inhabited, so that it would have been possible to ask their permission to visit the place and thus simultaneously accomplishing the goals of visiting an important landmark and a Libyan family.

However, the consulates had changed completely, and not by turning into residential houses. One of the consulates had become a tannery and the Marshal would have to endure the awful stench of the place if he insisted on visiting it. Another consulate, owned by a Jewish merchant, had become a brewery that produced a cheap local wine called bokha. As for the British Consulate, one of its corners had caved in, so it was being restored.

You told Houriya the only Libyan family you knew
was the family of a shoemaker who had employed you as
his assistant. The man was bedridden and lived in a three-
room house with his wife, son and daughter, whose husband
had gone to Abyssinia.

Houriya thought this would be the ideal family for the
Marshal to visit. There was no point in him visiting wealthy
Libyans, for he had already visited similar houses. She added
that he would be very happy to make the acquaintance of
the family whose son-in-law had gone to fight in Abyssinia.

You did not explain your relationship with that family,
nor the misunderstanding that had arisen when you bought
them a gramophone. You realized you must clear up that
misunderstanding before taking Marshal Balbo to visit the
family, and you decided to make that your first priority.

You were less interested in impressing the Governor-
General than with impressing Thuraya and the effect this
visit would have on her opinion of you once she learned
you had come to her house with the man who ruled the
country. Naturally, Balbo's identity would not remain a
secret for long after the completion of the mission, and the
time would come when such a matter could be mentioned
without any fear or embarrassment.

You asked permission to leave work early that day in
order to see to the preparations and shortly after the afternoon prayer you went to knock on Haj al-Mahdy's door.
You hadn't prepared what you would say to justify bringing
a stranger into their home, though you had some ideas
you hoped to flesh out during your conversation with Haj
al-Mahdy. You went without any of your usual gifts. You
were certain that any parcel or bag, even if it were of
onions, would put them on their guard.

When Thuraya's mother opened the door and took you to her husband's room, you didn't ask about Thuraya or even mention her name, in order to indicate you had come for a specific reason and not merely as an excuse to see their daughter.

After asking after the Haj's health, you quickly cut to the chase saying you had met a foreign merchant who knew Haj al-Mahdy and had dealt with him in the past. When he had learnt the Haj was ill, he had insisted on visiting him, so you had come to ask their permission to bring the merchant the following day shortly before noon. Haj al-Mahdy asked you what the merchant's name was and where he came from, and you told him you had only met him briefly in a friend's shop and that your friend had informed him you knew his old friend's address.

You had put the family in an embarrassing situation which forced them to accept the visit, and before leaving, you informed them their guest was travelling and so would only be able to stay for a few minutes in order to wish Haj al-Mahdy a speedy recovery, and that he would consequently not be able to partake of any food or drink.

Although Haj al-Mahdy continued to insist on knowing the visitor's identity, you were unable to answer him since you didn't know how the Marshal would be dressed. You had fabricated this friendship between the Haj and the mysterious guest because you knew he had met many merchants in his shop and would not be able to uncover the spuriousness of your claim.

After leaving Thuraya's home, you went to a restaurant owned by Shlomo the Jew. It was situated under the Clock Tower and you ate a plate of fasuliya with tripe, for which the restaurant was famed. You intended to remain in the streets during the first hours of the night, freely roaming through the old city. After the shops closed and the streets emptied, you would be able to save time by not having to wade through the crowds. Similarly, returning late to the hotel would save you from al-Kubran's chattering, which had worsened since he had come under the gramophone's spell and endlessly attempted to possess it by any and all means, sohe could avoid having to buy one himself.

You didn't have time to get involved with it now and hoped to put it off until the day after the sneaked Marshal's visit. You snuck into your room after everyone had gone to sleep and woke up early the following day to continue your work.

You found a porter who had been born and bred in the old city. He was very happy to find a customer like you who gave him the money he took for carrying goods without requiring him to carry anything.

Together, you began the tour from Bab al-Huriya where the Sariya Arch formed a natural entrance to the old city. You then passed by the Mufti Arch and the al-Arba Arsat crossroads, after which walked past the landmarks the Marshal wished to visit. After reaching Bab al-Bahr, you went down a slope that led to the harbour district.

You returned along the same route and then left him to traverse the distance from starting point to ending point on your own. You took the route a third time and felt you had perfected the lesson the porter had taught you. All that remained was to spend some money on a haircut and a new suit so you would look presentable for the Governor-General.

When you showed Houriya the suit you had bought, she said they hadn't considered the visit would cost you money. As she felt the soft material of the suit she said, "Your taste in colours is just like mine. I also like pale blue and hate dark colours."

"Does that mean you approve?" "Do you want to try it on now?"

"I already tried it on at the shop and it fits me perfectly."

"Congratulations! I suppose you've begun to outgrow the driver's uniform and want to wear the clothes of someone with more stature."

"I consider myself fortunate to be your driver and I don't aspire to any higher status."

"Let's settle on the final arrangements for tomorrow's visit. You will come a little before ten o'clock. You will hire a carriage in front of the Palace and park it right in front of the building. Then you will come up to meet the Marshal, and take him by carriage to the place where you will begin your tour, after telling the coachman to wait for you where you will end your tour."

She then brought you a map of Tripoli and asked you to mark the route you intended to take with the red pencil she gave you. You drew the route the porter had recommended so she could show it to Balbo, who would make any necessary alterations or additions to it.

She warned you against saying anything that might reveal the Marshal's identity, and added that if there was any need to address him, or if some situation required you to introduce him to someone, the Marshal would instruct you how to behave in the matter when you saw him tomorrow.

Before leaving, Houriya opened her handbag and took out a wad of banknotes, asking you to hang on to it. When you hesitated, she explained that the money was to be spent on the Marshal if he needed anything, and for the carriage rides.

All you could think about after you left were the minutes on the clock that comprised the remaining time before the trip, and every second brought you closer to your momentous appointment with Marshal Balbo, which could be a terrifying and critical juncture in your life.

You went straight to the nearby shrine of Sidi al-Hattab in order to pray and ask the pious saint to protect and help you so the tour would go smoothly.

You slept fitfully that night and were haunted by dreams, all of which revolved around the next morning's trip. Balbo came to you disguised in animal forms: once as a huge bird that still had Balbo's human head on it as it came swooping down from the sky; then as an ox with two horns and military medals around his neck; then as an elephant with a rifle for a trunk and a military helmet on its head; and finally as a man wearing in the Air Marshal's uniform but with the head of a blue-fanged snake that chased you while you fled invoking Sidi al-Hattab's help.

NAKED RUNS
THE SOUL

ONE

You woke to the sound of dawn prayer, and couldn't go back to sleep. You performed your ablutions and prayers, and then lay in bed staring at the ceiling, waiting for nine o'clock to arrive.

Minutes after leaving your hotel you found yourself by the Miramare café, so you had a glass of tea with milk and ate two pieces of pastry called 'bread of the Nazarene'. You then took a carriage to Baladiya Street where Signora Houriya lived. You told the driver you were going to hire him until midday and he was to wait for you at a specified place even if you were late.

You avoided unnecessary conversation with him so that you would not reveal anything confidential. At ten to ten, you asked him to stop in front of the door of the apartment building. There were none of the customary signs of the Governor-General's presence in the apartment, however the plainclothes policemen scattered throughout the surrounding area clearly suggested he had arrived.

So at the exact time set to begin the trip, you leapt up the stairs, amazed at how calmly you knocked on the door. Just a few moments ago you had been as terrified of this mission as though it were Judgment Day. Houriya opened the door. Her face beamed, her eyebrows arched with gratitude, and she smiled her magic smile that was reflected in her eyes. You saw in her a presage of your success.

She looked you up and down and was satisfied with your appearance, thereby increasing your self-confidence. She asked you to be seated in the salon and left you for a few seconds, only to return with a handsome Moroccan man who was wearing a fez, the traditional Moroccan jalabiya and a pair of Moroccan markoub. His appearance spoke of both refinement and wealth. You stood to welcome the man and shake his hand without the thought that he was the Marshal in disguise ever crossing your mind.

The Marshal had succeeded admirably in concealing his identity, to the point that he seemed like an authentic Moroccan. His black beard had been dyed grey, which increased his dignified air, and he had chosen a pair of silver-framed sunglasses to cover his eyes, which completed the disguise. He spoke a few words of Arabic which he must have picked up during his governorship in Libya, like "Peace be upon you", "How are you?", and "That's excellent!"

You were told that whenever the occasion arose, he would whisper what he wished to say and you would convey what he meant as the situation required. The Marshal had approved the route marked on the map, and said he would not add anything to it other than what circumstances might demand. He added that he would not linger long in any place and that his visit to the Libyan family would be short.

It wasn't hard to guess the Marshal would not go anywhere without his guards, and perhaps their number would be even greater than during a public tour, although more widely distributed. The guards on this secret mission would all be dressed in civilian clothes; some would be following the carriage, while others would ride bicycles or walk casually nearby.

The Libyans who were members of al-Aufra police force had already gone ahead of the Marshal, and were stationed at their posts near the landmarks he would visit, without their necessarily knowing they were looking out for Balbo. They had only been informed it was their duty to protect a very important person from a safe distance. That anyway was what you were able to discern from the conversation that took place between Houriya and the Marshal as she bid him farewell and wished him a safe, successful trip.

It was obvious from the very beginning that the Marshal was thrilled with the adventure, for it appealed to his love for theatrics even more than the uproarious dancing parties he hosted in hotels and palaces, because he could immerse himself into his new role with the verve of an actor in a play.

When the carriage reached your destination, you and the Marshal entered the old city through the Sararay Gate, walking through its labyrinthine streets past and cryptically engraved arches, all of which were ancient places of heritage. The Marshal stared at the arches as though he were trying to read the engravings. He noticed the arches differed in size and style and he asked what could possibly have linked them to the architecture of the Roman cities, where the arches instead displayed unifying characteristics.

You figured he was simply thinking aloud, and didn't expect you to answer any of his questions. He divided his attention between the arches, the houses and the wide halls that never closed their doors, because the many people who lived inside them, a family per room, didn't have time to open or lock the door every time one of them went out or came in. So they hung a piece of sackcloth over the door to conceal what was inside, and sometimes the door was even left bare if the residents were non-Libyans, which gave anybody passing by the opportunity to peer inside.

The Governor-General was also uneasy about the security of these districts where the safety of locked doors was unknown. He conveyed his concerns to you in Italian, whispering so as not to attract any attention because Italian, which was the first language of the new districts, had no presence at all in the streets of the old city. Arabic, in its local Tripolitanian dialect, was the only language spoken by the children, the street vendors, the push-cart vendors, and the merchants who displayed their goods out on the pavements. The only foreign languages here were those spoken among the Libyan communities of non-Arab ethnicities.

You began to describe some of the features of the old city to the Marshal, and though you were certain he had already learned more than you about them from his advisors' reports and his books, you had your own part to perform in the play. You were the guide who had perfected his trade, so you drew his attention to the fact that the greater part of the old city was comprised of the Arab Islamic districts, and that its most important thoroughfare was Kushat al-Safar Street, which you were walking through at the moment.

You had read an article in an Italian magazine about

the Phoenician origins of Tripoli, which had then been succeeded by the Roman civilization, and they had laid the foundations upon which the modern city had been built. Walls had been erected around the city to repulse the Bedouin raiders who had come from the desert, and additionally towers and fortresses had been built to repulse invaders that came from the sea.

It occurred to you to mention these historical facts to the Marshal in order to confirm what he had said about the architecture of the old city's arches, but that was not the kind of information he wanted from you. His chief concern was inspecting the district in order to acquaint himself with its street life and atmosphere.

The Marshal noticed several matters that had eluded your attention, such as the kind of stones with which the streets were paved and the source of the stones, or the decorations on walls and the engravings on a wooden door, all of which you had considered unimportant and thus didn't have anything to say about them. You were interested in the curves and twistings of these alleys, these walls covered with the rust of years, and the cavities in these arches where lizards and grasshoppers lived. You didn't understand why anyone used to opulent palaces like that modern marvel they called 'Balbo's Palace', which stood in the heart of the city with its golden domes, parks, fountains, lights and vines that climbed pristine marble arches, would take an interest in such things. And yet here he was, finding beauty in these dilapidated walls, raggedy shops, those street vendors in their filthy clothes and all the other signs of misery in this city, as though God had forgotten all about it. So why did Balbo hold it in such regard?

He took a studied interest in every stone as if it were

the most precious of gems, and if he found letters engraved on them that he couldn't identify, he would ask you if you could read to him. Most of them were on gates from the Turkish era with the words "In the Name of God" written at the top.

The Marshal looked so curiously at every lowly push-cart vendor it was as if he were selling the elixir of life. You were surprised and rather concerned when he asked you about the sahlab beverage that a street vendor was selling. He asked you about the roasted corn on the cob. He looked at these sights in the same way that he would look at a Punch and Judy show. He watched a water seller carry two vessels full of water hanging from a wooden pole he carried on his shoulders.

An approaching dervish thought the Marshal was a Moroccan Sheikh, meaning he and the dervish shared the firmest of ties. The dervish was wearing a green jubbah and carried a brazier from which smoke rose. He was muttering inarticulately and spittle flew from his mouth. He circled around the Marshal shrieking in frenzy. You immediately gave him a ten-franc note so he would go away, but when he saw the Moroccan Sheikh's affluence and how much more money he might be able to attain from him, his motions became even more frenzied and he whirled the brazier in the air over and over.

The situation had become distressing for both you and the Marshal, especially as the live coals from the brazier threatened to land on the Marshal's clothes, which would probably send the alarmed secret policemen rushing to save their master, attack the dervish, and end the tour almost as soon as it had begun. Without hesitating, you slapped the dervish sharply, which brought him back to his senses.

Howling, he fled from sight, which proved he was not a genuine dervish but a minor scam artist in disguise.

You turned to face the Governor-General only to find his reaction wasn't what you had expected. He was furious and in Italian muttered with suppressed anger, "Don't ever do that again."

You realized you had made a mistake, for he had been enjoying the unfamiliarity of these settings. You hung you head and resumed walking next to him silent and confused until you were saved from your embarrassment by your arrival at the focal point of the old city.

The four ancient Roman columns known as the al-Araba Arsat were what remained of ancient Oya and stood as a testament to the passing of the ages. The Marshal gazed at the columns, and walked around them searching for Roman writing that had been worn by the elements. He squatted on his heels, looking at the engraving of a man playing a harp, and then, as if he had stumbled upon treasure, he shouted, "It's Apollo!"

When the Marshal saw you didn't understand why he was excited, he told you Apollo was a god worshipped by both the Greeks and Romans. He added that there had been a strong link between Apollo and ancient Libya. He had named Libya after one of his daughters and one of the two biggest temples in the world had been built by the Greeks for Apollo in Libya, on Jabal al-Akhdar in in Cyrenaica, where it still occupied a whole plateau.

The second largest temple had been built by the Romans in Tripoli, "Oya", but its location was lost once it fell into ruins. The Marshal believed those four columns had been part of the missing temple. The gods had granted these four columns to the island of Mineous, where Apollo was born, in order to protect the island from sinking into the sea, and ever since his birth, Apollo's fame had been connected to those four columns. Breathless and silent, the governor continued to stare at these columns until some children and passers-by began to gather around you, so you were both obliged to leave the Temple of Apollo and continue on your tour.

The route took a right turn and soon led you to the consulates, which had all been built adjacent to one another. The French consulate was situated next to the Spanish Consulate, and then you came to the British Consulate, then Venice, Austria, Greece and Tuscany until at last you came to the French Consulate, which bordered the Bab al-Bahr district, which you had designated as your final stop.

The Marshal chose to begin his visits with the British Consulate, in one of Tripoli's largest and most spacious houses, which resembled a fortress., It was still owned by the British government, which had recently announced it would renovate it in order to prepare it as a headquarters for a British company that worked in exporting esparto and sponge.

The only person in the British Consulate was the guard who had received you the day before and agreed to your prospective visit. You had discovered he regularly received visitors interested in studying the ancient landmarks in Tripoli, and he was paid for his assistance. Moreover, when the guard accompanied his visitors inside the consulate to ensure the consulate's belongings would not be tampered with, he also acted as a tourist guide, expecting extra compensation for this service. You, the Marshal and the guard passed through the great main gate that led to a covered gallery, which ended at another gate, which in turn led to yet another gate. The guard said these gates would have prevented angry mobs from storming the consulate during times of crisis.

You then entered the house's inner courtyard. Part of it was roofed, while the other part was open and consisted of two gardens, one of which had tiled squares and the other which contained trees and plants that had become desiccated into straw and dry wood.

Next you entered the first and largest hall in the consulate, whose walls were covered with cracked wood panelling. However, the portrait of Queen Victoria which was painted in resplendent colours and hung high upon the wall was still intact. She stared back with eyes that burned with youth and intelligence, despite the signs of old age that had begun to show. Up against the wall in a case with a shattered glass door was a telescope, which according to the legend attached to it, had belonged to the famous British Admiral, Lord Nelson.

The Marshal couldn't understand the guard's comments, as he spoke in Arabic mingled with a few words of Italian, which he attributed to having attended an Italian school for two years. You suggested he talk to you in Italian, which would be easier to understand than his patois.

The guard was delighted with your suggestion and began to speak in fluent Italian about the history of the consulate.

"There is where people drank clean water in the time of cholera."

He lifted the cover off of the well dug in the centre of the courtyard that you had come to through one of the hall balconies. He explained that many people had come to the consulate in terror of a cholera epidemic that had broken out more than a hundred years earlier. Warrington, the consul, had offered them food and water and those people had remained in the consulate until the cholera epidemic had passed.

Talk eventually shifted to the first night the guard had spent working in the house and his fright upon hearing the voices of men and women crying and wailing inside the consulate. He had heard the sound of their footsteps as they went up and down the stairs and the slamming of doors as they were opened and closed. The same thing had happened night after night until he became used to them and was no longer terrified. He also said that he had seen a woman's ghost leave the house and then return to it by walking through walls and locked doors on more than one occasion.

The guard only discovered the history of the catastrophes that had taken place in the house, especially during the reign of Ali Burghul, much later on.. Ali Burghul and a number of his guards used to descend from the fortress and attack shops, loot them and chase the shop owners who had fled to the British Consulate with whatever money and gold they had been able to carry. They had sought sanctuary in the British Consulate, but Ali Burghul and his men broke into the consulate and tortured and killed the men in complete violation of diplomatic accords.

The Governor-General chimed in that Ali Burghul hadn't been a ruler, but a pirate who had exploited the discord during the Qaramanli era and arranged with some thieves and pirates to forge an edict, claiming it was from the caliph, to appoint himself viceroy over the entire country.

Nothing about the guard's appearance suggested he had

any patriotic inclinations, and his comment on what the Governor-General had said was completely unexpected.

"Ali Burghul was an inconsequential pirate who came and went in a few years, but what can one say about the pirates of today, who have pillaged this land for a quarter of a century, and continue to kill, plunder and starve its people without a glimmer of hope or salvation appearing in the heavens?"

You wanted to say something to deter the man, but as you glanced at the Marshal disguised as a Moroccan sheikh, he motioned you not to do anything by a look in his eyes and a gesture of his hand. Instead, he steered the conversation back to ghosts, asking the guard if he had ever communicated with the ghosts he had mentioned during his long tenure.

The man remained silent for a moment and then said that there were many secrets which he would never have discovered had he not spent a long time with those ghosts, one of whom was the cat you had seen sleeping beneath the stairs, who was none other than the spirit he had seen passing through walls as if they were merely air.

He had mentioned the story to a British researcher who had come to visit the consulate and study its the documents in its archives. The researcher had named the cat Miss Tully, after the woman who had been a relative of the consul and lived in the house with him, writing her memoirs during the time of pestilence that had befallen Tripoli. So the guard had also started to call the cat by this name.

The Marshal expressed his disbelief at the guard's story and stated that the cat was more likely the ghost of a girl called Sara, who had been the daughter of Consul

Warrington. He added that the girl had been raped and then committed suicide. The souls of those who had committed suicide clung to this world, since they had given up the ghost before their natural deaths.

In order to test the veracity of his account, the Marshal called to the cat.

"Miss Tully. Miss Tully."

The cat didn't move, so he called her again this time by the other name.

"Miss Sara."

And the cat got up from her nap, looking around as if she were searching for whoever was calling her, and when Balbo called her again she went over to him and stoppe at his feet, rubbing her head against the hem of his jalabiya. Her eyes shone with intelligence as if they were the eyes of a human being, and when you saw her open her mouth it seemed entirely possible to you that she would address the Marshal by name, saying, "Hello and welcome to our house, Marshal Balbo."

But it only opened its mouth to let out an anguished and plaintive meow.

You were surprised that a secular Fascist leader might have any interests in matters of a spiritual nature. People are not always what they seem.

TWO

The rooftop garden was your next stop. Trees had been set in large stone planters, and although the leaves had dried out and the planters had crumbled, the colourful ceramic tiles still sparkled, in spite of the heaps of dirt in the corners, as a result of the rainwater that washed them clean them from time to time. There was also a stone barbecue and a bar counter where drinks were served, which confirmed that the roof had been a venue for social gatherings and celebrations.

The roof was higher than any other roof in the vicinity, which had allowed Warrington, who had lived in that building for more than thirty years, to see everything that happened in the port with his binoculars, or even with Lord Nelson's telescope. He was therefore able to see every ship that entered or left Libya's territorial waters, in addition to being able to see everything within the city limits, and even beyond. That had been a useful advantage during the clashes between the governor and the people of the countryside, who had rebelled against the levying of further taxes.

The Abu Leila Tower could be seen atop an island rising out of the sea beside the port wall. The sight of the tower inspired the guard to inform you all about it. He said that Abu Leila, after whom the Tower was named, was no more than a highwayman and the leader of a gang of criminals during the reign of Ahmed Pasha. He had terrorized the people, attacking from both land and sea, and the government had been unable to stop him until Sidi al-Haddar had managed to make Abu Leila and his men repent and become pious God-fearing men.

The Marshal completed the narrative with information the guard didn't know and said that the historical documents he had read, clarified that Abu Leila and his men were an unofficial extension of the state apparatus. Ahmed Pasha himself had established the group with the intention of using it as his secret, unofficial weapon against his enemies. He had wanted it to be a force that could assassinate its enemies, and he had previously murdered a number of them in his country home where he had invited the Janissaries at the beginning of his reign.

Ahmed Pasha had previously massacred some of his enemies among the Janissaries at his countryside home, and now saw he was in need of a new method to put an end to his enemies once and for all, so he could steal from whomever he pleased and kill whoever he wished. Through this gang, he even kidnapped a woman whom law, tradition and religious custom denied him, snatching her from her husband's bed.

As you listened to what the Marshal said, you wondered whether Balbo had taken his cue from the stories of Libya's former rulers. You dismissed these thoughts so they would not poison your relationship with the Governor-General.

You looked at your watch and realized you had spent more time during that visit than had been scheduled, but there was nothing you could do until the Marshal himself decided to leave the British Consulate. He seemed to be making the most of this opportunity to speak Italian, because he knew he might not have another chance like this for the rest of the tour.

There were a number of nearby consulates, which were no less famous or historically significant than the British Consulate. But out of them all, the Marshal chose to visit the Spanish Consulate which had become the most disgusting place in the old city after it had been converted into a tannery. The hateful stench penetrated the walls and reached the neighbouring houses even though the actual tanning took place in underground cellars. Perhaps the presence of these cellars was why the place had been chosen to become a tannery since very few buildings contained basements like this. On entering the tannery, you saw faded paintings of coats of arms hung up on the walls. The Marshal said the Spanish Consulate was an old building that went back to days of Spanish rule, when the knights of Saint John had reigned over Tripoli during the sixteenth century. The building had fallen into disrepair and all but crumbled except for the lower floors, which included these historical cellars that had motivated the Marshal to visit this particular consulate.

When you asked the Marshal why the cellar was historically significant, he said that Count Pedro Di Navarro, the leader of the campaign against Tripoli, had dug a tunnel connecting this building to the beach where his ships had been anchored. He had wanted an easy escape in the event his soldiers failed to repel the angry mobs trying to storm

his house and avenge the massacres Di Navarro had perpetrated when seized Tripoli.

Although the owners of the tannery didn't mind letting
you go down to the cellar to find the tunnel the Marshal
was so eager to discover, the stench coming from the basins
used to cure the hides became more noxious with each
step. It was enough to cause the Marshal to abandon his
plan and return to the street, leaving the search for the
tunnel for another day.

The Marshal told you he had decided that a specialized
and trained team should be sent to search for the tunnel
in order to assess whether the tunnel could be put to good
use, either as an underground road or for sewage.

In the street, you found a number of curious onlookers
wondering what the Moroccan man's relationship to the
tannery was. When you told them he was a merchant
looking to make a deal for a large purchase, disappointment
registered on their faces because they had thought the
Moroccan merchant had come to establish a factory for
Moroccan clothes, which they admired, to replace the
tannery that made their lives miserable.

They had written dozens of petitions to the government without hearing any response because, according to
them, it was an imperialistic government that existed to
burden and oppress the people, and not to relieve them of
their burdens. You thanked God that the Marshal hadn't
understood what they had said about his government,
although he later told you he had realized their anger had
been due to the tannery in the residential district.

You led the Marshal to the nearby Turkish Market, .
Goods from all over the world were on display in its wide
spacious shops. Although the street in that market was paved,

covered, and only used by pedestrians, it was much wider than the normal streets. The problem that faced you once you entered the market was that since the Marshal was disguised as a Moroccan, he would not be able to remain silent, nor would he be able to mutter unintelligibly and claim that he didn't know the local dialect, since most of the merchants in the market understood the Moroccan dialect from their travels to Morocco to buy clothes and materials. Even the merchants who hadn't travelled to Morocco had mingled with the Moroccan merchants who had come to Tripoli to sell Moroccan robes, jalabiyas, fezzes and cloaks.

The presence of such a dignified-looking Moroccan merchant naturally aroused the curiosity and interest of the merchants in the market, and as soon as they saw him, they came out of their shops and welcomed him in the Moroccan dialect. They asked him if he had come to Tripoli to sell his goods, and one merchant offered him a cup of mint green tea prepared in the Moroccan manner while another shook hands heartily with him, and tried to persuade him to sit in his shop. A third merchant insisted on inviting him to lunch because he hadn't forgotten the feasts that the merchants of Morocco had treated him to in Fez and Meknes.

The Marshal was surrounded by merchants and his forehead had begun to perspire. You intervened and told the merchants that the Moroccan gentleman had a doctor's appointment that couldn't be postponed, promising them that he would come back the following day.

Quickly you pulled him out down the first alley you saw, which led you to other alleys where the shops sold handmade crafts the Marshal was able to admire to his heart's content without anyone disturbing him, for every single craftsman was engrossed in his work.

You passed through the turban market, the saddle market, the silk market, and the sieve market, after which you reached a small yard that enclosed a number of bakeries selling local pastries. At this stage, you feared you might lose your way so you resorted to asking a passer-by for the way to the Naqah Mosque. Instead of pointing you in the right direction, the man asked you to follow him through alley after alley.

Before reaching the Naqah Mosque, you passed by a small mosque where people in green jalabiyas were congregated. You told the Marshal those men belonged to one of the Sufi orders for which the old city's smaller mosques were renowned. You explained to the Marshal that each Sufi order organized processions that circled around the streets carrying their respective banners as they chanted and sang Andalusian melodies.

When the self-appointed guide stopped and pointed to the Naqah Mosque, you realized you had reached a point where you could pick up your old route again. A giant fig tree stood in the mosque's courtyard, spreading its branches in every direction and extending its shade both inside and outside the mosque, which gave the visitor a sense of having reached an oasis of tranquillity after traversing the innumerable alleys, arches, and halls tiled with granite.

It was the hour before the call to noon prayer, a time which was set aside for Quranic lessons. Little boys holding wooden slates sat in a circle around their Sheikh, who wore a Libyan summer cloak and held a long cane made from the branch of a palm tree. A boy recited the verse he had written on his slate and then the Sheikh dictated the next verse. Before the little boy had finished writing, another little boy had finished writing his. Sometimes they all recited verses in unison and the Sheikh was able to distinguish their voices and corrected whoever made a mistake by rapping their hands with his cane.

You had always been amazed at the ability of a Quranic instructor to recall any verse from the Quran and easily dictate it to his pupils, until you yourself had taught the Quran in the Sunni Mosque of Awlad Al Sheikh. You had discovered that God made the task easy for you, so you could do what the rest of the teachers did effortlessly, which convinced you that teaching the Quran was a blessed profession and that God made what was difficult easy.

The Marshal said, "So this is the oldest mosque in the country."

He said this as he stood beneath the outer arches, watching the Sheikh and his pupils from behind an open door. He added in a low voice that he was sorry Libyans refused to send their children to the modern schools the Italians had built for them. You made no comment, since the situation didn't give you the chance to talk to the Marshal in Italian, for someone might overhear.

You knew the real reason why Libyans refused to send their children to Italian schools, and what had happened in your village had happened everywhere else. Whenever the government opened a primary school, all the lessons were in Italian, without regard for the people's language or religion.

Yet you didn't say anything and directed his attention back to the mosque. You told the Marshal you thought it had been built during the Islamic Conquest of Libya by Amr Ibn al-Aas. The Marshal corrected you, saying the mosque that had been built by Amr Ibn al-Aas had fallen into ruins, and had been removed by Safarday, a Turkish governor, and Ahmed Pasha had later built his famous mosque on the site. As for Naqah Mosque, it had been built at a later date after the Islamic conquest, but was still the oldest existing mosque in Libya. "I find that places of worship everywhere, regardless of religious differences, have something special that sets them apart, an aura that emanates from within, and envelops the visitor in a sense of peace, even if he belongs to another religion."

Balbo had a map of the city which he unfolded and examined whenever there weren't many people close by, and decided he would like to see the old Court of Justice, located between the mosque and the Faneedqa Hotel, after which the district was named. You were surprised to discover the building was occupied by many Bedouin families, which was obvious from the traditional cloaks worn by their women. A small tent was pitched in the building's courtyard in preparation for an occasion, and its door was open as if it were a shop in a fair. The court-yard was like a school playground, crowded with women and children. You saw a woman chopping parsley on a stone block.

"How many families do you think live in this building?"

"I know that families coming in from the countryside make do with one room per family."

"There must be a lot of families then. This house has no fewer than fifty rooms. And this place is truly deserving of visitats from ghosts, not the British Consulate."

"Why is that?"

"Because no other place in Tripoli has witnessed such atrocities. Do you see this stone block where the woman is chopping parsley? That is where they severed the heads of criminals, rebels, and renegades, and many of the rooms were used for interrogations, where the accused were tortured using Ottoman methods like impaling."

The Marshal's depiction of the disgraces of the Turkish period wasn't new to your ears, for in the Italian media it was regularly narrated how the Italians had come to save Libya from the rule of the Dark Ages.

According to an article in one of the newspapers, the Italian name the Marshal hated the most was Graziani's, who had, as a result of his brutality, ruined the previously favourable comparison between the brutality of the Turks and the benevolence of the Italians.

You felt the time had come for you to convey the Marshal to the home of a Libyan family, but you didn't want to do so before first becoming familiar with the atmosphere of the old city and its local flavour. But you couldn't postpone the visit any longer, otherwise your arrival would coincide with lunchtime, which would have embarrassed both the family and the Marshal if he were offered any food.

You asked the Marshal's permission to buy a box of sweets as a gift for the family you were about to visit, and told him the story you had told the family about him, that he had visited the country before and met Haj al-Mahdy in his shop, so when he had learnt that the Haj was ailing, he had desired to visit him and wish him a speedy recovery.

The Marshal smiled at the fiction you had concocted to arrange the visit of a governor to the house of one of his poor subjects. He believed that had the master of the house known his true identity, his joy would be indescribable and that the visit would be the source of the family's pride and glory for generation after generation.

On your way to Haj al-Mahdy's home, you apologized for the family's humble status and said their house wasn't representative of a typical Libyan family's home with its sitting room and balconies. Still, they were indicative of the life and living standards of a normal Libyan family. There were four of them: the father, his wife, their young son and their married daughter, whose husband had gone to fight in Abyssinia.

You knocked on the door. The preparations for the visit were obvious. The stairs had been cleaned spotlessly, washed with water and soap, and the sweet scent of incense greeted the visitor as soon as he stepped up to the threshold.

The boy opened the door and led you and the Marshal to his father's room, where the Haj was sitting on his bed. He was wearing a complete Libyan outfit with a blue waistcoat and a red skullcap, and a golden-coloured chain dangling from the buttonhole in his waistcoat indicated he was wearing a pocket watch.

Two chairs you had never seen before were placed next to the bed and there was a small table covered with an embroidered cloth. A blue tableau with the Throne Verse written in golden letters had been hung above the bed, and the floor was covered with mats, one of which was brand new and covered half of the room. It was obvious that the family had borrowed some of those things in order to put forth a respectable appearance for the foreign guest, because it was highly unlikely that all those articles could have been in the possession of the family and yet had eluded your attention.

You tried to read the Marshal's face to see if he was

pleased or displeased with his visit to Haj al-Mahdy's family, for the future of the family depended on his impression of them during his short visit. You were delighted to notice he was very interested in all he saw, for he took a keen interest in all the details from the very minute he entered the house, wanting to learn about the trappings of common people's lives.

Thuraya and her mother entered, wearing their national traditional clothes that covered them from head to toe, except for a small slit through which they could see. Thuraya placed a tray with three cups of coffee on the table. The coffee cups were porcelain with a gold band running across the elegant white, and the smell of cardamom rose from the cups. Thuraya's mother put a plate of cakes on the table along with some of the sweets you had just brought. Both women then greeted the guest, whom they believed to be a friend of Haj al-Mahdy, and then left the room while the young boy remained standing in the room to wait upon his father's guest.

The Haj was in full possession of his mental faculties, brimming with curiosity and vitality despite the illness that prevented him from walking. He shook hands with his guest, as though he were meeting an old friend. He searched the features of his supposed old friend for something he could recognize.

The Marshal repeated the four or five Arabic words he knew and you filled the many empty silences in their conversation. You also did your best to relieve the Haj's perplexity as he continued scrutinizing the man's face, trying in vain to recognize him. You told him that a very long time had elapsed since his guest's visit, when he had been in his prime. You added that his guest had been so impressed by the hearty welcome he had received at the Haj's shop that he had never forgotten him. That didn't necessarily mean that the Haj would recognize his guest, for his facial features had changed much over the years.

These words eased some of the worry visible on Haj al-Mahdy's brow and he seemed to accept it as an explanation for his inability to recognize the guest. He sipped his coffee without scrutinizing the Marshal's face, while you quickly sipped your coffee quickly so you could drink the Marshal's cup after placing your empty cup before him without anyone noticing you. But instead, the Marshal reached out, picked up the cup and drank it slowly and with great pleasure. It was obvious he had taken a liking to the house and the family so he had foregone caution and ignored his security guards' recommendations.

The Marshal indicated he desired to give the master of the house some of the money you had in your pocket. You were about to take the money out and give it to the man, who you knew needed it more than anyone else, when you remembered what had happened when you had tried to offer the family the gramophone as a gift. You were certain they would refuse again and the visit would be ruined.

You ignored the matter of a monetary gift and told the Haj that his guest was one of the richest Moroccan merchants and that he wished that the Haj would ask him to perform any service that the Haj might need. Haj al-Mahdy said that he was only an ardent believer in the faith of the Moroccan people and of their proximity to God and that he wanted his pious guest to bless his home and family with verses from the Holy Quran and pray to God, together with the people of this country, to ask him to spare them His wrath and liberate their land from the cursed blasphemous Italian occupation.

Before the Haj was able to say anything else, you interrupted him and said that the Moroccan Sheikh had recited the opening of the Quran as soon as he had crossed the threshold of the house and his silence meant he was invoking God to bless their home and family and heal the master of their home.

Words of thanks and praise flew from the Haj as he stretched bothhis hands out, clasped his guest's and leaned forward in order to kiss it. The Marshal, however, pulled his hand away quickly and stood up ready to leave. Wishing to raise the morale of the sick man, you declared that his health had improved, which went to show that Sheikh Al-Balbal's visit had had good results. He agreed with you and said his only problem was the flight of steps that led up to their flat and that he couldn't go down them nor walk up them. Were it not for that problem, he could have walked to his shop leaning upon the walls on his way and could have worked instead of remaining idle at home. He nevertheless said he had great hopes that the blessings and invocations of his Moroccan guest would be accepted by Almighty God.

When you and the Marshal left the house, he asked you whether or not you had understood his gesture to leave a sum of money as a gift to the sick man, so you explained to him that a man like the Haj would never accept money as charity despite the fact that he was in dire need of it due to his illness. You added that the man suffered because if he weren't living on the top storey of the house, nothing would prevent him from going to his shop to resume work, even in his ailing condition, because of their desperate situation.

You were able to recognize the secret bodyguards who belonged to the Al Aufra police force standing near to Haj Al-Mahdy's home, ready to act if they had detected anything happening inside the house.

THREE

The Marshal had seen enough of the Arab district, so he suggested you should lead him directly to the Jews' Alley, but then he remembered that he wished to visit the American Consulate. The American Consulate had been built only about a hundred years earlier, so it wasn't situated in the same district as the other consulates, but was instead located near Bab Al Jaded. It had no historical or archaeological value and had only been used for a few years, during which nothing of particular significance had happened, nor was it linked to any important incidents or events.

Balbo had read the memoirs of Mrs Porter, the wife of the first American Consul in Tripoli, where she mentioned the city landmarks she could see from the roof of the consulate. Her account had piqued the Marshal's curiosity, who had then wished to see the extent of the differences between what Mrs Porter had seen and what a century of changes had done to the cityscape.

The Marshal looked at his map and pointed to where the American Consulate was situated on his map. It was on a street that branched off Sidi Umran Street. You didn't tell him of the possibility that it had become a brothel like most of the buildings in that district, but instead led him in complete silence through empty back alleys where there were no crowds or street vendors until you reached the American Consulate.

The Consulate was a large building that resembled a fortress, but time had left its mark and robbed it of the noble grandeur of fortresses. It had indeed fallen into the hands of those who traded in pleasure.

The Consulate's main gate opened onto a wide and spacious yard and many inner doors with a number of men gathered around each door. The sight of the brothel's women, who moved about freely in their underwear in front of the men indicated without a shadow of doubt that the building was one of the brothels that had an official licence and was thus run under the auspices of the Governor-General. The district's government representative was a patrolman who stood near the building in his official uniform to keep the peace.

You wanted to tell the Marshal that your presences in the district, especially outside this building, would lead some to wonder how a pious Moroccan Sheikh could possibly come to such a place. Fortunately, the suspicion reflected in the eyes of everyone around you saved you the trouble of having to say anything. A dwarf who worked in one of the brothels next to the consulate came and clung to the hem of the Marshal's clothes trying to pull him towards the brothel where he worked, offering a safe place for the noble Moroccan gentleman to sit, away from prying eyes, where women as beautiful as nymphs would be at his service.

After you had driven the obstinate dwarf away with some money, the Marshal said, "For the first time, I realize that I'm ignorant of many things in this city, and I'm sure no one would believe me if I told them that I knew nothing about this red light district."

"Sidi Umran is a famous landmark in the old city."

"I don't know if this district existed during the Turkish reign. I'm certain it must be one of Foulby's 'achievements', since both Di Bono and Badgolio are too puritanical to have issued licences for the establishment of such a district."

The Marshal had to give up on going up to the roof to see the city from where Mrs Porter had seen it. He was very upset, not only because the building had become a brothel, but because it was in utter disrepair and there no one to ensure it wouldn't one day collapse on its residents and visitors.

You prayed to God that Nuriya would not suddenly appear and disgrace you in front of the Governor-General, so you hastened to leave the street, heading towards the alley that led out of the district.

It was almost noon, and according to the original plan you would have to speed through through Jews' Alley and Bab al-Bahr before the shops closed, and see the narrow lane where Arabs and Jews lived together. It was very difficult to walk along the narrow streets when a vegetable-seller pushing his cart passed you or when a water carrier with two pails dangling from a wooden pole over his shoulders blocked your path. You and the Marshal constantly had to look for doorways to stand in to avoid passing carts or donkeys.

The farther you penetrated into the lanes, the more you noticed that the number of push-cart vendors almost surpassed the number of other people who either bought goods or loitered in the lanes. One man sold roasted corn on the cob, another sold Sahlab, while a third sold prickly pears. A fourth vendor sold padlocks and keys, while other vendors sold beads, garnets, combs and mirrors to say nothing of the second-hand bric-a-brac carts. It was as if the market came to the people and not vice versa.

The wider alley you escaped into next had an indefinable aroma to it, composed perhaps of the many kinds of incense and perfumes used by Jewish women, and the oils they used for their bodies and hair.

Here, noticeably and in contrast to in the Arab quarters, women were as visibly present as men, except in one respect, which asserted their greater importance. Whereas Jewish men neglected their appearance, the women took great care of theirs. They were clean and elegant, they wore necklaces, gold and silver bracelets, bangles and anklets, and long, silk embroidered dresses.

The houses in the Jews' Alley were no different from the other houses in the old city, and their doors were left open most of the time. The shops, however, were much more diverse, and had a sharp professional appearance to them. Here was a knitting and embroidery shop specializing in women's cloaks embroidered with ribbons and silver threads. Nearby was a shop where perfumes were distilled and placed in small bottles, and next to it was another shop that made and sold jewellery and trinkets, and catered to a wide female clientele.

There were shops that made and sold kettles of fired clay, copper and tin. Then there was a modern windmill whose engine-operated stone querns ground wheat and barley, and not far away was a small brewery that sold wine, as well as numerous butchers, grocers and bakeries.

The synagogue was the largest building in the district. Its walls were high and the bottom half was decked in marble. You stopped in front of it because the Marshal wanted to look inside, but the presence of one of the synagogue's guards, who had the build of a wrestler and held a heavy bludgeon, made the Marshal change his mind, especially as the guard had begun to track the two of you with a threatening stare. You thought perhaps the guard was there in order to drive away the Libyan youths who attempted to flirt with women heading to the synagogue.

The Marshal's attention was drawn away by the sight of a young Jew coming out of the synagogue wearing a black shirt. The Marshal said, "Fascists are more tolerant of Jews than are the Nazis for they accept them as members in the Fascist Party."

Then sarcastically, he added, "There is no need for a person to be both Fascist and Jewish at the same time, since the one dispenses with the other."

Before you had a chance to ask him what he meant, he asked you if you knew the whereabouts of a decent café where you could rest a while before continuing the walk up the sloping road that led to Bab al-Bahr. The small cafés in the Jews' Alley weren't to his liking, so you kept going until you reached the crossroads between the Alley and Bab Al Bahr and found a café shaded by an arbour with grape vines growing on its trellises in the middle of the courtyard of an old castle.

The Greek owner had restored its walls, paved the ground and put out stylish chairs and tables. The café's appearance was clean and pleasant. Making use of the Greeks' neutrality, both Arabs and Jews frequented the café.

As soon as you sat down, the castle came into view. It had fallen to ruins and become a place where sailors stored their old rotten boats, but the castle's ravaged garden, its dried water basins, its crumbling fountains that had become heaps of stone, and an ancient copse of palm trees that had staved off neglect and drought, evoked its former splendour.

The Marshal wanted to inspect the ruins after examining his map, and discovering that it was Yousef Pasha al-Qaramanli's castle. However, the café's owner warned him that a fierce dog guarded the boats.

You noticed that ten people had entered the café, after you and the Marshal had been seated. They sat separately nearby, so as to take up all the vacant seats around you. You didn't have to guess who they were, they were members of the Marshal's guards, who had accompanied you since the beginning of the tour.

You had asked for tea for yourself and a bottle of fruit juice for the Marshal, which you would drink in his stead. The Marshal began to explain his point of view about why Jews didn't need to be Fascists.

"Fascism isn't a scouting organization, and it isn't a sports club, it is first and foremost a way of life. An innocent youth who is ignorant of the realities of life takes up Fascism and it opens his eyes to those realities, helping him to understand the principles of struggle that govern societies where only the strongest survive. It gives him strength and resilience, imbuing his soft body with a coat of cruelty that is necessary to face life.

"Jews, owing to a long history of oppression, are born tough, aware of the facts of struggle in the world from the beginning. He would not need the Fascist Party to nurture the toughness that nature endowed him with, because if he did he would suffer like someone who is circumcised twice."

While the Marshal was talking about the Fascist Party,

you remembered how your application to join the Fascist Partyhadn't been finalized, so you told him that you had been accepted, but that your work had prevented you from going to swear the oath of allegiance and receive your membership card.

Balbo said, "Party members hold a special status to me. The party is one big family to a Fascist. You must be proud of your membership."

You replied ingratiatingly, "Indeed, I'm very proud."

"I initiated my reign by establishing the Libyan branch of the Fascist Party in order to prove that there was no difference between Italians and Libyans, which every Libyan should understand."

The voices of muezzins rose up from the minarets of the mosques in the old city to call the noon prayer and to announce midday, as did the chimes of nearby church bells that mingled with the sound of the call to prayer. You both stood and walked away, ascending towards the squares in Bab al-Bahr, which somehow seemed more spacious than the ones in the other districts.

The scents of benzoin and incense disappeared and you began to smell cumin seeds and other spices used to season fish since it was lunchtime and fish was the chief staple in that district. They had perfected the art of grilling fish, as was clear from the small restaurants scattered along the seaside road that specialized in it. Many Greek and Maltese families sat out on the ground in front of their houses, especially those whose houses were situated in the middle of the yards and squares.

You passed by Santa Maria Del Angelo Church, the oldest church in Tripoli, which had been built in Bab al-Bahr, and where the Marshal said he had attended New

Year's Mass the year before, though he hadn't been able to visit any other churches because it had been a rainy, stormy night.

Your path sloped as you crossed the plateau near the sea until you reached a district that had become merely a heap of rubble, when the district had been bombarded by the Italian navy at the beginning of the invasion. The Marshal expressed his astonishment that such a beautiful district had remained in such a wretched condition for more than a quarter century.

The desolate ruins had become a refuge for the multitudes who had come from the countryside and found nowhere else to live. The women hid behind their Bedouin cloaks and the men leaned exhausted upon the rocks. The boys looked like skeletons, wearing filthy clothes that barely concealed their genitals and begged alms from everyone who passed by. Some of them ran towards you, so you took out a sizeable amount of francs from your pocket and gave it to them. This in turn led to them calling other children and you suddenly found yourselves in the midst of a throng of human skeletons who were covered by flies and moaned as they begged.

From afar, you noticed that the people who had prayed the noon prayer had begun to leave the Gorgi mosque, so you and the Marshal headed towards it followed by the young beggars, whom you finally lost in the crowd. It was an opportunity for the Marshal to see the mosque which was famed for its distinguished architecture.

The Gorgi mosque was the architectural highlight of Libyan mosques, not just because of its numerous domes and its tall eight-sided minaret, but it also owed its fame to its decorations, and the arabesques in its mihrab and wooden minbar. You wondered what would happen if anyone discovered that the Moroccan Sheikh who stood contemplating the mosque's engravings was none other than Marshal Italo Balbo, the Italian ruler of Libya.

It was a far-fetched possibility, but you were stil apprehensive as he walked about the mosque contemplating the columns topped with ornate captical. Your apprehension increased as he walked up the marble spiral steps in order to examine the unique cylindrical style of the minaret. You looked behind you as you followed him up the steps, fearing that someone might be following you, until you reached the many-faceted balcony, from which one could see Tripoli's landmarks, including the harbour, the Corniche and the Red Palace.

You couldn't rid yourself of your apprehension as you waited for the Marshal while he walked around the circular balcony, and you only felt relieved when he decided to go back down and leave the mosque. Outside the mosque, the Marshal put on his shoes, which he had left before entering the mosque. That was the last stage of your tour and you thanked God that no disasters had occurred.

You wished that the Marshal would grant you a couple of minutes during which you could perform your ablutions and prostrate yourself twice to thank God for having concluded the tour safely and without any complications. But there was no time and you would have to pray later. All you had to do was put on your shoes and follow the Marshal to the Clock Tower, where you would find the carriage waiting for you.

You had bent over while putting your shoes on to tie the laces, when you felt a large hand clap you on the back and heard a voice greeting you and reproaching you all in one breath. You immediately recognized it as Abdel Mowlah's. He had been leaning on his crutch outside the mosque in his tattered clothes to beg from the people who entered the mosque. You tried to evade him, but he got hold of you and told you he had heard about your exemption, as had your family in Awlad Al Sheikh. They had charged him with looking for you and informing them of your whereabouts. He added that he had been looking for you for the last few days and now had come across you now purely accidentally. He would not leave until you told him your address and how you were faring, so that he could convey news of you to your family on his next visit to the village.

You couldn't imagine what the Marshal would think of you when he saw you restrained by this beggar. You were certain that the situation both irritated and surprised him for he stood in silence waiting for the scene to come to an end, so that you could both be on your way. You wanted to say something to apologize to the Marshal, but were unable to because the entanglement Abdel Mowlah had forced you into would not allow it, even if you could think of an appropriate word to subtly convey your apologies. You begged Abdel Mowlah to let you go as you were busy with this Moroccan merchant, who had an important appointment to keep.

As soon as Abdel Mowlah learned that you knew the Moroccan merchant, his face lit up with pleasure. He said he had been waiting years to come across a Moroccan from Fez capable of treasure hunting and dealing with its djinn guards. He said that he and only he knew that a treasure was hidden in an ancient well near the hut where he lived. You rebuffed him and told him these were just fanciful delusions, in any case the Moroccan merchant sold clothes and had nothing to do with unearthing treasures. You finally told him he would have to let you go to your companion now, but that you would meet him the following day at the same place and at the same time.

Abdel Mowlah nevertheless followed you and the Marshal saying that there was no Moroccan who couldn't discover treasures. He added that if the Moroccan needed a Negro boy with the Seal of Solomon in his eyes to slay as a sacrifice to the djinn guards, he could attain such a Negro boy and bring him without troubling the Moroccan sheikh. The beggar addressed the Marshal in Arabic believing he was Moroccan and assured him that the treasure was real, and that Libya concealed in her bowels the greatest treasures since the Roman era.

The beggar said that this information was known to the Italians who held fast to their occupation of this country and made sacrifices in order to maintain it. They weren't fools who did all that for the sake of a desert of sand, but rather they did it for the treasures marked on maps they had inherited from their ancestors. Governor Balbo supervised stealing these treasures himself and sent them to Rome on Italian ships with the aid of sorcerers whom he summoned from Fez, Shanqeet, Timbuktu, Kano and the Valley of Gold. He then offered to split the treasure with you and the Moroccan merchant before Marshal Balbo and his sorcerers could discover it themselves.

Marshal Balbo was a little surprised to hear his name mentioned more than once, and he exchanged silent looks with you. The scene had begun to attract a number of people, some of whom were no doubt Libyan secret agents who were listening to what the beggar said about Italy and the Governor-General. In an angrier voice, you told him to leave you alone once more, but he leapt to kiss the Marshal's hand and grasped it, begging him to accompany him to his hut so that he could show him the treasure.

The carriage was still quite a distance away, and you felt you had to do something to put an end to Abdel Mowlah's harassment before matters became more complicated. The Marshal had begun to show his disgust at the beggar's stubbornness and you saw no recourse but to do what you had thus far avoided doing to Abdel Mowlah in this grave situation. You took two steps back then stepped forward and kicked him as hard as you could in his leg, which caused him to scream loudly and sent him spinning. You turned away to continue on your way with the Marshal.

All of a sudden, Abdel Mowlah came up behind you, and jumped on your back, encircled your head in his arms with a strength that you didn't expect from a malnourished beggar. The two of you fell to the ground wrestling and trading blows in the dirt. People came and crowded around you, some of them intervened and pulled you apart. You stood up, brushed the dust off your clothes and looked around you but couldn't see the Marshal anywhere. You tried to catch up with him, but there was no trace of him.

You couldn't go to Houriya's flat in your dishevelled condition to verify he had got there safely. You were certain his men had surrounded him once the fight had broken out with Abdel Mowlah, and taken him back to his world and his true identity. But no matter how confident you were that the Marshal was safe, your duty was to make doubly sure he had reached Houriya's house safely.

FOUR

You were furious with Abdel Mowlah for having put you in such an embarrassing situation after the tour had been a great success, so you didn't shake his hand, extended as a peace offering after the fight, but instead left him and went to your hotel. He followed you in order to know where you lived and then went away.

You quickly got out of your new suit which had been covered with dirt from your fight with the beggar. You changed into your uniform and hurried to Houriya's house. You didn't wait to ask anyone's permission, and ran up the steps of the building and knocked on the door. Houriya was standing in the middle of the flat facing the door, so you saw her before seeing Morgan, who had opened the door and was standing behind it. She seemed to be in a state of agitation as she asked you the dreaded question, "You have come alone? Where did you leave the Marshal?" You froze in your place and looked up at the ceiling where the ostrich egg was dangling, imagining it was the hangman's noose around your neck. Houriya noticed the confusion and fright that consumed you, so she told you, smiling, to sit down and wait for the coffee she had ordered Hawaa to prepare for you, because you were entitled, she said, to your fair share of relaxation after all the effort you exerted to make the trip a success.

Houriya's smile assured you somewhat, but you wondered how she knew the tour had been a success without having seen the Marshal. Houriya told you the Marshal had arrived at his official residence and had telephoned her to assure her of his safe return and express his deep gratitude and admiration for what he had seen during the tour. He had said that even when one of the beggars got in your way, it hadn't ruined his appreciation of the tour.

You didn't tell Houriya that it hadn't been merely a beggar passing by, but rather a friend and relative who had embraced you and said that the Marshal had emptied the country of golden treasures buried underground and that he used sorcerers who sacrificed Negro boys with the Seal of Solomon in their eyes to facilitate unearthing these treasures.

You called Morgan over. The boy came and you held his face in your hands searching his eyes for anything that resembled the Seal of Solomon, so that you could advise him to escape before the Marshal found out and offered him as a present to one of his sorcerers.

Houriya asked you why you had been staring into Morgan's eyes, and you told her it was just a meaningless notion that got into your head. What was important was for her to tell you what the Marshal had told her about you. But she told you *she* was the one who wanted to know your impression of the Marshal.

"Now you've seen him and known him from up close. What is your honest opinion of him?"

"He is unlike anyone else."

He had in fact made a positive impression on you. You had seen a side of him that differed from the image of a wanton tyrannical ruler who looked down scornfully at others, as his Libyan enemies described him.

Of course, you couldn't say you really knew him because he had been playing a role while you accompanied him. This character, which he had decided would be a Moroccan sheikh, must have affected how you saw his manners and actions. There would have been a lot of acting mixed in with his real persona, and it would be difficult to tell them apart.

Despite these reservations, you couldn't help but admire his profound knowledge of Libya's history, and his kind treatment of you, in addition to the warm moments you had shared during your tour. You also couldn't avoid feeling profound sadness when you remembered Sheikh al-Balbal's prediction he would be assassinated by his own soldiers.

"This tour will be a mark of distinction in your life," said Houriya.

"I will always remember it with feelings of the greatest respect for the Governor-General, and gratitude to you for choosing me for this task."

"It will greatly influence your future."

"The future lies in the hands of God, and in any case I hope it will."

You suddenly remembered that the carriage driver was still waiting for you at the place you had specified for him, however late you might be, and that every passing hour meant more money would be owed him, so you asked Houriya's permission to go and let the carriage driver be on his way. Before leaving the house, you decided to give her the money she had given you. All the money was still in the large envelope, except for the small sum you had given to the beggars, and what you had paid for the box of sweets you had taken to Haj al-Mahdy's house.

"And do you really think the Marshal would accept that money?"

"But I took that money from you and I now I'm returning it to you."

"There is nothing to call into account between you and me, and you still have to pay the fare the carriage."

"Whatever it ends up being, I will pay for it. It won't be more than ten francs, not ten thousand francs."

"But you are entitled to it."

"I will accept it on the condition that you accept the gift I'm going to buy for you."

"A gift is not in its monetary value, but in its symbolic value, so do not buy anything expensive. The Marshal does not leave me in need of anything."

Only three or four days passed until a lot of things began to happen in the old city because of the Governor-General's visit. Decrees were issued relating to what he had seen there. The first ordered all the residents of houses licensed to practise their profession in the prostitutes' district to move from Sidi Umran to the new housing project beside the Trade Fair. The emptied houses were repaired and a system was to be set up for their maintenance, as well as for the maintenance of any other building threat-ening to collapse in the old city.

Another decree transferred the tannery from the building it occupied in the middle of the residential district to a plot of land that was granted to the owner of the tannery, along with a loan for the construction of a new tannery.

Yet another decree concerned the people who lived in the ruins next to the seashore and reserved places for them in the humble housing project of the Tajura district. The ruins were to be transferred to a department that encouraged tourism, so that the site would become one of Tripoli's tourist attractions.

A decree concerning Yousef Pasha al-Qaramanli's Palace was issued in order that the Palace be repaired, renewed and restored to its original condition, in order that it become a museum to the heritage of the old city.

As for the last decree, it granted Haj al-Mahdy a house on the ground floor in the Janan al-Nuwar district, and a permit to open one of the rooms of the house that faced the street as a shop for making and selling tradional Tripolitanian shoes. The Haj was also granted the right to regain his land in Tajura that had been confiscated, after proving that the land hadn't been deserted, since the confiscation law only included lands that had been deserted by their owners. The decree also granted Haj al-Mahdy the right to be treated free of charge at the military hospital.

You were chosen to hand the decree to Haj al-Mahdy, inspect the new house with a military accompaniment, and pick up its keys and deed of ownership.

You went to Haj al-Mahdy's house on your own and all the members of the family gave you a cold reception. They, including Thuraya, looked at you suspiciously and then the Haj asked you in an angry tone who the man that you had brought into his home was.

"I wouldn't have brought him except he told me he was an old friend of yours."

"How could he be an old friend when I had never seen him in my life before you brought him?"

"Why would he say that he knew you and insist on visiting you then?"

His wife said, "You are the one who has the answers to these questions."

The Haj added, "We want to know the truth about that man and why he came here, and how he could claim to know me, when he didn't utter a single word about how and when we had known each other."

You were very surprised by this interrogation and didn't know what had made them suspicious, because the visit had gone as well as it could have with the Haj uttering only words of gratitude and welcome to the Moroccan guest. That meant something must have happened after the visit that had aroused their suspicion, so you asked the father.

"God forbid. Has something happened to upset you?" Thuraya answered you this time, finally clearing up

your confusion.

"The city is full of rumours about a Moroccan sorcerer searching for a treasure, and as you know my father is a pious God-fearing man who would hate to have anything to do with magic or magicians."

Then her mother reproached you, "And why would the sorcerer come to our house? God forgive us."

The father pointed at you furiously. "That's his friend in front of you. Why don't you ask him?"

"Ask what, sir? Do you really think I brought a sorcerer to seek treasure? And this treasure hunter, did he come just to drink coffee and leave? Wouldn't he have made an excuse to search the house and dig in its corners or recited incantations to summon djinns or slaughtered animal sacrifices or some other nonsense? Did you see anything like that happen in your house?"

Their faces were still gloomy, for although what you had said was perfectly true, it didn't erase the idea that had been firmly planted in the Haj's mind: that you had deceived him when you told him the guest was an old friend of his. In fact, he was absolutely certain he had never met the man before and, knowing his suspicions were true, you felt embarrassed and worried, for your role in the matter had been revealed to the Haj and his family.

Your only consolation was that you had deceived them in order to help them. The decree in your pocket, together with the keys to the new house, would surely transcend this dilemma.

You said, "I beg you, Haj, not to believe the rumours, for that man's invocations have been answered, as you will see with your own eyes."

Here you were once again entangling yourself in lies, but it was a lie that would bring great happiness to this family. So you took out the decree that authorized their possessions of the new house and the keys of that house and asked Thuraya, her mother and brother to come close.

"Can you read this decree? It is signed by the Governor-General of Libya. Marshal Italo Balbo has granted you a new house on the ground floor in the new de luxe housing project in the Jinan al-Nuwar district, so the Haj can now go out of the house to the street and resume his work in the shop attached to the house. Here is the key to the new house."

They looked at each other incredulously, so you took out another paper from your pocket, as if you were a conjurer pulling pigeons from your shirt sleeves and said, "And this is a permit from the Italian Military Hospital for the Haj to be treated in the Orthopaedics Department, free of charge, until he is completely cured. There is a new piece of equipment in the department that treats the bones by electric radiation. That hospital is the only one with that device and its results are said to be miraculous."

The first reaction was disbelief because, as the father said, echoed by his wife and daughter, how could the government possibly have known about their state of affairs and their need for such a house and such medical treatment, when they had never written any petition or complaint nor asked for any aid?

Paying no heed, you informed them of the third blessing to add more fuel to the fires of bewilderment.

"Do you remember the land that was confiscated in Tajura? It will be restored to you, or you will be compensated for it. The choice is yours as soon as you present documentation to prove your ownership."

It was hard for them to take in all the good news at once. The only thing that would remedy their bewilderment was hiring a carriage to take the whole family, including the ailing father, to the Jinan al-Nuwar district, so they could see the house themselves.

They were delighted when they saw the spacious rooms, the kitchen with modern conveniences – like gas piped in to light the stove, the water heater and electricity in every room. There was a back garden and the room that opened onto the street would be Haj al-Mahdy's shop. They walked through the house, their eyes glued to the high ceilings, hardly believing that this state-of-the art house would really be theirs.

"Why are the Italians doing this only for us?"

"Why do the lights of serendipity shine on some people on the Night of Power, but remain hidden from others?

To be blunt, it's because others are not visited by a pious Sheikh like the one who visited you all a few days ago."

As if mention of the Moroccan Sheikh aroused the suspicion of the Haj once again, he asked you if that meant their old house would be taken from them. You understood what he was getting at, since this new house could just be a strategy to remove them from his old house where the treasure was buried.

Haj Al-Mahdy leaned against you with one hand and placed his other hand against the walls as he walked through the rooms of the house, which still smelled of fresh paint. After they were sure of the veracity of what you had said to them, you felt that the time had come for you to reveal who was responsible for these favours, the man without whom their dreams would not have come true. You waited until they had finished inspecting the house and had gone outside to sit in the small back garden, where a few herbs and the seedlings of the trees grew only a few inches high.

You then answered the father's question, addressing the entire family.

"You know the extent of my love and loyalty to you and your family, which I consider like my own. When I saw how you were suffering, I couldn't sit idly by.

From the very first day I saw you were sick, I did my best to find a solution to your problems. I pursued every available avenue until, by the Grace of God, I was able to bring your case to the highest power in the land, namely the Governor-General himself.

"His investigations confirmed what I had said to him about you, so he issued decrees for your new house, your free medical treatment and the return of your confiscated land. Do you really believe that such a ruler could possibly

need your old shop or your old house? They are still yours
to do with as you please."

The Haj's eyes brimmed with tears. They were tears of
joy mingled undoubtedly with tears of regret for having
treated you with such suspicions today, and for having
subjected you to an interrogation as though you were on
trial. His tears were more eloquent than anything he could
have ever said.

After returning the family to their old home, you gave
the Haj one thousand lire, saying that it wasn't a gift but
a loan to cope with the expenses of furnishing the new
home and opening a new shop. You added that he could
pay you back whenever his circumstances permitted.

As you resumed life at al-Kubran's hotel, buying whatever you needed from the shops in the old city and praying
in the mosque, you discovered that the tale of the Moroccan
magician, who had visited certain districts in the old city
searching for treasures, had become a well-known story.

People also gossiped about what had happened to the
tannery after the Moroccan magician had visited it and how
the poor people who lived in the ruins in Bab al-Bahr had
been given new homes. They said that the Moroccan stranger
had sat at the café next to Yousef Pasha al-Qaramanli's Palace
and that it was now being renewed. They didn't forget to
mention that the Moroccan Sheikh had visited his old friend
in Kushat al-Safar and that the family had been showered
with many blessings.

Everyone in the old city believed the Moroccan stranger
was a man of miracles, spiritual mysteries, and had relations
with djinns who carried out his orders and commands.
Some people knew you had accompanied the magician on
his tour and taken him to pray at the mosque, so they came

to your hotel and begged you to arrange a meeting for them with him so that he could bless them too and solve all their problems.

You couldn't find any answer that would satisfy them. When you told them the Moroccan Sheikh had returned to his country, they refused to believe you, so you told them that he would return in the very near future to make them leave you in peace.

Abdel Mowlah had gone to the hotel to visit you when you had been absent and had learned that you had bought a gramophone. This only further fuelled his obsession with the Moroccan sorcerer who discovered treasures and pots of gold. The fact you possessed a gramophone was proof that accompanying the Moroccan magician had been fruitful, and that you had received your share of the secret loot.

You could not get the gramophone back from a al-Kubran, who wanted to buy it at half-price. You hadn't accepted his offer, but you had agreed to lend it to him until he found a second-hand gramophone, or saved enough money to buy a new one. When you returned to the hotel, you could hear the sound of Oriental songs being played in the street through the hotel walls. You headed to al-Kubran's office, and he lowered the volume of the gramophone to say, "Your beggar friend came to visit you today and he hopes to get some of pots of gold that you and the Moroccan magician divided between yourselves."

"I never imagined your foolishness would reach new heights. Do you believe what he said as well?"

"Yes I believe him, and I also believe in the saying that the yard's palm tree casts its dates outside the yard."

"I don't know what you mean."

"Is it acceptable that you should accompany the Moroccan magician to all manner of places in and out of the old city, so that everyone benefits from his visit except those at the hotel that shelters you?"

"The man is not a magician. He is a merchant who wanted to see the landmarks of the city and to meet some merchants."

"That's what people thought, until all these wonders and miracles happened after his visit."

"They're just coincidences."

"If only you had come here with him, I would gladly welcome the coincidences that follow his visits."

Al-Kubran's companions were sitting with him and laughed as he continued talking.

"This Moroccan awoke something more than emotion in my breast, because all I want is a quarter pot of gold to create a new world in place of the old one you all know. If only our brother Othman were convinced of my words and brought this magician to us."

"He has already left the country, most regrettably." "Do you know what? Have you heard about the island of Atlantis for which the world has been searching for hundreds of years? It sank into the sea with all its treasures and there is only one person in the whole world who knows its exact location and that person is this humble man before you now.

"Atlantis is several miles from here. A German sailor's submarine sank during the war and he died in my arms after we spotted him floating in the sea and tried to save him. He told me in Italian, which I speak fluently, that he had seen Atlantis on the seafloor and he explained how to find it. His face lit up as he described the city despite the approach of death. I dream of the day I can lead an expedition to recover the treasures of Atlantis. Then you'll see what I will do with the world."

He slapped his palms to his cheeks.

"If only you had brought that Moroccan magician here!"

FIVE

You left al-Kubran dreaming about a new world, and went to your room. Your mind was incapable of explaining how popular imagination had endowed the Moroccan magician with supernatural powers that could alter the shape of destiny.

Ripples of the Marshal's tour were relayed to you by common folk with overactive imaginations. Rumours spread that in addition to Haj al-Mahdy's acquiring a new house, and the wealth that had suddenly rained down on him, he and the Moroccan magician had also split a treasure they had found buried under the doorstep of his old house. They invented stories about fictional characters wrumoured to have experienced the same luck as that of Haj al-Mahdy and had become suddenly wealthy after meeting the magician. These imaginary people were said to include a street vendor in Kushat al-Safar, a porter in the Turkish market and a carriage driver who lived in Bab al-Bahr.

To say nothing of the special attention the magician had reserved for the prostitutes' district, as if he had found his long-lost mother in the district, so they said.

He had answered the prayers of the district's women

and had replaced those decrepit buildings with refined houses in the city's finest district.

To explain these events, people added that magicians like him who dealt in black magic had close ties to the world of sin, just as the djinns that these magicians employed were usually infidels and atheists, who were deferential to prostitutes and would not scorn serving them.

Another malicious rumour circulated that seemed to be based on Abdel Mowlah's idiotic words about his willingness to slay a Negro boy as a sacrifice to the djinns who guarded the treasures. People said that a Negro boy, barely ten years old, had been missing from one of the Quranic schools, and they accused the Moroccan magician and his companion, whom they had seen visiting the schools, of having kidnapped him.

You heard about this evil rumour from the old black man who owned the cleaners where you took your new suit to remove the marks of your fight with Abdel Mowlah. The old man also said he had heard a man say that he had seen the Moroccan magician and his companion trying to lure a Negro boy who was a pupil in Sheikh Madany's Quranic School, near the Naqah Mosque. The man who had related this incident had shown himself and surprised them, and vanished without being able to kidnap the Negro boy, but that they must have succeeded in kidnapping another Negro boy from somewhere else.

You said nothing to correct the man about the Moroccan magician or his companion. You didn't tell him you had been the magician's companion and that you knew these tales were lies. You laughed at what he said, certain that more and more of these rumours would be fabricated and spread in order to entertain people in their spare time.

Houriya had informed you of the Marshal's appreciation of the old city and the lurid descriptions he painted
of the landmarks he had seen, in addition to the emotions
he had felt as he had walked in the streets that exuded the
scent of ancient history, a fragrance particular to this city,
deposited with the passing of the many ages, eras and civilizations since the city's founding, six centuries before the
birth of Christ.

You had been moved by the Marshal's reaction and
resolved to make another tour of the very districts you had
visited, so that you would be able to see them in the light
of this new understanding. This time, you would do it for
your own benefit.

You started to go around the alleys and lanes, flowing
from one to another spontaneously, like water, without any
aim other than your strong desire to be near the spirit of
the city and become acquainted with the uniqueness that
the Marshal had seen, but you couldn't, partially because
of the familiarity of the places, but also perhaps because of
your ignorance of the historical value of the landmarks,
which had dazzled the knowledgeable Marshal.

You gave yourself up to this spider's web of narrow
roads and alleys that melted into each other. You enjoyed
the sight of the small grocers' shops and the spice-dealers'
shops, whose appearance and architecture differed from
shops in other markets, like the al-Rabaa and the al-Laffa
markets, where the shops all looked alike.

Various goods were displayed on benches and on mats
in front of the stores, while the shopkeepers sat between
their goods as if they were part of the decorations. Whenever
they got up to serve a customer, they moved with great
slowness, as if they were performing an unpleasant duty.

Although you noticed a great difference between the shops in those markets and the perfume shops in the alleyways, there was nevertheless a certain conformity and harmony among all the buildings in the old city, whether they were shops, houses, markets or the lanes themselves, their roofs, walls, small balconies, and high windows covered with dovetailed blue wood. People behind these windows could see through the small holes known as zarzour eyes, and look out onto the street, safe in the knowledge no one on the street could see them.

The city seemed to have been built according to a single blueprint and under the supervision of a single architect, despite the fact that it was actually the accumulation of eras and generations that still preserved their characteristics and identity irrespective of the passing epochs.

You walked down the alleys that sometimes curved around into one another, or sometimes ended in a wall that blocked the way without any sign to indicate that it was a cul-de-sac. On the contrary, these obstructed lanes were often unnaturally wide as if whoever built them had intended to trick you. No doubt whoever had engineered this neighbourhood in such a manner hadn't done so out of whim, but had wanted it to be a maze for strangers and outsiders. It was a technique for self-defence employed by people who had been terrorized by invaders from the sea and desert, and thus had wanted their city to be an incomprehensible labyrinth.

As you attempted to discover the beauty beneath the rocks that had endured the vulgarities of time, you noticed that eyes were watching you with some wariness. You didn't doubt for a moment that the rumours that had linked you with the strange Moroccan man were behind their suspicious glances, since many people knew who you were. In fact you saw one person putting his head close to a friend's so he could whisper your name into his ear. It upset you to think that, in the future, you might have to disguise yourself as the Marshal had done whenever you entered these quarters.

After your tour, you went to work at Houriya's house and discovered you too had become one of the many people to benefit from the supernatural powers of the Moroccan magician. There was an invitation for you to attend an important function the following day at the headquarters of the Libyan Fascist Party in the Trade Fair building. The occasion was your official appointment as a new member of the ruling party. The function was to be held under the auspices of his Excellency the Governor-General, Marshal Italo Balbo, member of the Supreme Council of the Fascist Party.

Houriya considered your membership of the Fascist Party a new step on the glorious path that awaited you, and thought that the Marshal's attending the function was proof of the importance of membership. She also assured you that she would personally be the proudest person in attendance. The invitation stipulated you were to go to Party headquarters the following morning in order to receive your Fascist uniform, which you would wear at the function.

When the time had come, you discovered there were more than twenty new Libyan members who would have the honour of receiving their membership cards from the Governor-General. They were all your age and wore black shirts like yours. You weren't upset that so many young men were going to be honoured, on the contrary, you were happy because that meant that you weren't the only one to take this path and many other Libyans were hoping to ensure their futures and livelihoods, and had therefore actively striven to gain the favour of the governing Fascists.

Marshal Balbo entered the hall surrounded by his officers and advisors. He was wearing his Air Marshal's uniform and had pinned every medal he had been awarded on his breast. He sat and listened to the new members swear the Fascist oath in Italian and Arabic. When your turn came, you swore the oath of loyalty to Italy and to its leader Mussolini. Then you walked to the dais, as the other members before you had done, to receive your membership card from the Governor-General, who also pinned a badge to your uniform with the first letters of the motto written on it, the motto of the party, above which was written the initials of the Libyan Fascist Youths' motto, el Litorio.

The Marshal detained you for a moment and informed you he had examined your military file and issued a command to promote you to sergeant. He would not announce your promotion here, because you were present in your civilian capacity.

The audience of officers, of the veteran members of the Fascist Party, Italians and Libyan alike, all applauded you, and from the middle of the front row of guests, Houriya stood up to wave and congratulate you for having joined the Fascist Party.

You had donned the black shirt and white trousers of the Fascist Party an hour before the ceremony. From the moment you left the hotel, until you reached the head-quarters of the party, you had felt the burden of that uniform. You noticed the contempt and disgust in the eyes of the

Libyans who saw you, which contributed to your haste to be rid of it.

On your way back to the hotel, you avoided the crowded streets to avoid being subjected to what you had experienced on the way to the ceremony. Neither the applause you heard when you received your membership card, nor your promotion, which would increase your salary

slightly, nor even Houriya's congratulations, could ease the cloud of gloom that weighed heavily on your heart after the scorn you had seen in people's eyes.

Just before reaching the hotel, you noticed a crowd of people standing outside its front door. At first you thought the crowd had formed because some porters working in the harbour had come to receive the work permits that al-Kubran sometimes distributed. But despite the darkness that had begun to creep over the world, you were able to discern the presence of women wearing their traditional cloaks among the crowd, and that indicated the crowd was there for some reason other than work in the harbour.

Once you reached the hotel, you still felt ashamed of having to cut a path through the crowd while wearing your Fascist uniform, which invariably aroused people's hatred and contempt. You were therefore surprised to learn that the crowd had gathered for you, because as soon as they saw you, they rushed towards you so fast it scared you and made you think of fleeing, in case this gathering turn out to be a vengeful demonstration people had organized to protest against your joining the Fascist Party.

Instead you remained in your place, neither retreating nor advancing, especially when you sensed, after a brief while, that the crowd was peaceful and posed no threat. Instead, they came towards you meekly, some of them advanced with their heads bowed, while others who were closer tried to kiss your hand.

The only thing they had in common was that they all held papers in their hands. They humbly begged you to look compassionately at their requests and complaints. Some of them were merely teary-eyed, while some of the women wept bitterly, all of which gave you the impression that there must be some mistake. Perhaps as a result of your Fascist uniform, they had mistaken you for someone of authority.

When you looked at the papers they put in your hands, you discovered they were all addressed to the Governor-General, requesting work or a solution to some problem or financial aid. You couldn't understand why those people had sought you out for these petitions and you stood perplexed, not knowing what to say to them or how to escape their entreaties.

Al-Kubran came to your rescue, pushing the crowd away from you with his massive body and clearing a way for you to the hotel. The people followed you and al-Kubran told them to form an orderly queue in front of his office, and then ushered you inside. He lit the gas lamp and instead of saying anything, he took out the newspaper *al-Raqib al-Atid* and pointed to a front page story. The newspaper stated that *Le Courier* in Rome had published an article from its Tripoli correspondent saying that the Governor-General of Libya was so concerned for the welfare of his Libyan subjects that he had disguised himself as a Moroccan merchant and had visited the old city of Tripoli. He had seen its archaeological and religious landmarks, in addition to observing the living conditions of its Arab and foreign inhabitants, accompanied throughout his tour by a Libyan who worked in the government. After his visit, the Governor-General had issued a number of decrees aimed at developing the old city and saving certain architectural monuments from falling into ruins in response to the needs of their inhabitants.

That article solved the mystery of the Marshal's visit, dispelling the myth of the Moroccan magician who was able to work miracles and giving birth to a new myth, namely, you. The people who had previously linked you to the Moroccan magician could now connect you to the Marshal, as you had been his guide and companion when he had descended from his lofty place among the stars down to the alleys and lanes of the old city.

That crowd of petitioners was only the first wave, which would be followed by more and more according to al-Kubran, who expressed his regret at not having known of the distinguished standing you enjoyed with the ruler of the land. He accused himself of being stupid for not having understood that your presence in his humble hotel had been for the sake of observing the affairs and the needs of the inhabitants of the old city on the orders of the Governor-General before he himself came to inspect their living conditions and see their way of life up close.

At the crowd's insistence, al-Kubran came out of his office and collected the petitions and complaints, promising them that the Marshal himself would look into them so that all the requests and problems they raised would be resolved in less than a week. He added that with the Will of God and with the assistance of the Marshal's friend, who stayed at this hotel, they would all soon receive good news.

Al-Kubran managed to send the crowd away and returned with a broad smile on his face because he had managed to temporarily save you from their clutches. He told you he was at your service and would manage your affairs, assuring you that he was skilled at working with large crowds because of his experience as a foreman at the harbour.

You explained the facts that had escaped him, saying that you were only a driver who worked in the government, and that there was no relationship or friendship between you and the Governor-General or his office. Pure chance had made you his companion on his tour of the old city, since he had needed a Libyan guide who knew the streets and alleys of the old city. Whether al-Kubran actually believed you or not, you had told him the truth of your identity and then went to your room.

The following morning, you woke up to the sound of wailing outside your room, so you opened the door and saw two people in tears. One was Abdel Mowlah and the other was Nuriya, whom you hadn't seen for more than a month and a half since you had last quarrelled with her. You invited Nuriya in and sat her down on the bed, and asked her to stop crying so you could talk with her and learn why she was crying. Throughout this, Abdel Mowlah begged you to save him from being put to death for what he had said to the Governor-General about his plundering the treasures of the country. He was certain the Marshal would sentence him to be hanged.

Abdel Mowlah beseeched you as his blood relative to save him from the gallows. He had only done and said what he had in order to bring you and himself good fortune when he thought the Moroccan sheikh really was a treasure hunter.

In order to get revenge for all the trouble Abdel Mowlah

had caused you as a result of his ignorance, you said to him in a serious tone, "Actually, you will be put to death twice. Once for falsely accusing the Governor-General of theft, then once more for threatening to murder a Negro boy. Take the advice of a good friend who wants the best for you. Recite the opening Surah of the Quran so that God will have mercy on your soul starting now."

When you realized the wretched man believed you and intensified his wailing, you told him you had been joking and that he should stop crying and refrain from telling such wild lies. The Governor-General had more important matters to attend to than his stupid remarks.

Nuriya hadn't known you were still in Tripoli until she had met Abdel Mowlah the day before. He had told her that had been the accompanied the Moroccan magician everyone was talking about. She had later found out who the magician was, and that you had been responsible for the moving of the girls of Sidi Umran to the newer districts.

She was proud of you, and happy that you hadn't gone to war, instead attaining such prominent standing in the eyes of the people. She wept tears of joy upon having finally found you, after thinking you were suffering the dangers and horrors of war in Abyssinia. She admitted she had been wrong to ask you to stay with her. She now realized you had risen far beyond her and that you belonged to a sector of society to which despite her true love for you, she couldn't aspire to, any more than the eye can surpass the veil.

Nuriya assured you she would never again ask you to live with her, content instead to live the rest of her life with wedding singers, and to remain at your service whenever you wished to spend some time with her. All she wanted from you was to be treated as considerately as you had treated the women in Sidi Umran, for an old friend like her was more entitled to your consideration than anyone else. She then conveyed the greetings of Sherifa and the other women, who begged you to come visit them. She looked forward to you visiting her in her new elegant home, which she said would be fitting for a man of your standing.

SIX

All of a sudden, you realized that people considered you the second most important man in Libya. You burst into laughter at the thought.

The second most important man of Libya. Why not? After all, you didn't need a decree signed by King Victor Emanuel and Benito Mussolini, in order for you to become the Vice-Governor-General of Libya. All it took was the word of a woman named Nuriya from the brothels of Sidi Umran and a beggar named Abdel Mowlah. Hadn't al-Kubran also accorded you such a status the previous night, as had the crowds of petitioners outside his hotel? You had declined that honour, but why ? Why strip yourself of the raiments of power and authority these wretched people wished you to don? Why not allow them the pleasure of placing you in whatever standing they liked while you made the most of it? You were Marshal Balbo's deputy and would continue to be such in the eyes of the people so long as you played along with what they said. You would reap the rewards of the status they conferred on you without having to live up to its responsibilities.

You laughed loudly, much to the astonishment of Nuriya

and Abdel Mowlah, who couldn't understand what could have prompted such an outburst. Then your laughter proved infectious and they also started to laugh. You had already reaped the first fruits of your new status now that the woman who had once struck terror in your heart by threatening to follow you had relinquished her claim and had become obedient and content with her lot. Her highest hope was that you would visit her in a decent house commensurate with your standing.

You didn't want to disappoint her or deny that you really were the second most powerful man in Libya, so instead you gave her a large sum of money from the envelope in your pocket to reinforce the idea. You also gave Abdel Mowlah a similar sum of money and told him not to visit you again until he had rid himself of these filthy clothes and put on clean ones.

Nuriya pulled a petition from under her cloak, which bore the fingerprints of the women who lived with her. They all begged the Governor-General to take pity on them and grant them a new house as their current abode threatened to collapse at any moment.

When Nuriya handed you the petition, she asked you not to tarry to visit her, but you feigned fright, telling her that the state of the house as described in the petition was too much for a man like you who didn't have the courage of the artists who lived in the house.

Nuriya laughed and said, "Did you really believe that the house was on the brink of collapsing? It's sounder than Balbo's own palace. That's just the way petitions talk."

Tucking the file with all the petitions and complaints under your arm, you went to Houriya to show her the overflowing file, which had all come in that day. You asked her if the Italian article quoted in the Libyan newspaper had been published with the Marshal's knowledge, because according to your understanding, he had been insistent on keeping the visit a secret.

Houriya's answer was yes and no. She explained that the Marshal was in the habit of surrounding himself with journalists, so it was no wonder that one of them had learned of his tour and published it without his permission. But while he hadn't known it would become public knowledge, he wasn't angry about it. So you told her that a number of developments had resulted from this news, one of which was that people had begun seeking you out with their petitions wanting you to submit them to Balbo since you had accompanied him on the tour, all of which left you in an embarrassing position.

Houriya was wearing a short-sleeved, sky-blue blouse and a close-fitting white skirt that accentuated her slim waist, emphasizing her curves and uncovering the splendour of her arms that shone in their nakedness like two streams gleaming with the joy of life. She turned the petitions over curiously. She asked you to read out some examples, but you told her you had read them all more than once, and you could give her a general idea about their contents.

You told her about the petition of a widow who had not yet received compensation for the death of her husband, who had been killed fighting for the Italians several years earlier. Another woman complained she hadn't received the compensation a court had awarded her for the death of her husband, who had died in an accident when the harbour was being expanded.

There was the petition of a labourer who complained that the Italian owner of the farm where he worked had

fired him without paying him his due. Another man's petition implored the Governor-General to release his son,
whose only crime had been attempting to form a union
for the workers at the harbour. Many of the other petitions
were from people who requested they be moved into the
new housing projects.

"Why do you seem embarrassed at what has happened?"
"I'm afraid someone will think I've usurped their role, or
aspire to something I'm not. That's why I came to tell you
what has happened, and ask you where I can redirect them
to."

"Usually people take their petitions to the leaders of
their tribes or to the Commander Basher al-Ghiryany, and
it takes a long time before they ever reach the Marshal."

"Then my embarrassment had some justification, since
there are people who are responsible for dealing with such
petitions."

"We will try and relieve you of your embarrassment."
She walked to the other end of the hall towards the telephone. She made a call and exchanged a few words with
whoever was on the other end. Whether she was standing
or sitting, her alluring beauty had now become a hurricane,
her whole body swayed, and her feminine magnetism
exuded a lethal seductiveness as she walked quickly over
to the phone and then returned.

"I don't know how to apologize." You were still staring
at the living proof of divine miracle embodied in the beauty
of this woman who moved gracefully in front of your eyes,
and you failed to take note of the significance of the
sentence she had said. It took you a few moments to climb
down from your reverie. "Why should you apologize? God
forbid!"

Houriya replied, "Because from this very minute you have lost your job as my chauffeur."

You stood up feeling humiliated and furious. "Is what I did a crime that warrants being fired from my job?" Houriya replied, "Sit down and let me explain to you what I mean, for I've only told you half of what I intended to tell you. The other half of the matter is that the Marshal has agreed to appoint you to the post the people have chosen for you." Despite her reassurances, you returned to your seat preparing yourself for the worst.

"And what position is that?"

"You have just been appointed in charge of the office of the people's complaints, and you will work out of the Government Palace. Congratulations."

"Is this a joke?"

"Can assuming such important responsibilities possibly be a joke? Stand up so I can congratulate you."

You stood up and she embraced you with her bare arms, making you feel as though you were encircled by a ring of fire. The fire blazed brighter as she brought her face close to yours and kissed you on both cheeks, so you kissed her forehead and then kissed her hands in gratitude.

"This is more than I deserve."

"You deserve more, and God Willing, you will achieve it. When I suggested appointing you to this post, I had my own interests in mind too because I do not want to marry a chauffeur, but a man who occupies a much more important post than that."

You murmured indistinctly, "Yes."

"I want my children to be proud of their father, who will be an important government official."

"God Willing" was all you could say. "Thus matters take their intended course."

"What gladdens me most are your embraces and kisses. What saddens me the most is that it will deprive me of the joy of constantly being at your doorstep."

"I do not want you to neglect coming to this house, not even for one day. I'm not the only one who says this, but the Governor-General himself has ordered it, because you will not be able to meet with him in your new post. A senior administrative official will oversee your work but will not inform you as to the results of your efforts. That's why I will unofficially help you, especially in the cases that require the Governor-General's intervention."

"This is hard to believe."

"It's a working relationship, and later on it will be up to you if you want me to continue in this capacity or not." "What do you mean? How could I ask you to stop helping me to solve people's problems?"

"I mean after our marriage, because I will never do anything you don't approve of, and I will not take up any job that displeases you."

Once again you let the topic of marriage hang in the air without commenting. You neither agreed nor refused. You didn't say you didn't want such a relationship, as you had previously refused Nuriya, and you intended to leave the matter off as long as you could.

Houriya's reference to marriage hadn't surprised you, for she had often hinted at it. The truly surprising development was your new post, which exceeded even your wildest dreams. An official at the palace! You had never entered the Government Palace and had even feared passing by its imposing bulk in Italy Square, the main square in Tripoli.

The building was awe-inspiring and represented a new fortress that the emperors of the current Italian era had added to the old fortress, which had been built by the ancient emperors.

The Marshal had linked the two fortresses with a bridge, connecting the heritage of the past to the present-day achievements, uniting the glories of the ancient and modern worlds.

You wondered what kind of work you would be assigned. You feared the weight of your responsibilities. Houriya must have exaggeratedly praised your skills to the Marshal to ensure he would promote you to the post of a government official. As she intended to marry you, perhaps she didn't want her old colleagues at the Caneval Hospital gossiping that she had married a chauffeur.

The truth about your qualifications would soon be discovered along with the fact that your education was limited to the few years you had spent in the religious school in your village. Your knowledge of Italian was still very modest, especially when it came to writing it. Perhaps the best course of action would be to avert any scandal and decline the new post. You were happy being Houriya's driver and you felt that you would not be at ease in another job.

You told Houriya this, and begged her to dismiss the idea of appointing you to the new position and keep you in her service. Rather than reply, she just laughed and made fun of you because she couldn't believe anyone would refuse a higher standard of living or a higher post and status in society. She wanted you to be strong and ambitious, capable of riding the tallest waves fearlessly.

As Houriya said this to you, she didn't conceal her

pride that she was the one who had lit the auspicious star of fortune on your horizon. She said that she would always guide your path and open the gates of happiness and success for you.

SEVEN

It never occurred to you that your tour with Marshal Balbo, which had opened the doors of professional advancement, could also expose you to potential harm and suffering.

As you were returning to the hotel one night, you passed through the Blacksmiths' Market, which was shrouded in darkness, not only because the shops were closed, but also because ashes and soot had settled on the walls and ground, turning the whole place pitch black.

Suddenly a hand dragged you down an alley, and three men whose faces you couldn't make out in the dark took turns hitting and punching you in every part of your body as they called you a contemptible Fascist. They said this was the reward for having brought the Italian ruler to the old city and allowing him to enter the Naqah and Gorgi Mosques, desecrating those holy places.

You cried out in pain, and luckily a police car was passing through the main street, so the three assailants fled into the dark, after leaving you stretched out on the black, muddy ground. The police car didn't stop, nor did you make any attempt to stop it. You forced yourself to stand up, leaning against the wall and doubling over in agony.

Your clothes were soiled with soot and mud, and you preferred to remain where you were for a while so that the streets were empty and the people in the hotel had gone to sleep, including al-Kubran and his friends, before you returned home.

Again luckily, the only trace the beating had left was a slight swelling under your left eye. However, you woke up exhausted the following morning and could feel the pain from your bruises all day long.

You kept the door of your room shut that day so that anyone who might call on you would think you had left the hotel. You spent the whole day lying in bed, lost in a fog of apprehensions and delusions. You didn't attach too much importance to the previous night's incident and you didn't want to search for the perpetrators or report them to the police, because that would only ruin your reputation and become propaganda material for the extremists who wanted to harm you.

They had considered the Marshal's visit to the old city a violation of their sacred places, although his visit had in fact opened a door for the mercy of God to save many wretched and needy people. So what had really enraged them? Whoever was truly concerned for his homeland and wanted to register his objections, let him object and repudiate the ideology of a foreign colonialist government. This was the kind of action you could understand, the kind that had propelled people to war against the Italians in the past, even though it had depleted their energies until they dropped their weapons in desperation, surrendering to the will of fate.

So if a group of people, after all these years, were convinced that they had regained their strength and were in a position to resume the struggle, let it be a real struggle like the one this nation had witnessed for twenty years. Men bearing arms had taken up the call, mounted on horseback and raided the camps of the invading army. As for attacking a harmless Libyan citizen in one of the city's shadowy alleys, you couldn't consider it part of a greater struggle, but was instead simply bullying.

Of course, it was your fault as you hadn't requested to keep your pistol after you had been transferred to a civilian job. One shot in the air would have been enough to strike fear into the hearts of those cowardly brigands.

The sound of the gramophone reached you from the ground floor as part of the clamour of the world outside the hotel. Your ears had become accustomed to it until it became nothing but a skin for these worries that dominated your thoughts.

Only one song caught your ear, which went, "In order to rise higher and higher and higher, then we must be humble, humble and humble." You couldn't say anything to Houriya about the marriage. She always referred to it as if it were a given, while you lowered your head and kept silent, even though you wanted to fully express your love and respect. You would never dare hurt her feelings after she had treated you so kindly and affectionately. On the other hand, you would not be happy getting involved in something that would change Houriya's life for the worse.

The relationship between Houriya and the Marshal was an excellent arrangement that should not be ruined by any arrangements that would not add anything to the happiness that Houriya and the Marshal shared. Houriya said she wanted a child, and because according to Libyan traditions children only came after marriage, she must first find a husband.

Although you understood that Houriya's desire was reasonable and legitimate, why couldn't she postpone the matter as long as she was happy with the Governor-General? She should wait a few years before opening the gates to a storm that could sweep away the foundations she had built her life on. Who knew what time would bring?

Whether you agreed to marry or not wasn't the issue. The decision lay in her hands and the Governor-General's. Suppose she found a man like you who belonged to her religion and satisfied the conditions of Islamic Law. What would the Marshal's reaction be? Would he stay away and let her live her life with her husband? And once he left, would the leisurely life she led not also leave with him, if her husband was unable to replace it?

There was only one solution: marrying a man who would give her a legitimate child in keeping with the stipulations of society without obliging the Marshal to leave, thereby allowing her to retain her life of luxury. It was the perfect solution for Signora Houriya, and that was what the man whom she had chosen would have to accept.

The balancing act would achieve its goal. The glory of motherhood would most certainly erase the image of a woman who lived a life of sinful love, and her legitimate relationship with her husband would be a splendid cover for her illicit relationship with the Marshal. You hummed the couplet from the song, "In order to rise higher and higher and higher, then we must be humble, humble and humble."

The partnership between the husband and the Marshal in sharing the delicious fruits of Houriya's heavenly orchards would have to spring from friendship between the two. The husband would most definitely gain favours and wealth.

If you agreed to be that husband, you would indeed become the second most powerful man in Libya as Nuriya and other simple folk had called you.

You heard the gramophone fall silent, meaning everyone had gone to bed.

There was a knock at the door.

You checked the clock in the dim light of a lighter. It was one o'clock in the morning. Who would knock on your door at this hour? Perhaps it was one of the extremists skulking through the shadows to finish the job he had left unfinished the previous night. You thought about not answering so that whoever was knocking would think that you weren't in your room, but you were curious to know who it was what they wanted.

You stifled your voice in a yawn as if you had just woken up and asked who was at your door.

"Open the door, Othman! It's al-Kubran."

You opened the door and in the weak light saw that he wasn't alone. He had come with Nuriya.

"How long have you been here? This woman came at sunset to ask for you, so I told her you hadn't come back yet and asked her to wait. She has been waiting since then without anyone knowing you were in your room. I couldn't let her return alone through the dark streets at such a late hour of the night, so I asked her to stay until I finished work, and said that then we would check if you weren't in your room. How did you get here and when? Were you wearing an invisibility cloak?"

"Come in."

"You know that visits from women are not allowed, but necessity sanctions the forbidden."

Al-Kubran left after giving you this unparalleled

MAPS OF THE SOUL 479

authorization that made it possible for Nuriya, who had waited for so long at the hotel entrance, to exchange the time spent waiting for a night spent with you.

At such an hour, the only visitor you would have welcomed was a woman like Nuriya. You turned the gas lamp on and asked her to come in. She had brought a small parcel of hot food that had long since gone cold. It was a couscous cooked with a medley of vegetables and topped of with a big piece of meat. You would eat it even though it was cold, and you would eat it gratefully because you hadn't eaten anything all day except for a few dates.

You only had a small single bed in your room because you hadn't given any consideration to physical pleasure when you rented it. You showed Nuriya the size of the bed and told her that if she wanted to spend the night with you she would have to endure sleeping in a tangle of arms and legs. She took off her clothes she had been wearing, standing in the silk slip she had been wearing underneath.

She got under the covers and when you tried to fit your body beside hers you couldn't, so she stood up, leaving you the whole bed.

"And where will you sleep?" "I will sleep here."

Then she gracefully slid on top of you. As you embraced her, all the bruises you had received the previous night awoke. The pain increased with the rocking of the bed and its rapid rise and fall, though it was mixed with a great deal of pleasure.

The following morning, you got up feeling rejuvenated. Despite being cold, you ate your plate of couscous for breakfast and found it burned your tongue because of the spices in it. You followed it up with a plate of love in its

earthly physical form which was untainted by worry or
doubt. The night of lovemaking with Nuriya renewed the
circulation of blood in your veins and was a balm for your
wounded body and soul.

You went out into the noisy street ready to begin a
new stage in your life. It would be just like any other, full
of farce and futility, but the surprise this time was that you
had been promoted without striving for it. You had joined
the army of your own free will, and clawed through stone
with your fingernails until you were promoted and freed
from the limitations of the herd. By virtue of hard work,
you had broken through the suffering of military routine
to the position of temporary driver and God had crowned
your efforts with the postponement that had saved you
from going to war. Unlike your colleagues, none of whom
received such a postponement, you were able to earn the
esteem of Signora Houriya through diligence and devotion
to your work, until she accepted you as a permanent chauffeur. That had been the apex of your dreams.

Now, fortune had blessed you with an important position in the Government Palace, so you felt confused and
scared because this position exceeded your expectations for
this stage in your life.

You walked hesitantly and without the slightest enthusiasm to the Government Palace, trying to find reasons to
convince yourself of the advantages of such a post. Perhaps
these advantages outweighed the benefits you would personally enjoy. After all, thanks to this position you could serve
the wretched and needy among your people. Yet you were
unconvinced as you had long ago dismissed the idea of
sacrificing oneself for others, considering it a form of self-
deceit during times of crisis like these, when most people

were unable to help themselves. So why deceive both yourself and others?

This was what the realities of life said to you, and they also said that Italo Balbo, when it came to the final reckoning, hadn't come to this country in order to serve Libyans or pull them out of their misery. Balbo was here to serve his country's needs, which were to settle Italians in their new colony and provide them with a better future. No matter what sparks of light came from him here or there, they were like false lightning that would bring no rain to turn the earth green, in the same way that the Spanish and Turkish occupiers had passed over the land without leaving any seed behind them.

Amidst your whirling thoughts, you suddenly found yourself, in front of the Government Palace. You spun around terrified, as if there were a hyena waiting to attack and you were frantically trying to get away from it.

You then noticed many people entering and leaving the building, some of whom were high-ranked military personnel, while others were well-dressed civilian officials that had arrived in cars driven by chauffeurs, who held the car doors open for them. At the front gate was a red welcome carpet and two military guards in ceremonial uniforms.

Nothing could have increased your terror until you saw a luxurious car whose metal shone as if it were black gold and a lady stepping out of it, sweeping her dress over the red carpet surrounded by guards. One of the officers bowed to her and led her inside the palace. Everything confirmed your impression that you were out of place here, in a world where simple folk like you didn't belong.

You retreated to the streets to loiter a while. Although

you were wearing your new suit, which had been cleaned and ironed after your fight with Abdel Mowlah, a black stain that the cleaners had been unable to remove made you feel too embarrassed to enter the grand Government Palace. You suddenly remembered the envelope of money in your pocket, so you went to a shop in King Victor Emanuel the Third Street and bought a black suit, a shirt, a tie, a pair of socks and a pair of shoes so as to bolster your courage when you went back to the Government Palace.

You sat at the Miramare Café, sipping a cup of coffee and looking into the faces of the tourists that Marshal Balbo's propaganda had enticed to Tripoli. You inhaled the perfumes that wafted from the Italian women who paraded their beauty in the square, as they coquettishly walked past the café.

"Come on, hurry and tell me how the new job was." That was how Houriya greeted you when you went to visit her that evening. "I haven't gone yet."

"Why not?"

"It still seems too much for me."

"Don't talk like that. I know very well you are better than that post. I want you to get settled into your new position, because there are other important issues waiting for us, and a life together that we must begin preparing for."

Houriya asked you if you needed any more money. You quickly replied that you had more than you needed. You remembered you had promised to buy her a present. You thought she might be hinting that you had neglected to buy that present. Why had your memory betrayed you and made you forget to buy a ring or bracelet for her when you went to the market to buy your suit?

Houriya continued, "So don't come tomorrow and tell me you put off going to work. I want you to be there early tomorrow. After that you're free to come and go as you want, because you're the head of the office, and responsible for reporting how much time you need for office work and how much you need for field work. The creation of this new office will be announced in Arabic and Italian newspapers, as well as during the local RAI broadcast. Petitions and complaints will be sent to you so you can look them over and receive the plaintiff when the situation demands. Then you will issue a report on each case to the Governor-General's office and attach a recommendation to it.

"That's where your role ends and the administrative and security apparatus in the Governor-General's office will verify the truthfulness of what the petitioner says and contact other concerned parties. Depending on the results of these investigations, wrongs will be righted, and people will be given their due. But the first decision about these petitions is yours, because you will submit your opinion on what warrants inspection and ignore complaints that do not."

"It seems much more difficult than I had imagined."

"You won't say that after a week or two at work." "You know my abilities to read and write in Italian are limited."

"It's an office for the complaints of Libyans and their petitions will be written in Arabic. Likewise, you will discuss them with the petitioners in Arabic too. As for Italian, the Governor-General's office has a translation department that handles work like this. Do you need any more information?

"I'm going to be depending on you for guidance and direction."

What Houriya had said about announcing the new

office turned out to be true, because before even leaving her flat you heard the news from an announcer in an Arabic broadcast who praised the government for its zeal in seeingto its Libyan citizens' welfare. So as to improve their lives, the government had established an office especially to examine their complaints and demands and solve their problems. The announcer urged citizens to make use of this office and direct their inquiries to the Government Palace.

So the government was giving a lot of importance to this office and considered its establishment an accomplishment for the occupation government, entrusting it to you of all people. Who were you to decline this honour, that the master of the country had bestowed on you? You would take these responsibilities with enthusiasm and a sincere desire to see the new initiative succeed. You would gain the trust of the people in the petitions office, which would be the beginning of a new era of friendship between the government and the Libyan people.

You went to the head of the administrative department on the first floor of the Palace carrying an envelope full of citizens' complaints and handed them over to the man as Houriya had instructed you. He introduced himself as Signor Calvi, and told you how he had lived in Tripoli for more than twenty years, having come as a soldier with General Kaneefa at the beginning of the Italian era. After being shot in the foot, he left the army and turned to work as a civilian, remaining in this position until he became an expert in the country's affairs and an encyclopaedia of its administrative history.

As he moved about his office, the signs of his old wound appeared clear in his gait. With his first step, his body leaned until his side almost touched the floor, then he righted himself only to lean at the same angle with his second step, and so forth. Despite his kindness, you feared he might be capable of evil. You expected the wound he had received twenty years ago from Libyan resistance fighters would affect the way he treated you, but during the hour you spent together, you encountered nothing but respect, which manifested itself in his readiness to offer any help you might need.

EIGHT

Before you left Signor Calvi's office, he handed you the decree authorizing the office's establishment, which listed its goals, regulations and the specific responsibilities of each official. He also gave you a copy of the decree transferring you from the military to the office.

Signor Calvi explained that petitions would come to his office along with all the other mail that was sent to the Palace, at which point they would be recorded and turned over to you. After examining them and writing your recommendations, you would return them to him so that he could send them to the Governor-General's office. He concluded by saying you would pursue your work under his direct supervision.

Signor Calvi pressed the button that rang the bell outside his office and a soldier entered to take you to your new office. Signor Calvi bade you farewell and wished you the best of luck.

You discovered there were other flights of steps than the grand marble staircase covered with luxurious carpets that you had ascended after passing the main gate. Most of the workers, officials and civil inspectors came to the palace by an alternative back entrance, which you were told to use in the future as well. The soldier led you to your office on the ground floor at the back of the building. The offices were like wooden boxes because the whole floor was one hall that had been divided into small offices by wooden partitions.

Your office was a small room, with only enough space for a desk and two chairs. There was a black telephone on the desk and behind it was a window that overlooked the back courtyard. Several shelves had been mounted on the walls to hold files, and there were two photographs, one of the Duce and the other of Balbo.

The soldier drew your attention to a waste basket under the table, and then recorded everything in the office on a piece of paper and asked you to sign it. He informed you that the telephone was connected to the switchboard through which you could receive and make calls, and he showed you the button you pushed to summon the orderly.

You sat down in the chair. You realized it revolved, so you spun around in it a few times until you felt dizzy. The chair was comfortable, made of black leather, and moved left and right on axles. You had never sat on a chair like this before, nor in an office like this with an Italian soldier at your command!

You stretched your hand out, pressed the button and heard it ring in the outer corridor. The soldier came and greeted you, saying "Pronto."

What should you say? You had just rung the bell to feel that you could give orders to an Italian. Then you remembered you needed a cup of coffee with which to begin your new professional life. The soldier left to convey the order to the coffee maker.

You opened the empty drawers of the desk one by one and then inspected the shelves. Some of them had small drawers, which you opened and found newspapers cuttings about schools and an advertisement for school supplies. You realized the person who had occupied the office before you had looked after educational matters.

You picked up the telephone and a voice immediately said, "Pronto Signor." You repeated the phrase, "Pronto Signor", and replaced the handset on the telephone. Everything was in a state of readiness, but you didn't know whom to phone. Houriya was the only person you knew who had a phone, but you didn't know her number.

An Italian boy came with your coffee. He put it down and left. The orderly came back carrying a cardboard box of pens, files, notebooks, and forms. He also brought you a large file that contained the petitions and complaints that you had left in Signor Calvi's office to be recorded. You signed the receipt and then he left.

The telephone suddenly rang loudly, as if it were an alarm bell, and you guessed it was the head of the department making sure you had received all the office supplies, since he was the only person who would know your telephone number. However, the voice that came across the wire wasn't a man's voice. It was a sweet feminine voice that you knew intimately, that delighted you as if it were a singing curlew or a bamboo flute. It was Signora Houriya, who had wanted to be the first person to telephone you and congratulate you on your new post.

Houriya asked you what you thought of your office and the work environment in the palace. You informed her of the polite welcome you had got from the head of department. You told her the best thing about the office was the telephone that had enabled you to hear her voice, and would be a good luck charm.

You told her there were many things related to your work that needed organizing and you would not be able to know what they were, or they wouldn't occur to you, until you applied yourself to the practical aspects of work. She suggested you visit her after work in order to discuss a plan and celebrate your first day.

After the telephone call, you remembered that Nuriya was still living with you and that she had been confined to your room for two days, doing nothing but waiting for you and preparing meals for you. No doubt she was waiting for you to have lunch with her. You didn't know what kind of excuse you could offer. After the first night she had spent with you, you had pressed her to go back home, but she had insisted on staying for two or three days, to make up for the melancholy she had suffered during your absence.

Perhaps it was a roundabout way of realizing her old desire to tie herself to you permanently, using an incremental approach in hope that you would become accustomed to her presence until you were no longer able to do without her. You had, in point of fact, begun to feel the difference between living alone and having a woman like Nuriya to wait on you, prepare your meals, and both make your bed for you and mess it up with you, in the course of satisfying the needs of desire.

The file that contained the complaints and the petitions still lay before you, so you opened it and searched for Nuriya's petition, which would be the first case to be presented to the Governor-General. You would support the petition from Nuriya, Sherifa and their companions to be moved to a modern house after the example of the women from Sidi Umran.

You would convince the ruler of Libya, pioneer of the age of aviation and the hero who had crossed the Atlantic Ocean in his private aeroplane, to neglect all his other duties and concern himself with Nuriya, solving her problems and finding a new house for her.

Among the papers Signor Calvi had sent, you found a form attached to each petition that condensed the work for you because he had left blank fields asking you simply to fill in the plaintiff's address, a summary of his problem, the other involved parties and then your recommendation.

In your recommendation, you wrote that the petition was raised by a number of artists who sang at weddings thus reviving the musical heritage of the city. You stated that you had previously inspected their house and had found it unfit for habitation. A budget would have to be drawn up for its repair and renovation. Later, it could be used as a clinic or as a police station, since the building contained many rooms. You finally recommended that the women be moved to the modern district where the women of Sidi Umran had been relocated.

You decided you had accomplished enough for the day, for you had taken over the office, become acquainted with the work environment, and looked over Nuriya's petition, the first of the citizens' requests. You realized you must go to your hotel to persuade the woman waiting in your room to go home so that you could keep your lunch appointment with Houriya. Nuriya was no more to you than simply a means to satisfy your lust.

Nevertheless, during the last two nights you had started to feel a connection with her. You had become capable of listening fondly to the stories she told you about her experiences. She told you about a sheikh who always filed law suits demanding Sherifa and her women leave the house, on the pretext that one of his ancestors had a claim on the house that these women sullied thanks to their conduct.

The women had conspired against him and followed him on his way to the mosque at night, exposing themselves to him until they were able to get the best of him and lure him into one of the rooms in the house. Then one of them was able to take all his clothes off and then push him outside the room to let the rest of the women push him naked out onto the street. It was nighttime and the street was empty, so he began to beg them to let him in and spare him the disgrace, but they would not do anything until they had obtained a written pledge that he wouldn't bother them ever again.

Convincing Nuriya to go home wasn't as easy as you had thought. She had cleaned and tidied the room, lit the burner, and had begun to peel onions, slice tomatoes and prepare the eggs to make a plate of shakshouka. As soon as you told her not to trouble herself as you would have lunch at the office for lunch, and she had to go home, her face clouded with sorrow and silent tears streamed down her cheeks.

You promised her you would visit her soon, and that her staying in the hotel for more than two nights would embarrass you with the owner, who would be subject to trouble if the tourist police were apprised of the situation.

Nuriya dried her tears, fixed her shawl tightly around her body and face, until only one of her eyes could be seen, with which she could see her way. She left, at which point you set out for Signora Houriya's house and thinking that there was a great difference between the two women. With Nuriya, you had the upper hand in any situation, whereas with Houriya, you were always the weaker party.

You had also never felt for Nuriya what you felt for Houriya. Her personality and beauty made you acquiesce and turned you into a subservient lover.

When you arrived, you saw that the table had been set for two. Hawaa brought a bowl of your favourite lentil soup and Houriya took the bowl from you, and served you herself.

"It's a simple meal. I asked Hawaa to prepare the meal that you liked best, and she suggested lentil soup and baked macaroni. I went down to the kitchen to help her cook the side dishes like the stuffed vegetables and mashed potatoes. I must know what food you like, so I can prepare it for you in the future. You haven't told me what the food is like in your hotel's restaurant."

Laughing, you told her that the hotel where you were staying was different from the big hotels she knew. Your hotel was a simple motel where people from the countryside came with their cattle.

"You should not go on in such a condition. And yes, the time has come for us to discuss details. Everything must be arranged with great care. You must state your honest opinion on every single matter, so that I will know exactly what you want and don't want at this particular stage. That way, we will set a solid foundation for our future life. That is very important for building a happy home. Don't you agree?"

You both finished your lunch and Hawaa brought you glasses of green tea with mint. You felt prepared for the discussion that you had been avoiding for a long time.

"My dear Houriya, I am confused by the situation.

There is a stable, happy life between you and one of the greatest men in history. You love him and he loves you. Why do you want to sacrifice that life? And why have you chosen a simple man like me to be your new partner? Of course, you know that my love for you is boundless and I know your noble feelings towards me, but is it possible that feelings alone are the incentive behind this fateful change in your life? Do you think you're making the correct decision to guarantee your happiness?"

After a moment, Houriya added that honesty was of the utmost necessity at this stage. She said that although her relationship with the Marshal was based upon strong emotions, it had been from the start a temporary relationship and that it could never keep her from her right to be a mother and enjoy watching them grow up as her consolation in old age. As for the Marshal, he had always said he would see through his term of office in Libya, and then he would return to his family and homeland.

She said there was nothing strange in thinking about her future. If you had any doubts about why she had chosen you, you should search your own heart for the truth.

You said, "When I search in myself, all that I find is a flood of love and gratitude for you."

You took her hand, planting a kiss on her fingers.

"So where does this confusion you speak of come from?"

"From one source. The opinion of his Lordship the Marshal in all this."

"Don't concern yourself with the Marshal's worries. He is understanding because he considers himself responsible for me. He is convinced you are the right person for me, because I tell him so."

You felt you should make yourself perfectly clear, so you said, "I mean, will your relationship with the Marshal continue after our marriage?"

"It will not be simply my relationship, but our relationship, yours and mine. It will continue, of course, and it will be a relationship of friendship."

You didn't voice your concerns about how she could guarantee her friendship with Marshal Balbo would remain within the limits of friendship, when this wasn't completely within her control.

Instead you said, "Will he continue to pay for the expenses of your household for the rest of your life without anything in return? Will he pay the rent of this flat from his private accounts or from the treasury of his homeland, in addition to the wages of Morgan, Hawaa al-Fezany, Mukhtar and the car? Or will he cease to have a hand in all that?"

"Why should he cease to pay these expenses? He is the ruler of the land and in that capacity, he cares for thousands of households and spends money on thousands of people, so what is strange in that?"

You had made her tense and she doubtless considered your questions to be more than necessary, since she was used to such matters being dealt with subtly, where hints sufficed without explicit candour. You choose to stay silent so as not to worsen her discomfort.

Houriya resumed the conversation saying, "Has your bewilderment abated so we can return to the simple questions, the first of which is 'when'?"

She waited for you to reply and when you said nothing she said, "In a few days the Marshal will travel to Rome. He will be absent for two or three weeks at his sister Clara's wedding in Ferrara. That will be the most suitable time for our marriage, so that when he returns, he will find that I've become the wife of another man. The next questions are how and where."

"Before talking about how and where, let us first discuss when we shall celebrate it, since the timing you have mentioned is too soon and I don't know for certain if it will suit me."

Houriya sat up suddenly in her seat and stared at you in amazement, as if she didn't believe what you had said.

"What are you saying?"

"I mean that I've to prepare myself before entering upon this new stage in my life."

"What preparations are you talking about? If you mean the expenses, it will be covered, and if you need something, consider my money yours. What's the difference?"

Your mind circled around the four corners of the earth searching for a believable reason to postpone the marriage, a noble reason to which a woman like her could not object.

"The psychological preparations may take some time."
"And how long will it take for you to placate your psyche?" she said with growing bitterness.

"I'm only asking for a short while to think it over." She got up and walked from the dining room to the salon and then to the front door of the flat. You followed her and with nakedly restrained emotion she said, "Take as much time as you want, and don't come back here until you reach a decision."

You realized what you had said had been cruel, and the distress you had caused her was written plainly on her face. You wished you could take it back and instead answer yes to every question she asked and appear eager for the day of happiness in which you would realize the dream of a lifetime by marrying her. But you were too confused to respond, and you stood up silently and grave-faced, and then tried stupidly to smile while you searched for the right words.

When you saw she had reached the door, all you could remember was the last topic you had come to discuss with her. Hiding your confusion behind an empty smile, you said weakly, "We forgot to talk about a work plan for the office."

Without showing any interest in what you had said, she opened the door and said firmly, "Good bye."

She slammed the door behind you.

NINE

There was a myth about the king of the clouds, whose seven daughters lived on seven red clouds near the source of light in the eastern sky. He built a splendid palace for each one and their palaces were surrounded by beautiful gardens. When they reached the age of maidenhood, he allowed his daughters, each of whom was ravishingly beautiful, to descend to earth in order to choose seven bridegrooms, provided the bridegrooms were destitute, so that they would rescue their future husbands from their wretchedness, and ascend to the springs of light with them to lead a life of love and leisure in the lofty paradises. God would reward them for their righteous deeds and bless them with a happy marriage. So each daughter descended to the seven parts of the earth, because the globe seemed like a seven-sided star to the residents of those sublime quarters.

Houriya's lot was that of those seven ladies, sired by the king of the clouds who made lightning, thunder and rain, for she had descended onto the southern shore of the Mediterranean Sea to a city called Tripoli and had chosen a poor undeserving wretch and wiped misery from his face with her angelic feathers. She had transmuted the days of famine into seasons of plenty. But the man's foolishness had overcome the wise physicians, who tried to cure him of it, and stupidity possessed his mind and heart, blinding his vision so that he refused this celestial gift and rejected this daughter of the skies, preferring to remain in poverty and misery.

Yes, that was exactly what you had done to yourself and what you had done to Houriya. She was a gift from heaven and you had treated her faithlessly, after all the love and affection she had showered upon you, in a manner not befitting even the lowest of people. You had wronged her and wronged yourself in the process.

As you walked aimlessly through the streets, you felt despair suffocating you. Panting, you stumbled, lost. Your necktie was a rope tied around your neck, it was strangling you, so you untied it and held it in your hand. Your feet sank into the ground as if the pavement had become quick sand.

The great irony was that the woman you were fleeing, whose favours you had refused, was the same woman for whom you yearned. No sooner were you apart from her, if only for a minute, than you felt the pull of your love for her. In the recesses of your heart, you loved her, and wanted to be with her always, residing in the sanctuary of the divine beauty that shone from her, as if she were a gem of the most precious metals shining eternally, day and night, no matter the circumstances. Whether she spoke, remained silent, moved, was still, was angry or pleased, asleep or awake, she shone from every angle, like a precious stone. You couldn't imagine yourself living far from her, expelled from the gardens of her love, deprived of her tender caresses and voice, that always soothed your wounds.

You didn't know what to do. How could you possibly rest, eat or drink, as long as you knew Houriya was upset at that moment, and that you were to blame for it?

You continued to roam the streets until it was dark. You were worn out, afraid to stop and find only more dark thoughts assailing you in murky packs like hyenas. Fumbling for some sort of human companionship, you went to Haj al-Mahdy's new home and to the only family you knew in Tripoli.

The family welcomed you heartily and the Haj embraced you with tears in his eyes. The house appeared to be more pleasant than the first time you had seen it, when it had just been bare walls without furniture or inhabitants. You passed through the house into the recently planted back garden, where Sheikh al-Balbal was sitting next to the master of the house, who had invited him to partake in celebrating the new home and reciting invocations and verses from the Quran to bless it.

You sat next to the two men and were amazed to find Haj al-Mahdy talking to Sheikh al-Balbal as if he had been the one responsible for granting them their new home, although you, more than anyone else, knew that the credit was due to you and the Governor-General. You learned that Sheikh al-Balbal had predicted, a few days before the family had moved to their new home, that they would be blessed by good fortune and that Haj would own a new shop. Therefore, when the new house and shop came, along with medical treatment and the return of his confiscated land, in the eyes of Haj al-Mahdy and his family it was nothing less than a miracle worked by Sheikh al-Balbal. Sheikh al-Balbal's presence upset you, for you were certain that he knew your real intentions, the story of your thwarted love, and therefore understood your motives for coming to this house and paying such special attention to the family. You decided to face the Sheikh and provide him with a clear opportunity to say anything he might have to say about your affairs rather than wait for him to disgrace you.

As you drank the second round of mint tea, you turned to Sheikh al-Balbal belligerently and said, "Would you tell me, oh venerated Sheikh, something about the future that awaits me, so that my heart can rest at ease?"

Before you had made that remark, the conversation had been all about the war going on in Abyssinia, and the stiff resistance from the Abyssinians who had risen violently against the invading Italian army, which of course included Libyan soldiers. Thuraya's mother asked you if you had any news about their son-in-law Fathy, who hadn't sent a single message to his wife since he had left Tripoli. You answered her briefly saying that all the ships had arrived safely, and that the reports that had been sent praised the courage of the Libyan soldiers.

You concealed from them the real news that you had heard about the extensive loss of life that they had suffered ever since the first battles, when Graziani had positioned the Libyans on the front lines. You changed the subject, asking Sheikh al-Balbal again to predict your fortune. His answer disappointed you.

"God only knows."

"But you are a man known for working miracles. People relate what you say about the future as if it were the God-given truth, because time has proven the accuracy of your predictions."

"They are not predictions. When a person is virtuous,

we ask God to reward him, and if a person is evil we ask God to punish him in this world before he is punished in the next. God soon answers the prayers one makes, so long as that person has true intentions."

You ventured a question.

"Do you see me as a virtuous or evil person, oh sheikh?" You put the question forth accompanied by a smile as

if you meant it playfully. He didn't return your smile, and on the contrary frowned as he said, "You alone know the answer."

Haj al-Mahdy had been listening to your conversation with the Sheikh, and noticed that his answer had upset you, so despite his respect for Sheikh al-Balbal, he intervened on your behalf and said, "I consider Othman a second son and I wish he could benefit from your knowledge and learning. I hope you ask God to bless him during your prayers."

Sheikh al-Balbal sat up and asked for an egg and an empty plate. Thuraya and her mother were very embarrassed because although there were empty plates in the kitchen, there were no eggs. He told Thuraya's mother to send her daughter to the kitchen, because he was sure there was an egg in the basket where they normally placed their eggs.

Thuraya went to the kitchen and returned, astonished, carrying a plate of eggs which the family knew hadn't been there before. They asked the Sheikh what had just happened, but he didn't bother to answer them and asked again for the empty plate and to return the rest of the eggs to the kitchen, since all he needed was one.

The Sheikh tapped the egg gently on your forehead to crack its shell, and then emptied its contents onto the plate. He recited incantations over the egg as he moved the contents of the plate with a stick and when he was done he asked you to look into the plate. You saw two big eyes made of the yolk and white that seemed to burn as if they were two evil flames. Around them was a jelly-like face with deformed features.

Sheikh al-Balbal asked you if you recognized the face and the eyes, and before you were able to reply in the negative, he told you it was the demon that followed people. You told him you had heard its name being mentioned by many people but hadn't had the chance to ask who this demon was or what it did.

The Sheikh laughed at you, and said to Haj al-Mahdy that you were the first Libyan he had met who didn't know who the demon that followed people was, because it was the fate of all Libyans to live in conflict with that demon while she pursued them as a nation, before she confronted them individually.

"But that doesn't matter. What we are interested in is your particular case. Search your life and you will know the demon. She is an evil spirit who follows you, ruins your plans, robs you of success, and whenever you plan, strive and come up with positive results, she comes and deprives you of them. Do you understand?"

"What should I do, oh holy Sheikh?"

"Do not think that anyone can defeat the demon but yourself through more prayer, remembering God, and reciting the Verse of Sincere Faith a thousand times every day." You were shaken and wanted to benefit from the Sheikh's knowledge and blessings, so that you would be delivered from that evil spirit that followed you everywhere. You were convinced that it must have caused all the bad luck you had suffering for so many years. It lay in waiting for you around the corners of your life like a highwayman robbing you of your efforts, and once again returning you to square one. But Sheikh al-Balbal, saying no more, put on his sandals and left the house as fast as the wind.

You offered the necessary congratulations to the family on their new home and the new shop that would soon open in this district, which the Governor-General intended should become one of the finest districts in the city, where the elite of officers and officials who worked at the Government Palace would live. Then you took your leave.

You returned to your hotel, and forgot all about the demon with the fiery eyes. The only issue that came floating up to the surface of your mind and memory was the choice that Houriya had presented to you so that she might know what kind of metal you were really made of. Thuraya's father had seen a pure, noble metal elsewhere in you, but Houriya wasn't deceived by appearances, for she knew that not all that glitters is gold.

In the darkness, the roar of the sea penetrated the silence of your room and the smell of insecticide hung in the air. You put yourself on trial, using yet again that "why" that had stuck in your mind.

Why not accept Houriya's marriage proposal? There was no other woman whom you knew better. You knew her inside out, body and soul, and throughout that period you hadn't seen anything, no matter how tiny, that lessened her value as a woman and a person. Had you ever in your life met anyone more refined or as well-mannered? Nor were there any who could rival her beauty. So how could you hesitate to accept such a magnificent offer that was like a banquet from heaven falling into your lap? Why were you incapable of comprehending the blessing that merciful fate had led to you? Did you dare shut your eyes to the sight of angels descending from heaven to sing heavenly songs of joy? They were the wedding procession bringing the bride to you.

And yet what about the illicit relationship that tied her to the Governor-General?

Call it whatever you wanted, no one would deny it was a healthy relationship, no less than any marital relationship. Rather, it was indeed a marital relationship if you compared it to the old ways of marriage before governments existed and marriage was established by civil offices and contracts. As for modern standards, the prevailing customs among foreigners permitted relationships like this and considered them a form of marriage. So you would not be in error in many ways, if you considered it the same as a divorce once she had left her companion. Being married to her would be even easier than with other divorced women, because she would not need to wait the required period of time before entering a new marriage.

Even if you said yes to burying the past, for better or worse, and looked ahead to the future, did you have any guarantees that the relationship between Houriya and the Governor-General would end then and there?

Even if you could be certain, many would not believe the relationship between them was over and they would consider you the husband of the Marshal's mistress. No doubt, the matter would reach Awlad Al Sheikh. How would you be able to face the people there with an identity such as this? How would a man like your father face the other men of the village? What about your mother and the women of the village? Even if you accepted the crime against yourself and decided to bear the responsibility for what you did, what right did you have to burden your mother, father and siblings with this weight and sentence them to live with their heads hung low in shame?

Houriya had assured you that the relationship with the Marshal would end, but you felt the reality of the situation would be the exact opposite. Even if she wanted to, she would not be able to, because Houriya had her house in which she lived like a princess. She would not want to give it up, and she would not be able to find another lover with limitless resources. What you really feared was that the marriage might be just a game which would guarantee Houriya a legitimate child with a legitimate Muslim father, and that her relationship with the Marshal would continue.

This suspicion of yours might be misplaced and Houriya might truly be confident of her ability to stay loyal. Regardless, you would be able to test her sincerity if you accepted her marriage proposal. The instant anything appeared to the contrary, you could wash your hands of her and divorce her.

What did you think of that solution?

You weren't able to make such an important decision so quickly. Nevertheless, you felt very relieved because you had taken a big step towards a solution and the issue seemed much clearer. You realized you didn't object to Houriya's lifestyle or her past relationships, and that you were indeed ready to a new life together as man and wife. You no longer saw the past a problem. Your concerns had been narrowed down to a single issue, that of making sure that the idea wasn't a charade.

TEN

People read the announcement about the petitions office in the newspapers; they heard it on the radio and it was spread by word of mouth, People came in droves to your office at the Government Palace. Some of them knew how to find you at your hotel, and in all this humdrum, you found a chance to engross yourself in something new to distract you from thoughts of Houriya.

Al-Kubran allowed you to use his office two or three hours every day for your meetings with the people who came to file their complaints. Those who went to your office waited for hours crammed together by the wall, opposite the Palace's back entrance. You hadn't thought that such an inordinate number of people might need your services.

Although you didn't have enough time to meet everyone who came bearing a petition, you tried as best you could to interview most of them, and to make the interview short and helpful at the same time. To this effect, you heard the person's story and read his petition at the same time, training yourself to read with half your brain and listen to the petitioner with the other half, hoping to understand all the facts before reaching a conclusion. You realized the hardest phase would be at the start, when the number of complaints and petitions would be at its maximum, but that it would begin to subside over time.

Work took up the entire day. Before your official working hours, there was the time before and after business when you would meet people in your hotel. You also didn't neglect your war against the demon that followed you, which required additional time each day, for reciting the Verse of Sincere Faith a thousand times according to Sheikh al-Balbal's advice, so you would be able to repel the evil creature.

When you encountered some difficulty counting how many times you had recited the verse, you bought a string of prayer beads. Once people saw you with the beads, they thought you were a pious sheikh proficient at handling the affairs of both this world and the next. It became an excuse for them to kiss your hand, blessing the prayer beads and their owner, though in reality you knew it was merely flattery.

The first time a woman lowered her head to kiss the hand that held the rosary, you didn't realize what was happening until she had sullied the back of your hand with her lips. Your whole body shuddered, and you snatched your hand away as if a viper had sunk its blue fangs into your hand and you felt its poison begin to course through your body. You started to condemn what had just happened, saying in a near hysterical tone, "I take refuge in God!" as if the woman had committed a deadly sin.

You were acutely aware that your hand wasn't of the same substance as those of the wealthy elites or the pious sheikhs. You feared that you had trespassed onto their domain. This blatant transgression against their expertise would infuriate them so you looked about, left and right, even behind you, fearing someone might have seen the old woman kiss the back of your hand.

You didn't mingle with any of the officials in the Palace and limited your relationships to the orderly, the café waiter and the telephone operator. You seldom went to Signor Calvi, the head of the administrative department, because the two of you would need time you didn't have to get to know each other. The amount of work was immense and every day you would send the final product to the administrative department.

Your happiness at having a telephone in your office ended after the first day. You didn't know anyone to call and nothing on the horizon suggested that would change after Houriya had slammed the door behind you over a week ago, and told you not to come back until you had an answer. More than once, you thought about going to her or looking for her telephone number and calling her, but you held off doing either because contacting her could only mean that you would say yes to her proposal. You were truly saddened that this "yes" refused to budge from your throat. Even if your heart wanted it, and it surely did, your tongue refused to say it.

Ever since your childhood in the desert, something had settled in the wrinkles of your brain along with the salts, calcium and lime that form the human skeleton. This thing prevented you from being honest with yourself and forced you to repress your emotions and desires out of fear of the ghouls who haunted the desert shadows and which people called custom and tradition, shame and honour, and capricious gossip. It was thus the rule to say "no" when you should say "yes", and to say "yes" when your feelings screamed to say "no". Even if that meant falsifying and murdering every beautiful emotion that throbbed in your heart, you had to appease the ghosts that would haunt the ruins of your soul from the moment of your birth till your last breath.

You wondered how you could possibly face Houriya when you weren't able to be the person you were, nor the person that tradition and customs wanted you to be. How could you make the decision according to what your burning heart desired with every beat and flutter, and forget the sham honour spoken of by the old hag, the wizened, the humpbacked, the shaggy-haired, the toothless. They are called traditions because they are blind and deaf and only know things by touch so they mistake gold dust for ash and ash for gold dust.

Like a coward, you went before sunset and sneaked into her house, asking the chauffeur and the garage guard about their mistress. They knew nothing about what had happened between you and Houriya, or why you had been absent the past few days, which was the first thing they asked you about when you arrived. You said that you had been extremely busy processing people's complaints and petitions.

Mukhtar said, "Imagine, Ayyad! Your friend Othman is responsible for looking after Libyans' problems."

You replied, "I'm only a mediator between the ruler and his subjects."

You didn't wish to appear to be boastful about your new post, or to give it more importance than it merited, and you were uneasy in the presence of the chauffeur, Ayyad al-Fezany, because of the resentment that lingered between the two of you., so you waited for him to leave before you asked Mukhtar about Houriya. He answered you quickly, as if he had just remembered something he had forgotten to say to you.

"You should say hello to her and ask after her health, because she sent for Sheikh Al-Balbal, who has visited her several times during your absence. She never sends for him unless she is ill or very upset."

"What do you think she summoned him this time?"

"I think that the relationship between her and the great Pasha is not going well, which has made her sad and down-cast."

"Have you gone up and seen for yourself how she is doing?"

"As you know, I rarely leave my place. But she has come down twice on her way to see a concert at the Miramare theatre. To tell you the truth, she didn't look good at all. Her face was the colour of turmeric."

"Who else has been to visit her other than the sheikh?"
"Her friend the nurse, and the fat Italian lady who meas-ures her dresses. As for the great Pasha, he has only come once since you stopped working here."

"I've only left my work here temporarily".

"Why temporarily? You have got into the Government Palace, so don't ever think of coming back here. Look ahead, move on and never look back, whether you're here or somewhere else. They didn't cut your umbilical cord to this place so that you could remain tied to it. Can you drive a car with your head on backwards? Of course not. This is the prerequisite of advancement and success. Let your motto be, 'Forward march'."

He then patted you on the back with fatherly affection,

saying "We want you to be our delegate in higher circles, a representative for the disenfranchised people like us."

"Even you say that, Uncle Mukhtar, you who know all about me. My work in the Palace is no different from that of a postman, so I'm also disenfranchised."

"Here you are working in the Palace close to the Governor-General. That in itself makes people respect and fear you. However unimportant your work may be, you are now better than Prince Suleiman al-Qarmanli who sits in the municipality building far from the Government Palace."

"A lot of people are displeased with my work, some of them even try to do me harm."

"I know that what Ayyad had heard at the Tumur Agency didn't come out of thin air. Always be on your guard for every blessed person is envied."

It was wonderful to hear this from a man like Mukhtar, because no one could equal the agony he had lived or the sacrifices he and his family had suffered at the hands of the Italians. Yet he blessed your work with them and urged you to do your utmost to succeed.

"Don't you ever hate the Italians?"

"The hatred is there, but I don't know if it's for the Italians or not. It's against injustice more than anything else. There were three Libyans serving in the camp with the Italians. 'Mountain dog', 'Greyhound', and 'Pit Bull', we used to call them. They treated us with a cruelty that the Italians didn't, and it was they who whipped and tortured us until death seemed easier than life.

"Once, while I was shovelling soil over the bodies of a number of dead women, I noticed one of the women's chest rising and falling under her clothes. So I pulled her out of the hole. She was unconscious, but still alive. I used ammonia to pull her out of her swoon. When she regained consciousness and realized I had pulled her out of the hole, she yelled at me, cursing me for what I had done, blaming me for saving her from death and returning her to the hell of life in the concentration camp. She then invoked God never to make me a successful man."

Mukhtar got up and went into the garage. After a few moments, he returned with two glasses of tea, giving one to you, and sipped his noisily before saying, "I've been on the brink of death more than once. There was a far corner where they had erected two shacks where they moved prisoners who caught infectious diseases to die, isolated from the other prisoners. One shack was for men, the other for women, and no one was permitted to go anywhere near them except the workers like me who buried the dead.

"We had to inspect the huts every day with cloths over our mouths. We were to bury whoever died in the mass graves, and we were to give whoever was still alive food prepared by their families. During my time in those huts, I contracted an intestinal fever and like other sick prisoners was moved to this place, from which nobody left except to be buried. I waited for death amidst the putrid smell of decay and excrement of the sick who moaned day and night. They died one after the other in that isolated shack, with only insects for companions. Every sick person with me in that shack died, and many healthy people outside it died too. I remained, as you see me now, living the extra years that God has granted me.

"When the people in the concentration camp saw that I had returned from the shack of death, they could hardly believe their eyes and thought I was a ghost that had returned from the world of the dead."

You recited a verse from the Holy Quran and said, "So glory be to God in Who holds the world in His Hand."

Mukhtar added, "A person who is alive is more important than a dead person, and Marshal Balbo is a different breed from that dog Graziani. All Italians are not the same, nor are Arabs."

You wished you could divulge Houriya's proposal to him. Perhaps a man like him, who had boiled in the cauldrons of pain, would be able to help you with an elucidating word, illuminating something before you in the darkness of the road. But it was a confidential topic, a secret that should not be disclosed unless an agreement to marry had really been reached. Otherwise, it was a form of slander that Houriya didn't deserve, and a wrong against her that you would not accept committing.

"You should go and visit Signora Houriya before it is too late."

Getting up, you said, "Maybe it is too late. I will come back to visit her tomorrow or the day after. Today I just came to chat with you."

"Won't you stay a while?" "Goodnight."

Your vision was clear now, because you had decided to renounce the lies in your life. Ever since you had begun your new job, you had realized that even if you succeeded in lying to people, you would never succeed in lying to yourself.

Therefore you were able to see reality stripped of delusions and an open mind, trying to make out your self-interests in stark clarity and guide yourself to them without regard for the interests of others.

But the matter was slightly different this time. Houriya clearly only wanted what was best for you, and the great Pasha, as Mukhtar called him, had given you his blessing. It was a safe path and there was no conflict between emotions and self-interests.

Nevertheless, there was a factor that entered the equation and unbalanced it, a factor you would have been able to overlook on any other occasion, but could not on the question of marriage. No matter how much the two parties gave priority to the marriage, it was a family occasion and it was utterly impossible to omit families from any calculations regarding this union. Indeed, prevailing custom was that the agreement of the parents was an indispensable condition.

Family in your case meant more than just your parents, it meant all of Awlad Al-Sheikh, from the most recently born baby to the most venerated ancestor, whose shrine was in the village and from whom everyone was descended. They all looked up to him.

There was no doubt that a marriage like this would have an effect, and you didn't want to do anything to incite the village against you. People had attributed miracles to some of your ancestors, both before and after their deaths. Your mother had always warned you that no good would ever come if they turned in their graves out of anger at something you did. And that's what would happen if your fears turned out to be true, and the pending marriage between you and Houriya was merely a sham to provide a lawful cover for the caprices of a woman who wanted to add the blessing of bearing legitimate children to her life of luxury.

Perhaps she had tired of being alone in her house

because of her status as a mistress. The Libyan community didn't accept such a status and didn't like to deal with women who fell into the category of mistresses. So she wanted to reintegrate into her indigenous community, under a new status as the wife of a Libyan civil servant, guaranteeing her respect and acceptance, even if it was only superficial, since social customs are only ever superficial.

Houriya was two women to you. One of them was the person whom God created as a marvel of beauty. None other but the Greatest Creator could work such an inimitable miracle. If someone like you got close to her, came to know her character and burned in the flame of praises for her beauty, he would live his entire life bewitched by her, one of the many prisoners begging not to be set free from her net.

As for the other Houriya, she was the Marshal's mistress and was governed by conditions and considerations you couldn't decipher beneath the calm shining surface of this relationship.

Similarly, you also had two identities, one of which was Othman the soldier, whom Houriya had saved from being sent to the horrors of war by choosing him to be her chauffeur. Then she had graced him with a promotion he hadn't deserved or expected, appointing him a civil servant in the Government Palace under her patronage. He was indebted to her for all the good that had come from her affections.

Then there was Othman al-Sheikh, son of the village of Awlad Al-Sheikh, descendant of the men in the shrines and mausoleums that people visited to receive the blessings of their pious occupants.

If you were free to do with yourself as you saw fit, you

weren't free to do whatever you wanted to the people of your village in the heart of the Hamada al-Hamra. Those villagers included beggars, the unemployed, criminals who had spent time in jail, and people who had joined the Italian army during the resistance.

All these people's actions, no matter how lowly or depraved, had been accepted. Every forbidden act was excused when the need arose for it, except one act which found neither excuse nor justification, for a woman to profit from selling her body or for a husband to profit from selling his wife's body. Whoever transgressed against this rule in Awlad Al-Sheikh could expect only death, either physically or socially.

Was there anyone who could reassure you that Houriya was capable of sacrificing Houriya the mistress for the sake of Houriya the wife and mother?

ELEVEN

You waited three days before returning to Houriya's house. Mukhtar was sitting on the bench outside the garage, deep in thought, when you suddenly appeared. Provoking him a little, you said, "I bet you're thinking of the past. Leave it alone a while in order to live in the present."

"Do you think anyone can escape from his past?"

"I don't know, but you are living proof that a person can escape from his present. You're the one who told me just three days ago not to look back and to always look ahead."

"Yes, because your future is ahead of you, but as for me, I've left my future behind me. Thus, you're entitled to look ahead, and I'm entitled to look back."

"Aren't there some happy moments you can return to and derive something to rejuvenate your spirit?"

"Of course. Would life have meaning if not for these moments of happiness that one snatches from the depths of these heaps of misery?"

"This is the very first time I have heard you say something like that. Then why have you always drowned us in talk of pain and misery and withheld from us these heart-warming moments?"

"Didn't I tell you about the woman I saved from among the dead bodies when I noticed she still had a spark of life in her? How could bringing someone back from the world of the dead not be a happy moment? One week after I saved her, I married her. She was a beautiful woman and she was single. She had been widowed during the internment and she had lost her child too.

"She was more than fifteen years younger than me, but despite that she loved me. She found out my first wife had died giving birth to our daughter, who was only six months old at the time I married my second wife. She considered my baby daughter to be a gift from God to compensate her for the loss of her child. She started to look after her and breast feed her, so it was only natural that I married her. We spent a happy, loving year together in the hell of the concentration camp. Her name was Um al-Kheir and she died of a liver disease, following the same fate as the other nine members of my family who were all eaten up by the al-Aqila Camp."

"But the child remained."

"When I was chosen, along with others who had also lost their families, to be the first to be released from the concentration camp, I passed through the gates of the concentration camp with only that one-and-a-half-year-old child in my arms. I carried her through the desert under the scorching sun, my only goal being to get away from that dreaded camp. I walked looking behind me, worried they would renege on their decision and send someone to bring me back to the camp. I couldn't believe I was really saved.

"Before I could get to inhabited lands, I noticed the little one panting. I sat beside a Retem tree and placed her head beneath the tree's meagre shade so she could catch her breath. I gave her the few drops of water from the canteen I had with me, but she died.

"I closed her eyes, recited the Shahada and read the Opening of the Quran. Then I used a dry branch from the tree to dig a grave for her. No sooner had I placed her in the hole and covered her with dirt than a patrol of Italian soldiers came aboard their military vehicles. They asked what I was doing with this pile of dirt in front of me, so I told them that I had buried my dead daughter and that this was her grave. They asked me if I had a burial permit.

"That was the first I had ever heard of such a permit, and I explained to them that I had just been released from al-Aqila Camp, where people died and were buried in the desert without permits. They checked the release papers, which had my name on them and the name of my daughter. Then the officer in charge ordered me to dig my daughter up and look for a cemetery to bury her in because this was a military zone where digging graves was forbidden.

Mukhtar brushed away the tears that trickled down his face as he concluded his story saying, "I still don't know what gave me the strength to remain alive and not drop dead over my daughter's grave, and I still don't know how I was able to dig her dead body out and look for another place to bury her. I didn't know what to do or where to go and I continued to walk in the desert carrying my dead daughter in my arms as I wept and wept until it was dark."

You felt as if a cleft had opened up inside of you after what Mukhtar had told you. His voice was tinged with the reality of what he had lived through seven years ago and he stretched his arms in front of him as though he were re-enacting the scene. His voice was choked with sobs and you were sorry that by asking him to recall his happy moments, one of his saddest had resurfaced.

At that moment, Signora Houriya came down the steps and stood outside the building, where she waited for the chauffeur. Ayyad al-Fezany was at the ready and pulled up in front of her, then got out to open the door for her. Your eyes met hers, so you got up, quickly went up to her and kissed her hand like the Italians did to their women, as if you were apologizing for your behaviour. Perhaps she saw traces of the tears, which had sprung up while you were listening to Mukhtar's story, and thought they were tears of regret because you had been waiting so long to come back to her.

Houriya said reproachfully, "Did you have to take so long?"

You didn't say anything, but stood there feasting your eyes on her beautiful countenance.

"Didn't you know the Marshal left for Rome over ten days ago?"

You didn't say anything, and continued to look uncom-prehendingly at the movement of her beautiful lips as they formed words and letters.

"And that he'll be back in another ten days?"

You didn't say anything. The moment was more precious than any words. On the other hand, she looked at her watch saying, "I don't want to be late for the theatre." She got into the car and sat in the back seat behind the driver, while your eyes were still fixed on her, searching for the colour of turmeric that Mukhtar had spoken of, but all you saw was rose and honey.

"Come on, get in. It's getting late."

You hadn't been expecting this invitation, you had been

waiting for her to take her car and go to her appointment, putting off the meeting between you and her until tomorrow, when you would have been safe from embarrassment and returned to Mukhtar to find out how he had been able to find a grave to bury his daughter at the end of his journey.

You saw no other option but to comply, open the front door, and ride beside Ayyad al-Fezany. Thank God there was a third person in the car with you, making it impossible for Houriya to broach the topic in his presence.

You sat in the car breathing in her mind-numbing scent without uttering a word or asking about where she was taking you until she told you to look at the giant advertisement posters that adorned Italy Square. For the very first time since you had arrived in Tripoli, you saw Arabic advertisements in the streets and squares monopolized by the Italians, where the posters hung on the walls had always been in Italian.

The coloured advertisements featured pictures of actors and their Arabic letters shone beneath the lamps centred above each poster. The graceful lettering spelled out the names of the actors and actresses in pastel colours. The play had been produced by a troupe called Ramses. The plays included "The Desert", "Children of the Poor" and "Rasputin" and would be performed twice a day by an Egyptian troupe at the al-Hambra theatre. After you had both got out of the car and were walking towards the theatre, Houriya told you that "Children of the Poor" was being performed that evening and that according to those who had seen the matinee, it was meant to be superb. She emphasized that the troupe was the largest in the East. She said that they were truly wicked and awful, and that the troupe leader was also endowed with a large share of what Houriya called wickedness and awfulness.

A big audience had come to watch the play, consisting entirely of Arabs. The ground floor was reserved for men, and the upper floor was reserved for ladies and families, among whom were a few Libyan and Jewish singers, in addition to several Libyan families, whose women wore their traditional cloaks. You sat with Houriya in the front row, which was reserved for invited guests.

As you looked around, you saw Nuriya sitting next to Sherifa and her colleagues. You didn't look around you again in order to avoid the embarrassment of having to talking to her in Houriya's presence. The atmosphere in the hall before the curtains were raised was festive. The audience was composed of the elite of Arab society, who had raised their standard of living above mere subsistence and so aspired to dabble in the refined arts, a privilege usually limited to Italian in Tripoli. That night, it was as though the Arabs of Tripoli had come to challenge this concept, and assert that they were no less refined or appreciative of the arts.

While waiting for the performance to start, Houriya told you she had been responsible for the authorization that enabled the Ramses Troupe to come to Libya. The Italian censor had feared the plays would kindle nationalistic sentiments and had recommended refusing the Ramses Troupe a visa. However, Houriya had intervened and refuted this reasoning with a single question she had had put to the Marshal. The troupe was on its way to Tunis, Algeria, and Marrakech, so why was the French censor more civilized and liberal than his Italian counterpart? She had thus been able to persuade the Marshal to authorize these performances with the provocation that Italy should be no less civilized or tolerant than France.

"You might not believe it, but this is the first time Arabic has been spoken on this stage."

"It's wonderful that the language of the Quran will ring out in this hall." "Don't you feel happy and proud when you see Arabic

letters adorning the walls of Tripoli?"

"I'm certain that the noble Arabic language will be extremely grateful to the lady who returned it to its rightful place after being exiled from the streets of this city."

"It is cause for celebration," she said.

You replied, "I wish these people knew you were behind all this."

"That's not important. I'm happy because the troupe is here, the audience is here, you and I are here. That's all that matters, don't you think?"

"Of course, of course. That is absolutely true."

That was Signora Houriya's magnanimous nature. She never made a show of the generous favours and gifts she granted others. There was another, yet more lavish favour waiting for you when the lights were turned off, the curtains raised, the show begun, and Houriya's soft hand clasped yours in the dark.

You held that soft hand in yours and a delightful tingling surged through your whole being for a few moments, during which you became completely oblivious to every-thing around you, time, place, the stage, the audience and actors. There was nothing but the soft feminine hand and its beautiful fingers, each representing a comet or ember which gave off a holy flame to illuminate the heart and set fire to the body.

Let all your reservations about marrying this woman crumble. And let fall all the empty, pedantic customs and traditions that wanted to deprive you of this joy. Let everyone in Awlad Al-Sheikh go to hell, they who would stop a happy union that the angels would celebrate from their celestial towers.

The actors in the play evoked the Egyptian countryside with all its problems. They depicted a society divided between landowning Pashas and destitute peasants who served these lords. And from within this abyss of class differences, sprang a story of impossible love between the son of a Pasha and a young servant girl.

The cruel laws that governed this society inevitably had to exact their revenge. The romantic relationship between the Pasha's son and the young servant girl had resulted in a pregnancy and the foetus had begun to move inside the poor lover's womb. Because it was impossible for the Pasha's family to let their son marry this servant, in order to conceal the scandal they had to find a victim from among the sons of poor peasant families to coerce him into marrying the girl.

As the family conspired to cover up the scandal, one sentence of dialogue stung your ears and was repeated again and again to the poor youth.

"This is what the great Pasha wants."

You remembered that Mukhtar had referred to Marshal Balbo as the great Pasha. It was easy for you to see Balbo reflected in the Pasha who plotted and gave orders that met only with obedience and submission. You also saw yourself in the role of the poor young peasant as the Pasha's family tried to degrade him by marrying him off to the woman the Pasha's son had defiled. Despite the fact he still wanted to keep her on as his mistress after she married this cuckolded peasant.

You suddenly felt a shudder rack your body violently. No, you would not be this oppressed, cheated peasant boy. You would not step into his humiliating position. You felt nauseous. Your intestines twisted and bitter acidic saliva filled your mouth. You hurried out of the theatre, crossed the street and went to a dark corner to vomit.

You felt better as you stood beside the playhouse regaining your breath, filling your lungs with air, inhaling and exhaling. You headed back to the theatre and made your way to the upper floor to continue watching the play. But as soon as your foot touched the first few steps, you stopped and turned back.

You left the theatre behind, and its lighted facade, and Italy Square, and the clamour of its shops, its cars and carts, the water fountain that washed the stone horses. You returned to the dark, empty streets and to al-Kubran's hotel.

You went up to your room. Without turning on the light, you threw yourself fully clothed onto your bed and broke into tears. You had known that this was the end of your relationship with Houriya and that you might never see her again. When you had met her just a few hours ago after two weeks' absence, you had hoped that she had relinquished the idea of concluding this deal. However, she had been even more insistent, saying that the next ten days was the deadline for reaching an agreement.

She had seen your coming to her house as a sign that everything between the two of you was going according to plan.

As you had sat with her in the car, you had realized that things had reached their final stage. There was no time to lose and you couldn't go on running through God's world naked, body and soul. Nothing covered your naked-ness but the lies you told yourself, self-deceptions that in trying to cover your nakedness only further exposed it, justifying an unjustifiable fall from grace.

All you'd needed to know the relationship had reached its end was the theatrical scenario which in the language and emotions of drama narrated a story like your own, a living rendering with actors, dialogue and props. You couldn't go on playing the role of the naive young man who didn't understand what lay in wait for him and what went on around him. Nor could you continue being the confused person who needed more time to find clarity.

You had known from the beginning that this wasn't right for you. But your burning desire for Houriya had made you procrastinate as much as possible. Now the rope had reached its end and the moment you had feared had come to pass. Your relationship with Houriya had been the most beautiful thing to happen to you since you came into this world, its intimate moments when she gave herself to you, were the most marvellous gift the angels of happiness had ever given you.

Houriya had wanted you to taste that heavenly food so that you would never be freed from her spell, and here you were still, spellbound, enthralled by her beauty. Yet you had left her while every cell in your body called out her name and burned with desire to encounter her sweet scent you had parted ways with only moments ago, realizing it was the last time you would savour it.

TWELVE

You continued to pursue your work in the petitions department unenthusiastically. During Marshal Balbo's absence, it was clear that none of the administration officials wanted this office or were keen on solving the problems of these miserable Libyans who sought it out. You knew that the idea of establishing the office had been born in Houriya's head, who had in turn placed it in the Marshal's.

If she had seen it as a means to ease the suffering of some, that hadn't been her only motive. Her first and fundamental goal, as she had told you, had been to raise you to a higher status that would qualify you to be her partner by preparing a civil position for you in the Government Palace. And now you had brought down this central pillar on which the petitions office had been erected, so nothing remained but to bring down the office itself.

Withdrawing from the theatre could only have been understood as a statement of refusal, a coarse uncouth statement inappropriate for a woman like Houriya who treated everyone most graciously.

You contemplated writing her an apology, but a letter written in Arabic would be of no use because Houriya would be unable to read it. Perhaps telephoning was the best way to convey your apology, but that would require the courage to face Houriya and be honest about your feelings. But you weren't brave, because you were still vulnerable to her spell. You could not hear her name mentioned or see her figure in your imagination without wanting to weep.

You let the days roll by without doing anything but reciting the Verse of Sincere Faith a thousand times, in order to defeat the demon that followed you wherever you went. The crowds of people coming to the office diminished owing to the absence of the Governor-General, since they wanted him to examine their petitions, and you did not want to be any less confident in his Lordship the Marshal than his subjects, so until he returned from Italy, you would disregard the papers you received.

You became introspective and didn't communicate with anyone, feeling no desire to visit the people you had promised to visit, like Nuriya in Sidi Umran, or Haj al-Mahdy and his family in their new house. You didn't even feel like visiting the Shoushan Agency in order to get news of your family in Awlad Al-Sheikh.

You contented yourself with the routine trip to the office, without staying there any longer than necessary. You received some petitioners in the hotel and listened to al-Kubran's vacuous ideas about reforming the decadent conditions of the human race.

You listened to al-Kubran's old proposition to discover the treasures of Atlantis, which was an obsession to which he regularly returned. He was infuriated by the disregard he met from higher authorities. But this disregard didn't prevent him from suggesting a new idea, which he thought more effective and beneficial to the people of the country.

He wanted to present it to the Governor-General so it could be carried out immediately. This new project of al-Kubran's was the reclaiming the desert, and returning it to its original state when it had been arable fields and forests rich with water and fauna.

To give your mind a break from other troubles, you pressed him on the point, laughing and saying, "And how would you do that happen?"

"It's all very, very simple matter. All you have to do is introduce me to His Lordship Marshal Balbo so I can explain to him how to begin realizing what every other generation has dreamed of."

"It took more than ten thousand years for the desert to become a desert, so how are you going to return it to its previous era in ten days?"

"All it will take is a number of those giant digging machines produced in the factories of Milan so we can dig canals from the sea to the major cities in the desert. They can be used as a network for travel by boat. Don't you see? This way we will renew the caravan trade in a modern, civilized way that offers speed and increases the volume of trade ten times over.

"We will also connect the far reaches of the country, and all this water running across the desert will begin to change the climate once the water vapour begins to create rain, and in a short while, we will all see how the desert becomes a paradise, God Willing. We can also set up basins in the desert ravines to raise fish to end the famines that desert people suffer from, and pasture lands fed with seawater can be used to raise cattle."

"You want to create fields and pasture lands with water from the sea?"

"And why not? You might not know that there are forests at the bottom of the ocean that are larger than any forests you've ever heard of, and in them are more trees and plants than exist on land. Do these plants live on rainwater? Aren't they nourished by seawater? So why not plant their species above ground?"

"You know the level of the land is much higher than sea level. What are you going to do about that?"

"That's not a problem. A hundred windmills, a thousand windmills, even fifty thousand windmills will solve the problem. They don't use fuel and they won't cost money. They can lift the water to the level of one of the plateaus overlooking the sea and then the water will flow downwards until the mountains of Niger and Chad turn it back at our borders."

You laughed. Al-Kubran thought he hadn't overlooked the slightest detail. He had taken your gramophone to play in the hotel in exchange for exempting you from paying your room's rent for a year, which was equivalent to the price of a new gramophone. It was a good bargain for you, especially because you were going through a difficult period in your professional life, and a room to stay in for a whole year gave you a sense of security during these days when there was no knowing what tomorrow would bring.

Al-Kubran noticed you were distracted and had not paid attention to his amazing project, which he was sure would herald a happier dawn for the human race if were carried out, so he reproached you saying, "What I'm saying is scientific, but regretfully Libyan minds hate science and scientific thought. That includes you, Othman, for I cannot see any enthusiasm from you for my project. It will change life on the face of the earth."

"Who says that we want to change life on the face of the earth or even under it?"

"I'm not joking. I tell you seriously that God created man, gave him a mind, and for that mind created three regions in the brain. The region in the back of the head is responsible for creating and producing ideas. The region in the middle of the head is for planning the necessary steps to carry out these ideas, and the third region at the front of the head is for carrying out these ideas and living our daily, practical lives.

"But God relieved the Libyans of two of these three regions, the part for producing ideas and the part for planning. All he left these wretched creatures is the ability to deal with things as they are so they can do nothing but react. That's why there is little hope that they become people like other human beings."

"Aren't you yourself one of those Libyans?"

"There is an infallible test by which you can be assured if a Libyan is a real Libyan or not. If he mentions a new idea, there must be a foreign element in his genes, and I'm no exception to that theory, for the descendants of my family were Europeans."

"You condemn Libyans because they do not believe in your delusional ideas".

"In spite of my respect for the imagination, my proposals re not a matter of imagination, but are well-planned projects that are ready to be carried out."

Al-Kubran's gang began to drift in one after the other. One of them had heard part of your discussion and said, "We don't want these ideas however great they may be because only the Italians will benefit from reclaiming the desert."

Another of al-Kubran's friends asked to hear the gramophone sing, for it was better than all their chattering, and
then put a record on before anyone could say anything.
The sound of singing rang out, spreading a cheerful atmosphere that silenced al-Kubran, leaving all his chattering
trapped in his throat.

With the gramophone on, you returned to daydreaming
in your private world, worrying about what the days would
bring and making use of the advantage God had given to
the Libyan people, since according to al-Kubran, He had
created them only for reactionary behaviour. Realizing that
naturally events would not take their ordinary route and
that new realities were bound to appear in your life, you
had to prepare yourself for the future.

Those new realities didn't take long to appear. A few
days after the Marshal's return, a large well-built man
appeared at your door while you were in your office
preparing the reports on the petitions. He was wearing
traditional Libyan dress, complete with waistcoat, white
cloak and a red skullcap with its blue silk tassel. Although
it was warm, he wore an elegant burnous over his cloak,
as it was the sign of wealth and authority. He held a shiny
brown walking stick and an string of amber prayer beads.
His ring's large precious stone shone from one of his fingers,
while his grey beard accentuated his solemn dignity.

Before you were able to stand up to welcome him and
ask how you could be of service, a thin man with a pale
pointed face that resembled a rat's, wearing a grey suit,
entered the office before him, and said in a voice that was
more a shriek than anything else, "Commander Basher Bey
al-Ghiryany."

The dignified man strutted into the room and looked

around at the four walls, then raised his eyes to the ceiling for a few moments, though there was nothing there worth more than a passing glance. Without offering any greeting, he addressed you in a voice dripping with contempt, "Are you the person they call Othman al-Sheikh?" You didn't know how to answer him, so you kept quiet. The man's name wasn't unfamiliar as he was one of the most prominent Libyans in the Italian government.

"What are you doing here?"

He hurled the question at you even though it was your right to ask him that. Still, you curbed your anger, taking into consideration the difference between your age and his.

"I work in the petitions office for people's complaints."

"Since when have you worked in this office?"

"A month and some days."

"And where were the petitions and the people before this month? Did they appear suddenly from beneath the earth? Or perhaps there was a palace, my palace, on the Western Avenue which over the years had received them and solved their problems."

You answered him calmly and coldly saying, "Your Excellency knows very well that I didn't appoint myself to this office, nor did I force my way into the Government Palace and establish an office for the petitions of Libyan citizens so that I could manage it for my own sake. For anyone who is displeased by the matter, there is an official in this palace whom they can speak with, but I'm not that official."

Basher al-Ghiryany said angrily, "I've already talked to him and the matter is settled. Fowzy will take charge of this office and will send me the complaints and petitions so that I can assess them, for I'm more aware of the circumstances of Libyan citizens than the Marshal himself. As for you, you can remain in the office provided that you obey the instructions given to you by Fowzy."

You replied, "I don't take orders from you or from your subordinate Fowzy. I only take order from the officials in this palace."

You wanted to turn him and his little rat out of the office, but you were certain that the man had support from some important quarters to behave and speak like this. They weren't empty threats and no doubt you would be the loser in a battle between you and him, but there still was no need to give him an easy victory.

You left the office and went the head of the administrative department. You barged in and in a choked voice asked him to protect you from the tyranny of an ignorant man named Basher al-Ghiryany who didn't respect the decrees of the Governor-General or the sanctity of the Government Palace.

Signor Calvi came around his desk, lunging left and right, and asked you to calm down. Taking your hand, he led you to a chair and ordered a cold drink to be brought to you, then said, "All Libya knows that Basher al-Ghiryany is a temperamental person, but he has a heart of gold, so don't be angry and consider what he said to you to be what a father would say to his son. He is furiously resentful that Marshal Balbo established an office without his knowledge since he had previously been unofficially in charge of the Libyan citizens' complaints and petitions.

"In order that the matter would not become a point of contention, Marshal Balbo suggested that Basher Bey visit you and reach an understanding about how to run the office under his supervision. That's all, so leave the matter to me for two days and I will learn how to arrange everything so that you can continue with your work in the office without anyone interfering with you. I will send the complaints that need Basher Bey's opinion to his palace myself."

You left the office, the petitions, the Bey, his subordinate the rat and Signor Calvi the cripple and went out to the street, followed by the evil demon with its fiery eyes. What had occurred had been expected and the promise given to you by the head of the department that you would continue working in the office was only meant to calm your nerves.

The road to the Government Palace had been blocked just like the one to Houriya's house. This was only the beginning of the storm that would wreck everything you had built your life upon in Tripoli. The demon's evil had defeated you in spite of all the times you had recited the of Sincere Faith, because the demon didn't work alone. He had an army of allies spread out all over the world, blocking every road.

You no longer knew where to go or what to do with yourself. All that remained was the damp room in al-Kubran's hotel that you returned to without knowing what to do inside it, then left it without knowing what to do outside of it.

After two days of spinning your wheels, you went to Signor Calvi to ask him what had happened. He told you to wait a little longer but assured you your salary would be paid in full just as if you were working regularly. You gave Signor Calvi a written application for a week's vacation so that Basher al-Ghiryany would not consider your absence to be abstaining from your work and ask the Governor-General to fire you.

People continued to bring their petitions and complaints to you at the hotel and you were obliged to accept them. You put the petitions in your room without bothering to read or discuss them as you had previously done. After a couple of days, they stopped coming to the hotel for one of the Commander's people had notified them that your relationship with the petitions office had been terminated.

Al-Kubran noticed that you left the hotel late in the morning, sometimes walking in a different direction from the one you used to take to work, and he knew that you were on a vacation from the petitions office, and that you spent it loitering on the beaches. So he drew a connection between this vacation and the project to draw tourists to Tripoli. The newspapers had written about the project and people gossiped about it, particularly about the area west of the harbour, which was neglected and deserted despite its perfect location.

Al-Kubran had seen you walking in that direction a few times, so he became convinced that the Governor-General had assigned you to choose the sites where the new tourist buildings would be built. Al-Kubran had an idea he believed would make Tripoli's tourist project a legend of the modern era. He wanted to build a hotel in the sea. He said that it would not cost a lot of money, because the Tower of Abu Leila, which stood on a plateau in the middle of the sea, was already there, as was a stone bridge leading to it. All that was needed was a blueprint to develop and modernize by adding more storeys above it, and installing amenities for it underwater. For example, a café and club in the form of a submarine with glass windows should be built next to the hotel, so that the customers could sit among the fish and the coral reefs. Such a hotel would have more tourist appeal than the Italian Riviera.

You remembered a song you had heard on the gramophone and said, "It looks like you've fallen under the influence of the gramophone and that song that says, 'In the sea I didn't leave you, but on land you left me.'"

"No, you're right, but the more important line is the one that goes, 'I didn't sell you for any amount of gold, but you sold me for some hay' because my ideas are as valuable as gold. Honestly, don't you think that it's a wonderful idea? It only needs a great man like Balbo to carry it out."

Al-Kubran was a good man who still believed in you even though he had seen wandering distractedly around the Tower of Abu Leila and the deserted Jewish graveyard. Should you admit defeat and quit the battlefield, fleeing from the Commander who had appeared like a snake out of some unseen hole in the ground? Or should you fight, try to regain your post even if nothing came of? You could at least be a source of annoyance, for like the Libyan saying goes, the fly may not kill a person but it can disgust him.

So your task was to play the role of a fly. You couldn't kill the Commander but you could at least disgust him, so much so that he would wish that he and his rat Fowzy had never set foot in your office.

It was then that you remembered that you had a connection to the Fascist Party, the most powerful institution in the country. You had received your membership card from the Governor-General himself. You hadn't attended any of its programmes, nor had you made any use of its privileges, so you decided to go to its office in order to find allies for your battle with the formidable Basher al-Ghiryany.

There was another old saying, that being bitten reminds you that you have teeth. The Commander had sunk his fangs into your flesh, and the Fascist Party were the teeth capable of giving bite for bite. The membership card was of no use if it couldn't come to your aid during these trying times. In preparation for going to the Party's main headquarters, you had your hair cut by an Italian barber, you shaved using expensive eau du cologne, donned the black shirt and white trousers and picked up an Italian newspaper, the first page of which was decorated by a large photograph of the Duce. You were the very image of a wellkempt member who followed the news and made his party proud.

By six o'clock you were at the Trade Fair.

THIRTEEN

You had been exempted from the military training course since you were a professional soldier, but you were obliged to participate in all the other programmes with the rest of the members, the most important of which were the political edification programmes and the regular shifts in the office, in addition to being on guard duty one day every month.

The other members were about to attend a lecture on politics, so you found yourself forced to attend it too. You entered a large hall where a crowd of black shirts were sat in front of a screen. As you looked around, you noticed the incompatibility between the black shirts and the Libyans' skin colour, most of whom were dark, some of them to the point of being black. You were certain that the founders of the Fascist Party had never imagined that dark-skinned people would ever wear the black shirts which had been chosen to suit fair-skinned Italians.

The lights dimmed, leaving only the beams of light streaming from the projector in the middle of the hall. The device let out an odious whirring noise as it imposed its light on the screen, and the Duce appeared, standing on a balcony high above crowds who hailed him hysterically. As he began his speech, his voice mixed with the whirring of the projector, so it came across distorted as he threatened the forces opposed to the onslaught of Fascism, saying that the Italy's power would defeat the renegade gangs and slave traders in Abyssinia, and contribute to the victory over the republican army in Spain, in order to unify the Iberian Peninsula and purge it of Bolshevists.

The Duce made a fleeting reference to Libya, which he claimed was blessed with stability and prosperity after the sweeping Fascist victory. The speech lasted for more than an hour, during which time five cinema film reels were used. You were already bored by the end of the first reel and tried your best not to fall asleep, lest one of the zealous Fascists report you and get you into more trouble than you were already in.

As soon as the speech ended and the lights were switched on, people began to leave the hall and you threw yourself into the crowds thronging towards the doors. You had gone to the Party's office in order to escape your feelings of distress and resentment, to find some assistance to lift the siege. Yet those feelings had only worsened after hearing the Duce's speech. You felt that the Duce was one of the demons that followed you and he too, with his wide heavy body, weighed down on your chest until you began to suffocate.

When the film had ended and the lights had come back on, you hadn't been able to believe that you had been released from its hellish nightmares. You ran into the street, certain that the Fascist Party couldn't offer you anything other than more servility and humiliation, especially after reading in one of the newspapers that the number of Libyans in the Fascist Party had reached ten thousand and was increasing every day, such that it would reach twenty thousand the following year. You would not be able to attain any prominent position in this mob of black shirts and blacker faces, every one of them aspiring to prestige and power like you.

You didn't know why, but Nuriya came to mind. What if you went to her? It was a little late at night, for it was almost ten o'clock, but you were sure she would welcome you at any time, finding a chance to show your Fascist uniform off to her friends.

You plunged through the shadowy alleys until you reached her house. The noisy district that had always stayed awake until midnight had become silent and dark after the official brothels had been moved next to the Trade Fair. They had moved to Dante Street, Virgil Street, Mazzini Street and whatever other poets who would be delighted by the company of these girls of love.

Silence and shadows lay thick about the house. You knocked on the door but no one answered so you knocked again and again, louder and harder, but to no avail. Perhaps an angry customer, who hadn't been satisfied with his visit, had reported the women to the police who had taken them to prison on the charge of working without a licence. The objection wasn't to the principle of prostitution, but to their manner of practising of it, because the government didn't like people who made money to keep it for themselves rather than paying their share in taxes.

Circumstances were against you that night, and even the woman who sold you entertainment by the hour had locked you out of her house. There was nothing left for you to do but to return morosely to your damp hotel room, but after a few steps towards your hotel, you suddenly remembered the Eastern Café in Musheer Market, which stayed open until late at night.

The singers, dancers and musicians there could put an end to your bad mood, but you feared that you might not be allowed to enter the night club in your Fascist uniform. There was also another problem. In order to reach the night club, you would have to pass through the district of Thuraya al-Saffar and Sararay Arch and your Fascist uniform might provoke the Libyan youths into trying to do your harm.

You decided to refrain from going to the Eastern Café, and to return to your hotel by way of the Jews' Alley whose residences would have already closed their shops and retired to their homes. You walked through the alley safely and went up to the plateau of Bab al-Bahr, where you stood watching the waves of the sea and inhaling the breeze that smelled of wormwood. The smell reminded you of your family in Awlad Al-Sheikh, who had used wormwood oil medicinally, and as a child your mother used to massage your body with its oil in order to cure your pains. You only found that smell near this part of the ocean by the old city, perhaps because it was a hilly region rich with vegetation. Or perhaps it was the trees that grew thickly nearby that gave off this sweet smell. Your body took it in and savoured it, because it reminded you of the steppes and the countryside to which you belonged.

The touch of the cold breeze on your face refreshed you, and the lights of ships appeared, anchored at a distance and covered by an opaque film of vapours rising off the sea. Above the sea, the moon lent some of its pallid colour to the horizon beneath it. The waves crashing against the rocks on the shore produced a pleasant din that contributed to creating the recital being performed by the creatures and elements of the night and the sea.

You went down to the shore to a pile of rocks that faced the Tower of Abu Leila. You sat there, the sea in front of you, the stars above you, and all around you the whole world was enveloped in peace and tranquillity. The quiet was broken only by the sound of the waves as they crashed against the shore and sent arcs of water flying in the air. The spray on your skin refreshed you. The battles and frustrations and resentments of the day dwindled away. You felt the peace and serenity around you trickle into your heart, and you decided to remain there as long as possible, in order to imbibe the ambience, which revived the soul and imbued you with a sense of contentment as if you had satisfied every one of your needs in this world and didn't want for anything or anyone more.

You remained sitting until the light of dawn began to show, and then you went to Gorgi Mosque nearby, where you liked to pray more than in any other mosque. You performed your ablutions and prayed the dawn prayer without waiting for the congregation, so as to avoid anyone who might look at your Fascist uniform in contempt and spoil the moment.

You returned to your hotel room to sleep, full of the idea that you didn't need anything from anyone. Not one of them could harm or help you, and you would not ask any of them for favours, for God Alone is the Master of the Universe and it is He who grants blessings to whomever He wills.

You felt that the only person worth visiting while you underwent this spiritual experience and its clear-sightedness was Sheikh al-Balbal, so that you could receive his blessings. He only dealt with the realm of the soul, and had nothing to do with worldly ambitions of the sort you had fallen prey to, chasing after them like someone trying to clutch the wind.

You would go to this sheikh craving penance and redemption from the burdens of the past. The following morning, after waking, showering, and having a breakfast of tea, bread and cheese, you entrusted yourself to God and headed to Sheikh al-Balbal's home in Shaib al-Ain alley, near the Clock Tower Square. You went down the steps, making for the hotel door, when Sheikh Al-Balbal came through the door on his way into the hotel. Your surprise at this strange coincidence almost froze your tongue, and all you could say was, "I was on my way to visit you, venerable Sheikh."

"I came here in order to save you the trouble of making a visit in vain."

"Why do you deprive me of your aid and blessings?"
"Because you will find no assistance except from yourself."

"Won't you be kind enough to grant me one word of wisdom?"

"How long has it been since you visited your parents? Don't you know that what pleases them pleases God?"

He had given you the word of advice you had asked for, and then disappeared while you went back up the stairs to your room. Without delay, you packed your bag with what you would need for your trip to your village, and set out for the Shushan Agency to look for a vehicle going to Awlad Al-Sheikh.

News about your relationship with the Italian governor had made you into an influential and famous personality in the eyes of the villagers. No sooner did they hear of your arrival than they all went to your father's home, where you were staying, so as to welcome you and congratulate you on what you had achieved.

Your father confirmed your high-ranking status by slaughtering a ram in your honour and inviting all the people who welcomed you to partake of it.

In recent times, your father had been making use of your reputation and, propelled by it, had carved himself a place among the village elders, so much so that his home had become the meeting place where these elders came to ask for his advice in managing the affairs of the village and to ask for his help in sending their petitions to the government.

Prior to that, your father had been an ordinary villager who squatted in his store and sold coal and kerosene, which he had later changed to sweets for children and candles and lanterns for people visiting the graves of their deceased relatives. He had never had any ties to the village elders and none of them had ever given him second thought.

From the moment you arrived, people came to you carrying petitions and complaints, hoping you would find a solution. You wanted to tell them you were no longer associated with the office that dealt with such matters, because you had left it in the hands of new supervisers and returned to being a soldier in the Italian army.

However, your father prevented you from going out to them and being so candid with words which were, in his opinion, premature. You still hadn't officially left the petitions office, and if you did, it would not annul your close ties to the Governor-General. The villagers knew about these ties, and they were proud of them. So if you refused to take their petitions, you would be letting them down.

Therefore your father went out to them and received their petitions, not hesitating to promise them fast results from his son, who would do everything he could to meet their demands. The elders brought their letters and official petitions to the Governor-General, in which they begged him to look kindly on their affairs and help rid them of poverty and unemployment.

They also requested authorization for a number of projects whose execution had been delayed. These projects included improving the road from the village to the regional capital, building a new clinic, digging an artesian well for drinking water which would stop the village having to drink the unhealthy water from the old well. Your father took all the petitions and assured the elders that his son would convince his friend the Governor-General to meet all these demands, since it was no benefit in being a responsible and influential official unless it benefited the people of his village before anyone else.

You had come to Awlad Al-Sheikh seeking peace and quiet far from the physical and spiritual exhaustion that had afflicted you in the city. But your problems had preceded you. Whatever relief you had found upon reuniting with your family had been spoiled, along with this simple, provincial environment devoid of the complications of the city or relationships based on gain and mutual self-interest. You had discovered that those same concerns had entered the most private and intimate connections, like that between you and your father.

He had closed his ears and mind to hearing anything to the effect that your friendship with the Governor-General was a just rumour and that other people had assumed the responsibility for the petitions office's work. You added that what had happened to you wasn't a disaster, for you were still alive and well and had a salary from the army which was more than enough for your needs and those of your family. So why claim what wasn't true? But your father stubbornly clung to his delusions.

You went to your mother to unburden yourself. In a simple language that she could understand, you told your mother everything you had told your father, adding that you didn't know how to deal with your father, who had begun issuing decrees to the villagers in matters of govern-ance. He had given the petitioners high hopes, and attrib-uted you with power and influence you didn't have.

Your mother's only response was to weep because tears were all she had to express happiness and sorrow, refusal and assent, or farewell and welcome. When you asked her why she wept, she replied that they were tears of joy for the high standing her son had reached in the government which made you important in the eyes of the villagers.

Your mother added that no matter how modest you were, everyone knew your worth, and some had seen up close the high standing you held among the people of the city. Their testimony was undeniable, and they had come bringing the good news and congratulating your family. She said that the first person to congratulate them had been Abdel Mowlah, who always praised you fervently for the many favours you had done him and for the good deeds you had done for the poor and wretched in Tripoli. "Let other people envy you if they want, but at least don't you envy them yourself."

All that meant was that your mother hadn't believed a

single word of what you had said. The truth was not what
you said about yourself, but what rumour said about you.
After the services you had rendered to strangers, she wanted
you to turn to your siblings and help them obtain government scholarships and salaries even if they were too young
to work.

You saw no use in repeating what you had said about
your modest position that didn't offer the luxuries she
demanded. It seemed to you that your family's humble
origins, whether on your mother's side or your father's, had
played a role in their attachment to this delusion. As soon
as they caught sight of a peephole in the ceiling of poverty
that they lived beneath, they thought that heaven had finally
taken note of them and decided to shower them with their
share of the treasures of which they had previously been
deprived. It was hard to convince them that this window
was a lie, or that the walls of poverty still surrounded them
and that heaven's justice would be a few generations late.

All you could do was tell your mother that your siblings,
her sons and your father's sons, were still too young to be
appointed to any government post. The only help they
needed wasn't in your hands, it was in her hands, because
the best guarantee for their future was to enroll them in
the Italian schools.

You said the same thing to your father when he too
mentioned your siblings' future, as they shared a psychic
connection despite over a decade and a half of separation.
So you weren't surprised to hear the same response from
your father that your mother had made. "Don't forget that
the Sunni Mosque is what brought you all this good
fortune."

And so on and so forth. Religious education, which

was antithetical to a secular Italian education, continued to be firmly ingrained in this generation of mothers and fathers. You yearned to escape from these delusions that trapped your family and to return to the safety of your room at al-Kubran's hotel before someone laid bare these lies. But the men of your extended family, which included your father's side and your mother's side, had agreed to hold a feast in your honour. So you yielded to their demands that you attend and sat among the aunts and uncles listening to them chatter about your impending marriage, which they had planned without your knowledge. They had even chosen the prospective bride and all that remained was to draw up the marriage contract.

"You must know that the Masaeed Tribe is the most important tribe in the region, and its chief, Haj Sadun is the richest, most powerful and influential chief around. Marrying into the Masaeed Tribe will guarantee your family in Awlad Al-Sheikh a powerful ally to turn to in difficult times, and Haj Sadun hopes to find a bridegroom like you for his daughter Shahla . . ."

Before they could finish talking, you asked permission to withdraw because it was time for you to depart. You had a lot of important duties that prevented you from marrying right now.

You took your bag and left the house without knowing whether there would be any means of transport to Tripoli. You had just wanted to leave that family gathering by any means, so you walked down the street that led to the city hoping to chance upon a lorry willing to let you ride to Tripoli atop its cargo.

Some young men from your family followed you and begged you to return, but you paid them no mind. You walked two or three miles before a military patrol car passed by on its way back from one of the surveillance stations in the desert. You stopped the car, showed the driver your military identity card and rode back to Tripoli.

As you sat next to the driver, you tried to discover the secret meaning behind Sheikh al-Balbal's advice to visit your family considering the trip had turned out to be so fruitless.

FOURTEEN

When you arrived at the hotel, al-Kubran informed you that Nuriya had come twice in the past two days, and had waited for you that very evening, but when you hadn't shown up, she had gone home promising to return the following day. Al-Kubran added, "She is very insistent on seeing you, and we were lucky that you weren't here because that gave us an opportunity to hear her beautiful singing."

"Who? Nuriya a singer? Are you joking?"

"Don't say you didn't know. You knew and didn't want to tell us, just as you know that her repertoire is vast."

"All I know is that she lives in a house of wedding singers."

"Maybe after giving us the gramophone, which performs recorded songs, you wanted to monopolize this kind of live entertainment for yourself."

"Well, I've failed, for you have reached her and I fear that you will confiscate her just as you have confiscated the gramophone."

"Her voice is a sweet as a curlew's singing."

"The song of a curlew in al-Kubran's hotel would draw

lots of people if you decided to hold a concert for her in the hotel," said one of the al-Kubran's friends.

Without giving any concern to his friend's proposal al-Kubran continued to praise Nuriya's singing saying, "I wish you could have been with us yesterday evening. Nuriya's sweet voice attracted all the customers in the hotel who assembled around her as she sang her new song about Balbo."

Then al-Kubran began beat out the rhythm of a song on the table in front of him and sang.

"I love you with the greatest love, you whose heart is gold. O Balbo! The ruler of our land and the master of the masters of our government. You raise our banner high and we will live a life of happiness and songs. I love you with the greatest love."

You wondered how Nuriya could possibly have known Balbo enough to sing about him and love him with all that love, unless al-Aufra had decided to meddle in the business of wedding singers and ordered them to sing songs that would encourage people to love the Governor-General.

But since when had Nuriya become a singer? Working weddings was a only a camouflage for her other profession which was far more profitable, the oldest profession of all.

Al-Kubran gave you a pile of petitions and complaints from people who hadn't heard that you had left the office. You took them to your room and threw them in a bag full of the petitions and complaints that had been brought to you before your trip to your village and the others you had brought with you.

You went to sleep and didn't bother to get up out of bed the following morning, enjoying a lazy day. You thought about taking a little walk to the head of the administrative department to enquire about any new developments, but thought better of it. He knew your address and could send for you if he wanted, so you might as well enjoy this forced vacation and stay in bed until the day was over.

The fact that Nuriya would visit you gave you something to look forward to with anticipation, not just because she would be sexual nourishment, but also because you were curious about her metamorphosis from a woman looking for a licence to work in the official brothels to a singer in the royal court of Tripoli for the uncrowned monarch, Italo Balbo.

You didn't know why, in periods of stress and tension, but sex had this curative property that freed the body from strain, or more than that in your case, for you felt an ecstasy that surpassed the normal pleasure of sex at times of safety and stability. It was as if sex were the secret cave you had taken refuge in from the demon that was following you, so you could enjoy a few moments of peace. And sex was the ointment that wiped away the sounds of the heart and soothed its pains, even if only for a short while. You felt as if it were a sweet morsel in bitter saliva, knowing that the bitterness would return to your mouth once the moments of sweetness had faded.

That was how you felt as you enveloped Nuriya's plump body in your arms and tried to lay her on your narrow bed. Before asking her about anything, you grabbed her and got into bed with her. With a woman like Nuriya, the priority was sex before anything else.

It was the sort of sex you could enjoy for its own sake, uncomplicated by concerns, delusions, or whispers about carrying out your duty, bearing children, or married life, nothing but a coupling of lovers, innocent and simple.

After the animal in you had been sated, you were dying to hear why she had come to the hotel day after day so persistently. Her answer surprised you, that she only came at the strong insistence of her peers and Sherifa, the mistress of the house, who had sent you an expensive woollen pullover as a gift.

As Nuriya took the woollen garment out of its wrapping and held it up, saying they hoped it would protect you from the cold of the winter in exchange for what you had done for them when you ensured that they would be protected from the cold for the rest of their lives, and had bestowed such kindness on them as they would never forget.

You were neither able to understand what Nuriya was saying nor the motive behind the gift, until she explained that the petition that you had submitted for her, when you had first started working in the petitions office, had resulted in a swift response from the Governor-General. The official committee responsible for relocating the district's residents had inspected the old house and decided it was an architectural landmark that required urgent maintenance.

A decree to move its residents to a house in the new project in the City of Gardens had been issued and because Marshal Balbo admired the art of music, he had given orders that Sherifa's troupe of wedding singers be encouraged to sing their popular folk songs at the local Arabic broadcasting station.

Nuriya added that the Marshal had also sent them a book of songs that glorified Italy and Italy's development of Libya. Among those songs was the song of love for Balbo that Nuriya had sung to al-Kubran and his customers at their insistence, in addition to many other songs which they had learned by heart and had sung at the broadcasting station. They had been paid a sum of money in advance for these songs and they intended to devote themselves entirely to singing these songs, for that was much more profitable than any other profession.

Balbo had yet again augmented his international fame, which had turned his name into Babollo in order to resemble the name of the ancient god Apollo, the patron of music and the arts. As if after discovering Apollo's ruined temple in the old city, the Marshal had wanted to celebrate by following in the footsteps of that pagan deity, who had loved this country and named it.

Although good fortune had let you down, it had nevertheless actively used you to do good for others like Nuriya, Sherifa, her women and all the women who had lived in the brothels of that ancient district. This important victory for Sherifa and her girls had been realized through a meaningless piece of paper that might have had the same fate as the papers that were heaped in a corner of your room and would remain there until the ink faded.

These women's dream of a new home had become a reality in the blink of an eye, to say nothing of their new respectable profession, which brought in more revenue than selling their bodies. The stars of happiness shone in their sky, whereas in yours, all the stars had gone out one after the other, until it had become dark. Fate, as it seemed, was enamoured of this balancing act. When one side of the scale drops somewhere, the other side must rise elsewhere. Thanks be to God from Whom all things come.

Yet you wondered how the Marshal could find free time to concern himself with the petitions of women wedding singers and find people to write songs for them in addition to sending musicians to play those songs and then granting them the opportunity to perform at the broadcasting station, all at such short notice.

There had to be a reason behind all this, and it occurred to you that maybe one of the women of the house had caught Balbo's eye and he had opened this grotto of treasures for her. But that was unlikely because you knew the women of the house and not one of them had what it took to catch the attention of Marshal Balbo, the womanizer.

The truth then flashed through your mind and you wondered how you hadn't realized it right away. In recent days, a few songs by Basher Fahmy, the famous Libyan singer who had emigrated to Tunisia and who had been angered by the new law that automatically made Libyans into Italian citizens, had become famous. So he had composed a number of popular songs denouncing the law and criticizing the Mufti of Libya who given the law his backing.

Because of their simple melodies and their appeal to people's anti-occupation sentiments, people sang them over and over again everywhere in broad daylight, fearlessly, even the children sang them while they played in the streets. The Italian administration was naturally enraged and Basher Fahmy and his songs were blacklisted. Even his romantic and comic songs that had nothing to do with politics were prohibited. The Italian censor issued a decree that any person who sang, heard, bought or owned any of Basher Fahmy's records or those of the Sons of the Desert was to be punished.

The petition that Nuriya and her companions had submitted to the Marshal had come during this wave of musical hostility to the Italian occupation, so he had seen the benefit in using the wedding singers, along with recruited composers and musicians, in a counter campaign to nullify the effect of the anti-Italian songs by flooding the market with a new wave of Italian propaganda songs. He also ordered that a new anthem be composed for the Libyan Youth Fascist Party, which was sung by a male chorus in a broadcast from the radio station.

"Congratulations on the new song about the hero with a heart of gold," you said to Nuriya.

"That's just for the radio. But how about I sing it for you and use your name instead of Balbo's?"

"I don't want to start a competition with the lord of the country. Let him have his song. All I meant to say is that Nuriya is not a fitting name for your fame, and we'll have to choose a name to match the new star of the music world."

"Of course! No one in the whole world uses his or her real name when they begin a singing career."

"What name shall your fans call you by?"

"We're going to sing together under the name Tripolitanian Music Group."

"And do you have more songs?"

"Of course. Tell me what you think of this duet sung by an Italian man and Libyan woman who are in love."

"The look in your eyes,
My Italian man,
Takes me to another world.

The magic in your eyes,
My Libyan girl.
Has lit my world on fire."

Nuriya exclaimed, "Isn't it lovely?"

"Indeed, especially when it is sung by an Italian lover. It's a romantic song that, at the same time, encourages peace and affection through a love affair."

"And is there anything more beautiful than love? But mostly it's for entertainment."

"There are politics behind this entertainment, Nuriya. It's a song meant to be performed by a man and a woman." "A chorus performance is what the owners of the radio station want. Do you know why?"

"Because it better expresses the spirit of the masses." "Please, don't make fun of me. I know I'm not an artist or a singer, but it's fate, and a gift from God. They know our real abilities, and singing in chorus is the best way to hide our voices. That's what's really behind it."

"Believe me when I tell you that I'm very happy to hear your good news, and please thank all your companions for their wonderful gift."

"That won't do. You must come to thank them yourself, and attend our housewarming party."

"And when will this party be?"

"You are the guest of honour. Choose whatever day is best for you."

"Well, then there is no need to rush."

"No, there is a very good reason to rush, because the lamb is inside the house and no one can sleep because of his constant bleating."

"Should we say tomorrow?"

"Yes, tomorrow in the evening for nightly entertainment and singing. We'll invite our Italian neighbours, so none of them object to the noise we will make, and it's no problem if you want to bring a friend with you."

"Al-Kubran for instance?" "Why not?"

"He greatly admires your singing."

"Every Libyan man is quick to praise any woman's singing, even if she doesn't deserve it, because the goal isn't the singing, it's something else."

"Was his admiration insincere?"

"It was sincere, but he moved quickly from admiration for the beauty of the song to admiration for the beauty of the singer and invited me to spend the night with him. Of course I refused, because I came to this hotel only for you."

"What a scoundrel."

"And his size frightened me. I said to myself, 'If this barrel gets on top of me, I won't be able to breathe.' Still, don't hesitate to invite him if you want. What he did with me any other man would do as well. Don't think anything of it."

Of course you were going to invite him, because you didn't want to be the only male among all the women singers, or the sole male object of so many females' attention. Al-Kubran's sense of humour would add a playful atmosphere to the evening's entertainment, especially if he talked about his imaginary projects.

But developments that unfolded the following day prevented you from attending the party. At midday, two members of the al-Aufra secret police came to your room and ordered you to accompany them to the police station where you would be interrogated. You hadn't noticed those two watching you earlier that day when you had accompanied Nuriya to the confectioner's shop to help her choose the sweets and the cakes for the party, and when you had later hired a carriage for her to take her home.

You had thought that those men had been sent by the

people who had taken over the petitions office to find out what measures you were taking to return to your post so they could thwart you. So you were surprised when they followed you up to your room, informed you they were from al-Aufra, and then proceeded to search your room, which took very little time and effort owing to its meagre contents and tiny dimensions. They took all the papers in the room and then led you to the headquarters of the secret police on Milan Street.

The interrogation officer informed you that Basher Bey al-Ghiryany had accused you of taking official state documents, including petitions and letters, to the government office, withholding those papers, wrongly impersonating a government official, and conducting affairs with citizens through this falsified identity.

You informed the officer that you had never impersonated or falsified any identity or done anything against the law, because you were still officially responsible for the aforementioned complaints and that every petition you had received had been part of your official responsibilities.

The interrogation officer took a piece of paper you had never seen before out of the drawer of his desk. It was a decree signed by the Governor-General that charged Basher Bey al-Ghiryany with the supervision of the petitions office and his subordinate Fowzy, instead of you, with the responsibility for the office's daily work.

Although you explained to the officer that you hadn't received any notification of this decree, he didn't think this defence justified exempting you from culpability or cleared you of the allegation, which the papers seized from your room proved. So he ordered that you be imprisoned and later attend a court hearing.

Nothing that happened to you was surprising. Although you hadn't expected things to reach the point of such shameless slander and false accusations against you, nor had you expected to be led to prison like a criminal, still you were prepared and would not find any kind of punishment strange even if it came as cruelly as this. When you heard the word prison, you didn't feel the kind of panic you would have expected upon having that word flung in your face. You accepted everything calmly, without any anger, shock or bitterness.

On the contrary, you were able to see the irony in the situation, because once news of your imprisonment on charges of impersonating a government official reached your father, after he had refused to listen to the truth and instead continued to deceive himself and others, he would realize what a fool he had been.

As for your mother, you didn't worry about her because she had nothing to do with people outside her own house, even if she too needed a taste of this lesson.

FIFTEEN

They handcuffed you and told you to climb into a black motor car that transferred prisoners. A police guard sat next to you, watching you until the car reached the central prison whose name, Porta Benito, derived from its similarly named locale. They put you a single cell that smelled like dead cats and locked you in. You felt as though you had been placed in a putrid, tightly sealed tin box.

There was a small opening, the size of the palm of a hand, high up on the wall near the ceiling, but it let in neither air nor light. After your eyes got used to the darkness, you looked around, thinking to find the dead cat but found nothing. It was clearly the smell of urine, mixed with other offensive odours that had accumulated over years. There was nothing in the cell but a straw mattress and a filthy blanket.

The stench in the cell stifled your breathing, and magnified from something perceived only by the sense of smell, to something you could taste. You could feel the revolting taste stuck in your throat and on the tip of your tongue. You wanted to vomit, and you tried, but your stomach would not turn anything up.

Only then did you begin to grasp the reality of what had happened to you. At first, you had at first accepted it with a certain mockery because you hadn't known how ghastly it would be. You couldn't imagine what grave crime you had committed to warrant being in this cell.

You had done your best to serve the masters of the country and put yourself at their disposal, so what had you done to the Governor-General to fall so far from his graces, where you had sat singing and swinging your feet, thinking that you were utterly secure. Then suddenly the clouds melted, vanishing in the blink of an eye, and there you were, fluttering through the air, falling into this putrid hole.

You knew you had refused Houriya's marriage proposal, which had always seemed more like a game to you than it had been a serious relationship. Houriya wanted to replace her relationship with the Marshal, who gavehereverything she needed materially, spiritually and physically.

You were also aware that you been flippant with Basher Bey al-Ghiryany, although you hadn't uttered a single insulting remark, despite his humiliating treatment of you. But did your actions warrant being thrown in this prison, in this solitary cell which had to be the filthiest cell in Porta Benito? You couldn't imagine there being a more cramped, disgusting cell in all the world.

There had to be other, unknown reasons that had warranted this kind of punishment, because the worst you had expected had been to be fired from your position, or pay cut. Anything except fabricated allegations and imprisonment.

You picked up the sound of human voices coming from the other cells and the screams of people being tortured in what seemed to be a distant part of the prison. Their screams were soft and faint like they were coming from tunnels beneath the prison floor. You also heard the rattle of weapons somewhere, as if it were an execution squad preparing to open fire on their victims. Your fright intensified.

You tried to pace around the room instead of standing pressed against the door, thinking someone might open it and tell you to go because you couldn't accept that this was your new place of residence. The space in the cell was no wider than two steps in every direction. You found yourself bumping into the walls. Scribbles and lines had been scratched upon the four walls, and in the dim light you tried your best to read them, but they had become almost illegible.

You focused and squinted. Some were names, probably of people who had been imprisoned in that cell. Most of them were words of hope or requests, "Salvation comes when the crisis reaches its worst", "Everyone who came left. Happiness follows tribulation", "Happiness will come after distress" and "Prison is for men and heroes".

One of the prisoners had seen a connection between that cell and al-Aqila camp, so he had written verses from Sidi Rajab Abu Huweesh's poem.

"My only ailments are the house of al-Aqila, the tribe's imprisonment and the distance from my origins."

The other writings were Quranic verses, prayers to saints, and pleas to Sidi Abdelsalam al-Asmar, Sidi al-Haddar, Sidi Sha'ab, Sidi al-Hattab and Sidi al-Misry. Other prayers included "Invoke God against the unjust" and "Deliver me from the evil of women".

People had written words to treat the disease of despair and fallen spirits as they lived in the middle of this box of filth, which robbed people of their humanity. What really encouraged you was that these imprisoned scribblers had all been educated people and some of them had probably been resistance fighters, or dissidents against injustice in the present time, which represented a continuation of the injustice that had begun with the occupation over a quarter of a century ago.

As you moved to another of the four walls, you discovered that a black tree had been drawn among the lines and scratches on a wide patch of the wall. Upon closer inspection, you realized it wasn't black, but a deep red. A shudder of horror ran through your body as it became clear to you that it was the blood of victims who had been tortured in this cell.

You came face to face with the language of tyranny and power, which no sooner said something than it was done, even if it was written in prisoners' blood. It differed from the language of the other writings on the walls, which the prisoners had written themselves using the language of misfortune and hope, begging God's saints to light a path to deliverance. This was the other face of the Governor-General, the one that the many mirrors in his mistress's house didn't reflect.

You sat on the straw mattress, not knowing what to do with yourself. The small window in the wall went dark and an electric light in the corridor came on, its scant light slipping into your cell through the iron barred window in the door. Night fell and the voices quieted except a faint and distant moaning.

You slept fitfully, the whole time feeling neither hunger nor thirst, nor any other bodily need until a guard came in the morning to take you to a primitive bathroom. Then he returned you to your cell, and gave you your breakfast, a chunk of bread, and a small amount of cold tea in a tiny copper cup.

Although you were certain the guard knew nothing, you tried to wring any information from him that might shed light on these mysterious circumstances. It seemed that you asked him a forbidden question or one he wasn't used to hearing, for he looked behind him in terror as he pushed you into the cell and forcefully closed the door on you without saying a word.

After some time, you heard the sound of doors being opened and feet walking down the hallway. From the the snippets you overheard, you gathered it was time for the prisoners to leave their cells and go to the exercise yard. You predicted there would be instructions to prevent you from mixing with the other prisoners during break, as well as in the corridors, and to keep you isolated in your cell.

But a guard suddenly opened the door of your cell and ordered you to join the other prisoners. While you were in the yard, you learned that your cell was where a prisoner always spent his first day in prison before he completed a medical examination, as a protective measure to avoid what had happened in the past when new prisoners came with infectious diseases, such as tuberculosis or hepatitis, and spread them to the rest of the prison population.

You understood then why a sample of your blood had been taken before you had been imprisoned in your cell. But all you had to do was peer in the faces of these prisoners and knew that every one of them had a chronic disease. Their gaunt faces, their protruding cheekbones, their string-thin necks, their skeleton-like fingers, and their yellow complexion all indicated that they suffered from anaemia.

They also all had conjunctivitis, which ate away at their eyes and attracted hordes of flies. But the king of all diseases was poverty, of which they were all carriers.

When you asked any prisoner why he had been imprisoned, the answer was usually that he was a thief who had either robbed a shop or stolen a goat or grapes from Italian settlers. All were abjectly poor, meaning it made little different whether they were in prison or in their homes, which were no better than these cells. Nor was there any difference between the food they ate in prison and the food they ate at home, that is to say when they had food in their homes to start with.

You saw one of the prisoners staring at you intently as if he didn't believe it was really you. He cried out in astonishment, "Is it possible? Othman Al Sheikh with us in prison!"

The prisoner was a young man who at first you thought was overweight, perhaps the only overweight person among these walking skeletons. But on closer inspection you realized he just had a strong build, which he had gotten from drills, and from training like a wrestling or boxing champion. As you stared at him a while, wondering what had brought him amongst the lowest of the low, then you left him and kept walking. He followed you and said, "Don't you remember me?"

"No I don't. But there's no harm in reminding me." You shook his hand, which he had stretched forth to you. You felt that he was one of the very few prisoners with whom you could talk without catching a disease.

"I'm afraid that if I tell you who I'm, you will not want to talk to me."

His voice sounded familiar to your ears and you

remembered having heard it before. He looked at you from the corners of his eyes and you instantly remembered that you had seen that look on a night that you would not forget. It was the same look that had gleamed in the lights of a passing car the night three ruffians had lain in wait for you in the old city, and almost beaten you to death in the blacksmiths' alley. You were about to choke him, but you controlled yourself and said to him furiously, "Stay away from me for both our sakes'."

"Not before you hear my apology, because your being in this prison, whatever you may be accused of, can only mean that you are one of us and not one of them."

"I'm not waiting for a writ of innocence from you or from anyone else."

"Please forgive me."

"God forgives what's past."

"They found me distributing pamphlets issued by the Committee for the defence of Tripoli and Barqa that was established abroad. They took me to prison without trial. And you, what brought you here if you don't mind my asking?"

"You are fortunate because you know what you are accused of. As for me, believe me when I tell you that I don't know."

"As soon as I get out of this prison, I will continue my patriotic work, God willing. You are welcome to join us if you want to serve the nation."

"Can I ask how old you are?"

"Twenty-one. Omar al-Mukhtar, who died a martyr fighting the Italians, was over seventy. So what does age matter?"

"Omar al-Mukhtar fought from the beginning of the

invasion and died a martyr four years ago. His death terminated the resistance. He started out with an army supported by the entire nation, and ended with a small army supported by a handful of fighters. With what army will you make war?"

"The people are there, but they need leadership."

You realized the young man hadn't grasped the significance of what you had just said. If there were a legendary hero like Mukhtar, only a small number of those who had been worn down by a long war of attrition would be able to resume the resistance. But who would follow this young boy?

"And where are these people?"

"Let's begin with this prison. Every single man in it has a thousand reasons to fight the Italians."

"Why aren't they fighting then?"

"The people need organization and leadership."

You said sarcastically, "And where have you been all this time?"

As if he had taken your words seriously, he quickly answered with zeal, "The political leadership is there, but what we're lacking is military leadership."

"Well, I wish you the best," you said, trying to end this futile conversation.

"It must be a man with military experience, and he's here in this very prison."

You looked at him in astonishment and walked away from him but he stopped you, saying, "Don't look so surprised Mr Othman, sir, for you are that leader."

You couldn't stop yourself laughing. "Why are you laughing?"

"Because only a short while ago I almost met my end at your hands as an Italian agent."

"What's strange in that? Khaled Ibn al-Walid was the commander of the infidels' army before he became the commander of the Muslim army. Your experience working with them will be one of the points of strength that help us defeat them with the Will of God."

You decided to speak seriously to this youth who had become obsessed by the victories of the past and had forgotten reality, so you warned him saying, "That's enough. You'll be sentenced to death if the Aufra hear you. Concentrate on your studies or on a sport you like. That would be more useful than these delusions. As for me, I beg you to get me out of your head because I'm still a soldier in the Italian army."

A prison guard had come to lead you to the room where the visiting doctor examined the prisoners, so you followed him. The doctor placed his stethoscope on your chest and back, then examined your throat and asked you to cough and show him your tongue. After that examination, he decided you should be placed in one of the prison wards. The prison guard led you to the warehouse where you were given your prison uniform, told to put it on and hand him your suit. You were given a straw mattress, a blanket and a copper receptacle. When you returned to the prison yard, you found it empty.

The prison ward that the guard chose for you was packed, holding nine persons, though it was only fit for four or five. You stood next to the door, not knowing where to put your mattress for every inch of ground was covered with other mattresses on which the prisoners were stretched out.

Some of the prisoners had closed their eyes, surrendering to an afternoon nap, while others stared at the ceiling as if they intended to sleep with their eyes wide open. A number of them stared at you slack-faced, stupidly, without volunteering to utter a word to relieve you of your perplexity. All of them were silent and still as statues, except for the unthinking movements of hands shooing away the swarms of flies that settled on their faces.

You turned to the guard to beg him to take you to a less crowded ward or even to put you back into solitary confinement, but he locked the door and left you to deal with the cell's occupants. As soon he was gone, chaos broke loose in the ward.

The languishing prisoners jumped up from their mattresses like monkeys because their silence had been a show to mislead the guard. They returned to playing cards after dividing themselves into two teams, quarrelling and swearing at each other without paying you any attention.

One of them saw that you were still standing with the mattress and blanket tucked under your arm and the copper receptacle in your hand. Confused, he asked you why you were standing like that. He pointed to the cards, saying that you could join in if you wanted. You told him that you weren't any good at cards, so he told you to sit down since your standing in front of him was getting on his nerves and preventing him from concentrating.

You threw your prison effects at your feet and wormed your way into the circle of card players, trying to learn how to play, since that was their ritual method for killing time. After a few minutes, you realized you could never take part in this game because the stakes were cigarettes, which they used as a substitute for currency. You didn't know how they had managed to smuggle cigarettes into the prison, and so long as you neither smoked cigarettes nor owned any, you weren't fit to play with them. And perhaps those who had looked your way scornfully when you arrived without a single packet of cigarettes in your pocket thought you unfit to share their cell.

Mealtime came quickly. They gave you a ladle's worth of fasuliya in your copper receptacle and threw you half a loaf of dried bread, which you forced yourself to eat so you would not have to suffer the pains of an empty stomach throughout the day. You entered a ferocious battle with the swarms of flies that tried relentlessly to make you share the plate of cold fasuliya with them.

Despite the clamour of your cellmates' game, and going out to the prison yard for the evening break, then returning to the cell for another ladle of fasuliya for dinner, time passed slowly. You found out that some of the prisoners had been living like this for five or six years and you wondered how they were able to stand it all.

When it was time for sleep, they moved their straw mattresses and scrunched them together to make room for you to place your mattress next to the door. You laughed with your fellow prisoners at one young inmate who had a gift for imitating people. His victim that night was a Libyan judge known for fawning on Italians, following their orders even in issuing verdicts, so he imitated him as he went to his Italian master, who ordered him to give an innocent Libyan a life sentence.

The youth acted out the judge's confusion as he talked to the governor in Italian, but insisted on using Arabic grammatical conventions. So he pronounced "Marshal" as "Marshalun" and "Italians" as "Italiansun" because they were the subjects in their respective sentences. After issuing the shameful verdict, he seemed in a hurry to go to the mosque to pray in congregation, since praying in congregation brings a greater reward from God than solitary praying.

The play and entertainment came to an end in the cell, so you went to bed, sleeping soundly except for the stings of a few bedbugs that sneaked over to your body to suck whatever blood it had.

You expected your name to be called the next day either to inform you of the result of the investigation into the accusations levelled against you, or send you to court or interrogate you, or anything else that might give you an idea of what lay in store for you. But only two guards appeared, carrying canes. Before you had a chance to ask why they had come, they went to work, starting with you since you were closest to the door. They tied your feet to a wooden board and then one of them held them up to the other while he beat the palms of your feet ten times with his cane.

He counted the strokes aloud. With each blow your ability to master your pain diminished, and the screams you tried to stifle were forced out by the last strokes.

The other prisoners received the same punishment and they let out screams louder than yours had been, because for them today's beating came on top of past beatings. You learned that this punishment had been administered to everyone in the prison for the mere reason that an inmate in another ward had committed some error. They punished him, and along with him all the inmates in the prison, who numbered over five hundred. The reality of prison life gradually unfolded. The punishment the following day was not the bastinado, but depriving everyone of lunch and dinner, because another prisoner had committed some crime. When you asked your fellow prisoners about the nature of the mistakes that demanded such punishment, you were told that it didn't have to be any more than a word of protest from a prisoner against the brutality of a guard.

As for why the punishment was collective, the only answer was that it was a way of breaking the inmate whose unlucky stars had brought him here.

But what place did you have in the company of criminals who stole goats and robbed stores? You knew, as did those who had ordered your imprisonment, that you were no criminal, and you had committed neither a felony nor a misdemeanour to deserve this. So why had they brought you here among these people and subjected you to this cruel treatment?

The cruellest thing of all was that the second day passed, then a third and a fourth without any development concerning your case, which made you think you might be here indefinitely. You began to suspect someone had engineered this intentional neglect to keep you here without trial, to break your physical and spiritual health, so that you would be a wisp of a man when you finally got out.

The evidence for this hidden intent to beleaguer you, to implant the diseases of depression and worry in your soul, was that unlike the rest of the prisoners, you were prevented from receiving visits. When the time for visitors came, all the felons and hardened criminals went to meet their visitors and talk to them behind a wire netting. Everyone but you.

It was abnormal, because you had been arrested in al-Kubran's hotel, not the empty al-Hamada al-Hamra desert, in sight of passers-by from whom the news would fly to people who knew you. It didn't make sense that out of all those people no one would want to visit you, so the only explanation for the absence of visitors over the past four days was that they were prohibiting your visitors from seeing you, thus completing the conspiracy to isolate you before destroying you completely.

You had asked yourself the same question time and time again, what you had done to deserve such inhumane treatment?

SIXTEEN

On the seventh day of your imprisonment, an Italian prisoner was put in solitary confinement. The inmates didn't know what to make of it. Italians were always imprisoned in prisons reserved for their kind alone. The man piqued your curiosity, especially because his attire indicated a man who belonged to a distinguished profession such as a doctor, lawyer, or engineer. So when you saw him walking by himself in the yard during the prisoners' break, you decided to say hello and talk to him.

He welcomed you and when you introduced yourself as the former official responsible for Libyans' complaints and petitions, he was astonished that someone like you was imprisoned here.

You learned he was a journalist who opposed his country's policy of colonization. He had sneaked into Tripoli because the Italian authorities hadn't wanted to issue him an entry visa to keep him from writing about the prevailing conditions in the colony. When he had been discovered at the port of Tripoli without a visa, they had arrested him to return him to Rome. He had been placed temporarily in the Porta Benito prison until a means of transportation, either by sea or by air, could be arranged.

He had been imprisoned in a prison for Libyans and not in a prison for Italians because the Italians feared that he would convey his anti-colonial ideas to the Italian prisoners, and through them to a wider audience of settlers, which would affect their morale.

You didn't want to criticize his country's policy or utter a single word against the country's internal affairs. So despite all the questions he asked, all you mentioned was your personal predicament and that you had been imprisoned without having committed any crime. You added you were certain Marshal Balbo would never agree to such an injustice.

This journalist, an Italian citizen, could disagree with his country's government as much as he liked. As for you, who were you to express any objection to his country's policies or its occupation of your land? Any such remarks would only aggravate the troubles you were trying to find an answer to. All you could do was express your astonishment that an Italian could oppose the Duce, who was loved by all Italians.

"Who says that I oppose the Duce when I oppose the policy of colonization? I never write anything in my newspaper articles that isn't a restatement of the Duce's own words. All I'm doing is what the Duce himself did when he led the demonstrations against the occupation of Libya in 1911 and obstructed the path of settlers travelling to Libya. He was imprisoned for his opinions."

This was news to you, because all Libyans linked Fascism to two things, the violation of the truce that they had negotiated with the previous government and the subsequent resumption of the occupation by the most barbaric and violent of means. You wanted to ask him why the Duce had been forced to change his opinions after coming to power, but before you could finish your question, he said, "That doesn't concern me. My only aim is to find an outlet where I can express my ideas without being ground to bits."

You admired the noble, courageous Italian and felt sorry when he left the following day, though he promised he would raise your case to the prison officials, and would threaten to write about you as an example of the oppression practised against the people of this country. He said that imprisonment without trial, failure to appoint a lawyer to defend you, preventing you from receiving visitors, as well as the beatings you had been given were things that only barbaric regimes did, not those like the Italian government. which claimed to be civilized.

He added with a wink, "The Duce would never agree to that."

You didn't expect any good to come of the journalist's words, as he was also a victim of oppression. So how could someone unable to defend himself defend others? But your expectations, covered in the black pitch of despair, were proven wrong, and the siege around you began to collapse. The day after his release, visitors wanting to see you began to pour in one after the other.

Al-Kubran was the first to come and he told you that he had tried to visit you from the very first day of your imprisonment, but they had informed him that visits required a permit and that the permit couldn't be issued on the same day. He had come on the second day, and the day after it, and they had put him off until he had almost lost hope and stopped asking. But today they had surprised him by saying the permit was ready, so he took it and waited in front of the prison gate until visiting hour.

Al-Kubran added that your friends and relatives had all been treated similarly, day after day, until they had despaired of seeing you and stopped coming. But he would tell everyone that they could visit you now. He expressed his willingness to do anything to get you released and go to any important figure in the government whom you saw fit to contact for help, because he was certain that there was some mistake. He added that the Governor-General must not have known about your imprisonment, otherwise he would have intervened.

He said, "It's a conspiracy woven by Basher Bey al-Ghiryany. whose heart was eaten by jealousy of your success. He must have feared for his standing with the Italians."

You expressed your thanks to al-Kubran for his kindness and his visit cheered you up, for it seemed like a prelude to deliverance. You nevertheless told al-Kubran it was still too early to contact any important persons because you preferred to let the judicial process take its course, as you were confident your innocence would be proven without anyone's assistance.

You also asked him to put all your belongings in a cardboard box and to put it in one of the storerooms so that he could rent your room instead of leaving it unoccupied. But al-Kubran refused the idea before you could finish explaining it to him.

"Don't say that. The room will be waiting for you when you return, God Willing."

After al-Kubran, Nuriya came with Abdel Mowlah. Tears streamed down her face and she dried them with a pink handkerchief as she said, "It's the evil eye that's done this and ever since they arrested you in the hotel, I go to Sidi al-Haddar's shrine every day to light candles and ask him to help release you."

"You are a kindhearted person, Nuriya."

She burst into tears, and turning her face towards the prison gate, she lifted her hands in front of her and said in a choked voice, "O Sidi al-Haddar, you chose your shrine to be in the open air and didn't allow walls to be built around it, nor for there to be a lock on its door so that the stars and the sky would be its only cover. I beg you by the glory of God to hasten the release of Othman, son of Al Sheikh." Then she turned back to ask you what your mother's name was in order to facilitate the pious saint's task. You told her your mother's name was Mariam Al Sheikh, so she continued her prayer saying, "And the innocent wronged son of Mariam Al Sheikh; put an end to his ordeal." After Nuriya stopped crying, she told you that the feast in your honour had been postponed to a later date and added it would give them more time to prepare. She said it would be a double celebration, one party for their new home and the other for your release.

Nuriya was confident that everything she said would happen, because she believed Sidi Al Haddar would not let her down. She was certain of the truthfulness of the fortune-telling of a holy peasant woman who lived in Bu Mishmasha Alley. Nuriya told you the woman had foretold you would shatter your shackles, cross through boundaries, defeat your enemies and regain all you had lost.

You told Nuriya that these were all excellent prophecies except for the mention of travelling beyond boundaries, which worried you, especially if it meant going to the jungles of Africa. Abdel Mowlah said that the words uttered by fortune tellers weren't like the language of ordinary people, which could be taken literally. It was a language of ciphers and symbols, and the boundaries in this case were the boundaries of worry, misery, misfortune and suffering, which you would cross in order to enter the wide horizon of freedom and security.

You felt that all Nuriya had done for you and the amount of tears she had shed were definite proof that she had a pure soul no one could overcome. As for the body, it was the product of its world, wrestling with it, battling against the cruel circumstances in it until the body submitted to conditions, or conditions submitted to it depending on the force and malice of those conditions. But the soul, no matter the circumstances, could maintain its sublime purity and unbreakable strength.

Abdel Mowlah had come in a new guise this time. He was wearing a clean Arab outfit, sporting a red skullcap like the wealthy wore, and he also had a new pair of sandals. The filthy, tattered rags he used to stir people to pity and which he never shed except on his trips to Awlad Al Sheikh were gone.. As he usually left his face unshaved to give him an unkempt appearance for similar reasons, he also seemed soft-skinned by comparison now.

"What on earth has happened to you Uncle Abdel Mowlah? Why have you stopped wearing your filthy rags?"
"Those were tools of the trade that are indispensable for whoever works as a beggar."

"Are you trying to say that you've left that profession?"
"Blessings are from God but also from you, my dear cousin. I added the money you gave me to what I had saved from years of begging and bought a hand cart from

which I sell vegetables and fruit. What I earn is enough and blessed by God."

"That's a real miracle, Sidi Abdel Mowlah, because a beggar never stops begging even if he becomes as rich as a king. Haven't you heard about the poor girl whom the king of the Persia married and took to the capital of his country in order to make her the queen of his country? Well, she used to slip out of the palace in disguise every night in order to beg."

"Begging is not the profession for us men of Awlad Al Sheikh. As you know I've always hidden myself like a criminal from the people of our village. However, now my children can be proud of their father who is a respectable street vendor. The day before yesterday, I went to Awlad Al Sheikh in order to sell fruit and vegetables to a grocer in the village. I returned yesterday after calling on your family. They all send you their greetings and if I hadn't told them you weren't permitted visitors, all the villagers would have come to see you. Your father tells everyone that the important man feared for his post from you."

"You mean Basher Bey Al-Ghiryany?"

"No, he didn't mean him. He meant someone bigger than him."

"My father has gone raving mad from shock, so pay him no heed.. What matters is that I don't want anyone from Awlad Al-Sheikh to visit me, so tell them I will go see them there soon, God Willing. I'm sure my imprisonment won't last long."

"I will do that. Can I help you with anything else?"

"Just get me two packets of cigarettes and hide them inside one or two leaves of bread."

Other than the visits, your life in prison remained the

same as before. Nothing appeared on the horizon to suggest your fate would be any different from your fellow prisoners. Your punishment was exactly like theirs, including the bastinado, which was the cruellest and most humiliating of all the punishments. But when the guards heard you were a sergeant in the Italian army, they beat you less brutally than the other prisoners.

One day, you decided to experiment with your superior rank to the guard who beat you, and after you managed to control your screams of pain, you told him in a commanding voice, "That's enough beating for today."

The result was amazing, for he actually stopped beating you before reaching half the predetermined number of strokes and moved on to the next inmate. You started to repeat your order to the guards every time after receiving half the number of strokes and they all obeyed you automatically.

Despite the humiliation of being beaten, of occasionally being deprived of the break in the prison yard, and of food deprivation, which some people made up for by eating the food their visitors brought, the hope of being released was revived in you after you had been allowed to meet your visitors.

You began to think the day of freedom was near, as the pious woman in the alley of Bu Mishmash had prophesied. You would leave prison and enter a new world that would be very different from the world you had previously known. Or so you told yourself night after night amidst this dreary, desolate emptiness.

A new world. You would have to plan how to face it, because after your release you would not have as much find free time like in prison. A new world. You would see it for the first time with the eyes of someone who had lived through prison and knew what it meant to live life outside it.

It would be a world unlike the village world as you had known it through your life there. A world close to innate instinct, firmly connected to nature, differing from the city and its complications. It was a world you had grown far from, ever since you had moved to the city, joined the army, started working as a chauffeur for Signora Houriya, and associated with people of power so the spotlight of authority had shone on you for a short while. You had felt its warmth on you, but then its glare had intensified and turned into a flame.

Your connection to that world had come to an end, and now you were about to enter a new world. Its features weren't clear to you, and all you knew was that this was different from your previous worlds. You were also sure you would become a completely different person with different opinions and ideas after leaving prison.

It was a fact that you would come out of prison with different views than the person who had gone in. You would be freer because you were no longer hostage to anyone's authority. You would depend on yourself and make what you wanted of yourself, not what others wanted. You intended to employ the experience and knowledge you had recently gained for your own benefit, not for the benefit of a position or a government or a friend, or a girlfriend. From the moment you would get out, you would not work for anyone but yourself.

You therefore turned the prison they had wanted to crush you in into a means to break free of the chains that had bound you to them.

SEVENTEEN

After two weeks of imprisonment, Mukhtar and Ayyad Al Fezzany came during visiting hours, along with a woman you couldn't recognize, for her cloak was wrapped tightly around her face. You were surprised to see them because you hadn't expected that they would learn of your imprisonment after you had left your job at Signora Houriya's.

The woman wrapped in the cloak was Hawaa and as soon as you recognized her, you said, "Did you really have to come when these two could have conveyed your greetings?"

"And does friendship not extend to fallen places?" You said, "You are a faithful friend, Hawaa."

Hawaa told you she had heard passing mention from her mistress that you were in prison without hearing anything to explain the rest of the story, so she had agreed to visit you alongside Ayyad and Mukhtar.

When they asked you why you'd been imprisoned, you tried to make light of your imprisonment and said a small fight between you and Basher Bey al-Ghiryany had led to this regretful result, but that your case would soon be resolved.

They informed you of the many changes that had occurred in Houriya's house during the past month and that a new character had entered the pleasant peaceful place you had once known and completely corrupted it. Houriya had become involved with a member of the Libyan Fascist Youths who had grown up in an orphanage. He knew no father or mother except the Italian government and he only spoke Italian. This was the man that Houriya had married just two weeks ago.

You pretended to be clueless as neither Ayyad Al Fezzany nor Mukhtar knew you had almost been party to a similar arrangement. Only Hawaa had witnessed what had happened between you and Houriya, for she was more than a mere housekeeper, but was also Houriya's confidante. She knew you had been nominated to play the very role that this youth, culled out from the clay of the Libyan Fascist Youths, was currently playing.

There was one point you wanted to check before anything else, so you raised you voice and asked in a surprised tone, "Has the great Pasha been able to get along without the love of his life?"

Ayyad replied, "As a matter of fact, the Marshal's visits these days have become more frequent and as soon as he arrives, the girly boy sneaks out of the house and does not return until he is certain the Marshal has left."

Ayyad added in an angry tone, "I've made a request to retire in order to return to my family in Mirzuq as I can't bear to see what is happening here."

One of Mukhtar's comments shed light on another side of the sudden relationship between Houriya and this new youth.

"Ayyad is right. If I were in his shoes, I would leave.

That youth does not respect anyone, and his only means of communications is swearing and beating. Even Signora Houriya isn't safe from his profanities and violence."

"And what is forcing Signora Houriya to put up with all this?"

The three of them looked at each other and didn't utter a word. Hawaa was the first to break the silence and said, "By God, Houriya would not even have deigned to look at him from a window had she not been forced to marry."

You realized Hawaa was too embarrassed to mention the reason, so you hazarded to say, "Forced? Why? Is it because of the baby she's carrying?"

You hadn't known Houriya was pregnant and hadn't noticed any trace of pregnancy before. She must have still been in the early stages, or maybe not and she had managed to hide the signs. Her vehement insistence on a quick marriage made you suspect that more than her desire to be married, she had needed a lawful cover to have children because the first of those children had already begun to grow and develop inside her womb before the husband, who was to be the baby's legitimate father, had even arrived.

"How did you know? Did she tell you this?"

Despite the cloak that covered Hawaa's face and concealed her facial expressions, her eyes showed through the slit and widened until they were as big as saucers.

"Is there a secret about the pregnancy? Even if she considered it a secret, the signs are sure to show and reveal this secret."

"Don't talk about her that way. God knows the extent of her innocence and chastity."

"What matters is that she has taken steps to set it right

so that the signs of her pregnancy won't appear until she is already in wedlock."

"I wish you wouldn't be spiteful towards her, because Houriya is a gem to those who don't know her, Sidi Othman," she said, meaningfully.

You realized she was trying to allude to something and you didn't want to ask her what she knew in front of the others, so you waited until the time had come for them to go, and before they reached the hall's door you called her back to speak with her alone.

"What were you hinting at?"

"That you didn't know Houriya, which is why you belittled her and refused her proposal."

"Do you know that I'm in this prison because of her?"

"She's above such acts. She's not behind your imprisonment, because she is nobler and more refined than that. But of course she didn't intervene to protect you because you abandoned her."

"Would you have been happy if I had married her, then run away fleeing from the house when that man came?"

"It would have been different, because she loved you and wanted you. She sincerely intended to stay loyal to you, and you had agreed to turn the page on the past and open a new page before you went back on your promise."

"And has she remained loyal to her new husband?"

"Because he, in all simplicity, is not a husband, not even a man, or someone of her choosing. He came knowing what would happen, he would take his due and then go, because my lady hates no one in the world as much as she hates him."

"Please convey my greetings."

"You are the one who confuses me. Why did you agree and then run away?"

"Because Houriya wasn't able to explain how she could cut off her relationship with the man who pays her expenses. Isn't that impossible?"

"If you had waited a little, you would have understood. Houriya was going to turn a new page with you, built on trust, candour and love. She was on the brink of telling you how that man would continue supporting her, not because of the relationship, which she would have put to an end, but because of the fruit of the past relationship. This baby whom the Marshal knows is his. He would have continued to support the baby and its mother, even if he was unable to give it his name. Do you understand now?" As she turned to the door, you said to her, "Tell her

I'm sorry for any unhappiness I might have caused her." "I can't, because I didn't tell her, nor will I tell her about this visit."

You weren't sure what Hawaa had told you would change your change your mind about having pulled out of marrying Houriya. Perhaps what Hawaa said had actually confirmed your doubts and suspicions, . You would not occupy your thoughts with the past, its page had turned. It would do you no good hold your mind hostage to life-less events, which would only obscure your vision at a time when you wanted it to be clear, so that in the coming days you would know where to place your feet upon entering your new life.

Of course, it was impossible that Houriya had person-ally ordered your imprisonment or encouraged it, since those were criminal acts that required an evil disposition she lacked. All she had done was to withdraw the mantle of protection she had draped around you. That was all the good lady had done. She had given you her love, granted her patronage, and lodged you in the depths of her heart. And when she discovered you were undeserving of it, she had turned elsewhere and let the wolves run free and hunt you.

You had to put the past aside and look to your present, the reality you were living in this prison, to train yourself to accept it for what it was. You could try to find a solution to the cigarettes, and acquiring some of them would help make your stay more tolerable, especially when you learned that the guards could be bribed with cigarettes and would accordingly not mistreat you.

Abdel Mowlah brought you fine Italian cigarettes concealed in a loaf of bread, which secured you a better place to sleep than pushed up against the cell door. You were also able to join the rest of the inmates in playing cards. With enough cigarettes, you could force fear and respect onto the other prisoners, because here wealth was cigarettes. With each passing day, you learned the magic power of a packet of cigarettes, to the point that you asked Abdel Mowlah to bring you more every day.

A few days later, you learned that money had the same effect, or maybe a little more, on the guards. But you had to be discreet because giving money to guards was a clear case of bribery and buying favours, whereas using cigarettes would be looked on more leniently. With a few francs, the bastinado beatings tickled your feet and made you laugh instead of scream. Thuraya often came to you in your dreams and you thought about her during most of your waking hours, perhaps because Houriya's exit from your life in such a tragic manner prompted you to take refuge in dreaming about Thuraya. Thinking about her consoled you and gave you an opportunity to escape your wretched surroundings, the gloomy faces and revolting stench. You used the power of love to summon her sweet face and the memory of the perfume she wore to combat your depressing reality.

Thuraya's father couldn't possibly know about your imprisonment, otherwise he would have sent the members of his family to visit you every day. Had you wanted to, you could have sent Abdel Mowlah to inform Haj al-Mahdy of your plight and you would have found Thuraya before you the very next day. There was no one in the world you yearned to see more than her, but it would not be appropriate for Thuraya to come and see you. It would be better to be patient until these dark clouds lifted so she would see you under conditions better suited to your love for her.

You laughed at yourself for thinking of unrequited love and a woman whom fate had destined for another, but the heart is always blind such considerations, and it ached for a woman named Thuraya. Once you left the prison, you could see her whenever you wished, and within the prison walls, you would content yourself with evoking her image whenever you missed her.

Among the many writings on the prison ward's walls were love poems. A poet who had passed through this ward had written poems for his beloved, named Saliha, at the top of each of the four walls. In every poem he called her the heart's spring, though in one of his lines, he confessed he had never seen Saliha in his life. He had loved her through the matchmaker woman who had suggested her as his bride, and he would have proposed to her if this prison hadn't come between them and her family hadn't subsequently married her to another man.

This was the source of the fire in his poems. He had created an imaginary spring for his heart in the abyss of this prison, so why shouldn't you celebrate the spring of your heart when it was a real spring, fertile and alive?

The boy who had earned a reputation as the clown of the ward every night insisted on singing a sad folk song, which he called the Porta Benito Prison National Anthem, the words of which went:

> "Weep with me, you who have tears to shed.
> Weep tears of blood with me.
> People win treasures and plunder
> While I here sit in sorrow.
> Lean times avoid all but me.
> O you who have tears to shed.
> Weep with me, weep with me."

For the sake of variety, you suggested he should adapt the tunes of famous songs to the poetry written about Saliha on the walls of the ward, which all the prisoners had learned by heart because they were always in front of everyone's eyes. It was wonderful to see the poems sung to a melody and it was a great success. The young inmate chose cheerful songs that induced the prisoners to dance, clap their hands and beat their bowls with their spoons to the rhythm as they sang:

> "Saliha the precious spring of my heart,
> You have kindled stars of happiness in my thoughts,
> O Saliha come to me.
> You have kindled stars of happiness in my thoughts,
> O Saliha you are my one and only love,

> In the darkness you shine from above
> I heard the voice of love calling me
> You have kindled stars of happiness in

The prison guard angrily banged on the door and ᵥ
ened to have everyone punished. However, a five franc note
slid under the door made him disappear for the rest of the
night and he didn't reappear until the following morning.

The only difference between the conduct and behaviour
of people inside the prison and those outside its walls was
that people in prison lost their moral compasses. Qualities
deemed important outside prison, like pride, dignity, truth
and honour, lost all meaning. That was why cigarettes took
on so much power, and why you became capable of seeing
that things you had refused outside the prison walls weren't
so humiliating as to have warranted refusal.

For example, what if you had accepted Basher Bey 's
offer to let you Fowzy's subordinate? Wouldn't it have
spared you all that trouble? What had you gained by refusing
him?

When visiting hours came, you went to meet Abdel
Mowlah to receive your supply of cigarettes hidden in
loaves of bread, when one of the prison officers came and
informed you you had another visitor. You stood behind
the metal bars, looking towards the door visitors usually
entered from, expecting to see the person the officer had
so kindly announced.

But the officer motioned you to follow him, because
the visitor was in the warden's office. You told Abdel Mowlah
to wait, because perhaps you would be able to return before
visiting hours were over. Then you entered the warden's
office and found none other than Commander Basher Bey

-Ghiryany, whom all evidence suggested was behind your imprisonment.

He was sitting in one of the armchairs of the spacious office, with his greying beard, his broad red-tinged face, his full Arab suit on his massive frame, and a beautiful hooded olive-green cloak, which lent him even more dignity. He was the picture of health and wealth.

The office seemed wider and the ceiling seemed higher than it was, while the walls seemed to be extremely white and clean because of the narrowness and filth to which you had become accustomed. The window gave out on a splendid view full of green trees and blue sky which you looked at with eyes worn by the squalor of prison life. The warden wished to leave the office so that Basher Bey could speak to you in private, but the Bey asked him to remain and then indicated you could be seated with a gesture of his hand, which held a string of lustrous amber prayer beads. You sat opposite him and listened to what he had to say.

"My son, don't think I wished you any harm, for injustice is not in my nature. My duty is to redress injustice. I'm also very happy whenever I find a Libyan who proves to the Italians that he has intelligence and an upright character worthy of the confidence placed in him so . . ."

You interrupted him saying, "And that is why I've been imprisoned."

"Please do not interrupt me, for your anger is why you are here. You made a serious mistake when you refused to obey my instructions to continue to work in the petitions office. The post is not a shop you own for life, it belongs to the government and the government has the right to place you in any post it deems suitable. No one has the right to protest because the rules and regulations apply to everyone who works in the government, from the Governor-General himself to the youngest office boy."

You said, "One has the right to resign."

Basher Bey said, "You are still too young to talk like that. Where will you go if you resign, and why should you resign? You are still a soldier and no soldier can resign before their period of service is up."

The man stood up and leaned on his cane, saying, "I came here to warn you against being obstinate and to obey instructions next time, since rash conduct will not go in your favour. I've prevented your case from becoming more serious out of mercy for you and your family in Awlad Al-Sheikh, who came to my home and begged me to save you from being tried and imprisoned."

Before you had a chance to ask him which family members had gone to his home, he formally informed you that your assignment had been terminated and that you were to return to your former post in the army. He added that as soon as the necessary formalities were concluded, you would be freed.

You went back out to find Abdel Mowlah still waiting for you. Although visiting hours had come to an end, he had argued that his visit had been cut short by the warden's summons and so the guards had allowed him to stay.

You told him you would relieve him of bringing you cigarettes as Basher Bey al-Ghiryany had informed you your release would happen soon. Abdel Mowlah stretched his arms towards the iron bars as if he were trying to embrace you and congratulated you upon your forthcoming release.

Regarding Basher Bey al-Ghiryany, Abdel Mowlah said, "Thanks to him and may God curse him."

"Why are you mixing thanks with curses?"

"He deserved thanks because he came to tell you of your release, and curses because he was the cause of your imprisonment."

Before he left, Abdel Mowlah also reminded you that the first thing you must do after leaving prison was attend the party that Nuriya and her companions had postponed. All they were waiting for was a sign from you, even if you wanted it to be this evening. Then you would have to travel to Awlad Al-Sheikh to keep the promise you had made yourself to visit your family as soon as you were released from prison.

You had wanted to ask Adbel Mowlah who from your family had gone to Basher Bey al-Ghiryany's home to plead for you, but the question came to you too late and he was already heading towards the door, so it was easy for him to pretend that he didn't hear the question, to avoid discussing the impropriety of what had happened. In any case, an order for your release had been issued and Abdel Mowlah would inform everyone who knew you that you would be released in the very near future.

Abdel Mowlah came to the prison early the following morning in order to enquire at the prison's administration office about the exact date of your release. When it was time for visiting, you noticed he was upset because he didn't see a reason for this dilly-dallying, or what kept them from telling him what time you would be released so that he could inform your family and friends, who wanted to welcome you outside the gates.

You asked him not to do what wealthy merchants who had been released from prison did, namely, celebrating their release by slaughtering sheep, holding banquets and hiring musical bands to play music amidst the crowd of families and friends outside the prison gates. You added that your situation was different and your imprisonment had been a temporary imprisonment which you wanted to erase from your mind as if it had never happened.

You told him it would be best to stop worrying about the timing of your release and concentrate on selling his vegetables and fruit before they went bad. He would find you waiting for him at al-Kubran's hotel after your release, as would anyone else who wanted to see you, whether friends or family, because you didn't want to bother them by asking them to come here.

Abdel Mowlah left grumbling as if saying, do what you will with yourself. He had only wanted to do right by you and celebrate your release according to your people's customs.

EIGHTEEN

However, what happened after Abdel Mowlah's last visit was completely the opposite of what the Commander had told you in front of the warden. The second day passed without anything happening, then a third day, and now a fourth, all without any signs you would soon be released.

Your friends who had gone to greet you at the hotel hadn't found you there and had gone to the prison with al-Kubran to inquire at the prison administration office as to the reason for this delay. Abdel Mowlah came with them, as did several of your relatives from Awlad Al-Sheikh. They made such a noise that the warden heard them, and summoned you to his office. He informed you politely in Italian that you were no longer a prisoner and that the decree ordering your release had been issued. He said you could wear your regular clothes if you wanted and could have all your belongings back.

The warden added you could receive your visitors any time you wanted and that you were allowed to receive food from outside the prison. You were also permitted to leave your ward and sit in the yard any time you wished and you weren't to be included in any punishment. But you weren't permitted to leave the prison yet.

Before you had a chance to ask him angrily why not, he informed you that you had been ordered to join the soldiers travelling to Abyssinia in the very near future and you would remain in prison until the ship sailed from Tripoli the following Thursday.

In a stupor, you realized that you would be sent to Abyssinia in only four days. You knew it would be useless to attempt to obtain any further information from the warden, as he only cared about diligently carrying out his duties. However, you asked him why you should spend the remaining four days behind the walls of this prison instead of outside with your family. As soon as you finished asking the question, you felt the futility of such a question because it was obvious that the order was intended to deny you any chance to escape or to plead for an exemption so you would reach the transport ship as planned.

Before the warden could answer you, the telephone on his desk rang and he indicated that the meeting was over. You left his office and stopped. You were now free inside the prison, able to stand in front of the warden's office as you pleased, or sit if you wanted. You could walk, or lean against the wall, or lie down on the tile of this corridor, because you were free inside prison. You could return to the ward, or not return, eat or not eat, drink or not drink, talk to yourself or with others or dance like a gazelle in the desert and do what no other prisoner could do, because you were free inside the prison.

The plateaus of Abyssinia seemed to loom nearer than any place in Tripoli. They seemed nearer to you than the Red Palace, or Pasha Mosque, or Kushat al-Safar or Sidi

Umran or the Gorgi Mosque or Clock Tower Square or the Miramare Café. The Abyssinian Plateaus were definitely much closer to you than al-Kubran's hotel.

Your world in Tripoli had come to an end, and your new world in the plateaus of Abyssinia had emerged. The plateaus of Abyssinia were far closer than your village Awlad Al-Sheikh, which would fade into oblivion behind the smoke of the battles that awaited you in your new home-land. No one could escape his fate or what the angels had written upon his brow, as the saying went among mothers and grandmothers. So why did people deceive themselves and try to cheat fate?

When you went to see your visitors, who were waiting for you behind the grill in the visitors' hall, you surprised them by leaving the side reserved for prisoners and crossing over the barrier telling them what the warden had told you, that you were free inside the prison. You informed them that orders had been issued to retain you in prison until it was time for you to board the ship sailing to Abyssinia, to join your old military companions who were still alive. You would leave the following Thursday, which was the day weddings were usually celebrated in Libya.

Abdel Mowlah, al-Kubran and the representatives of your family stared at you in astonishment and couldn't believe what you had said. They couldn't imagine that the person they had thought was the second man in the land could sink to the level of the recruits sent to meet their deaths in the Abyssinian campaign.

They all knew you had been imprisoned due to the conflict between high-ranking officials in the government, but to be sent to fight in the war in Abyssinia was some-thing even the sons of servants fled from. It was undoubtedly far worse than living in prison for a few days. Dying in Abyssinia would be the lowest form of humiliation and misery because corpses there were food for tigers, hyenas and lions.

Al-Kubran was more shocked than anyone else, for he couldn't believe that you, whom the people of the city had seen working as the guide for the Governor-General, would meet such a wretched fate. He had built high hopes on his friendship with you, seeing it as a sure path to the Government Palace, and grasping at straws to save himself from falling into despair, he said "Are you certain your friend the Marshal is informed of what is happening to you?"

You told him, before withdrawing back into the prison to spend some time alone, "The decrees that assign a soldier to combat duty, like the decrees that postpone or exempt a person from military service, are signed by the Governor-General himself."

You felt that the four days that separated you from your departure were even worse than your being dispatched to war, because you could do nothing but dwell on the black thoughts that accompanied thinking about the unknown fate that awaited you. Time passed slowly, as it always had ever since you had entered the prison, but you suddenly found yourself wishing the days would pass quickly, so that you could meet your fate, for however terrifying it might be, it would be better than the constant empty waiting, which you saw as a barrier to setting out for the unknown.

You were now able to leave your fellow inmates in the ward and stroll around the yard any time you wished. You looked at the copper statue of the she-lion nursing her cubs, the ancient symbol of the Rome. You didn't see any significance to the statue being placed in the prison yard, but you considered its three figures witnesses to what went on in Porta Benito, and if you could talk to them, perhaps they would reveal the secrets of what they had seen.

An uprising had broken out amongst the inmates several years earlier. They had managed to disarm the prison guards and take their weapons. The government immediately sent a battalion that bombarded the prison with cannon and killed all the prisoners and the guards.

It was said that the prisoners took cover behind the statue of the she-lion and her cubs, so the cannons had targeted the statue, which had come crashing down. Nevertheless, the damage had been repaired and the statue was returned to its original place.

The she-lion was indeed the best witness to ask if they had indeed dug a hole in this very yard for all the dead renegades and turned it into a mass grave. Then you came, years after that massacre, walking alone above the skulls and skeletons of the dead, accompanied only by your shadow.

The silence was broken only by the sound of soldiers' boots in the halls of the administration building or the roof and surveillance towers.

The moans and groans that you had heard during the night vanished during the day. Every prisoner and guard you had asked about the moans and groans hadn't known anything useful. Like you, they heard the screams and moans, but didn't know where they came from. Some of them guessed there were underground tunnels reserved for the Duce's political enemies, whom he sent from Rome to be imprisoned and tortured. But no one knew the truth behind the muffled weeping that went on every night until the prisoners had got so used to hearing them they could only manage to sleep to this macabre lullaby.

There was another kind of crying and screaming that could be heard in the mornings, but its source was known to be bastinado. You remembered how you had previously been a member of the chorus that sang that miserable morning anthem, but now you merely listened to it.

The occupiers had intended the black metal she-lion as the symbol of the Roman revival in this land. The she-lion stood on her marble platform in the middle of the yard, nursing her cubs. Her head was raised and her eyes searching the ether, as though she were wondering what her fate would be so far away from her jungle home, a foreigner in a strange environment.

You felt a degree of solidarity with that she-lion, her strangeness, her loneliness and her uncertainty about her unknown fate.

"All strangers are related by their strangeness," you said to yourself, wondering at this strange connection between a human being and a metal statue.

You had heard the call to prayer several times when you'd happened to be in the yard at midday, or in the afternoon, or at sunset. So just to make use of this freedom that none of the other inmates had, you started to go to the yard so you could stand beside the statue, turn to face Mecca and pray. The call to prayer awoke memories of the relationships, images, and events that tied you to the city you would leave the following Thursday. Only God knew if you would return or not.

After finishing your prayers, you wondered if this was your final farewell to this muezzin's call to prayer, or to these people, or the vast deserts of your homeland and its scattered oases, like green stains on the red maze of sand. You wondered if your bones' final resting place would be some distant, dark mountain, and if this was the last contact you would have with your friends and family, who had begun to come to you in large numbers each day, wailing in the visitors' hall.

You met them, greeted them and exchanged kisses and embraces. You weren't surprised to see your mother weeping so bitterly it shook the prison walls, but you were astonished to see your father also cry as he held you close. You had never seen such a flood of emotions from a man who had always striven to seem capable of restraining his emotions at the saddest times, including the deaths of his brothers and sisters. As a result, you couldn't hold back the tears that streamed down your face, for you knew, for the very first time in your life, that your father had emotions for you he had never shown.

Your mother took out an amulet saying Sheikh Abdullah had made it especially for you. She told you he had written incantations on it that would ensure the angels protected you. She hung the amulet around your neck and told you to never take it off. You took the cakes, slices of cured meat, and the mixture of flour kneaded with oil and dates from her, so as not to hurt her feelings, but after she and your father had left, you gave it all to Abdel Mowlah. You told him you couldn't go to the ship carrying a parcel smelling of cured meat and sweets lest the Captain throw both you and the food overboard.

Next came Nuriya, her companions and their over-weight mistress Sherifa, who had always received you sitting down in the old house in Bahlool Alley. Now she wheezed from exhaustion, exhaling and inhaling noisily even when she was doing nothing more than shooing flies away or waving at her perspiring brow with her palm-leaf fan.

They had brought the lamb that had been waiting for your release party, slaughtered that day and still on the bone in two large cooking pots. You distributed the meat among the prison guards, the prisoners who happened to be in the visitors' hall and kept some for the other prisoners in your ward.

Contrary to the previous visits that had been rife with sadness, this visit was full of jokes and mirth. The large amount of cooked meat created a celebratory atmosphere in which the guards also participated as they filched large pieces of meat from one another, and then chased each other to regain what had been stolen.

You didn't let Nuriya ruin the cheerful atmosphere by crying, so when she took her handkerchief out of her handbag, you begged her not to cry because when you went to war you wanted to always remember her beautiful and smiling, not sad and crying, which ruined her pretty face.

Towards the end of the visit, Sherifa took you aside to thank you for what you had done for her and her girls. She wanted to give you a gift you would need more than anything else in the days to come. It was a metal box filled with musk powder, and when she realized that you didn't understand how or why you would use it, she told you it was genuine musk extracted from gazelle livers.

Sherifa explained to you that the musk powder would mask any hateful odour however strong it might be and spread a pleasant scent in its place. It wasn't the cheap kind of imitation musk available everywhere in the market, and she thought you would find nothing better than genuine musk powder to fight the odour of death.

When Sherifa saw the puzzled expression hadn't left your face, she added that Libyan resistance fighters had used this musk to preserve the dignity of their dead during battle whenever it was unfeasible to move and bury them. So they would cover them with musk powder to keep them from smelling of rot until their bones decayed. Real musk, she said, was one used to embalm the bodies of high-ranking people.

Although the mention of death reminded you of the horrors that awaited you, you took the gift with a smile and thanked her for concerning herself with the dignity of the Libyans who would die in the Abyssinian campaign.

When you returned to your ward, you decided to test the musk powder to see if it would get rid of the hateful odour that clung to the walls, ceiling and the floor. The result was amazing, for no sooner had you pinched a tiny amount of it and tossed it into the air than the rotten odour was gone.

When al-Kubran came to visit you the following day, he refused to come without bringing your gramophone, which he felt obliged to return. He said that since you were going to travel to the unknown jungles of Africa, you would need something like a gramophone to entertain and console you. He had also chosen a record that suited the occasion:

> "We left the palm trees behind us,
> Regret has caught up with us,
> How we wish we had turned away."

The gramophone sang out, reverberating through the prison, heedless of what the guards might say. But they said nothing and those who were on duty in the yard joined the others in the visitors' hall to hear the song that reminded them of the countryside they had left behind.

Three men from al-Kubran's gang had come with him, and he said that they had presumably come to say goodbye to you, but in reality had come to bid farewell to the gramophone, with which they parted ways tearfully. Despite that joking atmosphere, you couldn't hold back your tears when you heard that sad song depicting the cruelty of having to leave one's homeland, with its painful lyrics and clear melody that flowed like a brook.

Al-Kubran and his friends stopped fooling around and they were going to turn the gramophone off, but you asked him to leave it on until the song was finished. You dried your tears and wanted the cheerful atmosphere to return, so you told al-Kubran you would return the gramophone on the condition that he stop repeating the same old songs he had replayed dozens of times, lest the gramophone become bored and refuse to play any more records. After all, you said, these devices have feelings like real people, and one had to provide them with the newest songs on the market to keep them happy.

You then told al-Kubran to keep the gramophone as a memento. He accepted your gift but on one condition.

"I will keep it, but not as a memento, but as a deposit which I will render you on your return, God Willing."

All you could say was, "God Willing" because you knew that nothing in the whole world happened but by the Will of God, which would decide whether you would return or not.

Thuraya, whose beauty matched the Pleiades that bore her name, was your last visitor, accompanied by her mother and brother. They brought her father's greetings and a message, "My son, do not resent any thing that God has willed, but rather to try to use it for your good, whether it is imprisonment or going to war, because it was He who said 'Sometimes you may hate something, though it be a blessing unto you'. More often than not, trying experiences are a change to test our strength and bolster our self-confidence, though do not forget as you go to war that one's life is in God's hands, so no one in ever dies before his appointed time."

Thuraya's presence made you very happy, spreading a feeling of tranquillity and safety in your soul. You stood across from her, trying to memorize the limpid beauty of her face, to draw warmth from the light in her eyes to counter the chilly fear in your heart. You wished you could borrow her luminous energy, to help you bear the weight of the bitter experiences awaiting you.

Thuraya's mother wanted you to take some foodstuffs to her son-in-law Fathy. You apologized for not being able to take the bundle of food, which resembled your mother's bundle, under the excuse that no one was allowed to board the ship with food. But you promised her that you would search for Fathy until you found him and that you would send them a letter telling them how he was faring. You added that you would send them a sunny photograph of Fathy and yourself in perfect health, drinking coconut milk on a river bank.

You said all this to alleviate the ageing woman's anxiety about her son-in-law, evoking a peaceful image to replace that of war. You regretted not having taken advantage of the time you went out alone with Thuraya to take her to an Italian photographer for a keepsake photo that would have provided sustenance to you in the distant country. You felt an urge to embrace her, but since that was out of the question in the presence of her mother and brother, you just held her hand and kept it in yours, enjoying this blissful physical contact as long as possible.

Abdel Mowlah had brought your bag from your room in the hotel which contained some effects you needed for your journey. He had left the rest with your family in Awlad Al-Sheikh. On Thursday morning, two sailors from the Italian navy came to take you to the harbour in a military vehicle. They accompanied you to the ship and handed you over to one of the guards, only leaving once the guard signed off on your papers.

It was moving that such a number of your relatives and friends had come to say goodbye to you, all thanks to Abdel Mowlah who had informed them of your impending departure and gathered them at the harbour. Sheikh al-Balbal was there, carrying a green palm leaf in his hand and standing beside the stairs that led up to the ship. You regarded his presence as a good omen, as was the palm leaf, which people hung over their doors to bring them good luck.

You greeted Sheikh al-Balbal and thanked him profusely for coming to bid you farewell, but he joked with you in a manner that aroused your resentment somewhat when he raised the palm branch and beat you on your legs and feet as you climbed up the stairs. You were only saved from the blows when you ascended past the reach of the palm branch. You didn't know whether what he had done was a blessing or a curse. But who could explain the actions of a dervish like Sheikh Al-Balbal?

It cheered you greatly to see Haj al-Mahdy wave to you from the carriage he had come in. Nuriya hadn't only brought her friends this time, but also Warda, her seven-year-old daughter, whom she raised above her head so that you could see her. A group of women, whom you had never seen before, stood beside Nuriya waving their hands. You guessed they were women who had lived in Sidi Umran and had got new houses as a result of the Marshal's visit to their neighbourhood, so they had come to bid you farewell as a sign of their gratitude.

A crowd of people you didn't recognize surrounded al-Kubran and waved. You remembered al-Kubran had said people had been looking for you to express their appreciation for what you had done to facilitate their petitions.

Your father and a number of your relatives from Awlad Al Sheikh stood beside the ship. They stared in astonishment at the Tripolitanian women who had come to bid you farewell and couldn't imagine what could possibly connect you to such women. Your father invoked God to protect you, and as you stood near to him, he told you to take care of yourself and to return safe and sound.

You had to board the ship and as you leaned over the railing together with a number of other soldiers, who were taking one last look at their families, you could think only of the one woman in the crowd who had taken possession of your emotions and thrown her net over your captive heart. You felt ashamed because your mother was weeping bitterly, yet despite your love for her, no one commanded your feelings like Thuraya did, with her spellbinding power over you.

After staring at Thuraya for some time, you felt that the entire horizon had filled with her image, to the extent that even if you took your eyes off her, she would appear before you wherever you looked. And if you turned your gaze somewhere else, you would still see her smiling at you and waving farewell.

The crowning moment was seeing an Italian photographer on the ship taking photos of the families who had come to see the soldiers off. When you learned he was a war correspondent who was going with the soldiers to Abyssinia, you asked him to take a photograph of Thuraya and told him you would pay him whatever he wanted. However, he told you that he would not take any money from you, saying that it was the least an Italian journalist could do for a Libyan soldier who was on his way to fight in a war among the ranks of the Italian army.

The Italian photographer's quick response raised your spirits, even though your morbid disposition that day placed it in the same class as the final request of someone sentenced to death. He was sure to have his wish fulfilled and that had been your last wish before the ship lifted the anchor that moored it to the sea floor, pulled the lines that tied it to the pegs on the landing, and began its trip to far away shores.

The port shrank from view and the midday sun bathed Tripoli in a flood of white light. You bade farewell to the fortress, to the Miramare, to the Clock Tower, to the Grand Hotel, to Sidi al-Sha'ab, to the golden dome of the Marshal's Palace, to the minaret of the Pasha Mosque, to the Gorgi Mosque, to Ben Najy and to Mizran.

As the ship sailed away, the shore took on a brilliant form, assuming the shape of a huge shining crescent that encircled the blue sea with its green sheen, and the palm trees and water wells by the shore that blurred together into an arc of stones and leaves. The city became smaller and smaller, its buildings and the palaces of its rulers vanished until only the tops of the palm trees and the minarets of the mosques could be seen.

You told yourself that one had to sail away from Tripoli to appreciate its true beauty. How could one try to define this place, with its identity, personality and myriad colours, and then say to its Italian governor to remake it into a Western city? Tripoli would always remain one of the oases surrounded by barren land, and the red sand dunes around it would always shimmer in the scorching sun like two great crimson arms holding the green oasis and offering it like a sacrifice to the sea.

Everything swam in the glare of the midday sun, and everything around you seemed to dissolve. The ship distanced itself from the shore, and even the sea moved away from the horizon. You raised your eyes to the sky and saw white cottony clouds merge and then separate.

Your thoughts were filled with cars chasing and colliding into each other. And before you disappeared into the mist that surrounds the universe, when you saw Tripoli between those two bare red arms, you saw Mukhtar the garage guard carrying the body of his dead daughter into the wilderness, weeping and walking, looking for a grave where he could bury his daughter in that vast barren desert.

You saw Tripoli walking and weeping. The shore wept and moved, the ship wept and sailed, the sun wept and moved across the dome of the universe, and you too wept, walking towards your unknown fate.

ACKNOWLEDGMENTS

I should like to thank Graeme Estry and Ghazi Gheblawi for their efforts in editing and revising the translation.